Weeping Women

Springs

A Novel

by

Tamara Eaton

Published by Rebel Romance,

An imprint of Irksome Rebel Press

Los Angeles, California

Weeping Women
Springs

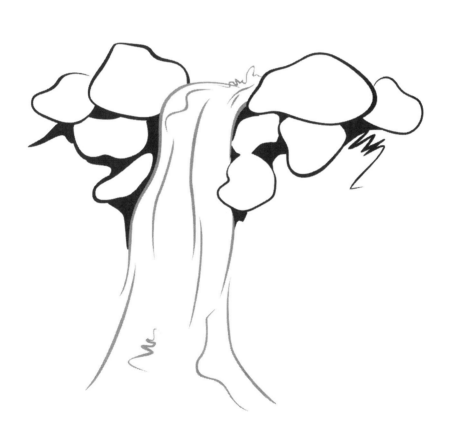

Published by Irksome Rebel Woman,
an imprint of Irksome Rebel Press

Cover Design by Kim Carmichael

Dedication

For my mother, who wept for two husbands and stayed strong always. I miss you.

For my beloved Chuck who was never one of the lost boys though he came awfully close in another war where too many more young men were sacrificed.

Lastly, for all those both on the Homefront and abroad who dedicate their lives to a cause greater than themselves.

Acknowledgments

Chuck Pride – My love, thank you for your support. Without you, this book would not be possible. Your help with brainstorming plot issues has made this a much better book. Your assistance with all things military was invaluable. Any errors are mine.

Kim Carmichael –Your loving encouragement means more than I can say. Thank you for your help to get this baby out into the world and for an amazing cover. Your friendship and acceptance of my quirks gives me warm fuzzies. We make each other better.

Davina MacLeod – Lass, thank you for your tough edit and your fearlessness in telling me the truth about the story. As an editor I know that had to be one of the most difficult things for you to do, but the story benefited from your sharp eye and strong sense of character and writing sense. You loved the story from the outset and made me a better writer along the way.

Ray Dyson – Thank you for a wonderful proofread. Your sharp eyes caught a lot of lingering issues, and thank you for the best compliment from an editor—you forgot you were editing as you were engrossed in the story.

Robert Schick, Amber Scully, and MJ Allen – Thank you all for beta reading the latest version and giving me your honest critiques.

Donna Mabry – For your early support as well as your help with getting the word out, thank you!

Beth Cato – For your help with blurb writing—the toughest writing gig for any author—my heartfelt thanks.

Patrice Horwitz – Thank you and your husband for help with Werner's German. Any errors are mine.

Critique Circle Crew – To the folks at CC, thank you for providing a safe learning environment for newbie writers. Thank you to critters Chuck Robertson, Dana Griffin and Barbara Humphrey specifically, for going through an early version of the story. Though it has changed dramatically since your critiques, you helped the story gain its legs.

Lia Hearn and the Triple A Team – Your help in promoting the book is much appreciated. Your generosity and enthusiasm have warmed my heart.

National Novel Writing Contest – My sincere gratitude for giving me an impetus to write my first novel back in 2008. This is the result of that initial foray into novel writing.

The following people provided names and or inspiration for several of the characters in the novel. Maxine Fiekens, we miss you dear friend; Peggy Cruse, we miss you serving as our postmistress extraordinaire, my friend; Bob and Linda Caldarelli, thank you for being such great friends; Harriet Perry, my adopted mom, thank you for everything; John Waterhouse, you were an inspiration for a strong character in the story, thanks for your friendship.

The list goes on for all the friends who have expressed their fervent support for this novel throughout the several years it's taken to complete. Thank you all.

A voice is heard in Ramah,
mourning and great weeping,
Rachel weeping for her children
and refusing to be comforted,
because they are no more.

Jeremiah 31:15

Weeping Women

Springs

Part I

The Static of the Radio

Chapter One

Liv

I DIDN'T ALWAYS WANT to hide. The Council made sure we hid the water from the start, but I would rather have gone out into the world. Hope Springs was a good place to grow up. Once I reached high school, I dreamed of going places. Did you know that? You came to town later, so I never shared that with you. The Council wants us to tell you the secrets so you can report everything that happened, maybe we won't be forgotten.

You only see what is left, middle-aged and old women who teeter on unsteady legs, searching for balance that is never quite there, the dusty roads, the faded buildings, the closed up businesses, all but Fiekens' General Store. Maxine always kept that open, even after—no I'm getting ahead of myself. Remind me to stay on track. It's always best to start a story at the beginning, then maybe you'll understand.

On that crisp December afternoon the air wafted over me cool and brisk. That morning I went to church with my family like every other Sunday. Maxine didn't attend church, not since her parents died in an accident the year before. Anna Frolander never did attend church much, but I couldn't pass judgment, not then or ever.

Maxine spent Sunday afternoons with us kids at the gym when the boys practiced basketball, and well, we girls practiced watching the boys.

I met up with Maxine at the store, but I'd seen the new carving, so I wasn't surprised when she shared the latest.

"Have I got news for you." Maxine's voice sang over the aisles of canned goods and staples. It was like my old friend was back, happier than I'd seen her in so long.

"Does it have anything to do with the new heart on the Sweetheart Tree? Spotted it this morning after church." I waited at the front door and hooked my arm into her elbow when she came up to me. We headed down the dusty street toward the high school. My friend almost skipped beside me.

Her face glowed. "Yes," she said with a little squeal. "Billy asked me last night. Liv, you'll be my maid of honor, right?"

I hugged her hard. "You bet. When's the wedding?"

"Not until school's out."

"Let's hurry. I'm sure Billy's eager to see you." I pulled her along faster toward the gymnasium.

On that quiet Sunday, few people were outside. We waved to my mother's good friend, Anna, who was sweeping her front walk. An early snow dusted the craggy mountains in the distance, but the moderate temperature promised a mild winter. The surrounding mountains and hills sheltered Hope Springs in a verdant valley. It made hiding easier then and later when it became more necessary. Our seclusion saved our lives or perhaps it ended them. I suppose you'll be the judge of that when the story's told.

We stepped inside the gym. The basketball players' shoes screeched on the wood floor. The boys practiced non-stop since the big game on Tuesday with our rival, Tularosa High, loomed in our future. We'd lost the last game with them, and we wanted to make the state playoffs.

The ball whooshed through the net.

"Billy made a good shot," I said and Maxine just grinned. "So tell me about the proposal. Did he get down on one knee?"

"No. He made my favorite sundae at the store and put a little toothpick with a flag on top. On the flag were the words, 'Will you?'"

Billy had loved her it seemed like forever, so I wasn't surprised, but his parents weren't a fan of the idea. "Did he decide to stay in town and run the store with you?"

"Mother and Papa would have approved, don't you think?" Her question came out breathless as she searched for confirmation.

I squeezed her hand. "I'm sure they would have."

The excitement of a moment ago faded from her eyes, replaced with the haunting pain of grief. At least while watching the boys, Maxine could be a girl again. I worried about her since she'd quit school to run her family's store. On Sundays and game days she closed the door and warmed a seat on the bleachers, cheering Billy Fiekens on. She hadn't lost her place in our class of 1942, though she wouldn't graduate with the rest of us. Without Maxine we'd only have thirteen on stage for the ceremony in May. She had confided to me she hoped to get her diploma after marrying Billy, if he could watch the store.

"His parents approve of it?" I asked.

Maxine closed her eyes a moment. The hesitation spoke volumes. Over the last year, I had watched her deal with the unthinkable. I couldn't imagine losing one parent, let alone both. My poor, gentle Maxine, who always had a kind word of encouragement for me whenever I grew tired of waiting to leave town, withdrew even deeper into herself after the accident. With the proposal, I saw signs of her sorrow lifting.

"They still want him to go to UNM?" I asked.

"Yes." Maxine clenched her green cotton skirt before smoothing it down. "I kept telling him to go ahead and attend school. Teaching is so important to him. He just said, 'If your parents were still alive, I'd do it, we'd go together and live in Albuquerque.' Then he'd mention selling the store."

"You could sell the store, but—"

"I can't do that, not yet. It's too soon. Besides, Billy's parents can't afford to support us both. Who would buy a store in the middle of nowhere, New Mexico?"

I laughed. "Or if the Council would even let you sell. I'm sure they'd have to authorize it."

The door at the end of the gym burst open and little Eddie Frolander ran inside. "The Japs bombed Pearl Harbor!" he shouted. "Melvin's dad heard it on his radio."

Everything went silent, all but the bouncing ball echoing through the gymnasium. The players surrounded Eddie and everyone began talking at once.

"Where's Pearl Harbor?" Maxine asked me.

"I don't know," I answered. We climbed down the bleachers to join the players.

Nine-year-old Eddie's words tripped over one another. "I dunno any details, but Mr. Bracht said to tell everyone. He said we might be at war and spread the word."

"War." The word was murmured repeatedly through the crowd.

"Pearl Harbor is in Hawaya. The president said they bombed the navy base there." Eddie's dark hair fell over his eyes.

Maxine rushed over to Billy and he threw a sweaty arm around her shoulders. At that moment, I longed for a shoulder to lean on too.

Donnie Frolander, Eddie's older brother, sidled up to me. "If we've been attacked, what will it mean?"

"Surely the president will tell us what to do." I said. "President Roosevelt has seen us through a lot already."

"Maybe we ought to head over to Mr. Bracht's house," Billy suggested.

"The Council was mad when Mr. Bracht bought a battery radio last year," Donnie said. "But maybe this is a good reason to have a radio in town. Imagine if we didn't find out until Tuesday when Tularosa comes to play the game. Boy, would we look dumb."

I itched to tell Donnie to keep his opinions of the Council to himself, but swallowed the urge. Too late anyway. The other young people muttered an agreement, falling into their common theme of whining about the Council's decisions. Uncle Jim's words echoed in my mind. "You youngsters have no real idea what it means to this town to keep us isolated as much as possible. Besides you have opportunities enough to get outside, go to Tularosa or over to Alamogordo to the movie house." Arguments of the young people wanting more freedom, and wishing to see the world, or letting more visitors in to see us always fell on deaf ears. Freedom wasn't in the Council's vocabulary.

From the time I started school, my parents and other adults in the community drilled into us the necessity of keeping the secret. On the verge of adulthood, me and my friends questioned the rules set up by the founding fathers. I pushed the thought away. War on the horizon? What did it mean to Hope Springs?

I caught my brother's eye across the group. "We need to let everyone know," I said. "Maybe we can all meet over at the Brachts?"

I yanked him away from Billy and the others. "Dewitt, I'm going to tell Mother. She'd better hear it from one of us. I'll see you over at the Brachts."

He nodded, but quickly returned his attention to the other boys. I ran the short distance back down Main Street to our house.

"Mother," I called. "There's terrible news. The Japanese have bombed the navy in Hawaya."

"Slow down," she said from the direction of the kitchen and I hurried to her.

"Mr. Bracht said we may be at war."

My mother dropped her dishtowel. "What?"

"We need to go to the Brachts to listen to the radio."

Mother grasped the kitchen table for support. "I don't think so. You go on ahead."

"But—" I didn't understand why she wasn't anxious to get the latest news.

"Go on ahead, daughter. There's nothing to be done for it now. You find out what you can, and I'll wait here."

"Could you go tell Uncle Jim? He'll want to inform the Council." Maybe they already knew. Sometimes the Council had inside information, though I could never recall them knowing about circumstances which didn't directly concern the town.

"Yes. Good idea." She removed her apron. "I'll do that while you go to the Brachts. Your father headed over to Jim's earlier. Decisions will have to be made."

By the time I arrived at the Brachts their parlor overflowed with townspeople and the rest spilled out onto the front lawn. I found Maxine and Billy along with the rest of our classmates milling around under a large tree in the yard.

When I asked if there was any further news, the others shook their heads.

A wave of "sh-sh," swept over the crowd.

Mr. Bracht's distinctive deep voice came through the open window. He sang in our church choir. "The regular programming has been interrupted. They are doing news reports, but nothing is certain. The president's secretary has issued a statement and says the president will address the people tomorrow."

The adults murmured. Again, the repetition of war traveled from lips to lips inside the house and out.

Little Susie Bracht pushed through the doorway. I smiled at her, a seven-year-old with blonde pig tails. She skipped up to me. "What's happening?"

"I don't know."

"What are they talking about, war?" she asked. "What does it mean?"

I couldn't explain very well. "War is when the men have to fight in the army to defend the country." The photograph of my father in his jodhpurs uniform from WWI came to mind. He'd come back from the Great War, back to my mother, and they'd started a family. Mother had always told me, you should have seen him before the war.

"But adults know better than to fight, don't they?" Susie asked. Her bright blue eyes opened wider.

I had no answer. Not quite an adult myself, I wondered when it was that a person received the key to unlocking the confusion. Adults always knew better. It's what we believed.

"I thought adults had all the right answers."

"Perhaps this is the right answer," I said.

"It doesn't make sense. Even our parents and teachers teach us not to fight." Her face scrunched up in disapproval only the young can have when they see the world in right and wrong, black and white.

Uncle Jim approached us. He smiled at Susie's words. "You're right, war doesn't make sense, but sometimes it's the only way." He addressed his next words to me. "Any further news?"

"No." My insides were wound tight, the waiting, the not knowing, the fears sent my head spinning. I clutched Susie tight and sat on the lawn. The dry grass needled my legs. It's funny how sensations became part of the memory.

"Do you think my daddy will have to go?" Susie tipped her head back to look at me.

A red dust devil skipped down the street. "No." Reassuring Susie seemed the right thing to do. Certainly Susie's father wouldn't go to war, but of course, I didn't know for sure.

For the next minutes and hours we waited, listening for further reports.

Reporter's Note: The above concludes the first taped interview this reporter conducted with Liv Soderlund in November, 1958. In order to share their story, the women of Weeping Women Springs, New Mexico, agreed to allow me to record them. After much contemplation, I decided that the transcripts of the tapes are the best way to tell their story in their own words, unedited, unembellished. – R.W.P.

Chapter Two

Liv

ON MONDAY, THE PRINCIPAL canceled school. By nine in the morning, everyone had gathered once again at the Brachts' home, intent on hearing the president's address. The crisp morning in the high desert would give way to a balmy breeze in the afternoon. If not for the air of dire expectations, I would have enjoyed the warmth of the sun as it peeked over the eastern mountains. If not for the dreaded tightness in my chest, I would have celebrated a day off school.

My mother and I weaved around the perimeter between the horses, wagons and cars lining the street. Ruthie Ackerman hung onto Joe Bauer's arm. When she caught my eye, Ruthie pulled Joe's arm around her waist, staking her claim. I shook my head. Ruthie had made the rounds of the males at Hope Springs High over the last four years. Joe had lasted longer than the rest. I pushed the thought away as it was no time for bitter jealousies. Since yesterday, the whole idea of trivial schoolgirl interests fell by the wayside.

I watched the boys from the basketball team, imagining them in uniform like that of my cousin, Leonard. Last summer, he'd enlisted in the navy and when he came home on leave me and all my friends swarmed over him. He was still Cousin Leonard, with his slightly crooked teeth and large nose, but somehow in his navy blues he looked more handsome and appealing.

Quiet settled in and the radio crackled. I could hardly remember a time when Roosevelt hadn't been president. Throughout the last few years, I had watched newsreels where he reassured the country through the hard times. Now, it came again as President Roosevelt addressed Congress, "Yesterday, December 7th, a date which will live in infamy. . ."

The sun warmed my skin, but a chill held my soul. Seven minutes later, the speech ended. I glanced around the gathering. No one moved for long minutes and then Dewitt, my brother, let out a whoop.

"Who's with me?" My little brother threw his baseball cap in the air. "I'm headed to Alamogordo to enlist."

Again the high school boys huddled together, joined by older men, married and single. Father approached them. Uneasy, I moved toward my father, confident he would tell them they should not go to war. His sensible speech would calm the boys' exuberance.

"The country needs us," he said. "You know I fought in the Great War. If Uncle Sam needs me again, I'll be there."

I stiffened. *No!* Dewitt's words, born of impetuous boyish excitement for an adventure, did not surprise me, but father waxing on about duty and country? All the silent mornings of my childhood rushed back to me. Father sitting at the kitchen table, unshaven, his eyes reddened from lack of sleep, and his coffee cup shaking in his hands. Hovering over him, my mother was always poised to embrace him or run out the door if the situation demanded it. Her steady voice would tell me and Dewitt to eat quickly and leave for school. But her eyes spoke of the churning whirlpool beneath the surface, the sleepless night she had shared with Father. Now, across from the group of the boys and men, my mother covered her open mouth.

The townswomen gathered closer to the porch. Mrs. Frolander called above the crowd, "I'll welcome anyone to my house this afternoon. We can start knitting scarves, sweaters and hats for the servicemen."

Uncle Jim stood at the top of the porch steps and lifted his voice. "Listen, everyone. The Council will be meeting this afternoon to discuss Hope Springs' war effort." He leaned toward Chester, another member of the Council. After a whispered conversation Uncle Jim continued. "Let's have a town hall meeting at the gymnasium this evening."

Reverend Unger waved a hand from the back of the crowd. "We'll hold a special prayer meeting this afternoon at the Methodist Church."

Father Gomez from the Catholic Church spoke in turn. "If it's all the same, could we all meet together for a community prayer service?"

Reverend Unger agreed. "At three, the Methodist Church will open its doors for anyone of all denominations to offer prayers for our country, the servicemen serving, those who have lost their lives in this brutal attack, and those enlisting."

How fast everything moved. It amazed me. Here we were in lethargic Hope Springs where my friends always complained that nothing ever happened, and the burst of activities swelled. The outpouring of support and the immediate necessary action almost overwhelmed me. The people were motivated by outside events as I'd never seen. Perhaps this tragedy would lead to Hope Springs entering the modern era. I smiled at the thought. It's what we kids had wanted for as long as I could remember.

Maxine walked up to me. "What are you smiling for? Seems a strange reaction."

"I don't think so. What if something good can come out of this?" I hugged her.

"Impossible." Maxine narrowed her eyes. "Already Billy is talking about heading over to Alamogordo tomorrow to the recruiters."

"Yes." I nodded. "He's going to the outside. Not just for shopping or the movies, but to interact with the outside. Can you remember anyone ever doing that before?"

Maxine shook her head.

"Even my father looks like he's gained new life. I guess that was the last time anyone from town left, during the Great War. Why is that?"

Maxine shook her head, but I saw the fear.

"I should get back to the store." She went to Billy.

He shook his head. Maxine put her hand on his shoulder and whispered something. Billy's face tensed, then he took her hands. Their foreheads touched and they stood like that for a moment, before she turned away.

I walked with her. "Do you think all the businesses will open again this afternoon?"

"Not sure." She pointed to the yellow brick building down the street. "The bank probably will stay closed, but Peggy will probably open the post office. I'm going to check my stock."

Behind us, the high school band played the national anthem. We stopped and put our hands on our hearts, facing the flagpole at the school where the flag flew at half-staff. Everyone joined in the singing. I brushed a tear away. Through the shock I promised myself to maintain a positive outlook. Something good would come of all this. On a cloudless day it was hard to believe otherwise. A soft breeze drifted through the street kicking up a little dust. When the anthem ended, we continued on our way.

"When will they go to the recruiter, did Billy say?" I asked.

"Tomorrow." She didn't look at me, but scuffed her toes in the dust. "Wish I could go with him, but I can't close the store again. Already Mrs. Frolander asked me if I had yarn for the knitting to be done."

"It looked like Dewitt and my dad will both be going to the recruiter too. Do you think they'll take the older men?" I couldn't imagine my father taking out his old uniform and marching off to a war again.

"If they need men, I wouldn't see why not. Are you worried?" Maxine brushed a wayward red curl out of her eyes.

"No. I felt all tight when the news hit yesterday, but seeing a light in Dad's eyes is sort of nice, and the patriotism brings a special excitement, don't you think?"

"Sort of. . ." My friend didn't seem too convinced.

"It's time some life came to Hope Springs. We're part of the bigger world, no matter what the Council says."

"Maybe." Maxine kept her gaze on the road.

Curious, but more than that I was determined to see the happy glow she had yesterday. I asked, "How will this affect your wedding plans?"

"Not sure yet." Unfortunately she wouldn't meet my eyes. Maxine was back to her quiet shyness. "Billy mentioned moving the date up. Shouldn't they graduate before they join the army? If they put it off, then we could get used to the idea."

I smiled. "And you could have your June wedding."

Maxine didn't return my smile and her gaze admonished me. "That's not important. Billy is."

I hooked my arm in hers. "Oh come now. Don't be such a silly goose. Of course, Billy's important, but so are you, especially to him. He'll do what you want."

She pulled away, and headed to the store, her keys already jingling. "I'll see you later."

That evening I set the plates on the table for supper. My mother mashed the potatoes with a shaking hand.

She was always strong, no matter how my father's mood changed. She made sure to dress for dinner, the way she'd been raised back east. She only came to Hope Springs as a teenager when her parents sent her to stay with her relatives while they went on a trip. That's how she came to stay with my Uncle Jim and Aunt Wanda. It was then that she met my father too, and why she never left. I always wondered how she with her elegance and eastern city manners made do in our little town, but she never seemed to miss the city.

It was odd, because most of the past year all I could think about was leaving Hope Springs as soon as I graduated, maybe for college, or maybe just getting a job at a paper. I loved writing.

I made a move to take the bowl of potatoes. "Let me help."

"No." She shook her head. "I can do it. Go call your brother for his supper."

"What's wrong?" I asked—a stupid question, but I couldn't handle her falling apart, not when things were so uncertain.

"Noth—" Done in, she collapsed in a chair and pulled at her earring. I knelt at her side, and she took my hand. "You've never known your father as anyone other than what you've seen. He was so like Dewitt. Happy, boisterous. Until the war. When he came home, things were never the same. The shadows never left. It was almost like I couldn't reach him. Sometimes he'd be all right for a while—when you were born his eyes gained new life for a while. Again, when Dewitt was born I hoped he'd be able to be the same joyous boy I'd fallen in love with before the war, but though he tried, he couldn't seem to shake them."

"What?"

"The war memories. The nightmares might leave for a while, but they always returned." She paused, her lips pressed together, trying to stop the flow of words or emotions, I wasn't sure. "I can't bear it."

"He seems better now, since yesterday." The feeling I had, that little hope flickered, not ready to give up. "Maybe something good will come of this."

"I'm afraid. I can't believe he's asking me to do this again, to watch him leave for war, not knowing if he'll come back again. It's too much." Never had I seen my mother so vulnerable, unsure. In one way, it scared me to death, but in another it made me feel all grown up—she was talking to me like another adult.

Needing to do something to help, I went to the sink and pumped water into a glass. "Here, drink some water. That might help." I filled another glass for myself. As always, the water perked up my spirits.

Mother drained the glass and a slight smile curved her lips. "It does the trick for now, but the fear is still there."

"Maybe Father will change his mind."

"Wishful thinking. I doubt it, though. It's the same look he wore before he went to Europe in 1918." Mother braced against the table, leaning on it for support to stand. "Go. Call Dewitt to supper. Your father should be in soon."

Her reaction puzzled me. Somehow she wasn't telling me everything. The nights and whispered mornings sprang once more to my thoughts.

My father arrived, grinning. Gone was the ghostly pallor. We sat down to dinner. Normally we weren't a praying family, not until the day before. We bowed our heads for grace.

"They'll be needing experienced soldiers." Father said, as soon as he finished the blessing.

"But Pops, they'll take younger boys, too, right?" In anticipation, Dewitt's eyes widened. He just started shaving his peach fuzz last summer, not that he needed to worry. A beard wasn't in his near future.

"Oh sure, course you'll need parental permission to enlist, son."

"That's not a problem, is it?" Dewitt asked. "Pop you'll sign for me, right?"

Mother's fork clattered against the plate. "No." Her whisper filled the sudden silence. "Not my baby."

Father grasped her hand. "Eva, he's not a baby. He's seventeen. Near enough to be a man. They'll need strong young men too."

I searched their faces for what they left unspoken. Some code existed between them that I never quite understood.

"We were attacked." Father's expression tightened, then relaxed. "This isn't like the last time. The time for keeping to ourselves is done."

"Mother, are you going to join the knitting circle with Mrs. Frolander?" I asked, desperate to relieve the tension. "Maxine and I want to go to Alamogordo to see if we can pick up some yarn."

Father stood and pulled the curtains closed. "Where are the blankets?" He faced mother once again.

She didn't meet his eyes. "In the hall closet upstairs. Liv, go get them."

"What for?" Dewitt asked.

"The blackouts," Father said. "We have to take care. There is the possibility the Japanese will attack the west coast. From there, it isn't far to New Mexico."

Preparing for the war started so simply, almost like we had been waiting for it.

Reporter's Note: In addition to the taped interviews. I was privileged to receive Anna Frolander's journal which included her first-hand accounts of certain events and her poetry. As the excerpts present another point of view of the town's stories, I'm offering several of them throughout the story as well. The first appears below. – R.W.P.

Anna Frolander's Journal

December 8, 1941

Listening to the president's short speech today sent a shock through me not unlike when Harold left for the war in 1918. My husband never a strong man, lacked what I thought might be needed in the hardships of a battlefield. However, nothing ever jolted me as much as hearing my Sam talking about joining up. My firstborn, by just a handful of minutes, has always been my heart's delight, no less than his brothers. His tendency to enjoy life, joking and making others laugh results in me favoring him perhaps a smattering more than his siblings. The boys were in their room talking in low voices when I heard Sam's voice rise. "Just think of the adventures."

In the twinkling of a moment, my boys have grown up.

The Day Following
The "Day which will live in Infamy"

Laced by radio static,
your strong voice reassures us,
a nation in fear.
You announce a war.
The pain of a young bride
becomes the agony of a mother
these twenty-three years later.
You ask for our sacrifice again
amidst waving flags
and trumpets raised in eternal clarion call.
Necessary?
Perhaps, but I'm a reluctant follower
much more unenthusiastic
now, than then.

Reporter's Note: Liv Soderlund, a woman of approximately thirty-eight with blonde hair and deep blue eyes, is one of several women you will meet within these transcripts. She possesses a strong countenance and fierce attitude which is evident in her narrative.– R.W.P.

Chapter Three

Liv

THE FOLLOWING MORNING, I scooted in the backseat between Dewitt and Maxine. Dad headed the car out to the street. Up and down Main Street other young men along with older ones piled into cars in groups and pairs.

I leaned across Maxine to roll down the window. "There's Billy. Isn't he going to town?"

"Not today," she said. "Says the recruiter would be too busy so he's staying home with his folks. He and his father may go tomorrow. I guess there will be time enough, whenever he goes." Her stony expression didn't invite any further discussion.

"Hey, Mike!" Dewitt called outside the other window to Mike Brennen. "You headed to Alamogordo? See ya there."

The day took on the quality of a holiday, as if everyone prepared to head off to a summer picnic in the middle of December, or perhaps on a community shopping day for Christmas. I hadn't thought about Christmas since Sunday. I wondered if holiday shopping occurred to anyone, despite the date. December 9. Only a little over two weeks remained. I couldn't remember a time when making gifts and buying goodies had not been my top priority at this time of year. Even when times were tight, and the last ten years had been exceptionally so, Christmas preparations took priority in December.

I nudged Maxine. "What are you getting Billy for Christmas?"

Maxine giggled. I joined her merriment, relieved she put aside her sadness. Taking the day off school to spend with my best friend was a good plan. When had we last gone shopping, or just goofed off? Certainly before her parents had died.

Determined to make the day a memorable one and a time for her to enjoy, I leaned in to her. "Come on. What gives? Surely you can tell me."

Maxine cupped a hand around my ear and whispered something.

"I can't hear you over the engine and the wind." The car rattled over the dirt on the way through the mountains. Trips to town were a big event. Many people don't understand, especially these days, but we had a lot of people in Hope Springs who were still in horse and buggy transportation.

She tried again, this time louder. "A typewriter. For school."

"But is—" I refused to remind her he wouldn't be going to college. "But isn't that expensive?"

"I've been saving for ages." Almost bouncing in her seat, she explained. "I've got just a little left and it'll be paid for. I put it on layaway at Sears Roebuck last summer."

"You've been able to keep it secret all this time?" My friend usually wasn't very good at keeping confidences as I'd learned when I told her I liked Joe Bauer. It was all over school the next day. I think she intended to tell Joe, but she told his friend Sam instead. Maxine never meant any harm—she only wanted everyone to be as happy as she and Billy were.

"He doesn't have any idea."

We settled back into our seats. The car descended the last hill to the main road heading northeast.

"Do you think Ruth and Joe will, you know?" I raised my eyebrows at her.

"What?" Maxine relaxed her head against the seat. "Go steady? I think they already are. Ruth seems happy enough this time. Maybe she and Joe will..." She sat up. "Oh, I'm sorry."

"It's okay. I'm over him. We didn't hit it off nearly like I had thought. I hope he's happy."

Our girl talk filled the car and though my parents carried on a low-voiced conversation in the front seat, I didn't pay much attention, though an occasional word drifted back now and then. "Europe...how long? Age?"

Dewitt grabbed the back of my father's seat, pointing. "Pops! Stop the car. I saw a—"

"Not today, son. We don't have the time to stop for you to tend the wounded rabbit." Father didn't need to wait for an explanation. My brother was a sucker for any hurt little thing. It was both endearing and infuriating if we were in a hurry.

"But—"

"No. Knowing you, we'd have to head back to Doc Brennen's for you to ask how to set a broken leg, or perform surgery." Dad's gaze met Dewitt's in the rearview mirror. "You can't save every little creature on God's earth."

Dewitt slumped back in his seat. I caught the look in his eyes. The pain there no doubt rivaled whatever creature he'd seen on the side of the road.

I patted his shoulder. "Cheer up, Dee. I'm sure you'll find some little animal needing medical attention on the way back from town."

Everyone in the car fell quiet, and we rumbled on along the ribbon of road that wove through desert brush spread out over the foothills.

When we reached Alamogordo, I unfolded my legs out of the seat and stretched.

"Remember—" Father started.

"Don't mention the water," Dewitt and I chimed.

Maxine laughed. "I remember Mom and Dad telling me the same thing every time we went to town, like I'd forget and suddenly start blabbing about the Spring."

"Sh—" Mother dipped her head near us. "It's not a joke."

We sobered.

"Where to first?" Mother's gaze followed Dewitt and Father striding down the street toward the recruiter before returning her attention to us girls.

"What branch do you think Dewitt will enlist in?" I asked.

"Not sure. Your father was in the infantry, so maybe he'll follow suit." Mother's expression dimmed and she closed her eyes. A moment later, she opened them, pressed her lips together and lifted her shoulders. "Well, young ladies, we're off like a herd of turtles."

We entered the General Store. I wandered the aisles with Maxine and mother, before stopping at the cosmetics aisle. I fingered the powder compacts and lipstick.

"Some blush on your cheeks would help," Mother said.

"Help what?" I stared at my reflection in the counter mirror. My blonde hair swept back from my face, secured with a pin. I wore my favorite lipstick. Though my face was sharper than I'd like, I always envied those movie stars with high cheekbones and big wide eyes, I couldn't complain about my appearance. Sometimes I wonder where that girl went when I look in the mirror today and see the beginning of lines. Back then we had no other real worries, except to make ourselves look pretty and get the best grades I could in school. It's probably cliché but a simple life is how we start off and simple is how I'd like to think we'll finish once more. Only the middle gets all muddled and complicated, especially for us girls who became the women of Weeping Women Springs.

Oh, there I go rambling again. I apologize. Where was I? Oh yes, Mother and her constant suggestions for what I offered to the world. I knew what her real motivation always was, as most mothers I'd guess.

"Oh, bring some color and highlight your lovely eyes." Mother's innocent wide-eyes didn't fool me.

"I doubt there are any eligible young men who aren't at the recruiter's today," I said.

"Doesn't matter. Who knows when some handsome young man will cross your path? Always be prepared."

"You and the boy scouts, eh Mother? The way to find a man, by Eva Soderlund." I caught Maxine's eye, and we dissolved into giggles.

"Someday, when you have a daughter of your own..." she said, but her voice contained no reprimand, and she winked. I must say she always made sure she was never without makeup and clean clothes, even during the worst times, genteel they called it.

"I won't hound her all day and night about finding a husband," I promised.

"There's no hurry," Maxine said. "Liv will find a nice boy and raise a passel of grandchildren to keep you and Mr. Soderlund busy in your old age."

"We can hope." Mother gazed into the glass counter filled with makeup.

"Thank God we have the Spring." I rolled my eyes. "We'll never lose hope."

The store clerk approached us and said, "Hope springs eternal. May I help you, ladies?"

I swiveled my head to see if anyone else had heard the reference. My heart almost stopped for a second.

"Sh— Livia Marie Soderlund!" Mother hissed.

Maxine paled. "Liv!"

"Sorry," I mumbled. How much had the woman heard? A rush of heat flashed through me. I avoided Mother's and Maxine's pointed looks. My mistake was unforgivable. "Um. Could I see your blush compacts?"

The woman went to retrieve the requested items.

"Not another word, Liv." Mother's breath brushed my ear.

The clerk came back. "Here you go." She placed several compacts on the counter. "With your beautiful fair skin—I'm guessing Scandinavian—am I right? I'd recommend a lighter pink. With some mascara to darken your light lashes."

I breathed a little easier and kept my eyes focused on the makeup. What would happen if the clerk had overheard my thoughtless remark? The Council would have to be informed, but what then?

"Where are you ladies from?" the clerk asked. "I don't believe I've seen you before." Her friendly smile took on the charm of someone intent on making small talk in the anticipation of a sale. As you might have guessed, Hope Springs people didn't mix much with the rest on the Council's orders.

Maxine pressed her hand against my back.

I drew strength from the contact. "We live a ways out. Don't get in to town very often."

"Girls, we'd better finish up here," Mother said. "We need to meet your father for lunch."

"But it's only ten—" the store clerk said. "Well, if you've come from a ways off, I'm sure you're ready for an early lunch."

"No." Maxine said. "You're right, it's a little early. Mrs. Soderlund, I'm sure Dewitt and Mr. Soderlund will probably still be busy, but we can go check. Miss, could I see the lipstick?"

I squeezed my friend's hand, thankful for her attempt to distract the saleswoman. "I'll take this one."

"Good choice. I'll wrap it up for you. Be back in a moment with the lipsticks."

"Let's go, girls," mother said. "Before she returns."

"We'll catch up to you, Mrs. Soderlund." Maxine said. "I think it better if we don't skip out. She'll be more likely to remember us then. I'm sure she's forgotten the earlier comment by now and we'll blend in with the rest of her customers for the day."

Maxine did some quick thinking and I nodded at her hushed explanation. "See you, Mom."

Mother walked off, glancing over her shoulder when she reached the door. I waggled my fingers at her.

The clerk returned with her package and the lipsticks.

"On second thought," Maxine said. "I don't need anything today."

I opened my pocketbook and placed a dollar on the counter. "Thank you for your help."

Outside, I patted my chest. "Oh my, I've never been so scared."

"You covered well. I don't think she noticed a thing," Maxine said.

We strolled down the street. Alamogordo was pretty quiet back then, before the army built the airbase, but bigger than what we were used to. Unlike Hope Springs, people here bustled along, going in and out of the businesses. Excitement unlike any I had ever experienced permeated the atmosphere. I attempted to understand the source. Though the holiday neared, this frenetic quality to everyone's voices and demeanor related specifically to the war news.

"Let's see what's playing at the theater," Maxine suggested.

"Maybe there's a Clark Gable movie. Or Cary Grant."

We rounded a corner. "Wow. Look at that." Maxine pointed.

More men than I'd ever seen in one place waited in line, shoulders against the adobe post office wall. Everyone, old and young, awaited their turn.

"Amazing."

"Your mother would be proud." She giggled. "It's like a line up. Take your pick."

Heat flamed in my cheeks. "Max! You're awful. Just because you have Billy."

"I'm sorry. I just want you to find happiness with a boy, like I have."

"Why is everyone in such a hurry? I'll find someone when the time is right."

"Don't worry." She threw her arm around my shoulders. "I know you will. This is normal."

"It might be some time before things get back to normal." I watched the men inch forward in the line. "The war changes everything."

"But it can't last forever."

A gust hurtled down the street.

At the cafe, the waitress delivered burgers to our table.

Dewitt joined us at the table and didn't stop chattering. "So they said they were sending a recruiter from Ft. Bliss. They're taking people in all the services. Maybe I can get into a submarine unit. I could be a medic."

"Submarine?" I couldn't imagine being confined to such a small space. "Isn't that like being in a sardine can?"

"Aw. It won't be that bad. Just think how thrilling it will be to dive undersea. It'll be like Jules Verne's story."

"The U-boats have been wreaking havoc in the Atlantic," Father said. "The supply ships to Europe are sometimes hit pretty hard. Remember the...last September."

We all quieted. The ship had sunk and all hands were believed lost. We thought the president would declare war, but the word never came.

I studied Father. His gray pallor had returned. That alone had answered my question about the answers he'd received from the recruiter.

"They said I'd be more useful on the home front," he said, "building ships or airplanes."

"Will you?" Mother asked.

"I'd have to go to California to do something like that. What would you and the children do?"

Mother fiddled with her fork and the quiet lengthened. "The same thing we'd do if you went off to war." The fork stilled, and she met his eyes. "If you wish to do it, go, Ed."

I didn't know what to think of her words. Everything was changing and whether it would be good or bad, I wasn't sure.

You probably think it's silly looking back on it from your stand point. As a reporter, you know what happened, but you've asked me how it happened, and I have to state the facts as they happened for us, not make it up.

LATER THAT WEEK, I arrived at school early for the Founder's Day planning committee. I entered Mrs. Godair's room to find my teacher alone at her desk.

"Where's everyone?" I asked.

"The principal said we were changing plans. The Council informed him the fiftieth anniversary fair was off and we'd hold a send-off parade for the boys."

I sank into a seat in the front row of desks. "Why would they cancel the Founder's Day anniversary? We've worked so hard all year on it."

New Year's Day in Hope Springs had always started with a parade, celebrating the founding fathers' rejoicing when they found the Spring in 1892. Last June, the Council announced the fiftieth anniversary commemoration would include not only the parade but a fair as well. The senior class planned the event, and it had promised to be the most exciting thing to ever happen in town.

"With the war, things have changed." Mrs. Godair peered over her glasses. "Liv, I know you and the others put a lot of effort in on the fair. Maybe someday we'll get to do it, but not now."

I slapped the desk. Maybe the other kids were right. The Council ruined everything. I almost said so to Mrs. Godair, but thought better of it. "It's disappointing. Have you told the others?"

"Not yet." Mrs. Godair stood. "Will you do it? They'll be arriving soon. I need to make some dittos for class."

"Fine." I went to the slate chalkboard and wrote in large letters: Founder's Day 1942 Canceled!

Ruth Ackerman, Sam and Donnie Frolander, and Billy Fiekens sauntered into the room.

"What?" Ruthie shrieked when she caught sight of the board.

The guys grumbled.

"Guess they decided we couldn't have any fun," Sam said.

"The war changes everything." I explained. "We're to have a send-off parade for the boys."

Sam perked up at that. "Hey guys, we'll be the honored servicemen. That'll be swell." He nudged his twin. "What do ya think?"

Donnie scuffed his shoe, stuffing his hand into his pockets. "Think we'll have enough marching to do." His lips frowned in disgust. Maybe Donnie wasn't so excited to be joining up. It surprised me. He was the first boy I'd seen that wasn't raring to go to war.

Sam punched his brother's arm. "Cheer up, kid."

"Did you and Sam enlist?" I asked.

"You betcha we did." Sam said. "I'm going into the army."

"I want to join the army air force, but not sure yet." Billy winced.

"Maxine said you're waiting to join," I said.

Billy wandered to the window, looking down toward the store. He nodded, then leaned a shoulder against the wall. "I'm going to marry Maxine. Nothing will stop me. I'll take my chances and wait for the draft board's letter."

"Dewitt's joining the navy." I informed them. "I think Dad is going to California to build airplanes. He's just past the age they're conscripting."

I watched the boys' faces. They seemed both older and younger all at once. From playing children's games of hide and seek on soft summer evenings, to sneaking a cigarette behind the store last spring, we had shared secrets and laughter from the earliest memories. Any moment, I could imagine one of the boys grinning and saying the war had been an elaborate prank. If I hadn't seen the lines in Alamogordo, I'd have been ready to believe them as well. Our years in Hope Springs had been full of life, of hope and childish amusements. The greatest threat the boys had faced before Sunday was a scraped knee or accidentally falling in a mining pit, not too likely an event, or the ominous warning from the Council, should anyone let word out about the Spring.

I clicked my nails on the desk.

"Please stop that." Ruth gave me a penetrating look. Always so quick to chide someone, she drove the rest of us crazy most times.

"Sorry. Everything suddenly seems uncertain. It's like we've always known something might happen, but now that it has—I guess I keep waiting for the other shoe to drop, or something. I can't put my finger on it exactly, but I feel things are changing, and it's not just the war, or maybe it is." My thoughts tumbled as I struggled to put the feeling into words.

Even discussing it now, I can't put a finger on the emotions running through me then. In hindsight, perhaps it was a premonition, but back then we had no way of knowing. Anyway, back to Founders Day.

"I told Maxine and my mother that I felt things were going to change. It could be a good thing, couldn't it?" I gazed around the classroom, seeking understanding and even agreement, but the boys didn't meet my eyes, and Ruth examined her nail polish. I ground my teeth. The boys I could almost forgive. They must have other things on their minds, but Ruth's vapid nonchalance, even disregard for anything serious, lacked the appropriate concern.

No one said a thing, but I went on as if someone, anyone had responded. "I mean, for so long we've wanted change around here. We wanted to get the Council to open up the town more, right? This might be our chance. Even though the town might not be any different, we're sure to be different if all our boys go off into the world." I shifted in my seat. "Just think of all the exciting things you'll see. You'll write home and it'll be like we get to experience it with you."

Billy turned from the window. "You bet if I went, I'd be writing Maxine every day."

"Sure, that's what I mean." I said. "You'll be able to take Hope Springs with you, but send a little of the world back to us."

Sam smiled. "Yeah, it'll be great. What an adventure we'll have, and we'll tell you about it too."

Mrs. Godair returned. "What adventure?"

"The army," Sam said. "Well, or navy or wherever the Hope Springs boys end up. There's a whole big world out there, one we've never seen. Heck, I've never even dreamed of going past Phoenix. What an opportunity to see the country."

"So you enlisted?"

While the boys told their enlistment stories, I flipped open a notebook.

Parade 1942 Send off, I wrote at the top of the page. This would be the grandest parade the town had ever seen. I would make sure of it. Since the boys would march in it, I'd enlist the gals to plan it.

You wouldn't believe the excitement we all felt then. Everyone except Maxine, that is. Here, let me call her over. She has her own view of things. I think it's best you get the fullest picture possible of our story.

Anna's Journal

Christmas is always a time of reflection for me. I try to make it good for the boys, but with so little at our disposal, it's difficult. They're such great sons and never mind that their shirts are homespun and the best present I can give is newly knitted socks.

This year of course we're knitting scarves for the military, hoping this bit of wool can keep them warm in the bitterest cold across the globe.

We went over to Elizabeth's for Christmas dinner. Lovely ham with all the fixings. In the kitchen at one point she said, "I worry so about you and the boys. I wish you'd allow us to help. You know we don't mind." I've accepted her hand-me-downs often enough. I know she doesn't mind, but my pride doesn't allow me to take money, though I know they can afford it.

My Sons

O male children of mine,
mere boys, possessors of my heart
you screeched in the night
troubled by unkind dreams.
Your grins brightened the sun
during the day.
You learn your ways
from peek a boo
to hide and seek.
You all buried your faces
in my skirts
one time or another.
If only
I could hide you
from the world.
An impossible task,
this lone motherhood
of boys to young men.

Reporter's Note: Below is the first of several interviews conducted with Maxine Fiekens. More introverted than Liv, Maxine is of similar age, thirty-eight with red hair. My initial impressions are of a kind woman who takes pride in her business, the local market.– R.W.P

Chapter Four

Maxine

I'VE NEVER REALLY UNDERSTOOD the excitement of New Year's Eve, even though I enjoyed spending the evening with Billy of course. Founder's Day is a different story. From the time I was a child, the excitement and celebration of the Founding of the Spring thrilled me. January 1, 1942 the Council canceled the Founder's Day Parade, and instead we had the send-off for the boys. It saddened me, but at least Billy decided not to enlist. He had to help with his folks' ranch and he spent plenty of time helping at the store as well.

Liv was in charge, and though I told her I'd assist, the store kept me busy. Billy came over in the morning before the parade and helped out with the stocking. We weren't open for business on the holiday, but I liked to make sure everything was set for business the next day. New Year's seemed to be a good time to start things off clean.

I placed the last can on the shelf and felt Billy's hands on my waist. He whirled me to him for a kiss. I fingered his collar. "Are you okay?"

"My best girl said yes, it's a brand new year, and I live in Hope Springs. What else could I ask for?"

He always looked on the bright side. It helped so much after my parents died. I was so grateful for him and everything he did for me, couldn't have asked for any better boy. Maybe that's why I felt so sad after, oh never mind me, but I will take your handkerchief, thanks.

Where was I? Oh, Founders Day 1942. I could tell Billy wasn't telling me everything, you know? I guess women always know these things, but his smile never faltered.

"You know I'll always take care of you, right?" His hands cupped my cheeks. "I wish I could do more, but until I finish school, Pa needs me to help out. Everything will be fine. In June we'll have our wedding. Sunshine, life will be good for us." The drumbeats echoed through the street.

"You ready to head to the parade?" he asked.

I nodded, and we went outside. Billy's folks sat in the Council seats placed at the front of the bank so we went over there.

Grace Fiekens pursed her lips at me. "Happy New Year." Her expression didn't do much for the sentiment, but I nodded and wished her the same. The woman was going to be my mother-in-law so I didn't want to make any trouble. Billy, the good boy he was, never noticed that his parents didn't like the idea of him marrying me. They had other plans for him, which didn't include running the general store with me.

Billy took my hand and we wandered down the street toward Liv who organized the parade at the end of the street.

The marching drums pounded out a marching rhythm. Liv waved an arm to start the parade. She wove between all of our young men dressed in their best clothes, not uniforms. Without the uniforms, I could almost pretend it was just our standard Founders Day Parade.

"Boys, when you get to the Council's seats, march in place and salute," Liv said to them.

The drumbeats thudded, keeping time with hearts and steps. "Good," she shouted. "Majorettes, you're on."

The girls twirled their batons and danced, skipped and marched down Main Street with the band close on their heels playing, "You're a Grand Old Flag." You know that music always gets to me, straight in my heart.

Then the boys, all forty-three of them, moved forward. Billy was the only hold out of the seniors and older boys. He'd promised me he wouldn't go willingly, though he prepared me for the fact they might draft him.

Once the parade was underway, Liv came up to us. "Don't they look handsome?"

I nodded but held tight to Billy's hand. Then Billy jerked away in a way he never did before. My breath caught when as the recruits walked by, he stepped into the street, falling into step with the others.

I stared at him, and then narrowed my eyes at Liv. "Did you put him up to this?"

"No. I'm sure I don't know what he's doing." Her open mouth showed she was just as shocked as I was.

A cheer went up from the crowd.

I returned my attention to the boys and swallowed hard. My Billy made his decision that day. I couldn't help but wonder what would happen to us, to our plans. "He belongs there with them."

Liv drew me close. "It'll be all right."

They continued down the street stopping at the Council and saluting. I nodded but didn't answer. The sun warmed the chilled air. I wondered if I would ever feel warm again. If Billy went into the service, what would I do? It was a thought that never left me.

THE MONDAY FOLLOWING the Christmas break, school was back in session. Since I'd quit school I hated schooldays. The Council told me they could make arrangements for the store if I chose to continue school, but after my parents—you know, the store was their life's work and my responsibility. It was something I'd accepted all my life, that when I was old enough it would be my job to take over the running of it. Things just happened a little sooner than I planned. Life isn't always fair, that much I'd learned on that terrible day over a year before.

On that January Monday, just like every school day, I worked at the store and watched the rest of the senior class walk by the store and go inside the brick school house. It still ached.

I swept the store and stocked the shelves, but Billy's actions at the parade had stunned me. I'd pondered it ever since and concluded finally that Billy needed to join the war, just like all the other boys. Duty called, and I had no doubt that along with patriotic duty, a certain amount of adventure and excitement lured them as well. But though I knew it, I really didn't like the idea much.

No customers yet, so I went to the backyard, to the Spring, the secret which held our town enthralled. Have you seen it yet? No? We'll have to take you out back later, right Liv? I never tired of the view, the small pond surrounded by rose bushes. My soul always seemed connected to this special place. Since the original settlers found it, the Spring provided both life and hope, gaining its name and earning our loyalty to keep its secret. The cliff rose above the pond and the Spring water ran through a crevasse. In winter the sandstone cast a shadow over the water. A short distance away a water tower had been built, a silent sentinel above the town. The normalcy of the water tower guarded our precious commodity. If ever anyone asked we told them about the well that we drilled, most people accepted lie as truth.

That day, I dipped a bucket into the pond, into the deep green-blue pool. From the tower, the water ran through the town pipes and I could open a faucet for all my needs, but I preferred dipping a bucket to bring up water directly from the pond. The powers seemed stronger at this point, closer to the source.

After drawing the bucket, I set it beside the pond and sat in the dry grass. I scooped up a palm-full to drink. The familiar zing of energy and vitality spread through my limbs.

A silent prayer accompanied the drink. I'd always considered myself fortunate to live with the pond, and honored to be the guardian of the well. My grandparents had taken their duty seriously, and passed on the task to me through my parents. The title, Guardian of the Spring, seemed mainly an honorarium by that time.

My prayer included acceptance of Billy's decision. A sense of peace overcame me. Yes, Billy belonged with the others.

Tomorrow, I'd go along with him to Alamogordo. But first, I'd fix something special for dinner.

"Hello!" came from the direction of the shop.

I rose and lifted the bucket, taking care not to spill a precious drop.

"May I help you?" I hurried to the front of the store. "Oh hi, Mrs. Soderlund. What can I do for you today?"

"I need some eggs."

"The Bauers brought in fresh eggs this morning. How many would you like?"

"I'm going to make an angel food cake, so I'd better take a dozen. It's Dewitt's favorite." The chirpiness in her voice didn't cover the worry I caught in her face. "He's headed out on the troop train Thursday. I thought we'd have a little going away party after the game. Can you come?"

I agreed. Then another thought occurred to me. "Mrs. Soderlund, would you mind the store tomorrow? I want to go to town with Billy. We'll be home before the game."

"Sure." Mrs. Soderlund plucked a can of milk from the shelf. "So, he's going to enlist as well?"

I nodded. "It's the right thing to do. I'm so proud of him. I couldn't keep him from it, nor would I dream of doing so. We all have our duties to perform."

"That's true enough," she nodded, "much as I hate to admit it. It's true."

"Will that be all for you?"

"Yes."

I noted the purchases in the ledger. "Seventy cents added to your tab."

"Thanks." She left and I returned to my work. I needed to place an order while in Alamogordo, so I took inventory.

The rest of the day I had a variety of regular customers until at precisely five after three the high-schoolers rushed into the store. Liv took her place behind the soda fountain to assist me. We served up Coca-Colas for the group.

Joe Bauer sat on the end stool and swiveled it around. Ruth perched on his knee and cuddled close with a little giggle.

Donnie and Sam Frolander mimicked her with a high pitched squeal.

Sam linked an elbow with Barbara. "Wish we had a jukebox. All we have is the old Victrola. Ah well, better than nothing. Wanna dance?"

He headed off to put a record album on. Artie Shaw's tune, "Dancing in the Dark," streamed out of the horn, and he bowed to Barbara and took her hand. They whirled around the small dance floor I had cleared in the back corner of the store.

Within a short time, me and Billy, Joe and Ruth and some of the others joined them. Liv smiled and tapped her foot to the music.

The music lifted my spirits while I cuddled close to Billy. When the drum solo came in the next song, Dewitt rapped his fingers in time on the counter.

"Darling, Not Without You" came on next talking about faraway places. Liv always dreamed of Mardi Gras in New Orleans, Hollywood in California. Hadn't we all dreamed of taking a long trip somewhere? I had too, before my parents died. But now, it would only be the boys going off without us.

Liv clinked a glass with a spoon to get everyone's attention. "Hey kids, Mother's having a sendoff party for Dewitt Wednesday evening. We take him to Cruces Thursday. He's headed to San Diego. So come on by our place after the game for a bit."

Sam whooped and ruffled Dewitt's hair. "So the youngest of us is off first. Lucky you." The high spirits spread through the crowd.

At the pause in the music, the bell jingled at the front of the store.

"What's going on in here?" It was Liv's uncle, Jim.

"Nothing much. We're just dancing." Liv said.

"Could hear you all clear down the street. Can't you turn down the Victrola?" With his hands in his pockets and his stern expression, he wasn't going to take no for an answer.

The boys grumbled. "Ah come on, Mr. Hoffman," Sam said.

I caught Liv's eye. The common complaint of the adults toward our music almost made everything seem normal, even though we were poised on the brink of the unknown, and everything would soon change. When the boys came home, they'd be different, transformed by their worldly adventure.

Would Billy change? How could he not going out into the world?

Mr. Hoffman scowled, but didn't move to leave.

"When will you get leave, Dewitt?" Donnie asked.

"Not before six weeks. Basic training."

"Will you write?" Barbara asked.

Dewitt waggled his eyebrows. "Sure. I'll write whoever wants to exchange letters. Especially girls."

Billy gave me a stern look. "You'd better not be thinking of writing any other boy than me, young lady."

I kissed him. "Hush, you."

The whole crowd laughed at that. My cheeks heated.

"Okay, young people," Jim said. "Isn't it time to head home for supper?"

The others groaned, but their hearts weren't in it.

"See you everyone." Liv drew her uncle to the door. "Let them have their fun. You know it won't be much longer and all the boys will be gone." I couldn't help but bury my face into Billy's shirt.

THE NEXT MORNING the bell jingled at the front of the store while I took out an iron skillet for breakfast. "Sunshine? You here?" Billy's voice called.

"In the kitchen. You want some breakfast?"

"Sure." He came up behind me and kissed my neck, sending heat up my face.

I laughed and pushed him away. "Sit. Tell me your news."

"How'd you know?"

"Billy Fiekens, you are at my doorstep before the sun." I removed a carton of eggs from the shelf. "Of course, you have news."

"Ma and Pa said they think you should stay here while they take me to Alamogordo."

At that I dropped the egg. The yolk puddled on the counter. So fragile, only a little fall and it broke. I whirled to him. "What?"

"Now, Sunshine. It's probably best. You have the store and I don't want to take you from your work." He picked up a rag and scooped up the gooey egg.

I clenched my fists. So this was the beginning. The distancing. For five years we'd been nearly inseparable, and now, he would disappear, go off to war, and then what?

"Is this how it will be when you leave?"

His forehead scrunched. "What do you mean?"

"Will you leave and suddenly you'll be gone, and everything we've shared will be gone." The thought tore up my insides.

"Huh? You're not making any sense."

I gnawed the inside of my lip. "I don't know. Everything's changed."

"I love you. That hasn't changed. Never will." He rinsed his hands in the sink and took mine. "You said you'd marry me. Are you having second thoughts?"

I shook my head. "I'm scared."

"We'll get married before I leave. Promise." He hugged me.

His words sounded good, but they didn't relieve the dark tenseness within my heart. My limbs felt heavy, almost the way I'd felt when the sheriff came to tell me of my parents' accident.

I forced a smile. "I know."

After he left I headed across the street to Mrs. Soderlund's. "You won't need to watch the store. Billy's parents are going with him to Alamogordo," I told her.

Mrs. Soderlund peered at me a moment before opening the door wider. "The store can wait a little while. Looks like you could use a cup of tea."

I backed away, but Mrs. Soderlund drew me inside. "I could use the company, and so can you."

I sat at the kitchen table. "How did you do it?"

"I won't tell you it's easy. I know Billy's going to enlist today. Dewitt leaves tomorrow and he's so excited. Somehow that makes it better in one way and worse in another. I remember when Ed left for the Great War. Dewitt reminds me so much of him. In 1918 he was thrilled to get out of Hope Springs. He wrote and told me how seasick he was on the troop ship going over to France.

"But that was only the beginning. Ed tried to keep his letters upbeat, but gradually I saw changes. It was subtle. I ached to see him get so worked up. One letter after another he'd write and tell me of another soldier he'd trained with being taken out of action. Wounded, killed. And then the letters stopped altogether for a while. That was the hardest, most difficult month I had."

The tea kettle whistled.

"What happened?" I asked.

"I cried and carried on. I was living with Aunt Wanda and Uncle Jim at the time. She was beside herself trying to comfort me, but I overheard her talking to my Uncle Jim one evening. 'Thank God she didn't get married before he left. I don't know what we'd do if she were with child.'"

"What an awful thing for her to say."

"I thought so, too, at the time. You see, I'd wanted get married before he left for boot camp, but there was little time."

She poured the tea. I wrapped my fingers around the warm cup. The coldness that invaded my heart seemed beyond the warmth.

"Billy asked me, you know? Did Liv tell you? He's promised we'll have the wedding before he leaves."

A sadness flickered on Mrs. Soderlund's face. "Congratulations. It's an exciting time for you. Please let me know if I can help. You're like a second daughter to me and—"

"Thank you." I grasped her hand, afraid she might mention mom next. Thinking about mom still hurt.

"I'm happy you have Billy."

"He's been wonderful, especially this past year." Every single day he checked up on me, helped with the store, and just held me on the days I thought I might not be able to go on.

"He's a good boy."

I stirred honey into the tea then sipped. Something about the Spring water tea with honey soothed as nothing else, and my spirits lifted. "I don't know what we'd do without the Spring."

"We're so fortunate."

"Did it help get you through while you were waiting for Mr. Soderlund?"

"Yes. I remember getting a letter from him." She ran a finger around the rim of her cup. "He missed the water and told me to drink some for him. It helped. I could never remain frightened or worried if I drank the water. Hope always returned."

I smiled. "It's exactly what happens to me when I start worrying about Billy. This morning was the worst. I feel like Billy is already gone in a way. Now, I can hardly remember feeling sad."

"You'll get through it." She squeezed my hand. Something about the comfort of someone who had been through similar circumstances reassured me everything would be all right.

"I know. I have Liv and the rest of the town. Besides, it isn't like Billy is the only one going. Everyone will be in the same situation. It's sort of nice, really, that we can support each other. Plus, what can happen to the Hope Springs boys? Right?"

Mrs. Soderlund offered me a piece of coffee cake. "You're right. Every one of the men returned to Hope Springs after the war. We knew then something special protected them. I've always believed it was the water."

A thrill ran up my spine. "I'm glad I came over to talk to you. It does help to talk to someone." After we finished our cake I gave her a hug and returned to the store.

I prepared the water cans for the game. It was my duty as the Spring's guardian—make sure no visitor drank the water. How often I'd wondered what would happen if someone did drink the water. It hadn't happened since I could remember, but Grandfather told me of John Waterhouse stumbling into town one day. The traveling salesman had been knocking on doors when he came into the store one day. In the storeroom, Grandfather didn't hear the bell. "I tell you, Maxi, when I came out of that storeroom and saw John holding a glass of water, I nearly knocked him down,' Grandfather told me. 'But it was too late. He'd already had a glass before that. I watched his face and knew the die had been cast."

Over the years, I'd heard the story dozens of times and always Grandfather warned me never to make the same mistake. "It turned out all right in the end with John, but imagine if he'd left without me seeing him. He could have blabbed all over creation. As it was, we were lucky he was a single man and distanced from his family. Otherwise, the population of Hope Springs could have increased by many more than one that time."

Would that really be so bad, I've wondered over the years. While I understood we didn't want a population explosion, a few newcomers might have been good. It wasn't my choice to make though. It's always been up to the Council.

Chapter Five

Liv

OH, I REMEMBER that game well. Don't tease me, Maxine. I see that glint in your eye. Why don't you go get Ruth? The reporter will want to speak with her too.

I'd been up in the stands watching the boys. The game was close, and we were behind by one basket. The final ball swept through the net and the crowd burst into cheers. It was deafening. I bounced down the bleachers to join the pandemonium on the court. Everyone was hugging and shouting. Hope Springs High had finally beat Tularosa. Donnie Frolander in his green silky uniform whirled toward me.

Swept up by the jubilant moment, I threw my arms around Donnie's neck and planted a kiss on his lips. The kiss lengthened and Donnie moved his mouth softly over mine. Suddenly it ended. I opened my eyes to stare into his. *Donnie?* I mouthed and blinked. No, not Donnie. Solemn, serious, studious Donnie? His twin, Sam, had always been the upbeat one who caught my attention and everyone else's too, while Donnie stood back, seemingly content in sparks reflected off his brother's radiance.

I walked away, glancing over my shoulder to watch Donnie, who had a rare smile on his face. He talked with his teammates, but his gaze didn't leave me. *What had just happened?* I joined Maxine who stood at the water table, making sure to hand Spring water to the boys and other water to the fans and team from Tularosa.

"What's wrong with you?" Maxine asked me. "You look stunned."

I hesitated. "I'm not sure." I didn't want to tell anyone yet. Instead, I held Donnie's kiss inside, letting the effervescent feeling bubble into gaiety, but not examining it too closely. I giggled and helped her hand out water.

Every few seconds I searched for Donnie, and met his gaze over the crowd. He milled around the court as people slapped him on the back, congratulating him for the winning basket. Finally the crowd dispersed, leaving only the team and me and Maxine. We packed up the water.

The team headed into the shower, but Donnie approached the water table.

"Want some water?" Maxine asked him.

Donnie shook his head. I fidgeted with the bottles in the crate, willing my hands to stop trembling.

Maxine stacked the crates on the hand truck, removing the last one from under my hands. "I'll go ahead and take these back to the store."

After a long moment, I asked, "Do you need any help?" I didn't meet her eyes, afraid of what she might see in them.

"Are you all right?" She cocked her head.

Heat flooded my cheeks. Great, why did I have to blush so easily?

Maxine's arm draped over my shoulders. "Are you feeling ill?"

Removing her arm, I ducked away. "I'm fine. Go on." She nodded toward Donnie.

After looking from me to Donnie, understanding came in the form of a grin. "Okay, I'm off then. Great game, Donnie. See you later."

We watched her wheel out the hand truck.

"Are you going to the after game party at Billy's?" Donnie asked.

"I wasn't planning on it. Still have to work on my essay for Mrs. Godair."

"Oh. Too bad."

The quiet of the gymnasium pressed in on me. He's just Donnie Frolander I reminded myself, the same boy I'd spoken with every day for years. Why couldn't I find something to say?

"Good game."

"Yeah." He was quiet for a moment. "That was some kiss."

A nervous giggle escaped me. I hardly believed that he'd mentioned it. "Yeah."

"If I write you, would you write back?"

"Of course. Donnie Frolander! How can you imagine I wouldn't write you?"

"Are you writing anyone else?"

"No one else," I assured him. "Dewitt, and Billy maybe, but he'll be writing all his letters to Maxine."

"Billy asked me to be his best man at the wedding."

"I didn't know that. I'll be Maxine's maid of honor." I wiped my sweaty hands on my skirt.

"Guess I'd better hit the showers." He leaned toward me and we bumped noses. The first kiss had flowed effortlessly, but it would not be repeated so easily. Our breath mingled. Then our lips connected and the tingle returned.

I can't help but sigh now remembering. Such sweetness and it was the first time I'd ever experienced anything like it. How did it happen in an instant? One moment he was the same Donnie Frolander, and the next he transformed into someone completely new.

The following night was Dewitt's party. I placed candles on the angel food cake.

"Why are you doing that?" Mother asked.

"Seems appropriate. Sort of like a celebration. Besides, he probably won't be around for his birthday this year."

I struck a match and lit the flames. "There, now doesn't that look cheerful?"

"You're right. Go on ahead and I'll bring the plates."

I took the cake down the darkened hall into the front room, where a small crowd gathered to wish him well. My little brother was soon off to be a war hero. I can't put into words how proud I was.

When I placed the cake on the coffee table Sam started singing, "For he's a jolly good fellow, for he's a jolly good fellow, for he's a jolly good fellow, that nobody can deny."

And so it went, everyone joined in, with Uncle Jim the loudest of all. How did adults switch gears from one moment to the next? They always complained that we kids were changeable, but it was nothing compared to an adult being strict and complaining one moment, and ready to celebrate the next. Sometimes it made my head spin. Uncle Jim had come in before the rest and spoke to my parents in hushed tones, all serious, but I wasn't able to catch what they said.

Father's face darkened as Dewitt's bright eyes glowed in the candlelight.

I couldn't keep my eyes off of Donnie. After the previous night's kiss, I didn't seem able to catch my breath whenever we locked eyes, and that was often. I don't think anyone else noticed at that point, but if I was going to get lovesick, it would be only a matter of time before everyone in town spread the gossip.

At the end of the party, everyone left, but Donnie lingered. He asked if I would accompany him on a stroll so I grabbed my cardigan and joined him outside. The night was clear, so brilliant with stars cutting little lights in the blackness. I knew how Juliet felt in the part of the play where she says she wanted to cut Romeo out in little stars so he would make the night so great everyone would fall in love with night. That's not exactly how it goes, but I understood wanting to show your beau off to the world.

Donnie held my hand then. Our hands fit together like we'd been meant to hold hands all our lives. How different things had become in just twenty-four hours.

We talked for a long while into the night, about nothing and everything. He held me close as the chill descended.

I dreamed that night of swimming in the cool Hope Springs pond. *The water slides over my body, giving me the sense of immersing completely in the well-being of the life-giving Spring. The seniors laugh and jump into the pond. Dewitt climbs the cliff and jumps into the pond from the top. The splash sparkles in the sunlight and the rings ripple away, lapping the edge. Donnie holds me in his arms.*

The freedom conveyed in the dream stayed with me upon waking. How odd. The Spring waters had always been off limits for swimming, though often we'd begged our parents to allow us to swim in it on hot days. The excuse they always gave, "It's our drinking water. We don't swim in the drinking water." Dreaming of the forbidden gave me an odd feeling.

After tossing off the covers, I went downstairs to the kitchen for a drink of water. Dad sat at the kitchen table in the dark. I lit a match.

"Don't."

"Hi, Dad." I blew out the flame.

"What are you doing up?"

"Had a disturbing dream."

"What about?"

I filled a glass with water and took a sip. "Not sure. It was about my friends." The swallow of sweet Spring water soothed and calmed my disorientation.

Father pulled out a chair. "Any details?"

"No." No good could come of telling about breaking one of the town ordinances. "Why are you sitting in the dark? Are you all right?"

Shadows below his eyes made him a gaunt stranger. Who was this man? Though he had lived all his life in Hope Springs, he had left for a while, during the war, and come back, but he never spoke of it. Our parents are always partly strangers to us aren't they?

"What was it like?" I said into the dim light. "Leaving Hope Springs during the war?"

He rounded his shoulders, his chest sunken to his body. Withering away.

"I don't like to think on it. When I left, I imagine I was much like Dewitt tonight. Us doughboys were out to save the world. And did, I'd say. But it wasn't enough. Never enough I'm guessing."

"Why did you go?"

"Had to. Duty. The country needed us. Just like it needs Dewitt and the others now."

"How did Mother stand it?" How would I stand letting Donnie leave after just finding him?

"She endured. We wrote letters constantly. I think she kept them somewhere."

"How did you live without the water?"

"That was hard. The best drink I ever remember was the first one I had when I came home." His lips upturned. I felt his eyes search for mine. "You know I was wounded, right?"

"No!"

He touched the back of his head. "Still have a lump there."

"Does it pain you?"

"No. Been a long time since it hurt, but it took some of my memory. One minute I was in the trench, knee deep in mud and the next thing I knew it was several days later and I was in the hospital."

I searched for his expression but with the drapes over the window, no moonlight peeked through. Only a dim glow of the open stove cast shadows on the wall. Though I saw him, his voice sounded disembodied, more spirit than man. I shivered.

"Well," he said. "We ought to be getting on to bed. Your mother will be missing me soon. You need your rest. To get Dewitt to the train, we'll have to leave mighty early."

His steps halted on each stair. Sometimes I wondered that he moved at all. For as long as I remembered father had crept along. Only when we went to Alamogordo had I seen him gain a little pep. He'd stood straighter, and almost ran down the street with Dewitt. Afterward at the restaurant, he returned to the same motionless man I'd known my whole life. The boys would change too, no stopping it.

Anna's Journal

January 16, 1942

My heart pours out in this journal, my fears becoming larger by the day. I catch the boys talking of when they will leave and everything grows colder around me. I can't let them see my face at such times. I hide the terror I feel at the thought of them leaving. Even if they come home safely, they will never be my little boys again. Tonight, Donnie came home whistling. I asked him why, as he's always been the more somber of my children, but he smiled and shook his head, unwilling to share.

Donnie

My quiet, serious boy
what glow has lit you from within?
Always your steps are tentative
not afraid, merely careful,
unlike your twin who
leaps too fast.
Yet you, too, within the shadow
of your boisterous brother
persist in talking of war, leaving.
I trust you, of all three,
will thrust deep roots into the soil
to keep us and you steady

Reporter's Note: The first of several interviews with Ruth Ackerman is below. Ruth is the last of the three women of the Hope Springs Class of 1942. Her dark beauty is reminiscent of a silent film star.

Chapter Six

Ruth

I WONDERED IF LIV and Maxine would allow me to talk with you. Liv said the Council wants you to have a full picture and whether she likes it or not I'm part of the Weeping Women Springs story. Of course, she has the Council doing whatever she wants.

Oh my, I may need a fan. Liv knows how emotional I get at times like this. It's been a few years since I thought about those days. I only came back a few days ago. I'll get to the reason I left, but as Liv said she wants us to give you the whole story, so we should start during the war.

On graduation day, we all wore our caps and gowns, all except Maxine, of course. I never quite understood her reasoning for not finishing out her schooling, but that was her choice. She was busy with her wedding plans anyway. She and Billy were rushing things in my opinion. You'd think they had a reason beyond the war to hurry into a marriage. Look at Liv giving me sour looks. Maxine didn't have a reason to rush— I'm not saying that, just they put everything together so quickly one might think they had a reason.

Graduation day in May was brilliant of course. We had the ceremony outside that year. I wouldn't let anything spoil the day I'd been waiting for all those years. I was valedictorian of our class and I gave a fine speech if I do say so myself. Still remember it. "In these times that try our souls we fought our own battle to graduate from Hope Springs High before our classmates were sent to the four corners of the world."

It was a trial to come up with something inspirational without becoming maudlin, as people under such circumstances are wont to do.

If you would like the text of my speech, I'm sure I have a copy tucked away somewhere. It was published in the Cruces paper.

After the ceremonies, everyone embraced and I held Joe close. His parents took our picture. Joe had asked me to marry him, and Mary and Sebastian were already like my own parents.

"Come on, Joe and Ruth," Mary said. "I want a good picture of the two of you before Joe goes back to the Army.

Joe had joined up right after Pearl Harbor and he had already completed his training in California, but he'd gotten lucky enough to come back for a weekend of leave. I made sure to tell the principal to schedule the graduation ceremony that weekend as well. It would never have done to have Joe miss my speech.

I smiled at the camera and linked my arm in Joe's. He smiled too. His parents thought the world of their only son. Of course, they didn't mind that I thought the world of him as well.

"Come on, you two love birds," Sebastian said. "Give her a kiss, boy."

I blushed, but Sebastian had such a twinkle in his eyes. He was like a little leprechaun, and so sweet. You never met such a sweet man.

"Just a minute," I told him and then I touched up my lipstick before they took the picture. I still have that too. You be sure to let me know if you want it for your article.

Joe was a year older than I was so he had graduated a year ahead of me. We weren't even going steady a year before, but a lot happens in a year, doesn't it? I didn't know it then, but before much more than another year I'd be out in California.

"When are you going to set a date?" Sebastian winked at us.

He was incorrigible. I'd made it quite clear that I would not have a rushed leave wedding. No. I wanted a proper church wedding with plenty of time to plan my dress and flowers and all the arrangements. The whole event would be written up in the society page, even in Albuquerque's paper. It's only once that a girl has a wedding, and it must be done right.

So that day Joe was so handsome in his uniform. All the girls said so, and I saw the envious looks they gave me. But his ring sparkled on my finger. It was his class ring, of course, as we hadn't had time to buy an engagement ring yet, but soon enough I would be wearing a diamond.

"Let's have a class picture, kids," Liv called. She was always the organizer. Some things never do change.

The class picture is hanging in the gymnasium along with the rest of them, well, it was until they packed it up. If you see it, you'll notice I'm the one in the center. My mortarboard is tilted at just the right angle to see my face without a shadow.

At the party, the boys grouped together, those who were still in town. Joe had gotten leave but Dewitt and some of the others hadn't been so lucky. They were all in various stages of training. Joe spent some time talking with the others.

I had the impression they were all in Hope Springs, but only in body. Their lives and interests were beyond the boundaries of our little town and even beyond the borders of the state. Soon they'd be beyond the borders of our whole country.

Sam Frolander and Mike Brennen were discussing the war in Europe.

"I read that the UK forces invaded Madagascar," Sam said.

"I heard that too," Mike said. "Of course, the navy is getting a grip on the Pacific. Those Japanese will be hating the fact they attacked us."

"It shouldn't be long before we head out." Joe said. "Between Africa and Asia, our American boys are going to be giving them hell."

It was a bit overwhelming to think about, but I determined never to let Joe's attention wander to other people and places. I'd heard of GIs getting married to girls just before they shipped out, girls they barely knew. I'd make sure he remembered what he had waiting for him in Hope Springs.

"Joe, are you finished with your talk of the army and war? It's my graduation party. Could we dance?"

He smiled at me, his brown eyes crinkled at the corners. Never had he looked at anyone else just that way, and believe me I watched him closely.

"Sure honey. Gimme a smooch and let's spring."

Joe knew how to kiss. He swept me into his arms and dipped me back. The boys hooted. I let him have his show. What's a girl to do anyway? It wouldn't do any harm, and we'd be married eventually.

He stood me upright again and guided us to the dance floor. I caught Maxine and Liv looking down their noses at us. It wasn't my fault Billy and Donnie were unable to get leave.

I turned my cheek into Joe's olive drab covered chest. If I tried, I could forget he was headed out in the morning with no news on when he'd be able to get another leave.

"Sweetheart, what's it like when you're away? Do you think of me?" I asked.

"Of course," he said. "I live for your letters, you know it."

"But what about—"

"No what about nothing. Ruthie, I love you. I've asked you to marry me. Don't you understand I'd marry you now if you would have me?"

"Joseph Bauer. It's not that I won't have you. I just want our wedding day to be special, not some trumped up affair to get hitched before you ship out. That's not fair to me, don't you see?"

"None of that stuff matters to me. You know that. You're beautiful whether you're in a satin gown or in your old dungarees. I'm not marrying your clothes."

Then he gave me that smoldering look, the one that told me he'd rather I have no clothes on at all. "Joe. Please don't." I couldn't meet his eyes when he looked at me like that. If I did, I'd give in to his carnal urges. The night before he headed out for training I had been so tempted. His kisses were so sweet, and I wanted to make him happy. What would he think of me if I gave in? Wait a minute. Maybe that's what he needed. After all, if he got what he wanted at home, why would he need to go looking anywhere else?

I couldn't believe I hadn't thought of that before. There was no doubt that he would marry me. He'd already given me his class ring and promised that we'd go shopping for a real engagement ring when he had more leave. He'd even offered to send me the cash, but I refused to shop for my own ring.

The more I thought about the idea, the more it seemed like the perfect answer. Of course, we couldn't go over the edge, but if we sealed our promise with making love, well, there would be no way he could fall into someone else's clutches at the USO or somewhere. I gave him a special smile.

"What's in that beautiful head of yours, Ruthie?"

"Oh, nothing." I couldn't keep the heat out of my cheeks though and he turned my face up toward his.

"Oh Ruthie, when you look at me like that I just want to—"

"Maybe you shouldn't have to wait."

"Are you saying?" His eyes grew wider.

I lowered my eyes. This step would be a big one, but if I took it, it bound him to me.

"Are you sure?" His arms tightened around me.

I nodded. "You love me and I love you. It seems that should be enough. Who knows when we'll be able to have our wedding, but nothing says we can't share our love. We have to be careful, but yes I'm sure. Something tells me this is right, we're right."

He whirled me around the dance floor then, spinning us both until I could hardly see straight. Nervous giggles burst from me.

He slowed down and leaned in close. "When can we get out of here?"

"You sure you're finished talking with the other boys?" The guys still seemed absorbed in intent conversation. The girls stood around the punch bowl at loose ends since most of the boys seemed more intent on war talk than on dancing.

"They won't even notice I'm gone. I get plenty of time with the guys at the fort. This is your day, Ruthie. If you'll let me I'll make it a night neither of us will ever forget." We drifted by the centerpiece on the table and he plucked a yellow rose from it. "For you, though nothing or no one can compare to your loveliness this evening."

I sniffed the sweet perfumed flower. The scent of roses still brings the memories of that night back to me.

"Let's go then, Joe."

He led me through the party and outside the soft breeze of spring carried the expectations of our future wrapped up in it.

THE FOLLOWING MORNING I accompanied Joe and his folks to Cruces. The train station was packed with servicemen going north, east, west—everyone headed somewhere. An excitement was in the air, but plenty of tears fell too. I felt strangely grown up. After our night under the stars cuddled up on a blanket in the field, my attitude had changed, evolved. I wondered if every woman who gave their virginity to the man they loved had this feeling. My body didn't seem to be mine any longer, not the one I'd known for eighteen years. Whenever I met Mary's eyes, I wondered if she could see our secret in them. Joe had changed too. In a grand way, I have to say. He held my hand the whole drive to the station, fiddling with his class ring on my finger.

"I wish you had more than my class ring," he said as we sat in the backseat of Sebastian's old Ford.

I laid my head against his shoulder and watched the sage covered hills. "We'll get it when you have more time."

"Yes, my next leave, we'll go shopping for a ring. All right?"

"Perfect."

All too fast the drive ended and we pulled up to the newly renovated station. He already had his ticket so we milled around the station while we waited for his train. A lot of airmen were coming to New Mexico, but just as many servicemen were leaving.

We spoke very little. What do you say to someone when you're not sure when you'll see him again. Of course, I'd never mention the possibility of him shipping out. While it remained in my mind, I refused to think of it. He still had months of training left anyway, so maybe the war might even be over before he got orders to ship out.

Mary gave him last minute advice, though heaven knows, he'd heard it all before. "Make sure you eat breakfast. I know how you like to sleep in, but skipping breakfast will do you no good."

Joe just smiled at her. "Mama, the army doesn't let you skip breakfast, or any meals. They make sure we get up at reveille. That's not an option."

"All right, dear. I worry about my boy, you know. I'll be sending you a tin of cookies soon. Is there anything else you want me to send you, son? I'll send socks and a scarf too."

"Now Mary," Sebastian put in. "You don't need to spoil the boy. I don't think he'll need a scarf in the desert of California, or Africa for that matter."

"Well, Dad, I'm not sure where we'll be headed, but Mama don't go to no trouble."

"No trouble, Joe." Mary looked down at her fingers. "I couldn't help but overhear you and Ruthie talking in the car." She removed her wedding band. "Why don't you and Ruthie use this as your engagement ring, until you can get another?"

"Mary, I don't want—" I stopped because I certainly couldn't tell her I didn't want her hand-me-down ring. "You don't need to do that. Joe's class ring will suffice." At least it was new.

"I insist." After placing it in Joe's palm, Mary curled his fingers around it. "It's a good ring, and I've been happy for the years I've worn it. Besides, when you get a chance to buy a new one, you can give it back."

Joe kissed his mother's cheek. "You're too good to us." He turned back to me and took my hand. "Ruthie, I'm asking again. Will you make me the happiest man in this station, and agree to be my wife?"

I cupped his cheek. "Yes, Joe Bauer, no matter how many times you ask, my answer will be the same."

He slipped the ring on my finger. It was a bit big, but I held it tight. "Thank you, Mary. I'll treasure it." It would remain safe in my drawer at home as I wouldn't wear it.

The conductor called the train for California.

"That's me." Joe stood and helped me and his mother stand. "You take care of one another, you hear? My best girls should be the best of friends."

"We will be, son," Mary said.

He shook his father's hand and hugged his mother, before turning to me.

The light in his eyes remained bright. "I love you, Ruthie Ackerman."

I knew I'd done the right thing the previous night. "Good bye, Joe. Dream a dream of me."

"Always you and no other."

I waved to him as he boarded the train and refused to let any tears fall. This wasn't a time for tears, but of celebration. He'd be home again soon.

Anna's Journal

February 23, 1942

Sam left today. My heart is breaking, but I must stay strong for little Eddie. In an effort to pretend all is normal I lose myself in daily tasks. Sometimes it works better than others. Today wasn't one of those times. Elizabeth and Henry came over along with Ruth to say goodbye to him. Afterward Doc and Mike offered to drive him to the train. Donnie went off to see Liv and Eddie off to play at Melvin's. Once they left, the house was so quiet, a hole in the fabric of our home. I used to revel in the silences after the boys went to bed or when they were all at school. Having time to oneself as a lone parent is a precious commodity, always has been.

Today was different, and Sam will be back after his basic training, at least that's what he said. My boy though, what he said to me just before he left told me more than anything he's all grown up. "Ma, I'll send most of my pay back home. Since I'll have food and shelter at the camp, I won't need much. It'll help with you and Eddie." Elizabeth mentioned afterward that I'd done a fine job raising him. At a time like that I don't know that I did anything except make sure he was fed and clothed as best I could. Love that boy more than I can say from the time I first held him and his brother in my arms.

Sam

My firstborn, heart's delight
Your perpetual grin
Challenges anyone
To remain somber
Near impossible
With an ever ready joke
You tease us out of misery

Yet on your quest
For life's adventures
I fear for you
Tossed on the winds of war

Woman's Work

A woman's work undone
Keep home stoves alight
Sustain loved ones with a meal
Clean-swept floors
Grime swiped off faces and counters
Clothes laundered and mended
Until tomorrow
all begins again
when all once done
becomes undone

Chapter Seven

Maxine

BILLY AND I GOT MARRIED right after graduation. I wore my mother's wedding gown she had packed away for the occasion. It kept my parents close for the special day they couldn't be part of, no matter how much I wished otherwise. Billy had been able to defer going off for his basic training since he had enlisted and wasn't drafted. They'd told him to finish school and he could come in August. He was anxious to make sure I was legally his wife before he had to leave. He would have married me before he finished school, but I didn't want him to be distracted from his studies, since I wasn't able to graduate.

No one knew when the war would end, but it might be a while before Americans would get into Europe. The whole world had gone a little crazy it seemed to me. Little Hope Springs suddenly had boys all over the globe, or at least headed there.

Liv and her mother, Eva, came over in the morning to help me get dressed. Instead of the church, we chose to get married out by the Spring pond. Perhaps it was a little superstitious of me, but I thought getting married by Hope Springs would make sure our marriage would be long and happy. As my favorite place, it held significance for both me and my family. The gazebo provided the perfect backdrop and the yellow roses bloomed ferociously that year. Their perfume wafted on the breeze and though I'd dreamed of getting married in June, the May flowers made it worth moving the date up.

My mother's wedding dress was simple white cotton with ivory tatting and lace.

"Simple but lovely," Eva Soderlund said as she lifted it over my head. "I remember when your mother wore this. You're as beautiful or more so than she was. She'd be so proud of you today."

My eyes filled with tears, but Liv dabbed a kerchief so they didn't ruin my makeup she'd just finished.

"Max, honey, the tears will make your mascara run," she said.

"I can't promise I won't cry when Billy puts his ring on my finger."

"Oh, hon, we'll all be crying when that happens." Liv squeezed my shoulders. "How long we've all waited for this day."

"Is everything set?" I asked Eva when she returned from checking out back.

"The reception hall at the church is streamed with ribbons and Anna delivered the wedding cake this morning. All that remains is for you to meet Billy at the gazebo. Reverend Unger is waiting with Billy there now. The guests are in their seats and Mrs. Bracht is ready with her violin."

I took a deep breath, but nothing could stop my trembling. It hardly seemed possible the moment I'd dreamed of since I was twelve had arrived. I nodded. "I'm ready."

Eva adjusted my veil over my face and left. Liv, as my maid of honor, dressed in a butter cream yellow dress and we both carried a bouquet of Hope Springs roses, though mine was much larger and covered my white bible. The strains of Mrs. Bracht playing Bach floated back to us.

At the back door, Liv stopped. "Max, I love you and Billy as if you were my sister and brother. I wish you both nothing but years of happiness." She kissed my cheek and readjusted the veil.

"Soon it will be your turn. Thanks for everything."

She marched down the aisle and took her spot in front of Reverend Unger. I clutched the bouquet to keep my hands from shaking and then started the walk. The moment etched in my memory, Billy standing straight in his charcoal suit. A yellow rose rested in the pocket and his bright smile welcomed me. His eyes never left me and as soon as I stepped next to him, he gripped my hand tight. The whole town showed up, but I don't remember seeing anyone but him.

Our voices quivered through the vows, but our feelings never wavered.

The reverend said, "I now pronounce you husband and wife. You may kiss your bride."

My cheeks heated when Billy kissed me long and hard. The guests started tittering before he finally lifted his head. His gaze bored into me. "I love you, Maxine Fiekens, now and forever. No matter where I may be, look up at the moon and I'll be thinking of you, always."

Of course, that started the tears I'd been able to hold back until that moment, all the joyous tears.

IS THERE EVER A GOOD time for a husband to leave his wife? We had only a few short weeks before Billy was scheduled to leave. His birthday was May 9th, and graduation was the 24th, followed by our wedding on the 30th. Though he was too young for the draft, when everyone else enlisted, he wasn't far behind. He didn't have to go because he was the only son, but he kept telling me, "Sunshine, they need men. I'm healthy and fit. It's not right that I not do my duty and serve when my country needs me."

My chest tightened every time he said it, but I couldn't, just couldn't, ask him to stay home. If he never went, he might blame me for the rest of his life. And I couldn't live with that. He would've stayed if I'd asked. That thought haunts me. But would he be the same person if he stayed? I'll never know.

During the early part of that summer, I played a game with myself. If I didn't think of the day he would leave, Billy would stay. Silly, girlish game, but even so I refused to speak of it.

One day about a week before he left, he came up to me as I was mopping the store floor. He put the mop in the bucket and took my hand. "Come on." He led me out to the pond. Quail scurried into the brush and for a moment I wished I could hide with them. He plucked a rosebud and tucked it in my hair.

"Sunshine, when I leave I want you to be strong. The sooner I go, perhaps the sooner this war will end. When it's over, I'll never leave you again, but right now I need you to be strong for me. I can't stand the thought of you crying for me. We'll write each day, and it will almost be like I'm here. You share all the moments of your life just like we do each evening over supper, and I'll do the same."

I swallowed my tears and nodded. "Okay."

He kissed me then, a bittersweet kiss of longing, when we both knew it would be one of the last kisses we'd share for a long time.

The week passed in an instant, like time does when you don't want it to, when you hoped it would stand still and the world would stop turning. If it stopped, the next day wouldn't arrive, and maybe just maybe he wouldn't have to leave.

But time never stops, does it? The world keeps going and he left. I shouldn't have let him go alone, but I was weak. Besides, his folks took him so he would not be alone. I couldn't stand the thought of kissing him goodbye and watching that train carry him away. It hurt too much. I've never regretted any decision as much as I regret that one.

In his army uniform, Billy was so handsome. You can see his smiling face in this picture.

We had our special goodbye at the Spring the morning he left. He took a photograph of me then. Let me find it. I look so young there, and of course, you can't see my red hair since it's in black and white, but that's the picture he took with him. You can see how worn it is.

"I promise to hold you close to my heart while I must be away from you," he vowed.

"Billy, I promise to pray for you each morning and night, and you know you are in my heart so deep you'll never really leave me."

He gave me a rosebud. "Put this between the pages of your diary, and when I come home I'll give you a whole bouquet to replace them."

The sun crept above the mountains, turning everything golden.

"This is how I will remember you, Sunshine. An angel bathed in gold with a rose in her hair." In the distance a coyote howled. "I'm going to miss that sound, but not as much as I'll miss you."

Too soon, only a few minutes later, he climbed into his parents' car and waved. I blew him a kiss and then he was gone.

Chapter Eight

Liv

BY THE FALL of 1942 Hope Springs was pretty quiet. Of course, the boys came home on leave every once in a while, but as they traveled around the different states for their training a lot of times they couldn't make the trip back.

October has always been my favorite time of year. The leaves of the cottonwoods shimmer golden and the sky is never more brilliant. The summer heat leaves us with a remnant of warmth during the day while we pull an extra blanket on the bed at night.

Dewitt was already gone. Donnie and Billy left earlier that summer. One afternoon Father came home from the bank.

"Eva," he said to my mother at dinner. "I'm going to California.

"What?" I asked.

"Told Mr. Ackerman today and he seemed to think with so many of the boys gone, things might be quiet at the bank as well. He said if he needs another teller, Mrs. Ackerman or Ruth could fill in. I can serve the war effort in the factories making airplanes or boats or whatever they need."

"But, Father—"

Mother shook her head in warning. I had to ask though. "Dad what will happen to us? How will we manage with both you and Dewitt gone?" Things were tight, had been as long as I could remember. Most of the men worked the mines, and they were doing okay, especially in the new war economy. If he left, maybe I'd have to go to work, something that I wasn't opposed to doing. Since I wouldn't be able to go away until after the war, it gave me something to do.

"I'll send money home, more money than I make at the bank, likely. Don't worry. Things'll be fine."

Of course, they wouldn't be but I tried to understand, accept the fact that he wouldn't be around.

After he retired, Mother and I sat in the parlor knitting another pair of socks to send overseas. "How can you just let him leave? He needs you. How will he sleep and take care of himself?"

"He has to do this. If I tried stopping him, he'd stay. I have no doubt of that, but like Dewitt enlisting, if I tried to keep him home, he'd resent me."

"But don't you worry about him?" The thought of Dad wandering around in the middle of the night in a strange place made me uneasy.

"Of course, I do, always have and I will when he leaves. Did you see the light in his eyes when he spoke of California?"

I slipped a stitch and sighed. "Yes. It was like Dewitt whenever he talked about the navy."

"Seems like the men want to leave Hope Springs," she said. "I wonder why that is. Can't imagine going away and not being able to have a pot of Hope Springs tea."

"True, but the boys have been called for their duty. Maybe it's time things changed around here." Not for the first time I thought about how things were shifting, but not for the better. Donnie had come home on leave the previous weekend, but unlike the rest of the boys, he didn't seem to want to talk about the war. Whenever the others came home, they grumbled about not being able to get to the front yet, but not Donnie. His eyes never left the cliffs, as if he drew strength from their solid unchanging nature and several times we visited the Spring pond and just sat staring into the deep green pool. Maxine never minded about people spending time in her backyard as she said it really belonged to the town. Though she was right—the Spring was not her personal property—not many of the residents ever felt the need to visit the Spring aside from Founders Day and the Day of Hope.

I shook my head. "Donnie doesn't."

"Doesn't what, dear?" Mother asked.

"He doesn't want to leave. I get the feeling he'd be real content to just stay in Hope Springs forever. Always surprises me to think that, really. All of the other young people can't wait to leave sometimes, even if they just go over to Tularosa. But not Donnie. He always found plenty to keep him busy right here whether it was hunting for rocks or helping out on one of the ranches."

"I always felt sorry for his mother. Poor Anna. Can't imagine having to raise three boys on her own like she has."

It was a town mystery as we never knew what had happened that day eight years ago. Donnie's father had left, leaving no word. Some wondered whether he left because of the shell shock from the Great War. Little Eddie had been but a year old when their father disappeared. Took the family car and just left. Others speculated that he was looking for work. At the start of the Depression a lot of men talked about leaving to get work, but only a couple actually left. The mines did pretty well. Those who left soon returned, saying that they couldn't stand being outside and not being able to drink the water.

"You know Mrs. Frolander better than anyone except her sister. What do you think her husband did?"

"She never spoke to me about it," my mother said. "Frankly, I stopped asking as she always got the saddest look in her eyes whenever I did."

"That's what Donnie says. He told me that they never speak of it at home. He just awoke one morning and his father was gone. Whenever he'd ask his mother, she'd just wipe her eyes and say, 'maybe someday we'll understand.'"

"You were both about ten when it happened."

"I remember everyone talking about it, almost whispering, but I never really understood what was going on."

"Some of the women blamed Anna," Mother whispered.

"No, why would they do that?" It shocked me that Mother knew something, what else might she divulge?

Mother put down her knitting. "I'm going to make some chamomile tea. Would you like some?"

I clenched my jaw, but said, "I'll put the kettle on." Obviously, she was not going to answer any further questions on the topic. I hoped perhaps that I might gain some insight into Donnie's family. I hungered for such things then. Of course, understanding came, but it was too late to do Anna or anyone else much good.

A CLEAR TURQUOISE sky marked my father's last day in Hope Springs before he took the train to California.

"Liv," he said after folding another shirt, "why don't we take a walk? It's been a long while." His invitation surprised me, not since I was about twelve had we taken one of our walks. Perhaps the teen years intervened, but in retrospect, it was probably more that Dad didn't do much besides work and come home and read.

I wasted no time in following him out the door. We walked without talking for a while, then headed up to the cliff above the Spring.

He helped me over the rockiest place, giving me his hand. "Liv, within the rocks around here there is gold and lead."

"Yes." I didn't say that was the most obvious thing anyone ever said to me. Everyone in the area knew that was what men brought out of the mines, along with silver and a variety of other minerals.

When we reached the top of the cliff, we sat overlooking the Spring. The pool was still, but lovely from this perspective.

"Gold is the most precious metal in the world so people value it highly from the ancient times to the present." He pulled a nugget out of his pocket. "They say there's lots of reasons for that, but basically it's found in its purest form and it doesn't oxidize. There's something to be said for something that holds a natural sparkle. Along with being pure, it's also the softest metal. It's easy to bend." He held the nugget up to the light and squinted. "What do we use it for? Jewelry, currency, and when things got tough, what did the government do? They shut down the gold mines. Always makes me curious when things like that happen. We upped the mining of other metals, lead, zinc all the things people build machines with, especially war machines. Interesting fact isn't it? Lead is also soft and bendable, but it isn't worth as much as gold, except in wartime. Now we need lead for bullets, so is it better do you think to have something pretty and shiny or practical?" Never had his focus strayed from the nugget in his fingers until he asked me the question, then he took my hand and placed the gold piece in my palm. Heavy and warm from his touch, it sparkled in the sunlight.

"Why can't we have both? Pretty things and the practical?"

For the first time in a long time Dad laughed. "There you go, girlie. I admire your attitude. Why not indeed? Practical is necessary, but the gold will be there after the war machines have finished their job, and then we'll have the time to make the shinies, but never forget, Liv, never forget that both have their times. Both have their uses."

I wasn't quite following him, but I made him laugh. That's one of my favorite memories of him. Later I'd understand what he wanted to tell me that day, but there, with the sunshine on my shoulders, I possessed what I'd always dreamed of, a father who shared with me, shared his heart and soul. I've always remembered the security I felt then, that everything would turn out all right in the end and the golden days would come once more.

Mother and I helped Father finish packing the next day. He hugged us both good-bye and with a glint in his eyes, he kissed my cheek. "Help your mother, Liv. And remember, I'll be thinking of you both. As soon as this war is won and the boys are back, I'll be back too, don't you worry."

Mother took his hand and walked with him to the car. They murmured something and then she cupped his face in her palms. It was one of the only times I saw them kiss. Our family had never been physically demonstrative. Mother was always more so than Father, and I suppose at such a time, she couldn't hold back her emotions—her need to embrace him and show her love. When the car rolled away, my mother stood there a long time before turning back to the house.

She smiled at me. "We have to let them go, you know."

Just those simple words, but I understood she meant all of the boys, our men. They'd all leave and have their adventures, do their duty, and someday they'd return to us.

Anna's Journal

December 26, 1942

Poor Eddie, alone on Christmas morning this year. In order to make it a little fun, I made arrangements for Elizabeth and her family to come over. It helped to fill the normally empty dining table, but nothing replaces the sounds of my twins' voices, their laughter and boisterous joy always lifted my spirits at this time of year especially. Now the vacant seats only added to my sadness.

At Christmas I always think of the man missing from our table. How long it's been since Harold left in 1933 bound to find work, where no work could be found. Word reached me several weeks after he left, but I never told anyone. Too painful to see the sympathy in their eyes. Too painful to remember the haunted misery in his face. Harold, too sensitive to have gone to war came home shell-shocked and unable to cope. So his memory remains with me, and the boys will never know a father or how difficult my life has been to care for them, keep them fed.

Not even Elizabeth [her sister] sees this heartbreak I keep hidden from the world.

Harold

My love, My husband
My joy, my woe
A pine tree torched
by a fire-bolt
while the forest quakes.
Only you extinguished, cracked.
The death blow, self-dealt
lashed out
in your last effort
to tend your own.
All we ever needed
you never gave us –
Simply, your return.

Part II

The Rumble of the Car with the Star

Chapter Nine

Maxine

THAT AFTERNOON IN MAY 1943, I clipped another yellow rose and placed it in a frayed basket. I tucked a wicker piece back inside the edge. How often my mother had used this same basket. Perhaps I should have thrown it out, but the memories were too dear.

Father had planted the bushes around the Spring to celebrate my birth, but I always associated them with Billy. The roses I'd carried at our wedding and the rosebud he placed in my hair and the morning roses he brought to the kitchen. I smiled at the memory. Hopefully, before long, he'd be bringing me roses again. A year had passed since our wedding and it saddened me to think we'd be apart for our first anniversary, but by our second anniversary, surely he'd be home.

A shadow flickered across the Spring, and then another, followed by a flurry of darkness. A murder of crows dove down to the Spring, interrupting my reverie. How strange, I'd never seen so many at one time. They crowded along the pond, dipping their beaks. Their "Caws" broke the afternoon quiet. I returned to the house to arrange the flowers into a vase. Then, I filled a bucket with soapy water, wrapped a head scarf around my hair, and headed to the storeroom to scrub the floor.

The bell jingled merrily at the front of the store, and I left the chore to greet the customer. Two army air force officers stood just inside the door, hats in hand, squinting. Behind them on the street, I glimpsed a car with a star on its door. I approached them with a smile, wiping my hands on my apron. "May I help you?"

"Mrs. Fiekens?"

I nodded.

"I'm Captain Richards, and this is Lieutenant Eldridge, the division chaplain. Is there somewhere we can talk?" I led them to the fountain counter.

Captain Richards continued, "I'm afraid we have bad news about your husband."

My legs went weak. I grabbed for the counter, knocking over the flower vase which crashed to the floor splattering water and I sank. *I'll have to clean the floor in here.* My mind fought for normalcy, but the familiar surroundings shuddered, everything off-center. Captain Richards caught me around the waist and guided me to a stool.

He removed an envelope from inside his uniform before he took my hand. "William was killed in action in North Africa. You should be very proud of his sacrifice for his country."

I stared at the envelope and forced myself to grasp it, but couldn't open it in front of these strangers. I strained to comprehend the captain's words. Releasing my hand from his, I whispered, "When?"

"April twenty-eighth." He touched my shoulder. "Please accept our condolences. Normally, the War Department would send a telegram, but Hope Springs doesn't have a Western Union office."

"I have to tell his parents." My thoughts tumbled over one another. Impossible—I'll never see Billy again? "Are you sure this isn't a mistake?"

The captain frowned. "No."

My eyes closed, remembering his last goodbye, his last words, his promise to be home soon. A moment later I opened my eyes and searched the captain's face. "What happened?"

He avoided me, his gaze on the floor. "I don't have those details, ma'am." Captain Richards glanced at the chaplain. "I have to remind you—don't mention his location. If he's written anything in his letters, it needs to remain secret. To protect our war effort."

I clenched my hands together until the knuckles turned white. "I understand." But I didn't, not really. Nothing made sense. Billy, my Billy, gone?

The chaplain said, "You'll receive his personal effects in a couple of months." He held out his hand. "I'd like to pray with you if you'd like."

Prayers? I'd said them every night since Billy's departure and look what had happened. Yet I nodded. My ears buzzed as he murmured words meant to comfort, and ended with, "Amen."

"Thank you." Why did I thank him? The buzzing filled my head, grew louder. For telling me my life was destroyed? For bringing me news my husband, my best friend was gone forever? I gripped the counter to keep from sliding off the stool.

The captain cleared his throat, obviously uncomfortable with his task. "If you need anything from the base, let me know. The address is on the envelope." After fiddling with his hat a moment, he glanced back over at the chaplain and then back at me. He cleared his throat again. "We, uh, we should be going back to base, you shouldn't be alone. Is there someone we can contact, a neighbor perhaps?"

I shook my head. "I'm sorry." My lips were too dry to form words. Not that the words made sense.

His murmur of concern penetrated the fog.

"Thank you. I'm sure you have a long trip back to your post. I'll be fine." The lie slipped out easy enough.

Not trusting my legs, I remained at the counter as they exited. The rumble of the car, the one with a star on its door grew more distant as it pulled away. I don't remember much of the next moments or it could have been longer. I returned to my scrubbing. On my hands and knees—dip, scrub, dip—I let automatic motions take over. The bell jangled once more. At the sound my tears fell. How odd because up until then, I hadn't cried. Beyond tears I suppose.

"Max? Are you here?"

When I recognized Liv's voice, I rose and slowly walked out to meet her.

"Were those soldiers lost?" Liv stopped, her mouth open. "Max, you're as pale as a ghost!" She rushed forward. "What's wrong? Are you hurt?"

"It's Billy. . .They said, the Captain. . .he said—" I sat on a counter stool. "Billy isn't coming home."

Liv gasped, then grasped my hand, and started rubbing it.

Through the haze of pain I sensed the warmth of Liv's touch, but a chill had entered me, a coldness I'd never felt before even in the depth of winter. "I'm never going to see him again. What will I do?"

"Oh, Max. I'm so sorry. I don't know what to say."

I ran a hand over my eyes and then pulled off my scarf. "Remember the beginning? The parade?" I hiccupped, stifling a sob. "So handsome they all were, and how Billy stepped out to join them. I think maybe I knew then but—I-we were so proud. What will I do?"

Liv remained silent.

I shivered. "When did it get so cold?"

"Oh, hon. You've had a dreadful shock." Liv coaxed me to stand. "Let me help you upstairs."

Liv guided me to the bedroom and tended me—removed my shoes, lay me against the pillows and covered me with the afghan Billy's mother had crocheted for us as a wedding gift. The bright blue and white pattern, always so cheerful before now caused me to wince against the pain of sweet memories it evoked.

Liv patted her shoulder. "I'll get some water, it'll help."

Billy smiled at me from the picture on my nightstand, piercing my heart. 'Here's the picture they took, my smile's for you, Sunshine,' he'd written. Tears streamed as I clasped the photograph to my breast.

After a few moments, Liv returned and held a glass to my lips. "Here. Drink this. It'll make you feel better."

Tears ran, salting the sweet Spring water. I sipped, but instead of the burst of energy which normally accompanied a drink of Hope Springs, sadness pressed down on my chest. I turned away from the glass and my friend.

Closing my eyes, I waited.

"I'll stay as long as you need me."

"No. It's okay. You can go. I'm just going to rest for a while."

"You sure?"

Without opening my eyes, I nodded. "It's fine. I'm so tired. I'll sleep then I'll be all right." But how could I ever feel whole again?

I pictured Billy by the Spring, smiling brightly. "I'll hold you close to my heart."

The next sensation I felt was the bed gently shaking. "Just a few more minutes sleep," I begged Billy. Then reality struck.

Billy wasn't bounding up the stairs calling for his sunshine to wake up and meet the day. The horror of his death hit me all over again.

Liv sat in a chair pulled up to the bed, but didn't raise her eyes from the book. I rolled over and rubbed my face against the damp pillow.

I SLEPT OVER THE NEXT few hours, and every time I woke, Liv was there. She held my hand, and wiped my tears with a cloth.

"Maxi, I'm worried about you. Let's get you out in the sunshine," she asked after a while, it must have been a couple of days. I rolled away from her, snuggling into the pillows once more, finding the sweet oblivion where Billy and I danced in the store and he never wore a uniform, never left me.

The next time I awoke, Liv sat me up, took my chin in her hand, forcing my gaze to her. "I've spoken with Uncle Jim. He says the Council will have a memorial service on Friday to honor Billy. They want you there of course, and I think this will help you, and help the town. Everyone is concerned about you, Maxi."

"I've got to open the store." I swung my legs out of bed, but Liv pushed me back.

"We've set up a rotation, well the Council did. The store is fine. Mrs. Frolander is taking her shift today."

For the next several days I slept and dreamed, always of Billy.

Friday, Liv led me through the crowd of townspeople to the front row of the gymnasium bleachers and sat next to me, stroking my back. "Have you been eating?"

Since she'd been with me every day she knew the answer. "I can't."

Patting my shoulder, she admonished, "You need to keep up your strength. Think of what Billy would want. It won't bring him back if you get sick."

"Nothing will." I turned away and gazed at the abundant floral display. The scent of yellow roses wafted through the air.

The organ music swelled. Several townspeople lined up to pay their respects.

Chester Fiekens, the mayor, fidgeted with some papers at the podium, his slight frame tall and slender. His gaze swept over the crowd before coming back to me. "He was so brave. Even though he had to leave Maxine, Billy joined the other young men of our community right after Pearl to defend our country. Hope Springs will honor him always. As mayor, I assure you—his sacrifice will never be forgotten."

A murmur rose from the bleachers and many of the women sobbed.

But I just stared out into space, unwilling, or perhaps unable to cry any more.

At the end of the speeches, Liv escorted me outside. People filed by me, offering words of condolence. My parents' funeral two years ago, now Billy. Never had I imagined I would be the center of everyone's attention at another memorial so soon. The words were much the same, but I sensed everyone's fear. If it could happen to Billy, their boys weren't immune either. Maybe his sacrifice would be the first and last Hope Springs would need to offer up. The thought raced across my mind, but I didn't want him to be a sacrifice, not even to save all the other boys' lives. I know it doesn't work that way, but such are the crazy thoughts of grief.

A disturbance nearby drew our attention.

Ruth Ackerman squealed at the center of a group of girls. "I got a letter from Joe. He says he misses me and loves me and will be home as soon as he can."

Liv put her arm around my trembling shoulders. "Pay her no mind. She's never had the sense God gave a goose as to appropriate behavior."

Liv's mother and her friend, Anna Frolander sent glares of disapproval toward the cluster.

Leading me away, Liv cast a dirty look at Ruth. She said, "How could you?"

Ruth turned away and started reading her letter to the girls.

The girls giggled with Ruth. Everyone else milled around talking and then a motor rumbled.

The army car with the star drove up the street, toward another home, another family.

We all stared at it. I'm sure everyone sent up a prayer that it wouldn't stop at their home. Already the fleeting thought I'd had earlier about Billy being the only sacrifice was in vain. He wasn't the last, only the first.

Chapter Ten

Ruth

POOR MAXINE, WE ALL tried to support her in her grief. Then came the Martinez family. Marco was a few years ahead of us in school, so I didn't know him as well. I felt sorry for all of them, but my correspondence with Joe was encouraging. I kept him abreast of the happenings in Hope Springs and especially his parents.

Since Joe left, I spent most of the time helping my father at the bank. Someday it would be mine, and I never forgot that responsibility. Mary and Sebastian needed help too as Joe was their only son. I visited several times a week, helped Mary with the everyday household chores. My talents have always been in the kitchen, though certainly not limited to the kitchen. Not with my brains.

On June 4th, 1943 I arrived early in the morning at the Bauer's. I knocked and Mary called out for me to come right in. I tied on an apron, and we worked most of the day canning an early crop of tomatoes—the scent of stewing onions, tomatoes and green peppers permeated the whole house. It's my special recipe and I could certainly provide you a copy for your paper if you like.

"I was looking at patterns for wedding dresses," I said as I sliced a knife through a crisp pepper.

"We could probably design one for you with little trouble," said Mary.

"I know." I scooped up the diced tomatoes and the juice dripped onto my white apron. "We have time. People probably think I'm stubborn, but I refuse to have one of those rushed leave weddings. I doubt he'll get another leave anyway. My wedding day is going to be special. I'll walk down the aisle in a beautiful silk satin dress. Maybe like Claudette Colbert's in *It Happened One Night*. It's a little dated, but in a classic way.

"It's your day, dear. You can wear what you like, but Joe will love you in anything at all. As long as you aren't wearing that." Mary pointed at my apron. "You look like you've been in a terrible accident. There's more juice on you than in the jars."

I giggled. "I sure am a mess. But that's what I like about you, Mary. You make me feel part of your family already."

A knock rapped on the front door. Still laughing, I went to answer it. My smile dropped when I saw two soldiers.

The taller one, who wore captain's bars said, "Mrs. Bauer?"

The tick of the cuckoo clock on the living room wall resonated in my ears. I trembled and no words came out right. I stuttered. "No—she's in the kitchen."

"Could you get her please? Is Mr. Bauer in?"

"He's out in the pastures."

"May we come in?"

The second man didn't say a word.

I brushed the hair out of my face. "I wish you'd go away, but you can't, can you?" I opened the door wider to allow them to enter.

"Will you get Mrs. Bauer? Please inform her Captain Richards is here to see her."

Without answering, I headed back to the kitchen. "Mary, you need to come." I hiccupped.

Mary wiped her hands on a towel. "What is it, child? You've gone white as a sheet. Aren't you feeling well?"

I choked back a sob. "The army car is parked outside."

Mary closed her eyes. "Oh, dear God, no."

Clutching one another for strength, we walked slowly out to the living room where Captain Richards stood with his companion.

Mary gestured to the davenport while taking a seat in the armchair. "Won't you sit down?" I perched on the arm of Mary's chair.

The officers seated themselves on the edge of the cushions. "Thank you, ma'am. My name is Captain Richards. This is Chaplain Eldridge." He fidgeted with his hat, running his fingers over the brim. "We're sorry to inform you that Joseph has been killed in action." He fumbled in his jacket before pulling out a white envelope.

Shaking, Mary groped for my hand. I clenched it tight, unable to speak.

"Where?" The word burst from me. "What happened?"

"We don't have those specifics." The captain handed Mary the envelope. "He died in the Battle of Attu."

"Do you need anything from the base? We can send a detail out for a memorial," Chaplain Eldridge offered.

Mary stared ahead. "I don't think so."

"The army will send his personal effects in a few weeks," Captain Richards said. "If you have questions about anything, please let us know."

Mary avoided his eyes and her hand tightened on mine. "I'm sure that won't be necessary. We can handle our own arrangements."

"If there's nothing else, we'll be leaving," the captain said.

Crying quietly, I led them out. I continued to watch as the car with the star on its side rolled away. Then I closed the door and leaned on it for support. The dream of my white silky satin wedding dress filled my mind. I refused to believe Joe wouldn't come home.

"No." The single word escaped through my constricted throat.

Mary held out her arms to me, her voice thick. "I'm sorry. You're too young to have to face this."

I accepted the embrace but didn't speak.

"Come sit down." Mary stepped back. "You're in shock." Mary grasped my hand, pulling me to the davenport.

"No." Did I mean, no, Joe wasn't dead, or no that I wouldn't behave as others might? I'm sure I don't know. The internal struggle of holding two images in my mind, the one of Joe at the station, smiling with the secret of our time that last night and the other him lying on the frozen wastelands of a godforsaken island in Alaska, the blood staining his uniform. One real the other imaginary, but both true.

A short while later, Joe's father arrived home. Mary stood, stroked my shoulder and reached for her husband.

"What—?"

"Sit down, Bast." Mary indicated the arm chair.

I patted the cushion beside me. "Dad, we have news." I mustn't let Mary tell him. He should hear it from me, his son's fiancée. In this way I could protect Mary. Besides, it was my right, my responsibility, to bear the news to others.

Sebastian's eyes searched his wife's face, and then he moved to sit next to me and I took his hand. "Dad, the army sent word. Joe died."

He covered his eyes with a rough calloused hand and his broad shoulders quaked.

I squeezed his fingers and reported what the captain had said. "I can't believe it. Mom and I were planning the wedding when they arrived. It's impossible to think there won't be one. I've planned it for so long."

Mary smoothed the doily on the end table.

I laid my head on his shoulder while Mary remained silent. "Make it not be true." I don't know if I was talking to myself, Mary and Sebastian, or God. "I'll have to tell my friends. You know, I share all his letters with them, so they'll have to know." I sat up. "Dad, would you take me home? I just don't think I can walk back to town right now."

The odor of burning tomatoes filled the room. Mary jumped up. "The tomatoes!" She ran from the room.

I sprang up and then froze. The tomatoes didn't seem to matter anymore even though they were one of my best recipes. Collapsing back onto the davenport, I needed more time to compose myself.

Sebastian stood. "I need to see to the horses." Without his usual energy, he shuffled out of the house.

In a few minutes Mary returned shaking her head. "Well, that last batch is ruined. We should have another harvest in the garden by week's end though."

"I don't understand how you can even think about next week when Joe is gone." I went to the window, fingering the lace curtains and watching Sebastian brush down the horses. "How is that possible?" Thinking back on it, there was probably a bit of an accusatory tone in my voice.

Mary didn't answer, but of course, what could she say? Thinking about tomatoes instead of Joe? How silly.

How long I stood there I don't know, but by the time Sebastian led the horses into the barn, I turned, and Mary was curled up on the davenport crying silently.

Sebastian returned. He wrapped her in his arms and sat with her, stroking her back. His eyes never met mine, and I sat in the chair about to say something, and then the strangest thing happened. It was almost as if they'd forgotten I was in the room.

His voice croaked with repressed emotions. "When I returned from the trenches in nineteen-nineteen, I promised myself I'd never leave home again, not if Mary Wilkerson consented to be my wife. Hope Springs'd be our home, and we'd raise a bunch of kids, but Joe was our one and only. Now he's gone in some war in some battle on an island no one's ever heard of. Sometimes it all seems so pointless.

"Don't know if I ever told him how proud I was of him, of the man he'd become. My pa never told me in so many words either. We're just not people who jabber on." He choked, a laugh, followed by a shuddered groan. "Now listen to me, can't seem to shut my mouth. Guess I'd better go milk Breezy."

Mary buried her face in his neck.

"Ah, Mary, won't you say something?"

Silence.

"Did I ever tell you of my first drink of the Spring after I came back?" Again no response. "It never tasted so good. Decided then and there to ask the most beautiful girl in town to marry me. My heart was already hers, but she'd never written me. Not once in the two years I was gone to war. I'd given up hope. Yeah, without hope or a girl. Then I saw you shopping in the store the next day and you smiled at me." He nudged a knuckle under her chin to bring her face up, but she burrowed deeper, refusing to look at him.

"Mary, I know this breaks your heart, mine too." His rambling continued. "But my job is looking after you. Promised I'd do that when I said, 'I do', back in twenty-one."

Silence. I almost said something then. But it was so awkward. Really, I think they had forgotten my presence.

Sebastian spoke again. "We'll get through this together just like we've got through everything else. The Depression. Even almost losing the ranch back in thirty-four. The loss of the first two babies. Yeah, I haven't forgot them either. I know what you're thinking."

This was too much. I cleared my throat and stood. "Sebastian, could you take me home? It's getting rather late." Removing the red stained apron, I imagined the juice as Joe's blood. I tossed the apron into the laundry, trying to forget the scene I'd just witnessed. It was too sad, and it made me uncomfortable to think about it too deeply. I went outside, giving them a moment together. Sebastian joined me almost immediately, but didn't speak.

I stood aside as he hitched the wagon. Did his hands tremble? I smoothed my skirt. At least no tomato juice had stained it. It was hard to believe he had such feelings. He was just an old rancher—Joe's dad. He couldn't be nearly as upset as me. After all, I'd just lost my fiancé. What could be worse than that? He'd lived with Joe for nearly twenty-one years, but I'd only been engaged to him for two years. The promises left unfulfilled knifed my chest. Sebastian still didn't speak to me. Well, what could he say, after all? Though I called him dad he wasn't my father. Without a wedding to bind us, who knew when we'd see one another again? I needed Papa. He'd know what to say to make it better.

I climbed into the wagon and studied my nails. They'd need to be polished before church. What would my friends think? No sense in falling apart. It would be better to just accept the news and the consequences without letting it affect my entire life. When Maxine had attended the memorial, she'd looked positively ghastly: pale and drawn, thin, a mere apparition of her former self. I refused to go down that road. After all, I had more class than to disgrace myself. I dabbed at a tear. Enough of that. No more tears. Another shuddering breath and I'd be back to myself.

We arrived at my house and I jumped down from the wagon bench. "Thanks." I offered a small smile, but he didn't return it, just gave a curt nod and snapped the reins to turn the horse around. Fine, I thought, it would be better this way, not to draw things out.

Surrounded by the familiar objects of my childhood home, Mama's crystal collection, and the Renoir painting Papa had bought her when I was a small child, saying it looked exactly like his sweet angels, I knew I would find the comfort lacking for me at the Bauers' farmhouse. Papa took one look at me and opened his arms. I buried my face in his chest. He smelled of money and home.

"Oh Papa, Joe was killed. Captain Richards came while I was at Mary and Sebastian's. Joe's not coming home. We won't have the most wonderful wedding I'd planned. What am I supposed to do now?"

"Ruthie, I'm sorry." He pulled away to look me in the eye. "Here, let's sit down. Tell me everything."

"He was at someplace called Attu. Do you know of it?"

Nodding, he clasped my hand. "It's up in Alaska. The Japanese have held the island since last June. People feared that taking an Alaskan island might mean they were planning to attack mainland Alaska or Washington state."

"He was supposed to be in Africa. That's what he said their training was for, North Africa. Papa, I can't believe this. It's not fair. Why Joe?"

"It's the nature of war, honey. We saw it during the Great War, and now it's happening again. Of course, that was before you were born, and Hope Springs was very lucky. We only had one boy die during that one. Already we've had two in this one. Perhaps that'll be the end of it."

"I can't believe I'll never walk down the aisle, after all my planning. I don't even have an engagement ring. I can't be a widow because we were never married. It's not fair." I winced unable to voice my fear. I wasn't a virgin. How stupid I'd been to give myself to Joe the night of graduation. Who would ever have me if I wasn't pure? My heart spiraled downward.

"Honey, try not to think about it. I'll take you into Alamogordo tomorrow and we'll get you something special. That will help ease your pain."

Mama came in at that moment. "What do you need cheering up about?"

I shook my head, so Papa answered. "The army sent word that Joe was killed."

"Oh my poor Ruthie." She rushed over and smothered me in a hug against her breast. "I know you had such plans for your life with him. It's okay to cry."

The tears wouldn't come though. Sometimes I think I'm bereft of tears. I've never been one for histrionics like some people I know. Life must go on, and we must make the most of it, even when bad things happen. Dwelling on it does no one any good, not me, and certainly not Joe. It was best to move on.

Chapter Eleven

Liv

IN LATE JUNE I dreamt, long, terrible nightmares which confused and scared me.

The most vivid one still haunts me. *I walk down Main Street on a brilliant spring day. From out of nowhere charcoal clouds shadow the town, turning the sky crimson. The rain falls in large drops which sting my arms and face. A black dog runs down the middle of the street, launching at me with its fangs bared. I run, but the dog follows and the heat of its breath presses close behind me as the dog grows larger.* Every time I awoke sweating and my heartbeat racing.

The first time I dreamt it was the night before Captain Richards' familiar car came to town after Joe Bauer had been reported killed in action. At the sound of a motor I rushed to the front window. The car stopped at Doc Brennen's. I sagged against the windowsill with a sigh of guilty relief. It wasn't Dewitt, not yet. Please, God keep him safe.

Poor Doc Brennen, he would be alone at home since Mrs. Brennen had died several years ago.

"Mother," I called. "I need to run over to Doc's."

A young man opened the driver's door and stepped out and opened the officers' doors. Then he went around to the front and pulled up the hood of the automobile.

"Why can't these people have a telegraph office like most of the known world?" the captain said in an irritated tone. Chaplain Eldridge stood beside him. The portly man wiped a handkerchief over his neck, but didn't respond. His red face contrasted with white hair bristling atop his head like a stiff brush. Captain Richards knocked on the screen door as I strode up the front walk. Doc Brennen's office door was open, indicating he was available to see patients. I rarely recall his office door being closed. It wouldn't matter if it was the dinner hour or Sundays, Doc made himself available for any patient who might require medical attention.

Doc's deep voice came through the screen. "It's open, come in."

When the men entered, Capt. Richards removed his hat. "Dr. Brennen?"

I scooted behind them.

Doc Brennen, with his bushy red mustache and matching hair, sat at a desk working on some papers. He didn't look up. "Yes? May I help you?"

The captain cleared his throat. "Is there somewhere we can sit?"

Doc raised his gaze to stare at the uniformed men. His forehead creased. Letting out a long sigh, he stood to lead the way. "Right here in the front parlor."

Once seated, Capt. Richards met the older man's eyes. "I'm sorry to inform you that your son, Michael—"

"What happened? I just had a letter yesterday."

"He was in a crash of a B-24 bomber at Wendover Air Base in Utah."

The doctor slumped into his chair. I rushed to his side. "Doc, I'm so sorry." He pulled away from me. "Liv, you should be at home with your mother."

"She'll understand why I needed to be here."

"I'm sorry, Doctor. If there is anything you need from the post, please let me know. We'll forward his personal effects as soon as we receive them."

"No. Nothing." He covered his face for a moment, then. "You'd think since I'm a doctor, it would be a little easier for me to accept death." He exhaled a long stream of air. "While I'm aware of the fragile nature of life, I never guessed my son would die before me. Even going off to war—and I know better, sure." He rubbed his forehead. "He just wanted to fly...my boy..."

Capt. Richards looked down at his hat, running his fingers over its band. "It's never easy."

Dr. Brennen lifted his shoulders and took a breath, his voice stronger. "I've been in your shoes, Captain. It's a difficult job."

"It's my duty during this war."

"War. Yes, but then Michael didn't even make it to war, did he?" He brushed a hand over his face. "Just a training accident."

"Yes, sir. Training to serve a country at war."

"No medals in that, are there?"

Capt. Richards shook his head, but remained silent. How did he do his job without showing any feeling?

Brennen sighed. "No medals, no heroics, just his sacrifice. Nothing. My son." The doctor's eyes bored into Richards' pleading for answers. "His life wasn't wasted, was it?"

Capt. Richards swallowed.

"Tell me! It wasn't wasted was it?"

The officer recoiled.

"No. Not wasted," Chaplain Eldridge offered. He lowered his bulk to kneel at Dr. Brennen's side, placed his hand over the doctor's. "A life is never wasted."

"He was at his prime, just finding what he loved to do. The last time he was home, he said being above the clouds was like being with God."

The room seemed to rise in temperature. Richards ran a finger around his collar. "Chaplain, perhaps you could say a prayer?"

"Certainly. Dr. Brennen, would you join us?

The angry surge of a moment before dissipated, and Dr. Brennen's stocky frame seemed to shrink beside me. "Yes, please."

The chaplain recited, "The Lord is my shepherd, I shall not want; He maketh me lie down in green pastures; he leadeth me beside still waters..."

FOUR DAYS LATER I peered out the drapes as the captain and chaplain emerged from their vehicle into the early summer afternoon and approached the door. The officers' previous visits had wielded devastation to my friends, but their relentless march toward my door could not compare. I squeezed my eyes shut to block what my heart already knew. The moment had arrived.

All week—my nerves brittle—I'd dreamed the awful nightmares, each one worse than the time before, but reality intruded—unstoppable, certain and callous. I kept my premonition secret, praying my silence would keep him safe. If I gave no voice to the horror, mother might worry less.

I opened the door, lowering my head. The captain gently took my hand and led me into the front room.

"No. My dreams can't be true. Dewitt has to be safe. He promised he'd be careful."

Capt. Richards avoided my hysterical outburst by focusing on the window. He rubbed the bridge of his nose. "Miss Soderlund? Is that correct?"

I wished it possible to deny my name, but any effort was futile. It wouldn't make the officer go away so I nodded, swallowing over the tightness in my throat.

"Who is it, dear?" came Mother's voice from the rear of the house.

"Mother, you'd better come to the parlor. Someone's here for you."

She entered the room, looking elegant as always. Through blurry eyes, I watched Mother's smile fade.

The officer removed his hat. "I'm Captain. Richards from Alamogordo Army Airfield, ma'am."

"Please sit down." Mother gestured to the chairs in the living room. "Get the gentlemen some tea, Liv."

The captain took a seat across from the women. "No, ma'am. We don't need anything. We came to inform you about your son, Dewitt."

"What?" Mother's delicate voice carried an edge of harshness.

"He was killed during a training mission."

She crossed her arms, rubbed them as if cold despite the ninety degree heat. "Dewitt isn't even overseas. I know his submarine is in Florida. It can't be Dewitt you're here about. There's been a mistake." She stood, indicating the men should leave.

For me, time slowed and the voices echoed, but I remained in frozen silence.

"I'm sorry, ma'am. It's not a mistake. Yes, he was on a training exercise in Florida. The submarine he was on was lost. All hands on board."

"When?" She perched on the edge of her chair.

"A week ago."

"How?"

"We can't give you any details, don't have many. Of course, you can't share any information you know about where he was stationed. It's for the safety of our other boys. You understand."

"Will his body be returned to us?" Tears brimmed her eyes and trailed down her cheeks.

"No, ma'am, it won't be possible. But his personal effects from the navy base will be sent to you."

I strained to hear my mother's whisper.

"How can you sit here so coolly when my boy is never coming home?" Her silent weeping continued unabated while her whole body rocked back and forth.

"Is there anything you need?"

She avoided his eyes and took a deep breath. "No, Liv and I will make do. We'll make the arrangements for the memorial."

"Yes, ma'am. If you need assistance, please contact me at the base, I can detail an honor guard to play *Taps* and give the twenty-one gun salute."

She nodded.

I couldn't believe my mother regained her composure so fast. Her face now void of expression, mother stood once more, indicating they could leave.

The captain stood, then fiddled with his hat, as if reluctant to leave. "You should be proud of his service." He reached out a hand toward Mother, but she refused to shake it. He moved to the door.

I resisted slamming it behind him, but how I wanted to crash it behind him, let him know how his visit felt. If I could have hit him, I would have. I clenched my fists. While he was just doing his duty, the news he dealt us destroyed our hope. Dewitt, the boy who ached over hurt bunnies, whose only desire was to help heal people, never would go to medical school. His navy corpsman training led him to a submarine, to his death. I wanted to hit something, someone. But there was nothing to fight. When I returned to the parlor, I stared across at Mother who crossed to the fireplace mantle and lifted

Dewitt's service picture. Her fingers traced the outline of his smiling face above his white sailor uniform.

In the still air outside, a crow squawked, disrupting the dusk.

A WEEK LATER I set Dewitt's plate at his place as I had done since he left for the war—a promise of his safe return. No, I had not lost all my marbles, I knew he never would eat with us again, but at least having that place at the table kept his spirit with me.

Mother picked the plate up. "No, not any longer."

"Mother! If we don't set the table for him, it's like he never existed."

"I can't bear it." Mother returned the plate to the cupboard. With an oven mitt covered hand, she placed the casserole dish of macaroni and cheese on the table.

"What about me?" I said, my voice shrill. "My feelings? He's my brother."

Mother whispered, "And my son." She smoothed a napkin onto her lap. "Sit down to dinner."

I ran out of the kitchen and thundered up the stairs, finally slamming the door to my bedroom. It wasn't fair. Mother acted like her feelings were the only ones that counted. My throat burned from the pain of hard truth.

Unable to be still, I stomped in a circle, stopping only to punch my pillow on each circuit. My head ached from the effort to repress my tears. I threw myself face down onto the bed and crushed the pillow in my arms. A shudder ran through me. For a long time I buried my head, sunk in blackness.

Then I flipped over with the pillow clutched to my chest and gazed at Father, dressed in jodhpurs, smiling down from the photograph on my wall. I went to my desk and reread Father's last letter.

Received your letter of 18 June, and am devastated to learn of Dewitt's submarine sinking. The words blurred as if he'd erased something, but I couldn't make it out. *Take care of your Mother. I know you're grieving, but she needs you desperately. The work here is so busy I will not be able to make it home for at least another two months. Remember what we talked about on the cliff on our walk. It brings me comfort to know you are made of lead, strong yet bendable.*

Strength seemed beyond me. When news of Billy's death reached Maxine, the euphoric pride I'd took in the boys' service dampened, and an icy fear entered my thoughts. Then Marco Martinez. Next Joe Bauer. His parents, Mary and Sebastian, were at church the previous week, but they didn't sing. They sat quiet and unapproachable. Doc Brennen didn't stop seeing patients after the captain brought the news of Michael, but no twinkle lit his blue eyes as it did before. And now Dewitt.

No one else should have to experience this anguish. Not in the way the captain had delivered the news, so uncaring, matter of fact, like it was just another day of his duty. I picked up a water glass from the nightstand and drank. The invigorating Spring water had always cleared my mind and helped me think. Before a test in school, I always took a drink. Superstition, Maxine had always said, but I swore on the tactic, especially when I received the coveted "A."

I swallowed another gulp of water. Since receiving news about Dewitt, the water tasted a little salty. Just a touch, but the familiar sweetness had disappeared. If the army car never came to Hope Springs again, the town would be better off.

I froze. *Would it be possible?* A plan formed. Yes, this could work. The call to action gave into the anger eating at me. For the first time since the captain's visit, I was motivated to action, and clattered down the stairs.

"Slow down, Liv," Mother's automatic call came from the kitchen. "Walk like a lady."

I smiled at the familiar reprimand—something normal at last. "Sorry, Mom. I'm headed out for a bit. Taking the car, but I shouldn't be too long." The door slammed behind me.

In the old wood shed that served as our garage, I grabbed a couple of tools—a hatchet and shovel should do it—and tossed them into the trunk before backing the car and heading out of town.

The sun at its zenith beat down in high desert intensity. I drove to the edge of the main road at the intersection with the highway. Taking the hatchet, I marched over to the first mesquite tree and hacked at the smaller branches I could reach. I piled them up in the road. Then I chopped down the street sign and the sign reading Hope Springs, Elevation 4650 feet—Population 564. It wasn't enough, so I continued chopping more branches. Within a couple hours pain shot up my arms and both hands burned with raw blisters. For the final touch, I tied some tree branches to the car bumper and dragged them over the dirt road to obscure the turn off. Several hours later I surveyed my work and nodded in satisfaction.

"I dare the car to find us now." I brushed my sore palms over my sun-reddened skin to remove some of the red dust, but nothing I did would hide the evidence that I'd been doing menial chores. Maybe Mother would be lying down, as she did so often these days, and I'd be able to sneak into the house and bathe before dinner.

A hot wind blew a dust cloud down the street when I walked over to the post office to collect the mail the following day. At midday, not many people usually came outside in the summer temperatures, but the desert sun warmed me deep inside. I could pretend nothing bad happened under such a gloriously intense heat. The boys at war in far off places under this sun could be safe in its comfort.

I pulled up short behind a group of women standing outside the post office door. "What's happening?"

"Read this." Ruth pointed to a sign on the door.

No Mail Today. Mail Truck from Organ didn't arrive. Gone to Tularosa to check. Peggy.

I could have kicked myself. Why hadn't I thought of that?

Peggy's car slowed to a stop on the street. She leaned out the car window and called out, "I'm back. Didn't have to go to Doña Ana to discover the trouble. Someone's blocked the road into town. Oddest thing. I'm headed to the mayor's now to report it."

The women surrounded the car, chattering all at once.

"Who would have done such a thing?"

"Why would he do it?"

"Maybe it's a prank. Y'know, the kids pulling a practical joke?"

"They should have thought about the consequences."

The women prattled on, but I didn't say a word. I'd have to confess, and make them understand this would help the town.

Maxine approached me. "You're pretty quiet. That's unlike you."

"Don't have anything to say," I snapped. "None of your business why."

"Well, you don't have to bite my head off." Maxine whirled away and headed down the street toward the store. I regretted hurting her, but I busied myself thinking about a way out of this predicament.

The women wandered away to their homes. I set out for Uncle Jim's.

When I arrived, Peggy stood inside the door of the front room with Uncle Jim. "It's like someone barricaded the road."

"What in the world? The Council will have to investigate. Sometimes, I wish we had a policeman. Doesn't seem like a big enough issue to call in the county sheriff. The Council will handle it. I'll get back to you, Peggy."

The postmistress nodded.

Once Peggy left, I said, "I know what happened."

"What's that, you say?" Uncle Jim tipped his head waiting for a response.

I swallowed, my mouth dry. "Uh. I hid the road."

"What were you thinking, child? Why would you do such a thing?"

Restraining the urge to snap at him, not the least for calling me a child, I took a breath. "I was so angry at Captain Richards. He's the one who brought the news about Billy, then Joe, Michael and now Dewitt."

"It's his job. Why be angry with him? Sit down, you're making me nervous with all your pacing.

The clock ticked away, an irritation in my ear. How could I explain? "Uncle Jim, uh. The captain only brings bad news. If we stopped him from coming, if we kept the town hidden, we wouldn't get the bad news. Maybe somehow, that could protect the other boys. You know, keep us hidden like we keep the Spring hidden from the world. Same thing, really."

"Not the same thing at all, young lady." He took out a cigarette and flicked his lighter, drawing smoke deep into his lungs before blowing it out in a cloud. "The founders decided to hide the Spring for population control and to protect the specialness of the water. We have no idea what kinds of things might happen if people outside of Hope Springs drunk the water. Maybe they'd all want to move here. If that happened, well, our town could be destroyed."

"That makes sense." I knelt beside him. "And Captain Richards with his devastating news could destroy the town as well, don't you see?"

"The problem, as you've seen, is that people need to find us. People need the mail and that's just one thing, what about deliveries to the store, the bank business?"

"Couldn't we just change where the mail gets delivered? If Peggy left the outgoing mail out at the turn off and they dropped the incoming mail there, it'd just save the delivery truck a little time. We could do the same thing for the store and the bank. Most times we're the ones making errands to Tularosa or Alamogordo anyway, so it wouldn't be much trouble."

He blew smoke rings before answering. "Guess that's possible, but it seems like an awful lot of trouble."

"Would you ask the Council? This is a good idea."

"I'll mention it to them, but no promises, Liv. In fact, you'd better stay for the meeting, at least you can explain your foolishness. They'll be arriving shortly. They may have questions for you. Your aunt should be in the kitchen fixing the tea. I wish you'd talked to me before you did such a thing. Hiding the road? I can't imagine what was going through your head. Young people, I swear. Now get out of here while I think."

I headed to the kitchen. "Hi, Aunt Wanda. I want to make the town disappear until after the war."

"Why?"

"The Council's going to talk about it, but basically it's to protect our boys, so we're going to hide from the rest of the world."

My aunt's lips thinned to a line. "I see." A knock rapped on the front door. "That's probably the Council. Would you help me carry out the tea?"

"Sure."

Grace Fiekens, John Waterhouse, David Fiekens, and Chester Pahl stepped into the dining room which doubled as the Council meeting room. I smiled politely at them and sat in a corner chair. The meeting began with a call to order and continued quickly with the minutes and regular business.

Jim raised a finger. "Have you heard about the road?"

Chester said, "Yes, my wife said there was no mail because someone had blocked the road. We have to find out who did this." He pulled up closer to the table, ready to attack someone, and I feared it would be me as soon as he heard.

"Well, that's something I want to talk about. Liv did it," Uncle Jim said.

The Council turned as one, to stare at me. All eyes bore into me and I fidgeted. What seemed like such a good idea while I was doing the work was going all wrong. I had to make them understand.

A barrage of questions followed.

"Now, wait everyone." Jim held up a hand. "Liv can explain her actions. Not that I'm convinced she did right, but she did have a reason."

The other members of the council nodded and returned their stares to focus on me.

Maybe I should go remove the barricade and forget all about it. I can't deny the thought occurred to me to just apologize and be done with it. But then the feeling of control I'd experienced while chopping the wood and brushing out the tire tracks gave me strength.

I opened my mouth, but nothing came out. Gathering up my courage, I tried again. "Captain Richards comes with bad news. That's all he brings and we have to prevent that news from getting to Hope Springs. I don't want anyone else to have to see the captain sit so calmly and give that horrible news that a boy won't be coming home. It's the worst thing that can happen to anyone. Already we've lost four boys. If he can't tell the news, the families won't be so devastated. So I hid the road. Took me most of the afternoon yesterday to do it."

Grace's voice carried understanding. "While I understand your meaning because my son Billy is one of the four you mentioned, you should have asked us first. This should be a Council decision."

"I was just so mad, I had to do something."

John pounded his fist on the table. "This is the most ridiculous thing I've ever heard."

"Now, wait a minute!" Uncle Jim stood. "It's not ridiculous. We already limit knowledge of the town. We keep the Spring secret, now don't we? It's not far-fetched to include hiding the town. Though it might not stop the car completely, it might slow it down. Give us time to prepare if there's any other telegram deliveries. All of our business is done mostly out of town anyway. The mail, well, we can make other arrangements."

"That could work," Chester agreed. "But how do we get the town to understand?"

"That's easy," Uncle Jim said. "We can just tell everyone this is a war measure. You know they're always eager to contribute something for the war effort. This is just another way they can do that."

"Huh? War measure?" John shook his head, his loud voice growing louder. "We've hid the Spring for years. I know more than anyone that it was a mistake I even drank the water. But since it happened, I've come to understand all the reasoning behind it. That makes sense, to protect our water source, and the special nature of the Spring. But hiding our town for the war effort? This doesn't make sense."

"Our Spring is special." Jim said. "We all know that. What's to say that our Spring might protect the rest of the boys if we make it difficult for the car to find us? There might be a connection. The Spring water and prayers could be the answer. Who knows?"

"But, if we don't try," Grace added, "we'll never know if it could have helped. If it could have helped Billy." She swallowed. "I say we should try it. Most everyone here has lost someone. Joe was my student when he was in third grade, Jim lost his nephew, Dewitt. I lost Billy, and Chester, well we all know Doc's your best friend, and Michael was like an adopted son to you."

Silence filled the room. The Council members closed their eyes, and I felt the memories of the lost boys drift across the room.

Grace was always a bit of a puzzle to me, as close as she was with her son, Billy, she never carried that feeling over to his widow. I wished they could have been a comfort for one another, but it wasn't my place to say anything. She tapped the table. "Another thing, and I know we've talked about this before, but I think it bears mentioning here. They're arresting Germans and putting them in the internment camps in Texas."

I gasped, wondering why she brought it up now. How awful for those people. I'd read a bit about it in the papers, but hadn't dreamed it could affect Hope Springs. And yet the Council had already discussed it? Pride swelled with my boosted confidence in the Council's governance. They'd do the right thing to protect the town.

"But none of our residents are German born citizens," John said.

"I know." Grace nodded. "But many, even most of us, have German ancestry and still have relatives living in Germany. Who's to say they wouldn't do to us what they've done to the Japanese? If there's a reason to hide our town, I'd say that would be it."

"We're American citizens," John said.

"She's right," Chester said. "My sister in North Dakota said they've been interning the wives and children, no matter where they were born."

"But aren't they voluntarily interned?" asked David.

"Yes," Chester answered. "But that doesn't mean they can voluntarily leave. Once they're in the camp, that's it."

No one spoke for a few moments.

"Are we ready for a motion?" Chester asked?

Everyone murmured an agreement except John. He remained adamantly opposed. "Hiding the Spring makes sense. That's a decision made long ago by the founding fathers of Hope Springs."

David in a slow and careful tone added, "This isn't rational, we're responding emotionally. Maybe we need to think about this a while."

"Exactly." John smirked and gave David a wink.

Grace covered her face with her hands, sighing. "John, what is it with you? You're always opposed to anything new or different. Can't you see...?"

John's voice rose. "See what? What do you want me to see?"

Wanda covered her ears. "I'm going to get some more tea. Anyone want a sandwich?"

"Good idea," Chester said. "Let's take a break."

I spread dressing on the bread while Aunt Wanda made a ham salad.

"You'd hardly know there's a war on with the food you're providing," I said.

"It's not great, but I try to make something a bit special for guests," Wanda said.

We returned to the council table with a platter and a pitcher of lemonade.

The conversation turned to the more mundane, what the ranchers were doing and who had gone into town. With everyone sated they returned to business.

Chester asked, "Now where were we?"

First, John objected again, followed by one of the others stating the necessity for the action, neither side willing to concede. David waffled. For one point he'd nod and agree with John, and the next he'd do the same for Grace. I bit back a reply. Since I wasn't on the Council, I could only watch the ongoing tennis match. Anger welled within me. They had to understand.

Uncle Jim grunted a half snore going into the fifth hour of the debate.

Stifling a yawn, Aunt Wanda nudged him awake and said, "I move that we hide the road leading to Hope Springs for the duration of the war."

"I second that motion," said Grace.

"I have a motion and a second to remove the road signs leading to Hope Springs. All in favor?" Chester asked for the vote.

"Aye." Five members raised their hands.

John refused to make it unanimous. "While it might not hurt anything, I still think it's ridiculous."

Chester pounded the gavel, bringing everyone to full attention. "The motion passes."

Chapter Twelve

Liv

A WEEK WENT BY, then another without an appearance of the army staff car. I allowed myself a self-congratulatory pat on the back. Thank goodness hiding the road worked.

One blazing day in early August, I made my regular trip to the post office. The hot wind dried perspiration before it had time to drip down my face.

Behind the counter, Peggy sorted the mail with methodical practiced motions. She'd glance at the envelope, sometimes squinting to read, before placing it in the appropriate resident's box. She blew a wisp of hair out of her eyes.

Peggy didn't skip a beat of rhythm when she looked up at me. "How's your mother?"

"She's fine. We're coping." No need for further explanation. Everyone had expressed their condolences, and yet nothing brought Dewitt back.

The postmistress gave a jerky nod and returned her attention to the next envelope. "Oh, no."

I stepped to the counter. "What is it?" In that instant, my senses went on high alert. The flag snapped outside the window. A crow landed on the sill and its shadow darkened the counter.

She held out a letter in trembling, ink-stained fingers.

The letter was addressed to Donnie's mother. The return address, Captain Richards, Alamogordo Army Airfield.

The room stifled and I fought lightheadedness that threatened to overtake me. "No, it can't be. Not Donnie. Not him too." Air wouldn't enter my lungs. "What should we do? Should I open it? Maybe it's..." I couldn't say his name, but touched the envelope gingerly, then flipped it over, wishing I had x-ray vision. Perhaps it was nothing, just a forwarded letter from Donnie, anything other than the same news Captain Richards brought.

"We can't open someone else's mail, but she shouldn't get this here." In a shaky voice Peggy asked, "Would you take it to her? You know her better. Your mother and Anna are lifelong friends."

After a long moment, I surrendered to her request.

Outside, the searing sun pulled all strength from my limbs. I hesitated in front of the store. I needed Maxine, her support, but I didn't want to upset her. She'd been reluctant to do much of anything since Billy's death. Determined to not do this alone, my friend's presence would comfort me and Anna. I always regretted I wasn't with her when the captain delivered her the news about Billy.

Maxine sat at the fountain counter, waving a hand fan about her face when she caught sight of me. "What's wrong?"

"I hate to ask you this, but I can't do it alone."

"What?"

"A letter from Captain Richards has come for Mrs. Frolander. It's got to be news about Sam or Donnie and she shouldn't face this alone, Peggy and I agreed. But I can't face this alone. What if it's—" It had to be Sam or Donnie. If it were Donnie, I'd die, but if it were Sam—I couldn't bear it for either of them. I stumbled over my words. "I couldn't just have Peggy put it in the box for her to receive without warning or friends around."

Maxine looked around the store, everywhere but at me.

"Max, I'm sorry, but I need you."

She put her hand out and I clutched it, seeking comfort, understanding, a reassurance that the news might not be bad.

"You're right," she said. "Mrs. Frolander should receive this news from people who care. You both shouldn't be alone when the letter is read. Maybe it will help since we've both been through this already. I'll lock up the store. Not much business today anyway."

"Thank goodness. I just don't think I could bear it alone."

We walked the couple blocks to Mrs. Frolander's house. Along the road, children played in yards under cottonwood trees.

"Summer doesn't seem the same these days," Maxine said.

I struggled to find a distraction. "Remember when we played carefree in the dog days of August? My favorite place was always over at your yard, in the Spring meadow. Always seemed a little magical."

Maxine nodded. "Certainly was the coolest spot, still is. I spend time out there."

We arrived at the Frolander's where ten-year-old Eddie Frolander sprayed his buddy, Melvin Bracht, with the hose. The red dust transformed into sticky mud clinging in cakes, clay shoes on their bare feet. Their giggles contrasted sharply with the possible news I carried inside the envelope.

Eddie waved at us. "Hi! Why're you here?"

I waggled my fingers. "Hey, Eddie. We need to see your mother. Is she inside?"

"Ma!" Eddie yelled.

"What is it?" came Mrs. Frolander's voice.

"Liv and Maxine are here! Go on in. She's in the kitchen." Eddie returned to his squealing when Melvin grabbed the hose and turned it on him.

"Hello?" I said.

"Come on back," Mrs. Frolander answered. She glanced up from kneading bread. "What a nice surprise."

I removed the letter from my pocket and handed it over without speaking.

"You'd better sit down," Maxine said.

Mrs. Frolander raised her eyebrows. "Why?" She glanced at it, reading silently. "Oh." She slid to the edge of a chair.

With shaking fingers she opened the letter. I waited, hope remained that the contents weren't about—I wouldn't let my thoughts continue the thought. I squeezed Maxine's hand until she gently removed it. Aloud Mrs. Frolander read with a quaking voice:

> Dear Mrs. Frolander,
>   Since I have been unable to reach you by any other means, I am writing this letter on behalf of the Secretary of War. I regret to inform you of the death of your son, Samuel, who was killed in action last week. Enclosed you will find the telegram from the War Department.
>   His personal effects will be forwarded to you as well as a

letter from his commanding officer.
Please accept my sympathy to you
and your family on your loss.

My sincere condolences,
Captain Wesley Richards
Alamogordo Army Airfield
US Army

The letter floated to the floor along with the telegram, which gave no further details.

Relief surged through me, awful I knew, but there is always a little joy when the bad news isn't worse news. Not Donnie, but Sam. I took her hand. "We're so sorry."

"How do I tell Eddie about his big brother?" Mrs. Frolander whispered.

I could only shake my head. My vision swam, still unable to believe Donnie still lived. Finally I asked, "Would you like me to do it?"

Mrs. Frolander's shoulders shuddered as sobs wracked her. "Could you? I just don't think I can."

"I'll do it in a bit," I said. "Right now we'll sit with you."

"Let us know if you need anything," Maxine said. "I can fix your dinner if you like."

Mrs. Frolander pressed her lips together and shook her head. "No." Her voice broke and she didn't continue. Sadness etched into Mrs. Frolander's face.

"Would you like to talk about Sam? "It helps sometimes." Maxine, the same age as me, was always so much older in wisdom.

Another cry burst out, Mrs. Frolander's face reddened and damp with tears. "No, I can't." She gazed at her hands, dusty with flour and bread dough, then waved them in slow motion, kneading the air. "I—I should finish the bread."

I stood. "Let me do it." I sprinkled flour onto the dough. Punched it violently, punishing it with my fury. How unfair for Mrs. Frolander, how unfair for Eddie. I felt so powerless against the news, against the rage fuming. How long I pummeled the bread, I'm not sure.

I would have continued indefinitely except Maxine

squeezed my shoulder. "Enough. Let it rest." She filled a glass with Spring water and handed it to Mrs. Frolander. "Here." Once again, my friend's gentle nature supplied the needed consolation for both me and Donnie's mother.

"It's good you have Eddie here, for company." I returned to the table. The woman's refusal to speak reminded me of Mother. The hush in the house pressed in until I leaped up unable to be still, the angry energy propelling me. "Do you think, well, I'm going to get Eddie."

Mrs. Frolander pressed her apron to her face, but muffled a soft, "Yes."

Eddie whooped with another spray of water at his friend. The boys' joy in their play did nothing to lift my spirits, rather faded, and Donnie's little brother must know about Sam. What had possessed me to volunteer to tell him? Then I remembered Mrs. Frolander's distraught face. How did you explain death to a child?

"Eddie, come on over here."

His smile froze in time while he considered me.

"Something's happened. Melvin, why don't you head home? Eddie will see you tomorrow. His mother needs him right now."

Melvin ran off and Eddie came toward the porch, his muddy feet scuffing the tufts of grass in the yard.

"Have a seat." I lowered to the step. "I need to tell you something." I took his wet hand. "You'll need to be strong for your mom, okay?"

His face crunched in confusion. "You're scaring me. What's wrong?"

"It's the war." A flurried rustle in the cottonwood drew my attention. Crows again. Lately, they seemed to be everywhere. I never saw so many as during the war. "It's Sam. We just got a letter from the army, the war department. He won't be coming home, well because he died."

Eddie shook his head. "Died?" His voice screeched too loud, not soft and quiet as the women's but all the unrestrained emotion of a little boy whose only connection to the far off events was his brothers' letters full of adventure and bravado in clobbering the enemy. Italy, or wherever, it didn't matter to this little boy. "Wait." He ran toward the bench under the tree and returned with a baseball glove and ball. "Sam and Donnie gave this to me before they left, said to practice for when they got home. I'm going to see if Melvin can play some catch."

"Could it wait, Eddie? I thought you might want to go in to your mother." I put my arm around his shoulder.

"Aw, yeah, she okay?" The ball slapped into the mitt, in a forceful drumbeat.

How could I tell him when I didn't know myself? "It's going to be tough."

"Sam's a hero. Our hero. That's a good thing I think."

"That's the truth of it. Don't ever forget it either." I ruffled his hair. "Come on. Oh, you'd better wash off your feet before you come inside."

FRIDAY AFTERNOON, RUTHIE and I sat in chairs placed on the gymnasium floor reserved for family members of those fallen soldiers being commemorated. I bowed my head. The Council organized another memorial commemoration for the boys, invited the whole town to pay their respects. While I hated the idea, the necessity of it, I admitted it might help my mother and the others by recognizing the sacrifices.

Next to me Mother placed her hands in her lap, a twisted lace-edged handkerchief worried between her fingers—the only sign of her grief at this public ceremony.

Sebastian and Mary Bauer and Doc Brennen along with the Martinez family were all in seats to the right of the stage area, with a clear view of the audience and the platform. An occasional cough or cleared throat was the only sound.

Councilwomen Grace and Aunt Wanda placed photographs of the young men in uniform on a flag draped table. Roses of all shades surrounded the stage area.

In front of the podium, the members of the town council stood. Chester Parks, as mayor, signaled the band director. The high school band played *The Star-Spangled Banner* while the choir sang in clear sweet voices. The words held new meaning for me. *Through the perilous fight—rockets' red glare and bombs bursting in air.* For the first time, the words evoked images of exploding bombs of war and the blinding light of a blast. Even the national anthem of my beloved country commemorated war as a noble and grand event. Was it? How could something which caused such pain be so glorious? Why had I never realized this before? While pride in Dewitt and my friends soared, I rubbed my clenched fist with my hand to keep them from trembling. My head hurt with the pressure of holding back the tide of sorrow.

Wanda handed a purple candle to each family of the deceased. I gripped the one for Dewitt so as not to drop it. The flare of a match from Grace lit the first candle and then each succeeding one until all five were lit. In deference to her loss, Maxine also received a candle. We proceeded to the front table, placed the candles in holders and returned to our seats.

"Please join us in singing *The Battle Hymn of the Republic* while Peggy plays the organ," Grace said.

Following the hymn, Reverend Unger and Father Gomez went to the lectern. "Please join me in prayer," Jim said, bowing his head. "Lord, God, you are attentive to the voice of our pleading. Let us find in Your Son comfort in our sadness, certainty in our doubt, and courage to live through this hour. Make our faith strong through Christ our Lord. Amen."

Father Gomez followed with another prayer, "May the love of God and the peace of the Lord Jesus Christ bless and console us and gently wipe every tear from our eyes. Joseph Bauer, Michael Brennen, Marco Martinez, Samuel Frolander, William Fiekens, and Dewitt Soderlund were violently taken from us. Come swiftly to their aid, have mercy on them. In the name of the Father, and of the Son, and of the Holy Spirit. Amen."

By the end of the prayer everyone was weeping. Other hymns and songs followed, sung by the women's choirs of the churches. Each song, *Goodnight Sweetheart, I Don't Want to Walk Without You,* and *I'll Be Seeing You* carried with it the memories of our young men who wouldn't return.

"And now we'd like to invite anyone to share memories of Billy, Joe, Dewitt, Michael, Marco, or Samuel," Wanda said.

I approached the podium. I hadn't addressed such a large group since high school speech class. My voice quivered, but I reminded myself this was for Dewitt.

"All of you knew my brother. He planned to return to Hope

Springs and then attend medical school to help Doc Brennen. We all know Michael Brennen had a great career as a pilot and the medical profession held no fascination." I looked over at Doc Brennen, who nodded with a sad smile.

"For Dewitt, healing came naturally. How I remember him bringing home all kinds of creatures that needed mending. Whether a bird with a broken wing had fallen out of the sky, or a snake seemed distressed, Dewitt found a way to try to help them. Mother and I never knew what we might find in his room." At this, the audience laughed quietly.

"Most of all, to me, Dewitt represented the best and worst of family. He teased me unmercifully when we were young, but if I needed help, I knew I could count on him. Dewitt, I'll miss you." My voice broke. Covering my mouth, I hurried back to my seat.

Mother covered my hand with her shaking one. "Thank you, Liv."

Several other townspeople took turns telling stories about the other young men and each anecdote brought both smiles and tears to me and the others.

Following the final hymn, Maxine, Ruth and I led a procession to the cemetery carrying fresh cut flowers in a strange parody of a bridal march. I felt far from a happy bride. Maxine's distress mirrored my grief, but Ruth showed no sign of sorrow. Her face remained impassive. No one else would compare this funeral procession to a bridal march. That I could even have such a thought disgusted me.

Along with our friends and families, we covered the tombstones with flowers and ribbons.

My heart lurched when young Melvin Bracht played *Taps* on the trumpet to signal the end of the formal memorial commemoration. The bittersweet, haunting melody followed me as everyone filed away in silence.

Chapter Thirteen

Ruth

AFTER JOE DIED, I worked in the bank for Father. The bank would someday be mine as I may have mentioned, but aside from summers where I helped count the tills, I never spent much time there.

Not more than a week or two following the Commemoration, several people came into the bank all on one day. Anna Frolander, Liv, Maxine—well Maxine came nearly every day—Doc Brennen.

I greeted them and transacted their business in the efficient way I always did. It was all going quite well until Maxine arrived.

Her eyes were reddened. Back then they were more often reddened than not. I never understood how she could never seem to get past the tears. Billy had been the first to die and it had been over six months and she still wept all the time. Every time I saw her I didn't know what else to say. I mean, it's just so uncomfortable for other people to be around the constantly grieving, don't you think?

Oh, Liv, don't get your hackles up. I'm merely stating what I thought then. Besides, one should not do activities that might compromise one's looks. Crying definitely affects one's appearance, doesn't it?

So I sighed when I sighted Maxine and motioned her over. Someone had to wait on her, and I didn't have any customers at the time. If she broke down into tears one more time, I just might have to slap her out of them. It wasn't like no one else wanted to cry. Of course, I did, but I had some self-control, some sense of appropriate public behavior.

Look over there, tears still fill Maxine's eyes. It's been more than fifteen years but her sadness continues. Am I so cold-hearted to confess that I never wanted to dwell in that grief?

That day she made her deposit as she did every day and I made some simple remark to make conversation. "I suppose things are going so well at the store because women have more money to spend from their husbands and sons' military pay, let alone the death benefit."

She stared at me as if I had suggested the Spring water turned to salt. "Ruth Ackerman, I cannot believe you would suggest that I prefer a thriving store to our boys being home and coming home safely." She covered her mouth and mumbled, "I'll be back later for my receipt," before stumbling out of the bank, nearly knocking over Anna Frolander.

"What has got into Maxine?" Anna asked. "She looks positively distraught."

I shook my head. "I'm sure I have no idea. Everyone seems a bit emotional these days."

Sadness crept into her eyes too. "Yes. We all have something to mourn after recent events." Sorrow laced her voice.

I thrust the receipt book at her to sign and finished the transaction. If she started sobbing too, I didn't know what I would do. My nerves were on their very last thread and I might just have to pull my perfectly coifed victory roll out of my hair, which would be a silly reaction and do me no good. The constant woeful distress possessing everyone pressed in at me.

As Anna left, I called to Father, "I need a coffee break."

I escaped into the cool fall afternoon. The golden cottonwoods flamed against a turquoise sky as they do that time each fall. In front of the bank, I paced, thinking of how things had changed since the previous year. Our town, always a tad stifling, was becoming downright oppressive. I wasn't sure how long I could stand it. Something had to change. Since the day Liv blocked the road, everything had closed in on us, on me.

It was time to do something. Since the Council had approved the isolation, and to be honest, I was not surprised at that decision after all the years we had kept the Spring a secret, the separation from the rest of the world altered in a way that smothered my spirit. The seclusion of Hope Springs for the duration of the war held an air of fear and pain I refused to submit to.

An idea had niggled at me for a long time, but after facing Maxine and Anna and their never-ending grief it became a firm commitment.

I must leave Hope Springs.

When I broached the subject at dinner that evening, Papa protested. "Ruthie, I won't be able to take care of you if you go."

"They need women in the WACs. I want to enlist."

Mama spoke then. "Darling, you would have to wear that olive uniform. I don't think it would suit you very well."

She had a point. The color would likely make me appear sallow. Makeup can only do so much. "Maybe I should join the WAVES then. I look good in navy."

"While enlisting is certainly a worthy thing to do," Papa's voice took on the tone it always did when he was going to propose something that did not coincide with my thoughts, but that I should listen and learn.

My hackles rose. If he told me to stay at home, I didn't think I could obey this time.

"Perhaps your skills would be better used in private business," he continued. "There are a lot of good jobs out there and you could use your banking skills to work in accounting or something like that."

"What do you mean? Where?"

"Well, I'd love it if you didn't go far, perhaps only to Albuquerque. Work for the state in Santa Fe or something."

"But Papa, I'd really like to contribute to the war effort. It seems the best way to," I searched for a way to convince him to let me go, "the best way to get past what happened to Joe and hopefully help bring this terrible war to an end. From what I understand, the big plants in California need workers. I've seen those advertisements in the paper."

"But it's so far away," Mama's large brown eyes widened, sending Papa a pleading look.

If she had a chance to get in her objections, convincing Papa to agree would prove that much more difficult so I rushed on. "It's only a day, maybe less on the train." The more

I thought about going to California, the more exciting it became. Movie stars, the beach, and good paying jobs. Who knew what might happen there? I could forget about the sadness of this little village and start over again. For the first time since hearing about Joe, I felt hopeful.

"When would you leave?" The fact Mama asked meant the battle was almost won. After all, neither one of them could ever refuse me anything I was intent on getting. Of course, I gave them no reason to reject any plan I'd ever made. I deserved to have their support in whatever I chose to do.

"By the end of the week. I bet Liv would be happy to work as teller. Since her father left, I'm sure they could use the money."

"All right, but you must promise to write every day. If I don't hear from you, I'll be on the first train out to bring you back home safe." He shook his head as he always did when he knew he'd lost the upper hand from the beginning of the discussion.

I couldn't help a little squeal. "Thank you, Papa." I jumped from my chair and kissed his cheek.

The train ride to California took almost a day and a half through the desert scenery. Locked in the valley of the Spring, I was accustomed to more greenery, not the starkness of the desert, well except when we went to town.

I'd never seen so many people as when I arrived in Los Angeles. They were everywhere and everyone seemed to be going somewhere. The electricity in the air sizzled. I'd made the right decision.

Within a couple of days I hired on at Lockheed where they made B17 bombers. The plant in Burbank didn't need any more office workers, even with my banking experience, so I ended up working the swing shift bucking rivets. A regular Rosie the Riveter. I made some good friends and within a couple of days moved in with another couple girls from the plant.

We had some good times together and I can't help smiling looking back at it. Getting out of Hope Springs was just what I needed. Like a breath of fresh air, though of course, it was in the city so there wasn't always clean air. On our days off the girls would head to the cinema to see the latest newsreels and there was a bit of pride that went through us whenever they pictured one of our planes. We were contributing to the ultimate victory.

Some days we went to the USO to volunteer. They were always looking for girls to serve doughnuts, dance and just talk. So many of the boys just wanted a friendly chat since they were away from home and headed overseas with no idea when they'd be back.

It was there I met Stephen Lloyd. He was a soldier from California. He asked for a dance one afternoon while I was on duty serving donuts.

"Hey doll," he said. "Want to dance?" He winked and smiled, reminding me of Tyrone Power. Such a handsome man, I could hardly look at him. That's not quite true, as I've never been one of those shy types like Maxine or even Liv who are almost afraid to say hello to anyone outside of Hope Springs.

"I have to finish my serving shift, which doesn't end for another hour," I told him.

"I'll have a donut then. Maybe more than one, so you'll have to talk with me."

I laughed. "You'd better find someone else to dance with. You wouldn't want to take more than your fair share."

"Fair share of what? Donuts or dances?"

I couldn't compete with that logic or charm when it was turned on full force and as soon as my shift ended we shared several dances. Each time another soldier would take a turn, Stephen would cut in. Finally, I had to tell him, "That's definitely more than your fair share. They don't like it much for one man to monopolize all our time."

"That's fine. When does your shift end?"

I told him it already had, but said I needed to catch the trolley back home before long. My work shift was scheduled to start.

"Let me walk you out. You have to let me call on you. It's only a couple weeks before I ship out. After I finish my training, it's so long US of A and hello South Pacific. You won't let a poor boy leave without someone to write to, will you?"

"I can't imagine you don't have a girlfriend back home." Most of them did have someone waiting. At the USO we just stood in for the ones they missed. It was frowned upon for us to get too close to them, but that smile. He made me weak-kneed as we stood at the trolley stop.

"No, and that's the honest truth."

"But not for want of any attention, I'm sure. There have to be some broken hearted girls back there."

He gave a shrug. "Doesn't matter, they aren't here and they aren't Ruthie Ackerman of New Mexico. Give me your number, please."

Shaking my head, I hopped onto the trolley, a little bit of regret that I wouldn't see him again.

"I'll be seeing you," he called out.

Reporter's Note: It is worth noting that Anna's Journal is blank for several weeks with no new entries.–R.W.P.

Anna's Journal

September 17, 1943

It's been a long while since I wrote. The desire to record anything left me when I learned of Sam's death. No poems yearned to be put down on the page. The most I could manage was making sure Eddie had a decent meal, but sometimes that chore was more than I could handle and when he asked to spend dinner at the Brachts I was relieved.

Today for the first time as I thought about the families, especially the women left to mourn their men, this poem came to me.

A Woman's Question

Why is it left for women
to lament,
to grieve
to tear at our hair
to tend the fire

Men leave

We women remain
tired
heartsick
struggling against
naught but our sorrows

Chapter Fourteen

Liv

WHEN RUTH LEFT, I started work at the bank, so it brought in a little money as well as Father's checks every month. He sent us what he could from Long Beach. His letters were both word from Outside, and a guarantee that perhaps life could return to normal someday soon, after the war. Whenever I went to Tularosa or Alamogordo I heard the same things. Everyone expressed the same sentiment. Time was counted by way of the war. When the war is over we'll take a vacation. Or, when the war is over we'll start our family or when my husband returns from the war we'll move to California. The whole world held its breath, waiting for the war to end. Yet in 1943 we were in the thick of things. Italy had surrendered, but it didn't look like the Germans would surrender anytime soon. Who knew what was happening with the war in the Pacific? All those island names no one had ever heard of before our boys fought on them.

One brisk day in October, I was chatting with Peggy at the post office when Mrs. Frolander entered.

Peggy looked up from the till. "Hi, Anna. How are you today?"

"Okay. I take them when I can." A whisper of a smile lifted her lips.

I squeezed Mrs. Frolander's hand. The woman's skin might have been a block of ice.

"You have a letter today." Peggy presented a tattered envelope. "Looks like it's been around the world."

After glancing at the return address Mrs. Frolander said, "I don't recognize the name. Wonder who sent it. She tore open the envelope and read. "Oh, I must share this with Eva." She bustled out to the street, and I followed anxious to hear what she might say to Mother.

"Mother, Mrs. Frolander is here." I guided her into the parlor.

Mother joined us.

Taking the letter out of the envelope, she gave a shaky smile. "I just received this letter. It's so touching, and I thought you'd like to hear it."

Dear Mrs. Frolander,

By this time I know you have received official notification about Sam. We called him Hope on account of his sense of humor and the place where he was from. He kept us laughing like Bob Hope, and well, as you know, he was from Hope Springs. I first met Hope when he was transferred to our outfit a year ago. Immediately he fit in our unit, cracking jokes and generally showing us a good time. He was a real pal. We spent some time together. I'm writing this on behalf of the men in my company. These are some things you won't hear officially, but I wanted you to know.

He proved the best of all of us, the best worker, the best soldier he understood better than any of us what he was soldiering for. When he had a job to do he did it with such determination that he seemed absolutely fearless.

I am not permitted to describe the details of the engagement in which he was killed, but the censor can't object if I tell you that he lost his life trying to save his buddies in this big engagement. I will never forget him. They probably won't give him any medals but his name will be remembered as long as I live. He was a real Hero, a man who did the right thing at the right moment. We who knew him in the barracks and on the battlefield will not forget him.

Nothing I say can make up for your loss, but you ought to feel very proud of him. I hope you don't mind me taking this privilege of writing to you, but I was told by a very good friend of mine to write to you. You will find a picture of some of the boys in the outfit. I want you to keep

them. I am the one in the center, Tex is on my
left and you know the man on my right.
   You have my deepest sympathy. God bless you
always. Best regards to you, and your other
sons.
Sincerely,
Stf/Sgt. Homer Sullivan

Her eyes brimmed with tears.

I met Mother's gaze and a tight smile curved her lips. "That's so wonderful. You're so fortunate Staff Sergeant Sullivan wrote you. How kind of him."

Anna sniffled. "Yes, that's exactly what I thought."

I unclenched my fists. While it was a good thing for Mrs. Frolander to hear such a thing, I burned with anger at the unfairness of everything, the war, the loss, the horrible sadness, and yet she got this nice letter from one of Sam's friends. Dewitt was drowned in a submarine with all his friends. We'd never get such a letter. It's hard to explain, it wasn't that I was even mad at her, just the situation and the always wishing things were different.

Mother patted Mrs. Frolander's hand. "Perhaps during the next commemoration you can share the letter. I'm sure the townspeople would love to hear it."

"Great idea, Mother." I said, but then thought, how stupid of me. Would there be another commemoration? Did Mother have some knowledge? Not for the first time I wondered if she had dreams foretelling the future also.

Rising, Mother said, "We're about to have some dinner. It isn't much but you and Eddie are welcome to join us."

Anna shook her head. "Eddie's over at Melvin's this evening. He spends half his time over there now." She bowed her head. "Sometimes I know he just leaves to get away from me and the silence of our house."

Every day for months, I plodded the dusty street to the white clapboard post office. The stars and stripes mounted on the front flapped in the wind, more tattered but still serviceable. Inside her little kingdom of ten by ten foot office space, the postmistress danced in tiny steps and hummed while sorting letters and packages. Visits with Peggy, filled with town gossip and exchanging the latest recipe one person or another had found in a woman's magazine, brought some normalcy—until Peggy's face paled and crumpled. I would round the counter and put an arm around her shoulders. We'd both cry, in a small mourning session before I headed out to deliver the news of one more boy who'd never come home.

Heartbreaking business, but it had to be done. Don't you think it was better for our people to hear the news from someone who cared about them, rather than the stranger from the army?

One day in October I received a letter. I smiled, taking the envelope, but on reading the return address in Dewitt's handwriting, darkness invaded my periphery vision. I grabbed the counter, and stared at Peggy until my vision cleared.

Peggy circled the counter. "What is it?"

I held out the envelope in a shaking hand. "It's Dewitt, Oh my God! - Dewitt's alive."

"Oh no, Liv. Look at the postage date. I'm so sorry."

My legs buckled at the knees, and I swallowed back nausea. The date, in red ink blared June 5, 1943. "No." My heart refused to let go of hope and I tore it open.

> *5-June-43*
> *Dear Sis and Mom,*
>   *I received your letter on the 2nd, but just now had the chance to answer. Can you imagine me writing letters at 6:15 in the a.m.? I'm sorry it has taken me so long to write back, but I've been so busy. I met a girl at the USO on my day off last week. She's swell and pretty, too. It is hot here, but nothing like home. The heat here is humid, not the dry heat of our desert. I'll write more soon, just wanted to get this posted.*
> *Love you both,*
> *Dewitt.*

I clasped my throat. It read like many of the letters Dewitt had sent. His energetic voice always brought him home to us. Who was the girl? No matter, if he'd met her the week before he wrote, they couldn't have been close. Yet, I couldn't remember Dewitt ever getting excited over a girl. He'd dated during school, but nothing serious. The fact he'd mentioned one at all was unusual; she must have been special. He neglected to include a name, so I'd never know this mysterious woman. The hope that had sung inside me for a few seconds evaporated. I smoothed the letter on the counter, inhaled deeply, but the tears flowed out anyway.

Peggy embraced me. "Let me get you some water." A few moments later she returned with a water glass.

I sipped the cold liquid. "Should I show my mother? It's so unfair. I can't bring her more pain."

"She has a right to read this. I think you know that."

Nodding, I folded the letter and returned it to the envelope and left.

The balmy desert breeze whipped my hair and dried the tears during the longest walk I'd ever taken. It didn't compare with all the trips to families all over town. When I opened the door, Mother paused her dusting. Her mouth opened but emitted no sound.

I held out the letter. "Mom—"

She snatched the envelope out of my hand and stumbled up the stairs. I followed a few steps behind, concerned for her state of mind. We entered Dewitt's room. Mother sat on his bed and read the letter while I remained at the doorway. Moments later, she folded the letter, placed it in the desk drawer, and then took a feather duster from her apron. She dusted the furniture with gentleness, lingering over the high school basketball trophy Dewitt had treasured. When she completed her task, she left the room, and turned the key in the lock.

That night, I thrashed about in bed, trying to wake from a nightmare. *Dewitt is trapped behind a door, calls to me and I struggle to free him. Water rises to my knees and still the latch doesn't release. The water continues rising and I drift away, unable to fight the current churning me farther from my dying brother.*

I awoke with my hair pasted to my head and neck. With shaking hands I threw back the blanket and went down the hall to Dewitt's room. During the time since he'd joined the navy, I'd found comfort in the place I felt closest to him. The door remained locked. I'd never be able to reach Dewitt again. Why did mother lock him away? I couldn't understand why. We shared grief, but everyone expresses it differently, don't they? For mother, she locked away the memories while I wanted to savor in the little things that kept my brother close to mind.

In the morning I went over to Maxine's. We sat at the soda fountain and I told her of my dream following Dewitt's delayed letter.

Maxine stomped a foot. "I'm so very tired of the sadness. The only time it's a little better is when I'm with other people, like the commemoration. Then I don't feel so alone. I've been thinking that we need something more."

"Like what?"

Maxine clenched her fists worrying the handkerchief in her hands. "What if the town set aside a time every day for meditating or praying or whatever? We'd not have to be together, but if we knew that at a certain time everyone was remembering in their own way, it could be a comfort."

I embraced her. "You might be on to something. Why don't we ask the Council?"

We approached the Council the following day. "The commemorations are monthly or at least have been lately," Maxine said, "but between those, we need something more to help us through the days. Having a time of contemplation will bring comfort to all the people here."

Chester nodded. "What do you have in mind?"

"If we have a time of meditation each day, it'll do two things," she explained. "One, the people will focus on their beloved soldier lost so they won't ever be forgotten, and two, they will be united in their sorrow on a daily basis, so I'm thinking it can bring a closeness we feel during the commemorations."

I almost expected Grace to oppose the idea because she never cared for Maxine, but to my surprise she immediately made the motion.

The Council voted to approve the Meditation Hour requiring all community members to observe an hour of silence each afternoon during which they could meditate and remember their lost loved one. They could do this in whatever way they felt appropriate, but the town would maintain silence during this time every day. It also left room for the churches to organize prayer meetings or services should they desire.

Following approval of the measure, Grace said, "I wonder if there are other things we can do to combat the possible depression of the residents."

John sighed, shaking his head. "Now what? I mean, I understand you all are trying to help, but we can't fix everything."

Ignoring John, Chester leaned his elbows on the table. "We already monitor the water, or try to."

"What do we do to help people not become depressed?" Aunt Wanda asked.

John said, "I have myself a good stiff drink every time I leave a Council meeting these days."

The Council members erupted in an angry rumble.

"I'm just kidding. But it is one way people cope."

Grace shook a finger in his face. "Stop being so negative. But that's something to consider. Maybe we should outlaw the sale and use of liquor except for medicinal purposes in order to prevent people becoming drunks."

John slammed a palm on the table. "This goes too far! Have we learned nothing? The country had prohibition and it didn't work. This won't work either."

I stood and at the mayor's nod I spoke. "Maybe the reasoning here is not to control people's behavior so much as to protect them from the possible effects of our grief."

"Exactly." Grace said. "And it wouldn't be like they couldn't use it at all. If Doc gave permission for a medical condition, alcohol would be fine. We're just restricting it."

John's elbow rested on the table and he rubbed his hair until it stood straight up. "I sometimes think the water has driven some of us around the bend already."

Clearing his throat, Chester said, "There is no call for nastiness, John. That's out of order. The proposal Grace mentioned about restrictions on alcohol needs a motion for us to go forward."

"I move we outlaw the sale and use of alcohol except for medical need," Wanda said.

John sprang to his feet, knocking his chair over. "Our country is fighting a war against fascism, and yet, you people are making a fascist town!"

With an exasperated sigh, Grace stiffened her shoulders. "How dare you! My boy, our boys have fought and died in this war. These are tough times. We must meet them with fortitude." She slumped back in her chair and continued in a voice barely above a whisper. "We have to help the people, both here and outside."

Chester rapped the gavel on the table. "We have a motion on the floor calling for an ordinance to prohibit the sale of alcohol except for medicinal purposes. Do we have a second?"

"I second," said Uncle Jim.

"All in favor?"

A round of ayes.

"Opposed?"

"Damned right I'm opposed. In fact, I'm beginning to think we're living in a miniature Germany. Would serve you right if you were all arrested as enemy aliens." John picked up his chair and resumed his seat.

The others grumbled. "John never understood." And, "You just don't get it."

The vote passed five to one, John the only hold out. I sat subdued. Something was at work in our little town, but I wasn't sure what.

When the muttering ended, Aunt Wanda raised a tentative hand. "Does anyone else think calling our town Hope Springs is strange nowadays?"

Chester tilted his head. "What's your point?"

She stared down at her hands clasped tightly together on the table. "I don't feel very hopeful. Coming to our meetings and discussing how to get through these times, it's not uplifting. I think perhaps calling our town Hope Springs...well it's just not appropriate anymore."

Stillness greeted her words. Everyone avoided one another's eyes. My heart caught in my chest and my throat constricted.

Grace closed her eyes for a moment and tears coursed down her cheeks. "Weeping Women Springs."

Wanda sniffed. "I move we change the name of Hope Springs to Weeping Women Springs."

The motion passed. My town changed forever.

Anna's Journal

October 21, 1943

 The oddest thing that I've ever seen happened today. Liv Soderlund blocked the road. Why in the world would someone think of doing such a thing I'm sure I don't know, but it's done. More strange than that, it seems the Council approved such a measure. They say it's all part of the war effort or something, but it doesn't quite make any sense, not that there's much never mind anyway because no one comes to town very often. Now no one will. It's the link to the Outside but it's broken now. I should know better than anyone that grief takes many forms, from my secret regarding Harold to make my loss private as anyone could ever get, to the lamenting over Sam's death most recent. Liv may have felt overwhelmed with the loss of her brother. Still, it's nothing like the loss of a husband, or son. You just never know how people will react to such circumstances.

The Road to Outside

Desert sands cover a path
brush blocks the once road
leading Outside,
a destination unwanted
by most
who, comforted
within a haven of hope,
remain wrapped in memories
of bliss
oppressed by sorrow unrelenting.

Part III

The Road Goes Quiet

Anna's Journal

December 21, 1944

The more I think of the cruel intentions of that man Hitler and what he's done to the world the more angry I become. Hatred has invaded my heart for the Nazis and the evil war they started. If not for this despicable world, my Sam would still be alive. How can a country allow such a leader to gain power? If I could get close to a Nazi, I'd shoot him.

The news we get is that our troops are making progress across Europe, but it can never be too soon. At least I still have my Donnie and Eddie

The Evil Spider

A huge black spider crawls
across Europe,
an infestation growing
attacking children
raping women
and always killing
our loved ones.
Stomp on him
and save the world
from the atrocious
Shadow of the Nazi

Chapter Fifteen

Maxine

NO ONE ELSE KNEW what happened that January evening of 1945, only me.

The crisp winter winds whistled through the canyons surrounding Weeping Women Springs. When I went out to the Spring the afternoon shadows stretched from the cliff rocks, throwing the yard into an early dusk.

After the Mediation Hour, I went out to prune roses in the backyard. I stopped short when I discovered a stranger sleeping by the Spring. A thin, bedraggled young man in rumpled clothes with sunburned skin lay under the tree. Even in his unkempt trousers, filthy shirt and unshaved face, I admired his physique—tight muscles hugged by his shirt. Where did he come from? More importantly, how had he found his way into Hope Springs without anyone seeing him? He smiled in his sleep and my heart fluttered. I hadn't had such feelings since Billy left.

My throat tightened. I wished this stranger peaceful sleep. In these times, it was so seldom one had good dreams. Billy haunted mine with happier times where we laughed together. I always awoke smiling before depression slid over my mind. Promises of those dreams would remain unfulfilled—Billy was still dead. The icy wind raised goose bumps on my arms and brought me back to the present.

I fetched an afghan from the house, and covered him with it. The light brush of wool on his skin woke him. He gazed at me with the brightest blue eyes I'd ever seen.

"*Bin ich gestorben und in den Himmel gegangen?*"

"*Nein, Herr, Sie sind* in Weeping Women Springs," I answered automatically, surprised at my high school German coming back so fast.

"*Aber Sie sind ein Engel,*" he countered.

"No, sir. I'm not an angel. I'm Maxine."

He shook his head, blinking. "*Fraulein.* How beautiful you are."

Heat flooded my cheeks. It had been years since anyone called me beautiful. Who was this young man? I was not accustomed to strangers and maybe I should notify the Council. Maybe not...he needed care. First, I could be a polite hostess.

I held out my hand. "What's your name, sir?"

Taking my hand in a caress, he said, "Werner Kohl."

"Hello, Werner Kohl. I'm Maxine Fiekens."

"I am pleased to meet you, Fraulein Fiekens." Werner swept his hand, indicating the yard and Spring, and I didn't correct the *fraulein*. "This is your home?"

"Yes. I live here. The Spring however, belongs to the town."

"Like paradise."

"It used to be, Herr Kohl, it used to be."

At his raised eyebrows inviting me to elaborate, I changed the subject. "Would you like to come in?" I searched around but saw nothing else. "Do you have a bag or luggage?"

He cast his gaze downward, frowning. *"Nein.* All zat I have, I wear."

"Oh. Well, some of Billy's clothes might fit you. He was about your size." Though it had been over eighteen months it seemed only moments ago that Captain Richards had informed me of Billy's death. I covered my eyes to erase the image and prevent the tears.

Werner stood, putting his hand on my arm. "It is all right. I do not need clothes."

"Billy doesn't need them anymore, so you might as well have them. At least they will get some use." I turned to go inside and gestured him to follow.

"I will wait outside. Too *schmutzig."*

"We'll get you a bath." I led him upstairs to the back bedroom. Opening the armoire, I inhaled. Billy's scent assaulted my senses. A shock of familiarity rushed through me, but I shook it off and sorted through the shirts, struggling against the picture of Billy in each sport coat, tie, pants. Quickly, I pulled out several items and handed them to Werner, afraid I might change my mind if I lingered.

"The washroom is through there." I pointed down the hall. "It's the first door on the right. You can take a bath and I'll make you something to eat. Don't have much, but I can put something together."

He studied me, until I wondered if perhaps he hadn't understood, and then he flashed a bright smile. "I do not want to be some problem to you, but some little food I would like."

I closed the armoire. "How long since you last ate?"

He held the shirt up to his shoulders and nodded. "Two days, Frau Fiekens."

"Two days? Oh my...I'll fix something right away." Forcing my gaze to his face I said, "And, please, call me Maxine."

Werner followed me out of the room. "Thank you, Maxine, I vill not take too long," He went down the hall.

I watched his broad back as he walked away. My mouth went dry. I cleared my throat. "Don't worry, take your time. It will be a few minutes before it's ready. When you're finished, come downstairs."

In the kitchen, I pulled out the coffee canister. Though I had only enough coffee for a couple of pots, I made some. I'd go without if necessary. A few eggs received from the Bauers would have to make a meal.

When he came downstairs I was cooking up an omelet. He'd slicked back his hair and he must have found Billy's shaving kit in the bathroom because the beard had disappeared. Taken back by the ice blue eyes of the stranger, I almost dropped the spatula. His square-cut jaw denoted classic good looks in true Teutonic splendor. His smile gleamed at me with perfect white teeth.

I blinked. He sure cleaned up fine. An almost forgotten feeling of gnawing desire flared within me. Pointing with the spatula, I said, "H-have a seat at the table. I'm almost done here."

I slid the omelet onto a plate with some bread I had baked earlier. After pouring some coffee, I placed the plate and cup in front of him.

His blue eyes widened. "Thank you, how vunderful this looks."

I shrugged. "It's simple, but it's better than nothing. With the wartime shortages, sometimes we don't get much delivered here." They had very little delivered these days, I added to myself.

Werner took a bite of egg, closed his eyes, and a look of pleasure washed over his features. After swallowing, he said, "Believe me, after what I have had recently this is a feast."

I chuckled. "I'm glad you like it. Have you been out in the desert long?"

Between bites, he mumbled. "Zwei weeks.

Sipping my coffee, I tried not to stare. "Why? Did you get lost?"

He stiffened and concentrated on his food. "Not really."

I swallowed my coffee too fast then coughed. "In that case, you knew where to find us?"

Putting down the fork, he stared at me. "Not exactly." He broke eye contact and looked down at the plate. "I vas wandering, but in the same direction vandering." His gaze darted up to mine. "I am headed to Mexico."

"On foot? Whatever for?"

Werner picked up the fork again and took another bite. "I didn't have an auto."

"Where're you coming from?"

He jerked his head toward the window. "West."

"Oh, you're coming from the big city, then."

Werner shook his head and dipped the bread to scoop up anything he might have missed on the plate. "*Nein.*"

"But there're over 60,000 people in Las Cruces now, especially with the military bases. That's what the paper says."

He brought the bread to his mouth. "Not Las Cruces. Close to Las Cruces." Chewing on the last morsel, he seemed to struggle between enjoying the meal and remaining stone-faced.

"Oh. Did you get into Las Cruces often?"

Avoiding my gaze once more he said in a stern voice. "*Nein.*"

I pursed my lips. "You're a mystery man."

"You are an angel still." He sat back in his chair and lifted the coffee cup. Inhaling deeply of the aroma, he brought it to his mouth and drank.

"Werner, how long have you been in the United States?"

Finally, he met my gaze. "A few months."

My hand twitched, almost knocking over the cup. "What? But the war has been going on for much longer than that."

He nodded. Yes."

I leaned toward him, putting my hand on his forearm resting on the table. "Were you in one of the detention camps?"

"*Nein.*" He looked down at my hand on his arm.

I yanked my hand away, and winced. This man confused me. No, not him, my feelings of desire. It had been so long since Billy had left. I stood, picked up the coffeepot and refilled both cups. "You came here on your own then?" As I said it, I began to wonder what would have brought him to America. His handsomeness had distracted me. Only one possibility struck me. To cover my sudden nervousness, I pumped water into the sink.

Werner studied his coffee. "No, not alone. I was on the boat."

I glanced at him over my shoulder. "During the war?" I still hoped my feeling was wrong—that there was some other explanation for his presence.

"Before the war," he said. He opened his mouth to say something else, but closed it again.

"Do you like it here?"

"It has been difficult...You see...I am..." He stopped. "You see, Maxine, I am prisoner of war."

"A prisoner of war?" I gasped and covered my mouth as my fears were realized. "But then how did you get to Weeping Women Springs?"

Werner reached toward me, but let the hand drop. "I escaped. Two weeks ago some of us escaped."

My gaze darted to the window. "Are they all here?"

He waved his hands, indicating no. "*Nein.* I was separated from them."

I winced. "Are the authorities looking for you?"

Werner cupped his hands around his mug and nodded. "I was not ever in war, but the Americans arrest me when war broke out."

"You've escaped them for two weeks already?" I reached for his empty plate, and took it to the sink.

He sat on the edge of his chair, poised to move. "I avoid the towns. This town is quiet, and I am thirsty and tired. I took a risk. I was lucky the spring to find."

I returned to the table. "It was quiet because it's our Memorial Meditation Moment." Maxine stared down at her hands blinking back tears. "We're in mourning for our lost soldiers. Every afternoon we have an hour of silent meditation time."

His eyebrow rose. "Oh I see. This is American uh..." He paused. "What is English word? *Brauch*?"

"I don't know *brauch*." High school English and my relatives in the Dakotas never went that far. If I knew I would be in this position, I might have studied harder.

"Ah, tradition. This is American tradition?"

"No. Only a Weeping Women Springs tradition."

Werner's bright blue eyes widened. "The soldiers are much honored."

I sat in silence. Could he understand? As a German, did he have any inkling of the pain this war inflicted? "We're trying. It helps us too...You see, when my husband was reported killed in action—" My voice broke. "I almost lost my sanity. I couldn't believe he would never come home." Tears slid down my cheeks. "We'd never have the children we dreamed of." Staring out the window beyond him, I shook my head. "We wouldn't have our life together. The meditation brings me comfort. During this time I remember him with sadness but also there's peace and acceptance. Well, most of the time anyway."

He took my hand. "That ist where you get the eyes of angels."

Heat rose in my cheeks. "I don't know about angelic eyes, but I am at peace with the loss. I'm still mourning of course, but it's more a feeling that we can't allow this war or any war to take any lives again. I'm determined to make sure our town or at least, our little corner of the world will never experience this kind of loss again. We're taking steps to make sure that never happens."

"How does one little town stop war?"

I slipped my hand out of his warm grasp. After walking over to the sink, I took a towel and wiped the counter, searching for the words to explain. "I don't know if we can stop a war. We can stop the hurt and loss it causes our community though."

"But if there is war, do not men have to fight?"

"Yes, Werner." I sighed. "They do, but we don't have anyone left to fight. All of our young boys signed up. They volunteered. Now they're mostly all gone."

Werner brought his coffee cup to the counter. "All gone? Surely some are here. Young boys—teenagers?"

"We have a few boys about ten or twelve but they're too young to fight in a war."

"In Germany young boys fight and many are too young. They are not ready to see war."

I clutched the towel until my knuckles turned white, unable to bear the thought of younger boys like Eddie and Melvin going to war. "Young boys fight in Germany?"

"Yes, of course. In Germany, many people fight. The *Fuehrer* authorized conscription so all men may fight—sixteen to sixty year old men."

"Sixteen to sixty? Even the old men? That's shocking."

"We do what we must." He lifted a shoulder in a shrug.

His words resonated with me. "I suppose so. Even here, we do what we must. We supported our boys. We still support them. It's just that we don't want anyone to have to experience this again."

He laughed. "That is women's ideas. Men like to fight."

My heart leapt at the cheerful sound despite his words. The man affected me, but was it just because I missed my Billy? "Why?"

Werner struck a mock fencing pose, brandishing a make-believe sword. "Men like the adventure. They like to use their skill in battle. Always been so. Will be so forever."

Far from being frightened, I repressed a grin, reminded of Errol Flynn pirate movies. "What if the women refused to let their sons go to war?"

He placed the invisible sword down and captured my gaze with his blue eyes. "Do you have sons?"

"No. Billy and I never had the chance." I broke eye contact.

He placed a finger under my chin to bring my gaze back to him. "Sons can be convincing. When your young men of this town went to war, did women want to stop them?"

Warmth shimmered through me. "No. We were proud of them. We *are* proud of them. They were so eager to go defend our country."

He let go of my chin and grinned boyishly. "Precisely. That ist how it works."

I giggled. "How did you get so wise? You don't look so old."

He gave a soft whistle, and then broke into laughter. "Not wise, just have experience. I am only twenty."

The lightness of the moment fled "Billy was just twenty when he died."

Tears prickled my eyes once more. It seemed as if all I did in those days was cry; it was all any of us did. I pushed the thoughts away. "Do you miss your home?"

He closed his eyes. "*Ja*, yes, I do."

I lifted a hand to touch him, but dropped it before he opened his eyes again. "Will you be able to go back after the war?"

"I do not know. Maybe."

"At least you aren't where the fighting is. You're lucky."

He gave a wry smile. "I am not lucky to be prisoner." His face brightened with a dazzling smile. "I am lucky to meet you. Maybe things change for me. Spring *und* nice pretty angel I find." He stifled a yawn.

"You said you were arrested when the war started. You were in the German navy?"

"No. A cruise ship. I worked on the ship, not navy."

"I don't understand." Then I remembered the internment camps where they were keeping German Americans, and Japanese Americans, maybe some Italians too. Many people who had not fought were in a camp anyway. "The whole world has gone a little crazy with fear." The setting sun cast a golden glow in the window. I shaded my eyes from the glare and pulled the curtain closed. "You must be tired. You could sleep in the spare room."

He hung his head a moment, and then met my eyes. "You are kind, but I go. I not want authorities to discover I am here."

I shook my head. "We only have the Council here and they wouldn't report you. I'm sure of it."

He shoved his hands in his pockets. "How do you know? They will not like having a German soldier here. Why you allowed me in your home, I do not know."

"Maybe not. But we don't have to tell them you are German." I thought a moment. "I could tell them you're my cousin visiting from North Dakota."

"North Dakota? Never have I been there." He rubbed the back of his neck.

My words rushed out. "That doesn't matter. All you have to know is that it's cold up there. Some of them speak with a German accent. My family does, in fact. It isn't exactly like your accent, but it's close enough. No one will tell the difference."

His shoulders relaxed. "Just for tonight. It would be good to sleep in a warm bed. The desert is very cold."

"All right. I'll go make up the bed." I poured more coffee in his cup. "You stay here and enjoy your coffee. I'll let you know when I'm done."

He grabbed my hand. "Thank you, Maxine. I will never forget."

"It really is no problem. If Billy were in the same situation I would hope some nice *fraulein* would help him. I'll be right back."

A few minutes later I returned to find Werner placing clean dishes in the drying rack. I looked around the kitchen. "You didn't have to wash the dishes. You're a guest, but thank you."

"No. Thank you. It was the least I could do since you provide me food and bed."

"Whenever you're ready for bed, you can go on up, it's all set."

He yawned. "Sorry. I am tired and look forward to sleep in a real bed."

"Follow me." I led him up the stairs and to the spare bedroom. "This is it. If you need anything, just call. You know where the washroom is, so that's all you'll need."

He bent over my hand to place a kiss. "Yes. This will be fine, wonderful. *Danke*."

The heat rose in my face. "Sleep well, Werner. I'll see you in the morning."

I closed the guest bedroom door, and headed down the hall to my room and secured the squeaky lock. It didn't hurt to be cautious. After changing my nightgown, I slid between the covers and reached for my diary. When Billy left for the war, I'd written him a letter every evening. For the past twenty months my diary had replaced them. Most days were similar. Here's my entry for that day.

> *January 10, 1945*
> *Dear Billy,*
>   *You'll never believe what happened! I found a German POW. Well I guess he found me. His name is Werner Kohl. He escaped from the prison by Las Cruces. He said he'd been out in the desert for two weeks. I went outside to the backyard and there he was by the wellspring. I was surprised to see a stranger, but I didn't know he was an escaped prisoner until after he ate some supper. He ate an omelet I fixed him and then after we talked a bit he went to bed. I told him he could stay the night. I wonder what will happen. If he drank from the Spring, he probably won't want to leave. I'll write more tomorrow. What would you think, me housing the enemy in our home? Even though he's not a soldier, he does come from Germany. It's difficult to think of Werner as bad. He seems normal, just like any other young man. Actually, he reminds me a little of you. And I hope if you'd been in Germany needing help that some German girl would have fed you and given you warm clothes. He's nice and asleep*

now in the guest room. Oh Billy, I'm so lonely
without you.

The next morning dawned cool and sunny. I rose from bed
and hurriedly dressed, taking a few extra minutes to run some
bright cherry color over my lips. While pinching my cheeks for
some extra pink, my thoughts wandered. Why primp for this
stranger? I finished combing my hair and stilled my shaky
hands.

At least I could prepare a good breakfast for Werner. It felt
so good to have someone to take care of and I wanted to make
every moment last. Every morning for the last two years, the
missing element of my routine had been someone to share the
day's plans with. Billy and I had begun our day by sipping
coffee while planning chores. Often we told one another our
dreams of the previous night. I missed the simple comfort of
having someone in the house. The surprising scent of fresh
coffee drifted up the stairs and I hurried to the source.

Werner, dressed in Billy's clothes, stood at the kitchen
counter. He welcomed me with a bright smile. "Guten
morgen."

My cheeks warmed and I dropped my gaze, but I berated
myself for acting so silly and lifted my eyes. "Hi. How did you
sleep?"

Taking a sip of coffee, he met my eyes over the cup. "Very
well — *Danke schön*. The comfortable bed slept me very nice."

I grabbed an apron and tied it around my waist. "I see
you've made coffee."

Werner sat at the table. "Yes. I saw the coffee pot here. I
want to make ready for you."

I reached for the cast iron skillet, then gathered ingredients
for breakfast. "Thank you." Beating eggs helped me fight the
temptation to stare into his eyes. "I'll have to open up the store
in a couple of hours. What are your plans?" I glanced over my
shoulder.

His gaze met mine. "What store?"

After drawing open the heavy curtain at the window, I
explained. "The front of the house is the community store.
Now we...uh...I just sell a few things people need. There's a
soda fountain, but not many people come by for a treat these

days." I frowned. "We don't have the makings because of rationing. Plus, I think people don't care enough to want to have one anymore, it reminds them of the past and it becomes too painful for them."

"I see." He sipped his coffee. "Do you have help working the store?"

I poured the eggs into the pan. "Our plan was to run it together, Billy and me, but since the war...well I guess I'm just going to run it myself from now on. Most of it is bartering these days. That's how I get eggs and milk."

He stood, almost knocking the chair over. "Maxine?"

"Yes?"

"Do you think?" Werner stepped toward me. "Do you think I work in the store to help?" He ran a hand over his hair. "In my grandparents' market I work when I was a boy. I help you."

My stomach fluttered, but I resumed cooking. "Don't you have to go to Mexico?"

Werner touched my shoulder. "I don't have anyone there. I thought perhaps..." He backed away. "*Nein,* of course. Not a good idea to stay." His shoulders drooped.

Pangs of sympathy shot through me. "I thought you couldn't stay in the United States." I finished toasting the bread, grabbed plates from the cupboard, slid the eggs onto them, and then buttered the toast.

He flopped onto the chair. "You are right. It would danger you if they find me. You would be comfort providing for the enemy."

"Werner, I'm not concerned about that. It's your safety I'm concerned about."

He shrugged. "They can't hurt me. They just send me back to the prison camp."

Leaning over him, I placed the plate on the table. I couldn't resist touching his shoulder, lingering a moment. "Are you sure? I mean, since you escaped?"

Werner grazed my fingers with his knuckles before I withdrew. "Forbidden by the Geneva convention. The prison can keep me, but they cannot punish." He reached for the strawberry jam on the other side of the table. "I guess they think prison is enough, neh."

I took a seat. "But you don't want to go back. Was it horrible?"

"Not horrible, but I am useless. At least I have, had job on the ship. Good job too. I like working with the passengers." He forked some egg into his mouth.

I stared out the window. The silence stretched out. I couldn't pretend. Billy died because Werner's country started a world war. Simple fact. And yet, sitting across from him at the kitchen table, I couldn't hate this good-looking man who washed my dishes, made me coffee and smiled at me like I was an angel. Billy's voice whispered in my mind. "Hello, Sunshine."

My throat tightened. Lifting my gaze, I met those blue eyes. Words wouldn't come.

Werner reached for my hand. He stroked it and touched my gold wedding band. "I am sorry about your husband." His thumb drew circles on the back of my hand. "You will continue the store to run and live here?"

The mesmerizing warmth of his touch made me slow to respond. "Yes. I don't have any other family, except my distant relations in North Dakota, so I'll stay here. Our town is like family." I pulled away. "Especially since the loss of the boys."

"I see." He sat quiet for a moment. "I should go." He made no attempt to move.

"I suppose so. You must go so you can make it to Mexico." I couldn't smile. My thoughts ran rampant. *Get a hold of yourself, Max. You don't even know him.* His company brightened my world and gave me something to do, someone to care for. I sighed.

A faint knock interrupted my longing. "I wonder who that is? I'll have to answer it. Stay here. I'll be right back." I pressed a finger to my lips to emphasize the need for silence before racing to open the door.

"Liv? What is it?" I resisted the urge to check over my shoulder.

"You know. We're headed to The Weeping Place. Aren't you ready?"

"Uh, no." I glanced back down the hall. "No. I'll be a few minutes. You go on ahead."

"Is that coffee I smell? I'd love a cup." Liv moved toward the kitchen. "Mother and I used the last of our rations a couple days ago."

I grabbed her arm, almost spinning her around. "I'm sorry. I just drank the last of it." My lie brought heat to my face. I didn't meet Liv's eyes.

"Oh. Well, that's okay. Did you need some help getting the flowers?"

"No." The word burst out sharper than I intended. "I mean, no thank you. It's something I like to do alone. You go on ahead. I'll be there in a little while."

"Are you all right? You're acting a little odd."

"I'm fine. Guess, well I guess I just overslept. Haven't had a chance to wake up yet, haven't finished my coffee." My words tripped over themselves.

"I can stay and help. Really it's no bother." Liv made another move toward the hall.

"Really, it's fine." I opened the door. "You go on ahead. I can go alone later." What would make her go away? "In fact, sometimes walking to The Weeping Place alone is a solace."

"Since when? You're always the one wanting company." Liv's brows scrunched. "What's going on?"

"Nothing. I'm fine, everything is fine. I just need some time alone." The last came out harsh.

"Well, okay then." Liv's smile faded. "I won't bother you any longer." She swept outside, her shoulders high.

Liv wouldn't understand, and it was important to protect Werner's secret. Maybe by the time I saw her again, I could explain my behavior away. I returned to the kitchen and smoothed my apron. It was a close call.

"Is there anything you need for your journey?" Liv momentarily forgotten, I opened the cupboard. While keeping busy, I wouldn't have to think about him leaving or about lying to my best friend. Was I crazy? I'd just met the man, for goodness sakes.

"Maybe crackers or bread? Something I could take?"

"Yes. I have the rest of the bread. I'll pack it up for you and I have some cheese. That'll keep as well." I bustled around the kitchen, sliced bread and cheese and wrapped it then handed him the brown paper package. You can take water with you too." I handed him a container. The Spring couldn't have any greater effect on him since he'd already drunk from it.

"I'll fill it outside."

He no sooner left than I wiped my eyes, admonishing myself for being silly, behaving this emotionally when I didn't really know him. Perhaps once he went away I could focus on what mattered—keeping Billy's memory alive for as long as I lived—I could never forget my purpose in life. Try as I would I couldn't stop the sobs.

Werner reentered the kitchen and rushed to embrace me. "Poor *liebchen*. What the matter is?"

"Nothing." I sniffled. "Nothing more than what has already been wrong for the last couple of years. Every day I think, perhaps I won't weep for Billy, perhaps I won't cry today. But every day I do. The tears come without warning. Sometimes I don't even realize I'm crying."

He leaned back still holding me within his arms. "I thought I made you sad."

I shook my head in denial. These tears were for Werner, due to his presence in my life, short as it was, but he could never know. I tried not to think how good it felt to have someone strong hold me. My palms lingered on his chest before pushing against him.

I stepped away. "I'm sorry. I didn't mean to cry, not now. You must leave. Today the townspeople are going to the cemetery to trim and adorn the memorials. It should be quiet for the next couple of hours if you head out of town in the opposite direction." Drawing an imaginary map on the table, I explained. "Once you get to the edge of town you will see a little path. That will lead to the main road. If you want to avoid the main road, continue on the path. A wash runs pretty much south here. If you follow it you should find yourself in Mexico in a few days. There are a couple little villages between here and there so you can find water or food along the way."

"*Danke*. You are a special woman. I wish something I could do for you."

"There is nothing you need to do."

I couldn't tell him what was in my thoughts. You've done enough, Mr. POW. You've changed my life somehow I can't explain. You've reminded me of the world outside. This world we want to hide from keeps calling us. You must return to that world, but I cannot follow. I have my tasks here.

He took a step toward the door. Then he turned and retraced the step. "You okay will be?"

"Of course. Weeping Women Springs needs me. Billy needs me. We'll be fine here." I reached for a towel.

Werner went back to the door, spun back to me, took three strides and swept me back into his arms. I let the towel fall. He kissed my cheek. "If I would stay, I could. *Aufwiedersehen*, Maxine. Goodbye. Be well."

I touched his cheek, brushing trembling fingers over his lips. "Goodbye, Werner. Be safe. You know you have a friend here if you should need one."

He kissed my fingertips. "Goodbye, *liebchen*."

Without looking back he walked out the doorway. Following him, I leaned against the door jam and watched him hike down the road wishing I could call him back, explore those tentative feelings. But I remained silent.

Wandering out to the backyard I found my clippers, and snipped yellow roses for Billy's memorial grave. They didn't send his body back, but a headstone rested in the cemetery to remember him by. Billy always said the roses reminded him of my sunshine smile. The tears came unbidden but welcome; my heart needed them. I welcomed the familiarity of remembering Billy. This felt normal. Best for me to remember it. There could be no young handsome man come into my life and replace Billy. Werner was a stranger—an enemy even. Billy continued to be the love of my life. I recalled Billy's embrace, but kept getting confused by the very real memory of Werner's arms around me.

My tears fell onto the petals of the sunshine yellow rose and I pricked my finger on a thorn. Despair filled my soul. *This is what my life will be like forever now. There will be no one left on earth to know me, to love me, to care for me. I am alone and will remain so for the rest of my days.*

Until that moment I'd never allowed the sheer aloneness to take over my spirit. It settled around me, taking away the small beam of hope lingering in the deepest part of my heart these past few months. From that moment forward I would not be the same person.

I finished cutting the roses and imagined them wilting before my eyes.

I held up the bouquet, the buds fresh and brilliant with life. I placed the roses in my basket and went inside for my hat then headed to the cemetery. Hopefully, no one would notice my tardiness or ask any questions. I took time to stop at the Sweetheart Tree and ran my fingers over Billy's name carved with mine. Never had I been as happy as when he cut them into the tree, and I struggled to remember those joy filled days.

Chapter Sixteen

Liv

AT THE END OF JANUARY 1945 I visited with Peggy in the post office.

"Here's a letter for the mayor." Peggy studied the envelope. "That's odd."

"Who's it from?" I asked.

"The return address says *Albuquerque Journal*."

"Wonder what that's about. Maybe I'd better take it to the Council meeting this afternoon."

I arrived at Uncle Jim's house just before the meeting and held out the letter to the mayor. "I thought this might be important. Would you mind if I stay?"

"It's fine." Chester smiled. "Have a seat." The dining room served as the Council's chamber. The dark wood shone from Aunt Wanda's recent polishing.

Chester read the letter to the Council.

```
January 27, 1944
Dear Mayor,
 My name is Robert Perry and I work
for The Albuquerque Journal. It has
come to our attention that your
town has sacrificed several young
men in the War. We would like to
honor their memories with a special
article. Would it be possible to
meet with some of the families to
hear their stories?
Sincerely,
Robert Perry, Reporter
The Albuquerque Journal
```

"I don't think we want to put the townspeople through that kind of thing," John cautioned in his booming voice.

Grace raised a delicate hand. "It could be a good thing. We could let others know how we've been hurt. We've lost almost all of our young men. Even though I'm sure other towns have experienced loss, I bet none have lost as much as we have."

John shook his head. "It won't stop the war."

Grace leaned her elbows on the table, inclining her head. "No, but it'd let people know the cost of war. It's been on my mind a lot lately. I think perhaps we can have an effect on others. Our boys' lives wouldn't have been given in vain."

John straightened in his chair. "Of course, they weren't in vain. They're keeping our nation free, but wars will happen. It's inevitable."

Chester rapped the gavel. "Do you want to put it to a vote?"

"I move we allow the paper to do a story on our townspeople," Grace said.

"I second," said Wanda.

"Wait!" John stood. "We are isolated for a reason. You're all going to just let a reporter waltz in and talk to everyone? This is a bad idea."

Grace leaned back in her chair. "It doesn't matter what we want to do, John opposes it. I still make the motion."

"We have a motion and second. All in favor?" asked Chester.

"Aye," chorused all members except John.

February 14 arrived and I have to admit it was a little exciting. I spent the afternoon checking outside every few minutes for the reporter. At the rumble of a car engine, I lifted the front drape. A blue Ford coupe rolled down Main Street and pulled up in front of the house. I dropped the drape and went out to meet Robert Perry to fulfill my assigned task for The Council.

The man stretched after getting out of the car. "Liv Soderlund, I presume." He grinned.

"Yes. The mayor said you would be coming out today. Mr. Perry, is that correct?"

He held out a hand. "Call me Bob. May I call you Liv?"

His friendly nature had me smiling back. "Yes, that's fine." I determined to keep a businesslike attitude. Bob's movie star good looks with ice blue eyes seemed to pierce my heart.

He took out a notebook and began jotting in it.

I tilted my head to see. "What are you writing? You just got here."

"Hmmm." He kept scribbling. A moment later he said, "I'm noting some initial impressions. It helps me add color to the story when I get back to my typewriter."

A tingle raced up my spine, just watching his handsome face. "Oh. Uh...how long have you been reporting?"

"Since high school."

"You didn't enlist or get drafted then?"

"No, 4F here." He winced, but seemed to recover quickly.

"Sometimes I wish that was the case for our young men." I couldn't keep the sadness out of my voice.

"Why? They served their country honorably. The country needed men like them. Unfortunately, they don't need me with a bum heart. Instead I'm here reporting about them." His lips twisted. He looked up and down the street, before returning his gaze to me. "Who did you lose?"

"My brother, Dewitt."

"What happened?"

I pressed my lips together. "Training accident. He was in a submarine."

He scribbled a note. "I understand that all of the boys of Hope Springs enlisted. Is that right? How many?"

"Yes. They were eager and proud to serve and signed up right after Pearl Harbor." I drew in a shaky breath. "Forty-four went."

"I know this must be a difficult question, but I have to ask. How many have died?"

"Forty-three. Only Mrs. Frolander's son Donnie is left. He's a tail gunner." I neglected to add Donnie was my boyfriend. It didn't seem appropriate to mention, and Donnie had been gone so long. That's not to say I didn't live on the hope he would be the one Hope Springs boy to make it back, and together we'd build a life together, a life where children played in the streets again.

"I'm sorry," he said. "But that's the reason my editor wants me to do a story on it. How big is the population?"

"Before the war, a couple hundred or thereabouts in the area, including the ranchers and all."

He jotted in his notebook. "Who will we be meeting today?"

"The Council lined up a couple of people to talk to you. Maxine Fiekens, and Mary and Sebastian Bauer. Of course, there is me and my mother too." I led Bob across the street. "We'll start with Maxine. She runs the store. Since it's late, we may not get out to the Bauers."

The bell jingled our arrival, and Maxine came out from behind the counter to greet us.

I pointed to Bob and introduced him

Maxine nodded. She extended her hand. "Yes, the mayor told me. It's nice to meet you." Her lips turned up, but her eyes remained listless.

Poor Maxine. I thought. What would the stranger think of her continued sadness? Everyone's continued sadness. The fact that we all seemed mired in it unable to move on angered me even more. The more I tried to fix things, the worse they'd become. Hiding the road just meant I had to deliver the news, while better than having the army do it, it didn't change the news.

Bob nodded. "I appreciate your taking time to meet with me. Who did you lose?"

I jerked a little at the abrupt question, wishing there was some way to protect Maxine. Maybe I should have set down some preliminary guidelines for him.

She drew back, drawing a wash rag across the counter. "My Billy. We'd only been married less than a year. He didn't have to go, but all the boys were doing it, and he didn't feel right about not joining up too."

"How old was he?"

"Twenty."

Bob gasped. "Me too." He rubbed his forehead and sat at the counter. "Wow."

I touched his shoulder. "What's wrong?"

He stared into space for a few moments before speaking. "It hit me, if I still lived in Hope Springs, I'd be the only man my age left."

"You lived in Hope Springs?" I said. "But I don't remember you."

"My folks moved away when I was still about two. I don't remember it of course." He rolled his shoulders. He turned to Maxine. "When did you get the news?"

"May first of last year. The army sent officers out to tell me. I still remember them."

"Why didn't you get the telegram they usually send?"

"We don't have a telegraph office or telephone lines in town." I explained. "We're sort of out in the wilds here."

He scratched something on his pad. "Well, a lot of our state is, but finding the place wasn't easy. Without the landmarks you gave me I would have missed the road. The twentieth century seems to be passing you by."

"Not completely."

Bob chewed on the end of his pencil. Finally he looked up. "Could I have a glass of water?"

"Sure." Maxine filled a glass from the tap and handed it to him.

He took a deep mouthful.

I caught Maxine's eye and drew her aside to talk out of earshot. "Maybe you shouldn't have given him any water. We don't want him to have to stay here. It's just not a good idea, for him or us." I bit my lip, torn by my thoughts. "He's a reporter." Of course, having a good looking young man in town held a certain charm. Maybe it wouldn't be a bad thing if he wanted to stay.

Maxine winced. "Oh, I didn't think. Will it be a problem?"

"Well, maybe not. If he lived here as a child, he would have already tasted it." I returned to Bob. "What about the water— do you remember it?" I asked him.

"It's really good. I was thirsty." He perked up. While up until now he'd been subdued, after sipping the water, he smiled and softened toward Maxine.

I exchanged a glance with Maxine. We watched him closely.

"Y'know?" Bob's forehead creased. "Come to think of it, this is odd. This water is really good. I remember my folks talking about the special water of Hope Springs. They lived here for several years after I was born and always talked about coming back. They raved about the water, almost to the point that it was strange. Now I know why."

The clock behind the counter chimed. "It's getting a little late," Liv said. "I don't know if we'll be able to make it over to Mary and Sebastian's. Had you planned staying overnight?"

"I hadn't, but is it a problem if I do? I need to talk to at least a couple of other people. I'd also like to look around the town." He winked at me. "It would be nice to spend some time here, especially with such pretty company.

"It's not a problem. You can stay at my place. My mother won't mind." My task of monitoring his communications hadn't included providing room and board, but having a young man at the dinner table might be fun. Of course, he wasn't hard to look at and having him stay at our place made sense. It had been so long since I'd had a chance to socialize with a young man my age. Oh, that's just silly, I admonished myself. He'll only be here a short while, and besides, what would the other girls think if I flirted with the first available male who came to town, especially when I waited for someone to return, praying for Donnie, writing him love letters daily. Why was his memory dimming?

"All right, let me finish up here with Maxine, and then we can go."

After a couple of more questions, Bob learned Maxine received comfort from special memorial ceremonies the Council organized.

"That's about all the questions I have for now. Thanks for your help."

"I'm sorry it is such a sad topic. I wish I could talk about happier times." Maxine's gentleness shone through, her sympathy for others at the forefront even after all her loss. I admired her so much on one hand, but despised the fact I couldn't help her snap out of her sadness.

"I understand," he replied. He turned to me. "I'm ready to go, if you are."

I led the way back to my place.

Opening the door, I called out, "Mother, Bob Perry's here. He'll be staying for dinner."

She came to the front room, approaching him with her hand out. "Hello, young man, I'm Mrs. Soderlund."

He shook her hand. "Liv said I could stay the night here. I hope it's not too much bother."

"No, of course not." Liv caught the wince on her mother's face before she spoke. "Liv, would you fix up Dewitt's room? We're having meatloaf for dinner. There's always enough for one more. In fact it'll be nice having a young man at the table. It's been so long." Her smile came slowly. "It will be a few more minutes before dinner is ready. Why don't I take your picture while it's still light? My brownie is right here." She opened the hall closet and brought out the camera.

"Mother!" I made a half-hearted grasp for the camera. "I'm sure he doesn't want to be your model."

Mother's too bright voice seemed forced. "Nonsense. He won't mind, will you, Bob?"

"I guess not." He chuckled.

"Great, let's go out to the street." Camera in hand, she almost dragged Bob outside, but his reluctance seemed feigned when I caught his grin.

"Stand by your car," she directed. He did and she snapped a photograph. I stood aside. A ghost of a smile appeared on his face.

"That's good. I think that will be a good shot. Liv, you join him now. I'll take another."

"Mother," I tried to protest.

He slipped an arm around my shoulders.

"Perfect. You look good together." She snapped another picture.

Didn't she remember I had a boyfriend? Sometimes I wondered if losing Dewitt had affected her memory.

"Dinner will be ready in just a few minutes. Liv, why don't you show him where to wash up?"

"Follow me."

A short while later he joined us in the kitchen. Mother took the meatloaf out of the oven. "Good timing, Bob. I hope you like corn. It's a simple fare tonight."

"Really, Mrs. Soderlund, this is fine. Good, in fact." He pulled our chairs out for us.

Mother asked me to say grace.

"Dear Father, thank you for this meal. Bless and keep our loved ones safe here, and bless those that are with You, especially our Dewitt. In Jesus' name, Amen."

I explained to my mother that Bob had lived here as a child.

"I'm trying to remember. I do recall some Perrys living here a while back. Margaret and Woodrow were their names, I think"," she said.

"Yes, ma'am. That's right. They're my parents."

"How are they these days?"

He looked away. "Dad died a couple years ago, and mom, well, she seems a bit lost without him."

"I'm so sorry to hear that. You'll have to give me her address. I'll sent her my condolences."

"I still miss him. But you know what it means to miss your loved ones."

"Yes. The war has been hard on Hope Springs. Perhaps after the war, you might come visit us again."

"Perhaps," he answered. He caught my gaze and beamed.

"How about some pumpkin pie for dessert? I happen to have a slice leftover from one Liv made yesterday. She's quite a baker, our Liv."

A rush of heat filled my cheeks. "Mom!" She never changed. Whenever an eligible young man came around, she wanted to plan a wedding. Only for the last little while since I'd been going steady with Donnie had she let up at all in the matchmaking department. I wondered at her sudden change of heart here.

"Thank you, ma'am. I would love a piece.

"Why don't you go into the front room?" I suggested. "Mother and I will join you in a few minutes."

When he left I leaned in close to mother. "What are you doing?"

Her eyebrows rose. "Nothing. I'm just offering the nice young man a nice home-cooked meal and friendly company. We both need a distraction these days."

I couldn't refute that logic. My heart seemed a little lighter that afternoon. The constant tension had disappeared or at least lessened.

"Go on in to him. I'll follow once the tea is brewed."

When I returned to Bob he was gazing at the memorial we set up for Dewitt, the flag, his picture and the framed letter from the navy.

"Were you close?" he asked.

"Sometimes he was my best friend, though he drove me a little crazy as well. I suppose it isn't surprising with siblings. Do you have any?"

"No. Just me and my mom."

"So tell me, what's Albuquerque like now? I've only been once, years ago, and it sounds like it's changed a lot."

"We're definitely growing, with the Kirtland Army Air Base there these days. It seems like overnight we've gone from a travel stop on the rails or Route 66 to a big city. With the air fields and training base, you probably wouldn't recognize it."

"It sounds exciting."

Bob grinned. "It is, I can't deny it. It's a great time to be a reporter. I'm on the cutting edge of everything. Most of my work takes me out of the city. Like this story."

His smile was contagious and I found myself feeling lighter than I had in the months since we'd learned of Dewitt's death.

"Here we go." My mother entered carrying a tray with the tea and pie.

I told Mother that the city of Albuquerque sounded like a place on the move.

"Fascinating. Do you ever get tired of the bustle, Bob?" She poured the tea and handed the plates and cups.

"No, ma'am. I love it. Wish I could be closer to the action of the war, but since I can't do that, reporting on the events in the state is just as important."

"That's true. Mother and I read the paper every week for news of the war. Everyone in town does. It's our lifeline to the Outside. What's the biggest story you've worked on so far?"

"Well, I investigated the bat explosion over at Carlsbad," he said.

"What's that?" I asked. "I don't remember hearing about it."

"They were making a bat bomb. I'm not sure of the exact details other than it involved bats and somehow they were going to set fires in places in Japan. You know their homes and buildings are made of a lot of bamboo and paper, flammable stuff. They were testing the project over at the army airfield and somehow the armed bats were released. Incinerated the test range and got under a fuel tank. It resulted in quite an explosion. My sources gave me the scoop."

"Wow." I couldn't think of any other response. "You lead an interesting life."

"It is. I don't get tired of it. Most recently, I covered a POW escape."

"They were all found, weren't they?" Mother asked.

"All except one. Most of them returned to the camp." He shrugged. "I guess it's more comfortable than a freezing desert night in January."

"How curious," I said. "I can't believe they escaped."

"Fortunately, nothing happened as a result, but it's to be expected. From what I understand, the security is not a big priority at the camp. It's mainly a work camp so the prisoners are out helping farmers and other activities that we don't have men to do with the war on. The one who's still missing was taken prisoner at the start of the war."

We continued talking as we ate our pie.

"Tomorrow I'd like to get a look at the town if that's okay?" he asked.

"Yes, we can take a tour." I couldn't help but experience a little thrill at getting to spend some more time with him. He was bright and friendly, and I know I've mentioned handsome, but it's true.

Mother gave an exaggerated yawn. "I'll go fix the bed in Dewitt's room."

I gave her a questioning look. "Mom, are you sure? You don't have to..."

"It's fine, dear. You stay here and keep Bob company." She bustled from the room with a strange smile on her face.

I shook my head. "I'm sorry. Sometimes she isn't very subtle."

Bob rubbed his chin. "What do you mean?"

"She likes to play matchmaker, so she's giving us plenty of time to be alone. She hasn't had an opportunity to do that in a while. Don't take her too seriously. I'm used to her antics, but she doesn't mean any harm. Back when I was in high school, no week went by that she didn't try getting me a date. Like she never trusted me to get one on my own."

"I can't believe you had any problem getting a date." His wide-eyed gaze traveled over me.

Heat flooded my cheeks. "Well, to be honest, I dated only a couple of guys, but until just before I graduated nothing had really been special."

"Now you have someone special?"

I hesitated. Donnie's face faded in my memory. It had been several weeks since I received a letter. Maybe he had met someone. "Remember Donnie, the boy I mentioned earlier?"

"The last boy?"

"Yes. We have been going together since before he left."

"I know several girls working at the paper who say they get pretty lonely without their boyfriends and husbands. I imagine it's difficult here where you don't have any social activities like a USO."

"To be honest sometimes I can't envision his face unless I look at his picture. I love getting letters, don't get me wrong. But lately with all the other boys gone, I feel guilty saying anything to the other girls."

He nodded and took my hand. "Don't feel guilty because you have someone to write to, someone to pray for, someone to care for."

My hand trembled in his and except for the ticking clock, everything went silent. So much he left unsaid, but I guessed he wished to be overseas with all the other boys yet was stuck on the home front covering local stories.

"So if you have Donnie, why is your mother playing matchmaker?"

I laughed, shaking my head. "I'm not sure except perhaps it's a habit she doesn't seem capable of breaking until she sees a grandchild."

"Was there a reason you didn't marry him before he left?"

"I just wasn't quite ready. We graduated in May and he left not long afterward."

"I betcha he's regretting that he didn't make it permanent."

"What makes you say that?"

"I just have to look at you, doll. Any guy who'd let you get away has to be crazy loco." He kissed the back of my hand then, and I swore I felt it all the way to the top of my head. "In fact, I look forward to spending the day with you tomorrow. I hate to cut this short, but I need to write up my notes from my interview with Maxine and some of my first impressions while they're fresh."

The stairs creaked as my mother came down. "The room is ready when you are."

"Thank you, Mrs. Soderlund."

"Liv, go on and show him up."

I led him upstairs to Dewitt's room. It was odd to have someone sleeping there again, especially after Mother had locked it up for the past few months. I fluffed the pillow and smoothed the blankets, before returning to the door and moving past him. "Goodnight. We'll go over to Mary and Sebastian's tomorrow."

"That's fine." He leaned a shoulder on the jam. "Sleep well, Liv and I'll see you in the morning." His eyes caught the lamplight.

My mouth dried suddenly when he leaned toward me, brushing his lips against my cheek. Before I could react, he stepped inside the room and shut the door. I knew what I'd be dreaming of that night.

OVER THE NEXT TWO DAYS, I resolved to keep Donnie in the forefront of my mind, but spending time with Bob distracted me from my best intentions. We took a hike up to the mesa the next afternoon. The notion that I'd met him on Valentine's Day did not leave me. Was it some kind of sign scrawled across my mind with hearts and arrows? Love shouldn't be so fickle, should it? I chastised my thoughts over and over, but whenever I caught the appreciative admiration in Bob's eyes, I blushed and giggled as if I were about fourteen instead of almost twenty-one.

"You're lucky you don't live in Albuquerque," he said when we reached the mesa above the Spring.

"Why is that?" I offered up a water canteen.

"Maybe I should say I'm lucky you don't live in the city. If you did, I'd be fighting for your attentions with every GI traveling through town."

The water drizzled down his dimpled chin as he tipped the canteen back. My gaze locked on the droplet, wishing to scoop it up with my finger. If the Spring had special powers of Hope, perhaps sipping the water off his skin might mingle with the attraction and form a bond. I shook my head, admonishing the direction of my wayward thoughts.

He must have caught something in my expression because he leaned toward me. The sun framed his head, creating a blazing crown. Certainly it had to be a joyful signal from the heavens that I could be joyful in this moment.

A slight shock of electricity preceded the kiss, a mere grazing over my lips. I jerked away almost before it started, searching for the memory of Donnie's first kiss, and yet it remained silent, out of reach like a dream dissipating upon waking.

Bob drew back. "I'm sorry. I shouldn't have done that."

"I should be sorry. It's just that I can't—" His fingers stilled my lips.

"Of course. No need to explain. You have Donnie. Since talking with his mother I understand you have an understanding with him."

"That's just it. I don't remember Donnie, his kiss, his arms around me. It's so long ago, everything." My muddled mind could not form the words for the confusion which swamped me.

"Could I ask one thing?"

I nodded, afraid what he asked I would not be able to grant, or in the granting some further light might be shed upon my predicament.

"Could we write? Can I visit on the weekend? Not asking for anything more than the opportunity to spend some time with you, to get to know you better. You may find it's not such a scary prospect, I hope."

"Give me time to write to Donnie. It's the fair thing to do."

"You got it."

I held his hand and we stared at the Spring's blue green pool below.

Before I slept I wrote a letter.

> *February 16, 1945*
> *Dear Donnie,*
> *I hope this finds you well. Things are*
> *quiet here.*
> *I'm not sure how to tell you this, but you*
> *need to know. A reporter came to town.*
> *The Council asked me to show him*
> *around. He works for The Albuquerque*
> *Journal and is doing a story on all the*
> *boys.*
> *I'm not sure of the future we might*
> *have, but it is only fair that I release you*
> *from any understandings we may have.*
> *Here is your class ring. I have no doubt*
> *you will meet a wonderful girl and when*
> *this awful war is over you will have a*
> *happy life. Please forgive me.*
> *Take care,*
> *Liv*

I posted it the following day.

A week later, the brisk February air bit through my jacket, a reminder winter still reigned. I tucked my chin into my jacket and walked over to the post office. I opened the post office door to find Peggy grim-faced and pale. Without saying a word, she handed me the familiar letter. I avoided Peggy's eyes, but stared at the wavering typewritten letters swimming on the envelope. *Not Donnie, too, please.* My mind screamed in denial. Had my letter initiated something in the stars so that across the globe, in Europe an enemy bullet, bomb or grenade found its way into Donnie? Silly thoughts to be sure, but a young girl often thinks the world revolves around her and her actions. The memory of that time still aches.

I stumbled out of the post office and down the road toward the Frolanders. For once the tears never came. After all those months of delivering the horrid news of loss when every letter brought more tears, more pain, at the news of Donnie's death, numbness seeped over my thoughts. The street was mostly empty as families prepared their supper. The scent of frying bacon wafted on the air. Normal, but it wasn't, not now. Nor, I feared, would it ever be normal again. A whole generation of our young men now lay dead around the globe. From Florida to Alaska, to the South Pacific, to Italy and Germany the blood and sacrifice of Hope Springs spread across the world.

I hesitated before knocking on the Frolander's door. I lifted my hand again, when it opened and there stood young Eddie. For a moment, my thoughts stalled. Eddie looked exactly like Donnie as a boy of fourteen.

"Hi, Liv." His gaze flicked from my face to the letter I clutched. He looked back up at me, his eyes wide. Then his smile disappeared and he slammed the door. I heard his voice behind the window curtain, "No. Go away."

It never got easier. Unsure of what to do, I lowered my head pressing against the door, my shoulders slumped.

A wail echoed from inside the house. "No!"

Called to action, I flung open the door and rushed into the kitchen. Mrs. Frolander hunched over, her arms wrapped around her waist. Eddie stood with his arm around her shoulders. His hollow gaze met mine over his mother's back.

Mrs. Frolander swayed from side to side. "It's a mistake."

I helped Eddie lead her to the kitchen chair. Eddie stood at his mother's side rubbing her back while Liv took a seat.

Taking Mrs. Frolander's hand, I squeezed it within mine. She pulled away. "No. Don't."

My heart mimicked the pain in Mrs. Frolander's face. At least I had not told her of the letter I'd sent. "There's nothing I can say. You know how I felt about Donnie. The whole town was praying for him."

Eddie didn't move. "What happened to him? Can we see the letter?"

"Of course." I still had it clutched in my fist. Releasing Mrs. Frolander's hand, I grabbed a knife from the table and sliced the envelope and read:

```
Mrs. Frolander,
 The Secretary of War has
asked me to inform you of the
loss of your son, Sergeant
Donald Frolander, in Europe in
defense of his country as
stated in the enclosed
telegram. A letter will
follow.
 Please accept my condolences
on your bereavement.

Sincerely,
Captain Wesley Richards
Alamogordo Army Airbase
US Army
```

Mrs. Frolander lifted a questioning gaze. "It's not a mistake? Both of my twin babies gone? I can't believe it."

The tone of her voice, the recognition of losing two sons broke my heart. How deep her pain must be. "I'll miss him desperately." The absent tears stung my eyes. "But I promise you as long as I live, he will not be forgotten."

An image of the twins I'd gone to school with flashed in my mind.

On the first day of sophomore year, our new English teacher Mrs. Godair arrived. Since our small town rarely changed teachers except when someone retired, it merited as a special occasion. The Frolander twins found it particularly fun. Ever since they were young, they delighted in fooling people, each pretending to be the other. After a while most residents clued in to their games and figured out some way to tell the difference. Mrs. Godair didn't have that head start. Donnie and Sam took full advantage of the poor teacher's ignorance.

At the beginning of English class one hid out in the hallway, and one sat in a desk just inside the classroom. When Mrs. Godair called roll, Donnie dressed in a bright blue shirt answered, "Present." Then she called Sam's name. With an expression of sincerity, Donnie said, "He's home sick today."

A few minutes later, Mrs. Godair turned to write something on the board. Our whole class watched Donnie and Sam switch places. Ruthie smothered a giggle. Sam wore a bright red shirt. When the teacher faced the classroom again, her gaze swept the room once and then back again, resting on Sam. Her forehead wrinkled, but then relaxed.

She asked for volunteers to answer the question she'd put on the board. Sam raised his hand. "Donnie? What would you do if your parents forbid you to see the girl you liked?"

"Uh, my name's Sam. But if my mom didn't like my girlfriend, well I'd find a way to see her anyway."

Mrs. Godair's brow furrowed. "Sam?" She reached for her roll book. "Your brother said you were absent." Her glance around the classroom took another moment.

Ruthie giggled and squirmed in her chair on the opposite side of the classroom from the door. The teacher's gaze froze on her. "Miss Ackerman, what seems to be so funny?"

Biting her lip, Ruthie shook her head. "Nothing, Mrs. Godair. Sorry." Another giggle escaped.

Mrs. Godair walked down the row of seats, pausing in front of Ruthie. While her back was to the door, Donnie slid into a seat next to his brother.

At this, we laughed, anticipating what the teacher's reaction might be. Mrs. Godair spun around. Seeing the mirror images before her, she looked from one to another several times before smiling in understanding.

Returning my attention to the present, I gave Mrs. Frolander a reassuring smile through my tears. "I know it sounds trite, but I think they'd like to be together. I have to believe they are together. Can you imagine? They're probably wreaking havoc on some unsuspecting angel."

The older woman pressed her knuckles to her mouth. "Maybe, but I don't understand. Why would God allow both my boys to be taken from me?"

"I wish I knew. It doesn't make sense. None of it does. This awful war. We never imagined when they left none of them would come back."

"What'll I do without my boys?"

Eddie kneeled at his mother's side, looking up at her. "Ma, I'm still here. I'll help you, I promise. You won't have extra work to do. I've been helping out for four years already."

"You're such a good boy, Eddie." Mrs. Frolander stroked her son's cheek. "I know you're here." She grabbed him in a fierce hug. "You're all I have left now."

My tears blurred the vision of the young boy and his mother. "I'll be glad to help in any way I can, whenever you need anything. Please think of me as your daughter, though it was never official." Guilt struck me anew at my words. Surely Donnie never knew I'd sent his ring back. Hopefully his mother wouldn't ever find out. I'd make it up to both of them. "I'll leave you now, but I'm sure my mother will bring over a casserole later."

I had another letter to write that evening. The promise I'd made to Bob Perry must be broken.

My fingers shook with anger as I wrote the words. The war had robbed us of every young man. With everything that had happened, I could not consider starting a romance with anyone else. The last words I'd written to Donnie had not been for him, about him, but had been selfish, uncaring. Amends must be made.

> *Dear Bob,*
> *I know what we promised one another*
> *last week, but I find it impossible to*
> *forget Donnie. It's impossible to forgive*
> *myself for allowing a moment's*
> *indiscretion to interfere in the future I*
> *had planned. Therefore, I request that*
> *you not contact me again. Donnie is dead*
> *too, and I must react as a beloved*
> *girlfriend, not someone who could so*
> *easily cast him aside for a fling with a*
> *handsome stranger.*
> *Everything is my fault, but I wish you all*
> *the best.*
> *Liv*

Reporter's note: Unlike after Sam's death, there is no break in the entries following the news about Donnie. Instead, the reader finds a change in the focus of her entries and poetry. The entries are short and mainly about the weather and everyday events and chores. What was going through her mind at the time can only be guessed. The entries have been omitted, but the poems have been included here.

Anna's Journal

March 1, 1945

O Spring!

O Spring of Hope
life-giving sustenance
salvation of our forebearers!
One sip of your essence
provides faith, courage
promise of a future
without strife.
Our sanctuary lies within
range of your reach
Why have you forsaken us now?

Escape

Just today,
needing to get out of the house
I took a walk--
A simple one foot in front of the other
gives time to clear my heart of despair,
my head of thoughts
better left unspoken
better ignored.
If only I could.

Back home,
the same ferocious
refrain of ghostly torment
plagues my reason.

Chapter Seventeen

Ruth

GOOD, LIV AND MAXINE are occupied across the way. The next part of my story is rather more personal, and I'd prefer they didn't know about it. I suppose that sounds a little strange given that it's been more than fifteen years since it happened. I can't believe I'm going to tell you this. Secrets? Yes, I have them, doesn't everyone?

From the time I arrived in California, I had done my best at the job and it showed. Ruthie the Riveter they called me. One day the floor supervisor said the advertising executives needed someone to model for some publicity shots. She didn't have to ask me twice. I knew I would be perfect. Remember the posters of Rosie? My photos were better, and I'm not convinced that Rosie person was even real. My face turned up in all the magazines and I figured Hollywood movies were just around the corner. I'd done a little acting for the senior play and I looked good in whatever I was wearing, even my coveralls. If things had been different, my movie career would have been the next step, but though I touched the dream, I never lived it. One of my only regrets, but it's no use crying over lost opportunities. My life turned out better than most around here, that's for certain.

Stephen showed up at the USO the next time I volunteered. Or I should say he was there when I arrived. The girls told me he'd been waiting for me every afternoon, not dancing, just holding up the wall beside the punch and cookies and scanning the crowd.

Of course, I spotted him the moment I entered. Dressed in his crisp uniform, he stood out in the sea of other servicemen. Why, I wondered, but when he caught my eye I nearly stumbled. The joy apparent in his expression left no question as to why he had been asking about me.

It never surprised me that the boys paid attention to me, but with Stephen my normal composure disappeared. My trim figure and perfect teeth, along with my large brown eyes never failed me, but watching him rush toward me brought a sudden flush of heat.

"Ruth? I've been thinking of you every day. You have to give a guy a break and let me take you to dinner after your shift. Promise?"

Most men might appear desperate what with the urgent begging tone he took, but Stephen coupled a confident wink with the plea. Charmed, I'm sure.

But a girl can't be too forward, or eager. I learned that a long time ago. I lowered my eyes and said, "Thank you for the invitation—"

"Stephen. You remember me, don't you, doll?"

"Oh yes. Thank you, Stephen. I've promised my roommates I would be home right after my shift."

"Shucks, Ruthie, you're killing me here."

"Do you have a car?"

He perked up then. "Mine is parked out back."

"Why don't you give me a ride home then, and I'll fix us something to eat."

That afternoon led to the next and the next and the one after that.

By the end of the week, we were nearly inseparable. Well, aside from my shift at the factory. Things were going well there too, with the photo shoots and interviews. They wanted to make it look glamorous, and they chose the right girl for the job.

One afternoon, maybe a couple of weeks later I came home from work to find Stephen on the steps waiting in his dress uniform, unlike the regular khakis he usually wore.

"I ship out the day after tomorrow." He knelt, offering me a small box with a beautiful diamond ring. "Will you marry me? I almost asked last week, but I knew you wanted time. I've known from the first time I met you that you were the girl for me. Please? We can get married tomorrow, if you say yes."

I took a step back. Marry Stephen? What if something happened to him? Granted, they said the war would soon be over, but no one knew for sure. I'd put him off so far, and no one back home would know if I married him or not. If I didn't marry him I was prepared to give him the gift I'd given Joe.

The least I could offer, a little comfort to see him along his way, and he would remember me forever, right?

I lowered to my knees. "You've made me so happy." It is always best to let them down a bit easy. "Don't you think we should wait? I've always dreamed of a beautiful wedding and we don't have time to do it right, not before you leave. Tomorrow we have an important shoot for the ad campaign. But if you write, I'll write every day."

It was the same promise I made all the GIs I met at the USO. So far I'd exchanged letters with several, but they drifted off so by this time I only communicated with a couple of them. Stephen proved to be different though, as you'll soon see.

"No, Ruthie, I won't take no for an answer." He stood and grasped my wrist tight within his fingers.

"Hush." I tried to lift my hand to his lips, but he held it firm, and bruising my wrist.

"You're my girl. You know that, have known it from the start. You wouldn't have been so willing to go out with me otherwise. I'd watched you for days before I approached you. You never gave anyone a second glance, not until me."

What was he talking about? My chest tightened, making it hard to breathe. The expression on his face had hardened, and the anger I saw in his eyes I had never seen before, not with him, or anyone else.

I opened my mouth either to laugh or to cry out for help. He covered it before I could do anything.

"We can be good for one another. You deserve me, and I want you. The rest of the world doesn't matter. Listen to me." His voice softened, but his eyes remained wild, darting from me to the house to the car. "We'll get married tomorrow and then have our wedding night. We're shipping out the next day. I've planned this for weeks. You had to know."

Weeks? Nothing made any sense. I tried shaking my head, but his grip held fast, and I only succeeded in wrenching my neck. Instantly, my life changed, and instead of planning the next photo shoot, I scrambled to remember when my roommates were due home. Not until later, much later and by then it would be too late to help me. I had to think fast. Blinking back tears, I forced myself to lean into him. I rested my head on his chest and he removed his hand from my mouth.

Though tempted to cry out, I gasped when his hand clenched my wrist tighter, cutting off circulation until my hand tingled. It served to warn me that he could hurt me before anyone could hear or react if I called for help. No, I'd have to treat him carefully and play along with his plan for the moment. If I could outlast him for two days, he'd be gone, boarded on the ship and headed out into the Pacific. I would be safe from any further contact.

"I care for you, and didn't mean to say we couldn't be together, but—"

He twisted my arm until it ached before abruptly releasing it. "You belong to me. We belong to one another. I've been patient these last weeks as you've played hard to get. But the time for games is over. I'm going to war in two days. You need to be taken care of, after all, what if something should happen to me? I'm not willing to risk that, or to risk you finding another flyboy or sailor while I'm gone."

My mouth dried while I searched for an excuse. "My parents. I couldn't get married without them there."

"This is the twentieth century, there is no need for an adult to need their parents' approval. We'll send them an announcement. Hell, we could even call them."

"They don't have a phone."

"Send a telegram then. When the war's over we can have a big ceremony and reception for all our friends and family. I'm not taking no for an answer. You care for me as you just said. There's no need to wait. Get your things and we'll head out to city hall. I already got the license."

"I need to leave the gals a note." Maybe he'd let me out of his sight and I could call for help. At least I could lock the door as a barrier. I stepped toward the house, but he blocked me.

"We'll be back soon enough. You're fine, and no nonsense about powdering your nose either." He grabbed my arm and pulled me to the car parked on the street. My head hit the top of the door frame as he pushed me into the car from the driver's side, never letting go of my arm.

I opened my mouth to call out, but he clapped a hand over it. "You're coming with me. No one can stop me."

The drive to city hall sped by, while I searched for an opportunity to elude him.

After parking the car, he growled into my ear. "One sound besides, 'I do,' and you'll regret it." Backing away, he continued with his eyebrows raised. "I don't understand how you could resist having the happily ever after every girl dreams of—believe me I know. My sisters all raved about it. I'm your knight in shining armor, and don't you forget it. Well, I suppose you'd have to say knight in green." He barked a laugh. "The Green Knight."

With that, he opened his door and dragged me out into the dreary mist.

We went to see the judge. The judge's secretary stood up as the witness. "Don't you at least have a bouquet?" She looked up and down my coveralls. Even in Hope Springs, I would never have been caught dead in such an outfit. It galled me to think of getting married in them. Old habits die hard I suppose, but really, out of control as everything was, at least he could have let me change into a dress. Maybe it was part of his plan to keep me on edge.

"No, we had to hurry, she just said yes today." Stephen sported a charming grin.

She gave me a little carnation from a vase on her desk to hold. "Here. Everyone should have a flower. I do hope you brought rings."

"Yes, ma'am." He pulled out the small box from his pocket. "Couldn't let my Ruthie go without the best. This was the best money could buy."

In a blur the vows were exchanged and he placed the ring on my hand. Heavy and unfamiliar, the words and the vows weighed me down.

"You may kiss the bride," the grey-haired judge said with a warm voice. His eyes never left us.

I always wondered whether he sensed something wasn't quite right, but he never said a word, and though I wished to give some signal, I could think of nothing that would not immediately raise Stephen's ire. My mind wrestled to fathom the stranger he'd become in the past hour.

The secretary kissed my cheek. "If you like, I can take a picture and send you the print and negative. I try to do that for all the brides who don't have their family around."

At her kindness, tears misted my eyes. I ducked my head.

"Thank you, anyway." Stephen offered me his handkerchief while gripping my other hand and pulling me into the hall. "We'll have pictures taken at the reception. Our friends are waiting for us."

"Best wishes to you both. I just know you'll be so happy together." Her words sang out but she didn't know the irony they held. No doubt she said the same things to every couple she witnessed in the judge's chambers, but how many women were in my position? Not very many I'd wager.

Back in the car, Stephen drove us to my house. "Go pack an overnight bag. I've made our reservations at the Beverly Hills Hotel. Money is no object when it comes to my wife. You'll never regret becoming Mrs. Stephen Lloyd."

My chance had arrived. I certainly could call for help and let my roommates know what had happened.

As I exited the car, he opened his door. "I'll wait inside, thank you very much. Wouldn't want you to get too lonely without me." Again, he barked that odd laugh. "I take care of my girl. Oh, and be sure to change into a nice dress. We have reservations at The Brown Derby. I want you to be seen by the best. Don't think I don't know of your dream of being a movie star. My family has connections and whatever my baby wants she's going to get."

It occurred to me then to ask for an annulment, but I didn't think that was what he meant when he promised me anything.

I went through the kitchen, where a note explained my housemates' absence. They were both on dates. After glancing over my shoulder to be sure Stephen was still in the living room, I reached for the phone.

"Hurry up, doll."

I jumped, before reaching again.

"Hey, I'm gonna get a Coke while I wait." He entered the kitchen and I pulled my hand back. "Do you have anything in the icebox?" His gaze traveled from me to the phone. "Uh-uh. What do you think you're doing? We'll send a telegram to your folks tomorrow with the big announcement. Go on. Get packed."

The fire flickering in his eyes chilled me.

I scooted into my bedroom. How long could I get by without raising his attention? I had to think. First, I pulled out my overnight bag and makeup case. If he heard me moving around, it could buy me some time. Making as much noise as I could, I slammed the drawers, clanged hangers and threw clothes on the bed. I calculated how much time it might be before one or both of my roommates returned, but I doubted I could waste an hour, not if he had dinner reservations. Who in the world could get reservations at The Brown Derby anyway? I'd dreamed of going there since my arrival, hoping if I did, I'd run into one of those Hollywood execs. My opportunity may have arrived, but the dream had faded behind the need to get away from Stephen. I sank onto the bed.

Not two minutes passed before he knocked on the door. "You don't have to pack the kitchen sink. Just a nightgown and your unmentionables and an outfit for tomorrow. We can come back and get more clothes. Hell, I can buy you a new wardrobe."

"Just a minute." Confusion muddled my thinking.

With every word and action, he seemed to reveal new mysteries. How rich was he? Before that day, I hadn't known a thing about his money. He never hinted at it on any of our dates. So far he hadn't hurt me aside from my wrist which could be purple with bruises tomorrow. If I kept him happy perhaps this peculiar marriage might end up being a good thing. I packed my bags and changed into my best dress. If I was to meet the rich and famous I didn't want to look like a Dumb Dora.

After freshening my lipstick, I opened the door. Stephen leaned against the wall. "Took you long enough, but—" He whistled. "Well worth waiting for. Glad you've come to your senses. Let's fade."

My roommates had yet to arrive. "Can I leave a note for them?"

"Sure. Just tell them you'll be back tomorrow. No need for any other details."

Went to Hollywood for the night. Back tomorrow. Nothing else came to mind on what I could add to give them a clue. Maybe if I added Beverly Hills Hotel, at least they might come look for me, but as I began the next word, he pulled the paper from my hand, leaving a big line scribbled across the note.

"That's fine. Come on. Our reservation is at seven so we'll have to hurry. You'll love the Derby."

"Do you know any famous stars?" Awkward as my circumstances were, a little thrill went through me at the thought of meeting some movie stars or producers.

A short while later we settled into a booth at *the* place to be seen in Hollywood. Already I had spotted Bing Crosby on our way in and the people sitting at the next table I couldn't believe my eyes. "That's Lauren Bacall and Humphrey Bogart," I whispered.

"Yes, doll. That's why I wanted to bring you here. You belong with the stars. My father knows a lot of the big producers. One should be in here this evening too. I want to introduce you."

A stocky slightly balding man walked up to our table. "Stephen, my boy. Your father said I might run into you here."

"Saul Bierman, please meet my wife." He introduced us and Mr. Bierman of California Bear Film Corporation, or CBF bent over my hand.

"You know how to pick 'em, boy. She has a beauty that needs to be seen on screen."

My cheeks heated.

"I knew it the moment I met her." Stephen squeezed my hand, making sure that Mr. Bierman didn't hold it too long. "I'll be shipping out in a couple days, but I was sure you'd want to meet her. She'd be perfect for that new film you have in pre-production, the one with the girl in the small town who comes to Hollywood to make her big break. What was the name of it?

"Working title is *Deluded Dreams*."

"Ruthie would be perfect."

"Why don't you stop by the studio tomorrow morning?" He handed me a business card. "Hand the guard this, and they'll let you right in."

"I'd love to, but I have to work at Boeing."

"She's a riveter." Stephen laughed. "Don't that beat all?"

"She won't be pounding any rivets once we get that face on the screen. We'll do a test tomorrow."

And so it began, the start of my own deluded dreams. They do say that fact is stranger than fiction sometimes, and in the next few months I would find that to be true.

I CALLED IN TO THE factory, saying something real personal had come up. Well it was true, I'd just married, but a girl certainly can't pass up her big break, now can she? My screen test appointment overshadowed the memories of my so-called wedding night. Stephen, after having received what he wanted—me as his bride—treated me with tender care. He took us back to the hotel where fresh cut flowers filled the room with the scent of spring.

He allowed me time alone to dress in my nightgown before knocking on the bathroom door. Rather subdued, he approached me with a gentleness I'd seen in him that first day I met him.

After kissing me, he led me to the bed where he drew down the covers and lay me back, stroking my arm. "I'll be careful, but I can't promise it won't hurt."

I swallowed. No use telling him that wasn't a problem. "Do it fast."

When it was over, he rolled off me and fell asleep, snoring softly. I don't believe he ever knew he hadn't married the virgin he expected.

He drove me to the CBF studios the next morning. I awoke early and made sure I was ready, dressing in the perfect small town girl outfit, the only one I'd brought with me and hadn't worn since my arrival. While perfect for Hope Springs, it felt out of place in Southern California.

In the car, he took my hand. "You're my dream come true. I'll be writing you every time I get a chance. But right now is goodbye." He really was a handsome man and when he got all romantic I forgot the way he manhandled me before the wedding.

He kissed me and I watched him drive away with mixed feelings.

At the gate, I presented Mr. Bierman's card and they couldn't do enough for me. The guard called up to the offices to announce my arrival. A secretary came to meet me and led me to a studio to do my screen test.

Mr. Bierman met us at the screen test. He was really a hands-on man. Well, not that hands on mind you, but nevertheless it surprised me when he showed up to watch.

I looked super, I don't mind saying. Honest. You've seen the classic movie actresses, Lauren Bacall, Katherine Hepburn, Claudette Colbert? The screen test they shot showed my features to the best light. My dark eyes held mystery yet the overall effect was an innocent girl prepared to meet the world. Next, they gave me a script. The actor reading opposite me was just someone they pulled in off the lot to fill in for the day. Let me tell you, it wasn't easy doing my best work with someone who had all the emotion of a door knob. Yet I persevered.

"Perfect," Mr. Bierman declared when they'd screened the test shot.

Just like that I was on my way. I quit the factory job and started making my film. In those days shooting a movie happened quickly. No television or other competition, and the theaters needed new features nearly every week.

My co-star was a B list actor you might remember, Andy Stocker? Anyway, he played the small town boyfriend who followed me, well Sadie, to the big city where I had moved to chase my dreams.

Talk about star struck. It hit me the first day of shooting when I first laid eyes on Andy. Suddenly our romantic scenes I'd dreaded to do in front of the cameras were something I looked forward to doing. Those blue eyes and dark hair, absolutely striking. I swoon at the memory.

He sauntered onto the soundstage as if he owned it. I was a goner the minute he smiled at me. "Hey, sweetheart. Stick with me and we'll sizzle on that screen."

We headed to the back lot in the afternoon to shoot the exterior scenes of the small town. I swear it was almost like being in Hope Springs. Somewhere I wasn't missing at the time. We wore our costumes, I dressed in this gingham dress and pigtails and he wore rolled up pants and suspenders. Sort of hokey looking but hey, it gave the feel for the scene of young and innocent.

"Okay you two," the director called. "Walk down the street and Andy, you really like her, but she doesn't know it yet. Ruth, Sadie is more interested in getting out of town. She doesn't even notice he's told her that he loves her. Hit your mark on the X and that's where the dialogue begins."

Once the cameras start rolling I was in Lakemeadow, Minnesota, and my name was Sadie, and Andy, well he was Joe. Isn't that strange his character's name was Joe? Seemed to me it was destiny. I don't mind telling you that I was lost in the moment. Joe had come back to me in a way.

The shooting went off without any problems whatsoever. I'd found my element. At the end of the day, we shot the last scene of the movie where Sadie and Joe come back to the small town. He carried me over the threshold of our little house with the white picket fence and kissed me. Our first kiss on camera and the fire lit up inside of me so hot I was panting by the time he pulled away. I wound my arms around his neck and just clung to him, unable to catch my breath.

"Cut!" the director yelled.

Andy gazed at me with a glazed expression. I must have looked the same.

"Let's wrap it up for the day," the director said.

We nodded but never looked away from one another. I'm not sure how many moments passed before he put me down.

"Um, want to grab a bite to eat?" he asked.

We went to a small diner, made sure it wasn't close to the studio. He might be B-list, but he'd be recognized by the press. Our contracts both specified we had to keep our reputations above reproach and we were careful.

That night we signed into the hotel as Mr. and Mrs. Lawson, Joe's last name in the movie. Until the day before the end of the shoot three weeks later, we didn't spend a night apart.

Look at Maxine and Liv glower at me. They don't know the half of what I went through, neither of them ever left this town.

Sorry, this part of the story still breaks my heart. So the movie went so went my life I suppose. I mean in the movie Sadie, the girl I played, finds her happy ending, but when the movie shooting ended I didn't find mine.

Pardon me, I think I need a little break. Maybe you could talk to someone else for a little while?

Chapter Eighteen

Liv

AFTER WE RECEIVED word of Donnie, all hope that was ever in Hope Springs died. On May 16, 1945, I made my daily trip to the post office then ran over to the store with a copy of *The Albuquerque Journal* in one hand and a letter from Bob Perry in my pocket. It wasn't the first I'd received from him, but important things first.

Opening the door, I called out over the jingling bell. "Max, you'll never believe it! It's over.

Carrying a crate of strawberries, Maxine emerged from the back room. "What?"

"It's over, the war in Europe. Germany surrendered on the eighth."

Maxine's legs sagged beneath her and she almost dropped the crate before I rushed forward to catch it. "Over? Really?" She grabbed the counter for support.

We set the crate on the counter. "Everyone's celebrating." I unfolded the paper and pointed to the banner headline along with the picture of a ticker tape parade in New York.

I hugged Maxine and spun her in a dance. We giggled. After such a long time of war, it was over. Well, at least part of it.

When the whirling moment passed, Maxine frowned. "Billy still won't come home. Ever." She sank to the counter stool.

Sitting beside my friend, I leaned an elbow on the counter and rested my chin. "You're right, nothing's changed for us. The boys are still lost. Nothing's the same as before the war. Besides, they're still fighting in the Pacific."

"Seems like forever, nothing but war and news of the war, and dreading the war."

We sat in silence, the brief joy we experienced made no real difference for Hope Springs.

From the papers it seemed everyone celebrated the end of the war, but in Weeping Women Springs we held our memorial. I'd thought that we had seen the last memorial service after Donnie died, but the Council ordered that we hold one every month. We still had the meditation, and then as a community every month we gathered in the gymnasium to commemorate our loved ones.

Maybe I should have sent Bob's letters back, but I never could. I didn't respond, but I read them each and every one.

```
Dear Liv,
    I was so sorry to hear of
your loss. My condolences to
you and Mrs. Frolander. It's
an awkward thing but,
sweetheart, I still hope we
can write. I will be in
Carlsbad later this week and
would love to call on you. I
could take you out for a show
over in Las Cruces. You're a
special woman, and I hate to
think of you in Weeping Women
Springs, cut off from
everything. You deserve more.
    I shouldn't tell you this,
but my editor is teasing me
awful, wondering what happened
in Weeping Women Springs. I
must be talking about you more
than I thought. Not
surprising.
    Please say you'll meet me on
Saturday.

Yours,
Bob
```

Every week Bob wrote me a letter. He never gave up for a long while. I never encouraged him. It was too much to think of people going on with their lives almost like nothing had happened, like forty-four boys wouldn't be returning to us. Weeping Women Springs was like a ghost town. Sure the bank was still there, the post office and the store. Most things didn't change, and yet everything had.

I promised myself, that it couldn't happen again, wouldn't happen again. We had to protect the memories of our boys. If that meant that I didn't get to go to the movies with Bob Perry, then that's how it must be. No one would ever be able to accuse me of forgetting Donnie, or any of them. My chest burned with the anger and unfairness of everything. What if I had met Bob first, before that kiss I shared with Donnie? Of course, why would Bob ever have come to town if the boys hadn't been lost? Such is life, isn't it? One event leads to the next, good or bad, but back then everything seemed to lead only to one end, we lost a generation of our young men.

At least Dad would be home since the war was ending. That brought me a little comfort. We could be a family again, if even a smaller one without Dewitt.

I suppose that's why women went into the nunneries in more ancient times. There's something about losing your beloved that permanently bruises your heart, you never forget and that same something makes you want to hide from the world.

Ruthie

ISN'T THAT JUST LIKE YOU, Liv, to think of the most downright depressing thing one could imagine? A nunnery? Hide from the world. While I won't argue that I wanted to escape the pain, hiding was never an option I considered.

I had other worries in California. Would you mind if I spoke privately with him? Thanks, Liv.

All right, I may be being silly to not share this information with Liv, when sooner or later it will all come out in your story or a book down the road. It's a little different if someone isn't watching you while you're discussing the intimate details of your life. You may decide not to use any of this information anyway. After all, your focus is on Weeping Women Springs, not Ruth Ackerman Caldarelli.

Anyway, we left off when Stephen shipped out and I fell for Andy. We had a wonderful three weeks. I swear our heads were spinning most of the time, which might be why we ended up the way we did.

Filming went fast. *Deluded Dreams* was almost finished, and we only had a couple more scenes to shoot. Andy waited for me on the backlot of the studio.

"I can hardly wait to get you home." Andy took me into his arms. It was always that way with him. While I tried to play hard to get, it wasn't easy because I liked him just as much as he liked me. Notice I never said love. That feeling was reserved for Joe and then...but let me finish this part of the story.

I buried my face in Andy's neck and inhaled the special cologne he wore. Yummy. Clean, and spicy.

Mr. Bierman's voice startled me and I jumped back, but too late. He'd already seen me in Andy's arms. "Ruth? What the—"

"Uh, Mr. Bierman, it isn't, I mean we aren't, I mean—" My mind went blank.

"It's okay, Mr. Bierman," Andy spoke up to defend me. Of course, I was the one who needed defending, not him. No, the man is never at fault, it falls to the woman to take the brunt of the mess when these kinds of things occur, doesn't it? Andy continued, "Mr. Biermann, it's not what you think. Ruthie and I are getting married."

"What?" Mr. Bierman's voice echoed through the little alleyway between soundstages.

"Ruthie and I are getting married as soon as we finish shooting."

That's when everything broke into chaos. Our secret was out, and then the real secret was out too. You see, as soon as I knew I didn't need Stephen in order to get a part in Hollywood, and well, truth be told, I didn't really trust him after he finagled me into that marriage, I divorced him. True it was still pending, but I had filed the paperwork stating extreme cruelty. I explained this to Mr. Bierman.

"So you've divorced Stephen, a man serving our nation at war? A young man who is the son of my good friend? You're divorcing him where he cannot defend himself in court against your charges?" If ever I saw fire in someone's eyes, it was in Mr. Biermann's gaze on that day. "Did you never think that your contract with our studio and the moralities statement you signed might have some bearing on your situation?"

"No, sir. This was a private matter only," I said.

"Oh, and how are we supposed to explain that one of our up and coming actresses, one who is playing an innocent young farm girl in a sweet love story on screen, is a philandering floozy? Ms. Ackerman, you can pick up your final paycheck. I am revoking your pass into the studio as of this moment." With those words he walked away.

In the matter of a few moments, my up and coming career in the movie industry was finished.

Andy stroked my back, in a half-hearted attempt to console me. "It's okay, Ruthie, I can support us."

"How do you think I could be happy with you now? You're going to go to work every day at the place I was happiest, doing the thing I've dreamed of doing and then come home and share your stories from on the set? That sounds like so much fun. Honestly, Andy, you're just as dense as Joe in *Deluded Dreams*." I pushed him away.

With my head down, and blinded by my tears, I went to the payroll office where they cut my check. That's how fast things happen when one of the big bosses starts the ball rolling. A guard escorted me to costuming where he waited while I returned the dress I was wearing and retrieved my things from my locker. He never left my side until we reached the gate.

From March until the end of May, that's how long my film career lasted. If not the shortest in Hollywood history, it sure would be a contender. They scrapped *Deluded Dreams*. I guess it was a sacrifice they were willing to make in order to not have to deal with the scandal. These many years later, I can at least be grateful my scandal never made it to the papers. Sort of a scandal that never was. The only good thing that came out of my broken dream was that my divorce went through, and no one ever was the wiser.

I never saw Stephen again, or Andy either for that matter. It didn't surprise me. His professed passion lasted about as long as the time it took for me to ride the bus back to my apartment. I'm guessing one of Mr. Bierman's men took him aside and explained the facts of studio life to him. If he wanted to continue working for them, then he had to shape up, and that meant no philandering floozies for him.

It wasn't possible to get hired back on at the plant. With the war in Germany already over, they figured the rest of the war would be over soon too. They may have resented the way I left also. My options were limited. Much as I wished to stay in California, I couldn't bear the thought of facing my roommates and having to admit my failure. That day, I packed and headed back to the train station, back to Hope, well Weeping Women Springs.

Anna's Journal

July 16, 1945

Awoke early with a tremendous flash lighting up the sky bright as day though darkness still lay on the land. The ground shook. Eddie told me later he was on his way to the Bauers when he saw the brightness in the east. He said Melvin saw it too and mentioned that it seemed as though the sun got up early. Melvin guessed that it might have been a meteor but Eddie said, no because he'd never seen one so intense. Later we found out the Martinez' house had some broken windows but that seemed to be the only damage in the village.

Liv

THE STEEL GREY STORM cloud covered the August afternoon sun. Lightning flashed on the mesa, followed by a clap of thunder. I entered the post office, shutting the door against a dusty gust.

"It's over." Peggy handed me the newspaper, while fluttering a fan about her face.

I read the headline: The War is Over! Victory in the Pacific. The war over, at last. For almost five years everything had hinged on and around the war. Finished. The sailor kissing the nurse in the street revealed an ecstatic nation's euphoria, but my heart lacked joy. A sense of futility engulfed me. I barely restrained myself from punching the door, anything.

I went to Uncle Jim's. The hot wind blew hair into my eyes. I blinked, brushed the strands away. The paper rattled as I scanned the other front page stories. Two atomic bombs dropped on Japanese cities instigated the surrender. The story came out about the tests, the atom bomb tested in our state. A new atomic age ushered in, the story read. I knocked on Uncle Jim's door.

"Come in."

When I entered the smoke filled the air, I stifled a cough. "The war's over."

His eyes lit under raised brows. "Really?"

"The Japanese signed an unconditional surrender to General MacArthur."

"Well, I'll be. Thought it'd last longer."

"They dropped some new atomic bombs. They say it's equal to 20,000 tons of TNT."

He clenched the cigarette in his lips and his words escaped like the smoke puffs. "We'll have to have a celebration."

"Celebrate what? The war may be over, but that doesn't change what's happened in Weeping Women Springs. I don't see us becoming Hope Springs again, do you?" The awful waste of everything piled on top of me.

Aunt Wanda stepped in from the kitchen. "What's happened?"

"War's over," Uncle Jim said.

Aunt Wanda clutched the tea towel to her chest. "Really?"

"Yes. But as I was trying to tell Uncle Jim, it doesn't change anything for us here. Dewitt won't come home, and neither will any of the other boys. We've known that since January."

"Still, we should have some kind of event to mark the occasion."

I tossed the newspaper onto the sofa. "Well, if you do, I won't attend. I don't see any reason to celebrate. We can hold—should hold commemorations. Just like we've done since forty-three."

"I'll mention this to the Council. Leave it up to them."

"Will you tell them how I feel? I'm sure I'm not the only

one."

"Sure."

"Guess I'd better tell mother and Maxine the news."

Outside the breeze had cooled, and another roar of thunder split the air. I passed a mesquite tree, and in a flap of wings, a crow cawed in displeasure.

Anna's Journal

March 31, 1950

Today I made some cookies for Eddie. As soon as he got home I told him to get some. We have a few minutes before Meditation. Wordlessly, he walked past me to the kitchen table. Sugar cookies fresh out of the oven were his favorite. He stuffed one into his mouth. He would always be my baby, even though he was near grown, he'd be eighteen in May and graduating soon after.

"Ma..." he said, with an earnest expression.

I followed his every move. "Yes?"

"Uh...nothin.'"

Though I wondered what was on his mind, the clock chimed three, and I reminded him that we needed to light the candles.

Eddie popped another cookie it his mouth before nodding and heading to the parlor. Sometimes his attitude left reverence out the door. He struck a match and lit the two purple candles set in front of the Stars and Stripes.

We sat in the arm chairs and stared at the photographs situated between the candles. The glass on the photos reflected the dancing flames giving the illusion of movement. My uniformed sons smiled through the flickering dim light. For an hour neither Eddie nor I moved or spoke.

It is at such times my poems come.

Today I recalled the excitement they both had before heading off to war. Even Donnie near the time he left had an urgency about him, as if he couldn't wait to see life outside our village.

Two Boys

Expectation fraught with courage
fills two boys
who long of manhood
too early.
Flag waving winds
blow them away
from hope
from a mother's empty arms

Eddie

Sapling of Youth
littlest yet sturdy
I place my joys in thee.
O son become my sun
dependent yet you bear up
under my need for support.
I thank God for you.

Reporter's Note: Susie Bracht is a fresh-faced young woman of twenty-six with a serious expression, and she squints at times, most likely from being nearsighted from the reading she does. This reporter was quite impressed by the breadth of her knowledge of world events. The following transcript is from my interview with her.

Chapter Nineteen

Susie

EDDIE'S VOICE CALLED OUT, "Hey, Mrs. Bracht."

At the sound, I put down the *Life* magazine I'd been studying for the past couple of months. I ran out of my room and came up short, face to face with Eddie in the living room. Every time I saw him was like the first time. It didn't used to be this way—I'd almost grown up with him and Melvin always playing around. Things had changed though, by the spring of 1950 whenever I looked at his sad smile and the dark shadowed mysteries inside his eyes, a strange blossoming occurred inside me, as if a bubble might burst and flood my veins with some sweet poison. I always wondered if that's what Juliet felt with Romeo.

"Hey, Suze. Thought you might like to go for a walk. Unless you're busy."

He didn't have to ask me twice. "Ma, I'll be back later," I called into the kitchen.

We wandered outside in a meandering stroll, going nowhere in particular. When his knuckles brushed the back of my hand I struggled to remain calm, with little success. My heart sped up—what was it about this melancholy boy? He captured my fingers in his and the world shifted. A quail squawked and several of his covey scattered over the brush with little chicks bringing up the rear. Eddie led the way and we clambered over red rocks, kicking the gravel to alert any rattlesnakes of our presence. On the edge of the cliff we sat, swinging our legs off the side. The town spread out like a pinwheel on a stick. The stick was the road leading out to the highway over the rise. Directly below them, the Spring pond lay tranquil, deep malachite green surrounded by yellow roses.

"Looks like we could jump into the pond from here, doesn't it?" I kept my voice soft, afraid to disturb Eddie's thoughts, or break the mood of the moment.

"Yeah. It's a great place to think. I often come up here to get away."

I leaned back on my elbows and stared at the surrounding hills. "So far away from the world and yet, not so distant. In *Life*, they had an article about the coming war and what would happen if we were hit by a nuclear bomb."

His head swiveled to watch me.

"Don't look at me like I'm crazy."

"I'm not," he said. It always amazes me that you think of those kinds of things. You're just a kid of fifteen. We hardly ever go outside Weeping Women Springs, and here you are thinking of a nuclear bomb. They wouldn't hit us. Besides that, we're not at war."

"Fifteen isn't so young. Only a couple years younger than you. You'd be surprised." I sat up straight, the energy from fear and knowledge fighting to explode from me. "We're close to the testing grounds. Maybe they wouldn't mean to, but it could happen. The town might not be the target, but the dust from the fallout could reach us, depending on the wind's direction. Add to that we are at war, or will be soon. The Soviets and us. The magazine had a picture of a nuclear blast. Looks just like the newsreels, you know?"

His dark gaze never left me, like he was really listening, unlike my parents or Mel. They all told me that I worried for nothing. When I talked to Eddie, he took my opinion inside of his mind, mulled it over and then accepted it as valid, whether or not he agreed.

"Yeah. S'pose so. I've been thinking a lot about the lost boys."

"You mean Donnie and Sam, right?"

"All of them." He brushed the front of Sam's letter sweater. "Sort of like your nuclear bomb went off right here in Weeping Women Springs. Nothing's been the same since the war."

I had no words to comfort him, so I squeezed his hand.

"What happened to Weeping Women Springs could happen to the whole world in the next war. I'm writing letters to the senators and our congressman. Think I'll write President Truman too. They have to understand we can't kill the whole world."

He shook his head. "They won't listen. Never do, especially to a kid. What can you say the great scientists haven't already said? Even Professor Einstein says we shouldn't be building the nuclear and hydrogen bombs—but it's like they can't quit. S'pose it's like the boys. They couldn't quit either, even though I bet they were afraid."

"Have you told your mom?" I asked.

"Not yet. I've been on the verge, but the words just won't come out. Don't wanna hurt her."

"She's got to know."

Eddie stared down at the Spring and nodded. "Guess I'm not very brave."

"Don't say that, it takes bravery to even think about leaving."

He stood, giving me a smile that never reached the dark depths of his eyes. "Come on. Got to get home for dinner. Thanks for listening."

Poor Eddie, my heart ached for him and not just a little for me too. When he left for college, what would I do? No one else understood me like he did.

The morning after the graduation ceremony for the class of 1950 I awoke early, determined to accompany Eddie and Mel to the Bauer Ranch. Both my brother Melvin and Eddie had received their diplomas, one more step on their way out of Weeping Women Springs. I was only sixteen so I had a couple more years before I had my opportunity to explore the Outside.

We hiked over to the Bauer place. He and Melvin helped Mr. Bauer on the ranch in return for a little pocket money, but more importantly, Eddie received foodstuffs, eggs, meat, and milk to help his mother. Mel also received some things too, but Eddie and his mother had little else to live on.

That day I tagged along, something easier to do since Eddie wanted me there. A couple years before, whenever I tried to follow they ditched me. Mel didn't like it much, but he saw how it made Eddie happier to have me around so he put up with it.

In the barn, Mel hefted a hay bale and lugged it to the stall. "You'd better tell your mom what you're planning so you can get all the paperwork into the college before you miss the deadline."

Pitching a forkful of hay, Eddie said, "Yeah, I know. But you don't understand. She's lost so much. If I leave town, she'll be all alone and I just can't bring myself to tell her." He leaned on the pitchfork. "You don't know how she looks at me. Such sadness in her eyes and I just know she's thinking my brothers should be here too, not just me."

"Everyone's lost someone. My mom lost someone too","" Mel reminded him.

"Yeah, but a brother is a little different than losing two sons." It was true, our family had been luckier than most. Uncle Henry was killed in the fighting in the Pacific.

"This town needs to just get past it," my brother said.

"They have in a way. This is how they have found to deal with it. Don't you get it?" My heart ached at Eddie's frustration.

Mel shook his head. "All I know is when I go to Tularosa, they know how to have fun. We shouldn't be suppressed just because we experienced a loss as a community. Carlsbad did too." Mel snarled. "You know, they have school dances too."

"They're different. Not one of our guys came home."

Mel flopped down onto the clean hay beside me. "Yeah, that's what the Council says, but still. We didn't do anything wrong, and it's like we're being punished. I can't wait to get out of this place."

Sebastian Bauer entered the barn. "So this is what I pay you for, lounging around on the hay?" The twinkle in his eye relieved the sting of his words. "Hey, Susie. Good to see you, are you keeping these boys out of trouble?"

"Not sure that's possible, sir." I grinned.

He winked. "I must say they usually get a lot more done when you're around. Mary's got some fresh peach pie waiting for you kids in the kitchen. Now I'm not so sure I should let you boys go since you're already on your break."

Mel scrambled to his feet. "No, sir, I mean—we were just talking for a minute, but we're about done with cleaning the stalls aren't we, Ed?"

"Go on with you."

At the kitchen table, I studied Mary Bauer. Shadows haunted her eyes, the same ones which I saw in most of the women. Mrs. Bauer's lips lifted in a smile whenever we spent time with her. However, I suspected she wished her son, Joe, sat eating pie instead of us.

"Thanks, Mrs. Bauer," Eddie said before biting into the warm fruit pie. "Mm, peaches taste better than they did from the tree."

She tussled his hair. "You're a good boy. I'm sure your mother is right proud of you."

"Hope so, ma'am. I'm afraid she won't stay that way though."

"A mother never stops being proud, Eddie. No matter what." Light glinted off a tear at the corner of her eye.

"Even if he does something that hurts her?"

The question must have startled her because her gaze jerked to stare at him. "I'm sure you could never do anything like that. But, yes, even if he hurt her. She still loves him, no matter what."

"See? Told you so." Mel spoke around a bite of pie. "You don't have any excuses now."

Mr. Bauer shouted from outside. "Melvin, Eddie come quick."

The boys raced out of the house, with me and Mrs. Bauer close on their heels.

"The mare is ready to foal," Mr. Bauer said. "Thought you young'uns might want to see. Melvin, you and Eddie go make a bed of fresh hay for her."

Eddie had been looking forward to this. He told me when his favorite stallion, Spirit, had bred with the mare that he wondered what their offspring would be like. The boys scattered bunches of hay in her stall.

"Now we'll let her be." Mr. Bauer closed the stall door and we leaned over the wall to see.

The mare grunted and huffed for maybe half an hour before the foal made his way out. Mr. Bauer assisted by ripping the birthing sac and making sure it breathed. If you've never seen a life coming into the world, it's quite a miracle. After several attempts it finally reached his mother's nose and they nuzzled. The sweetest thing.

They didn't name all their horses but a few. "Mr. Bauer, could I name him?" I asked.

"Sure, Susie, you have something in mind?"

"I do. Santiago." It seemed a fitting name for the son of Spirit and Carmella. "I like the name because it reminds me of saints."

Eddie put his arm around my shoulders. "I like it. Look at the white star on his forehead. It's a sign."

The early days of summer passed. They flowed into one another, and likely as not I'd be with the boys whenever they went to work over at the ranch. Eddie became very attached to Santiago. We both did. We enjoyed watching him romp around the corral and discover new things.

On that day in late June, Eddie and I had gone ahead. Mel, being a lazy bones, didn't roll out of bed, and I enjoyed the time alone with Eddie, even if we didn't talk. We walked hand in hand to the Bauers'.

Though I knew the answer to my question, I asked anyway. "Have you told her yet?"

He kicked a rock. "Darn it, no. Suze, don't be that way. You have no idea what it's like. She needs me so much."

"I know. But it isn't fair not to give her some time to get used to the idea of you being gone. Promise me, you'll tell her tonight?"

"Now that's not being fair. You looking at me with your pretty blue eyes and asking me to promise. You know I can't tell you no." While he might have been irritated, I know he needed the incentive my request gave him.

I was milking the cow and Eddie was pitching hay when Mel ran into the barn waving a newspaper. "It's happened. We're at war. They aren't calling it that, but the president is ordering troops to Korea."

"What?" Eddie grabbed the paper and scanned the

headlines. "Suze, you were right. You said war would come—never thought it would be so soon."

I froze, unable to move or speak. Yes, I had known it was coming, but it didn't mean I was more prepared.

Mel nudged me off the milking stool and grasped Lucy's teat. "We have to go." Squirts hit the metal pail in a quick rhythm, punctuating his words. "This'll be our chance to be heroes."

I covered my mouth and held my breath, while waiting to hear what Eddie would say. If he couldn't tell his mother he planned to go to college, he never would be able to tell her he was headed off to war. I bet he could avoid the draft as the only surviving son, so I let my chest relax.

"Donnie's friend, Homer Sullivan, wrote about how Donnie was a hero. Korea's distant and exotic. Far away from Weeping Women Springs." Eddie's voice took on a strange tone, as if he was speaking only to himself. "Donnie and Sam would have gone. Why can't I? It sounds like the conflict will only last a few months anyway." His gaze found mine. "I'll be back almost before Ma realizes I'm gone."

His mother was his main concern, not me. That's okay, even understandable, but I could see he waited for my approval. What was it he told me just that morning? He couldn't tell me no, well I didn't have it in me to tell him no either.

"We'll have a big party for Christmas when you two get back."

Mel whooped, startling Lucy, who mooed a complaint. I merely locked gazes with Eddie, who nodded.

On my sixteenth birthday I was reading *Dinner at Antoine's,* dreaming of what New Orleans must be like with all its old world charm. In books I traveled beyond the desert of Weeping Women Springs, my mind soaring to distant places. A sand-colored lizard skittered under the porch out of the searing late July sun. Though engrossed in the story, my awareness wandered to my surroundings waiting for Eddie and Mel's return. Mother had wanted some help around the house, so I didn't go to the Bauers with them. Each day that summer, he wormed his way a little deeper into my heart. The sweet pain of knowing he would soon be gone combined with the strong feelings I had for him. I felt sure he felt the same way about me, but he hadn't ever said anything. I smiled to myself—I'd been reading too many mystery novels and love stories, so I saw clues and love all around me.

"Hey, Suze." The subject of my daydreams tied two horses to the fence and opened the squeaky gate. "Too hot to go for a ride?"

"Never."

We rode in silence—first a walk and then when we reached the edge of town, we let the horses have free rein.

We raced until Eddie pulled up on the reins and guided us to a grove of cottonwoods. In the shade, the scant couple of degrees made a difference. While the horses munched on some grass, we sat in one of our special places.

"Happy birthday," he said.

Since my skin flushed from the heat, he wouldn't see my blush. "Thanks."

"Sweet sixteen."

"Not sure how sweet, but sixteen."

He cupped my chin. "So sweet, like strawberry pie."

His face leaned toward me until he blocked the horses and everything. He became the world. My eyes drifted closed. Our breath mingled and when his lips moved over mine, melding softly, I couldn't tell where his ended and mine began.

His lips left, but his face remained close. I'd remember him like this forever. "Mm. I love strawberry pie."

I giggled, hating the fact I let it escape. He'd think me a little girl for sure.

He held my hand and stared out at the valley. "Tomorrow."

If the kiss hadn't left me bereft of air, this announcement did. I found no words to tell him how I felt, to beg him to reconsider. The decision had been made. I just didn't know the timing.

"Mel didn't tell you? Thought he might've. We'll leave before dawn, and catch the bus in Cruces for Albuquerque."

"You told your mom then?"

"No. She'd just try to stop me."

I would have given anything to stop him, but he would hate

me for it. So I held fast to this moment, and the last. "Do you know where I can write you?"

"I'll write and let you know. I have a favor to ask, Suze."

"Anything." I wanted to do something for him, except what he was asking me to do, watch him go off to war.

"Be there for Ma, okay? She'll think the worst will happen, but we'll be home by Christmas. She shouldn't worry. And neither should you." My skin tingled under his rough hands which brushed my cheeks.

"Can't help it, but you'll be back soon. It's only a few months."

I left my bed when I heard Mel's door close and met him in the kitchen. "Is it time?"

He nodded. "Ed'll be here any moment."

"Did you tell the folks?" We were speaking in hushed whispers, so I guess I knew the answer.

"Nah. I gave Ed such a hard time, but now I know how he feels. It's hard to tell them."

"It's not fair though, that they can't tell you good-bye."

"That's what's got you up so early, huh? Gotta say good-bye to Ed?"

"Not just Eddie, big brother. Going to miss you. Are you sure you want to go? What if they use the bomb?" Even back then the nuclear bomb was never far away from my thoughts, anyone's thoughts I guessed, not since the end of the war.

"Just a risk we have to take. They'll need us over there."

A soft rap on the kitchen door broke the quiet and Mel opened it. "Hey, bud. I need to get something, and I'll be ready to head out."

He left the room and I embraced Eddie. "I couldn't let you leave without seeing you once more." I blinked hard.

"I'm gonna miss you, Suze. Hey, don't cry."

Such a blubbering fool, I was. "You weren't supposed to see that. I'd hate for you to just remember me crying."

"Smile for me then." He tipped my chin and captured my lips in a soft kiss.

Mel returned. "Hey, you two, don't get all mushy, okay?" He handed me a case. "Take care of this, will you? They'll need someone to play at the commemorations, right?"

"Your trumpet? You sure?"

"You're good, better than me, besides I can't take it with me and it should get some good use while I'm gone."

I hugged him. "Thanks."

Mel lifted his suitcase. "Ready, Ed?"

A hug couldn't last long enough, never long enough. "Be careful," I whispered.

I followed them out to the porch.

"Stay here, sis."

"But—"

"No. It's better to say good-bye here, not draw it out, you know?"

I nodded, any words stuck behind the lump in my throat while their images faded into the distance blurred by unshed tears. In the early morning darkness, a crow cawed.

Anna's Journal

August 15, 1950

Nearly a week has passed since I awoke to the note taped here.

> Dearest Ma,
>   Donnie and Sam served their country and now it needs me. Just like we couldn't let the Germans take over in the war, we can't let the communists win now. The war in Korea should be over in a few months and I'll see you when I get back. I'll write when I can.
> Your Loving Son,
> Eddie

I was stunned and stumbled back to bed. The betrayal struck me deep within and caused an ache in my soul. How could he after seeing his brothers taken from us in war? All things came clear, the silences and the half-started sentences. All of those signs I refused to see. Eddie was different, more sensitive and I read the unwritten words, he went because he too is haunted by their ghosts. I pray daily for his safety, to the same God who let Sam and Donnie die. I can only hope He has more sympathy for my prayers this time.

February 21, 1951

I received a letter from Eddie who never forgets to write. Every week I receive something. After his initial deception I've had cause to be eternally grateful for such a loving son. While Donnie and Sam wrote, they were never so regular as my Eddie. He's a dutiful son.

Dear Ma,

Sending my love to you. How are you getting along? I hope Aunt Lizzy and Ruth are helping you while I'm away. Don't forget to ask Susie if you need help in the yard. She's told me that she is more than willing to help with mowing or weeding in the garden. It helps to know both of the people I care most about in the world can be together.

I appreciated the gloves and scarf. They help against the cold here. Snow and ice weren't something I got used to back home.

Will write more soon. Thanks for the letters.
Love your son,
Eddie

Chapter Twenty

Liv

DATES ARE BURNED into my memory. After the war, I hoped no further dates would need to be remembered, but I was wrong. On September 21, 1951, in the afternoon, the rumble of a motor interrupted my meditation. Despite it being the hour of silence, I peered through the front window to investigate what car broke the stillness. Townspeople up and down the street rushed out of their houses to follow the vehicle, and I joined them. A strange the sense of déjà vu struck me when the dreaded army car pulled up in front of Anna Frolander's home.

En masse the people marched up the road; I nudged my way to the front of the crowd. I confronted the captain as he stepped from the car. "You're not welcome here."

He stared at me. "What's going on here? I'm on official military business."

While I didn't shake my finger at him, I sure wanted to. "We know what your business is, and we want no part of it. Years ago we had plenty of your business. We aren't going to allow you to do this again."

He shook his head. "How do you know why I'm here?"

"We saw this car during the last war. We took special actions so this car would never find its way to town again." I peered at him suspiciously. "How did you find your way here?"

"The army has its ways."

An undercurrent of growling murmurs rolled across the street.

One woman yelled, "Mrs. Frolander already lost two sons to your warrior games, she can't lose another." The crowd chorused an agreement.

The captain drew himself to his full height. "I'm here to tell her that her son was a hero."

"No you aren't," I said. "You're just here to say she has no sons left. You're here to cause her torment."

He maintained a stoic expression. "I'm here to offer help and condolences."

Not willing to give him any benefit of the doubt, I tapped my foot. "What condolences can she have now? Her son's never coming home."

He slammed the car door shut. "This isn't a favorite task of mine either, but it must be done."

"Why?"

"Why?" He leaned forward, his face mere inches from mine. "Why? Because a young man died to protect our country. Do you think we should ignore that? Men die all the time. Isn't that right? Perhaps another death doesn't matter to you. But it matters to me. This man could have been my brother."

I stepped back and bumped into Maxine, who placed a hand on my back. Maxine's unspoken support warmed me. "There must be another way to protect our country that doesn't involve the death of all of our young boys."

"The world hasn't discovered it yet."

"They haven't looked very hard. Maybe that's because all the young men keep offering themselves up for war. Perhaps because they keep sacrificing themselves. It doesn't have to be this way."

The townspeople muttered and nodded their assent to my words.

Sweat beaded his brow. "It's their duty as citizens of a certain age to be available for serving their country."

"You sound like you're talking directly out of a training manual," I accused.

He didn't deny it. "It's part of the agreements we make as citizens."

"We didn't agree." I swept an arm toward the crowd. "We weren't asked. We weren't asked to sacrifice our sons and our brothers and our husbands to this war or the last one."

"I understand that to an extent, but evidently Edward and Melvin understood this; they were proud to offer their service to their country."

Not just Eddie then, Melvin too? I brushed a tear off my cheek. "They didn't tell their parents. They just left. We don't understand why they felt the need to go since they had seen the devastation war caused for us here."

The captain shrugged. "They were adults when they enlisted, so their parents don't have to be notified."

"I find that interesting since you seem so intent of notifying parents now, when it is too late to help them," I countered.

"Normally we send a telegram, but we thought it would be better to come in person. Besides, you don't have a telegraph station here."

The crowd, more restless now, surged forward.

I held my position face to face with the captain. "Yes, we're well aware of your standard policies. We had enough of that during the last war."

He backed against the car. "Will you let me pass so I may talk to Mrs. Frolander?"

Silence answered his question.

Finally I dropped my gaze. "I don't suppose it will do any good to stop you at this point. I—we just want you to understand that it isn't just another marine to us. To us, Eddie and Melvin are our family."

"Believe me I know that. Now I need to speak with their families."

The crowd gave a discontented murmur, but didn't prevent the captain from passing through to Mrs. Frolander's front door.

"Someone should be with her." For some strange reason, my feet wouldn't move to follow him up the path. Twice before I'd been with Anna Frolander to deliver the news, I couldn't do it a third time.

Susie Bracht squeezed through the crowd. "I'll go." She hurried up the path. At the front window the drape moved. What use was the delay? Mrs. Frolander already knew the news. I half expected her to refuse the captain entry, but the door opened with a whispered creak. They entered the house and the door closed. No scream echoed from the house. Mrs. Frolander had no sons left, but no doubt she knew that as soon as the car arrived.

There was time later for more mourning, but at that moment I'd had enough. Enough. I raised my voice above the crowd. "As a community we have given everything we have left to give to these warmongers. These two, Eddie and Melvin, represent our next generation of youth taken in by the glories of patriotic fervor that led them to their deaths. I refuse to be a part of these war games. We must remember our heroes, but how can we allow more boys to be taken? Is there some way to prevent this?"

The townspeople bowed their heads.

Turning to my uncle, I continued in a lower voice. "Shall we have a commemoration tomorrow evening in the community center?" At his nod, I announced it to the assembly.

"Sandi," I said to a young lady next to me, "will you choose a couple of girls to work with the commemoration committee and help choose a couple of songs to remember Eddie and Melvin?"

Sandi nodded, overtaken by sobs as she realized what she was being asked to do. I weaved my fingers through hers. "We have to say good-bye to them properly."

Sandi's face reddened and she held back further sobs. Uncle Jim held up a hand. "Everyone, please be sure to light a candle for our two fallen boys in addition to your regular candles during these next meditations."

The crowd dispersed as the wind bumped clouds across the sky, hiding the sun. Drops of rain fell, marking the road with quarter-sized splashes and pinging rooftops. The rising breeze skimmed over the crowd. Their outrage and disbelief dissipated. Heads bowed, they trickled away.

"Uncle Jim, can the Council make a resolution to protect our boys?"

"We can resolve to oppose any future wars, but if the boys are drafted, the Council can't prevent them from going."

Black rage rose within me.

I walked back home with my mother while stuffing the anger deep within. Along the street, the windows one by one glowed with candlelight, as a second candle and then a third joined the others. Our remembrance candles were a poor substitute for the lives we'd lost.

Susie

AT THE DINNER TABLE the day we received the news, I struggled to control my tears. Not Melvin, not Eddie. They said they'd be home in six months. When Christmas came and went, I held on to the hope. I had no appetite, and my parents lifted their forks mechanically while they stared into space.

Every night since his departure, I'd fallen asleep dreaming of Eddie's goodbye kiss. What would happen to those dreams now?

"May I be excused?"

My mother's nod released me and I ran upstairs to my room. I pulled out a packet of letters wrapped with a ribbon.

It couldn't be true. I'd received Eddie's weekly letter only yesterday. No, the captain was mistaken, besides, Melvin and Eddie couldn't both be dead—too much of a coincidence, right? I'd sit down and write to him and it wouldn't be true. How often had he written that my letters gave him hope? We'd laugh at the silly mistake when he returned. What a story to tell our grandchildren. Wasn't it Mark Twain who had said something to the effect that reports of his death had been greatly exaggerated? I picked up a pen and began to write. I really believed that then.

The following evening, my parents and I joined the townspeople filing in to the gymnasium. Each family walked to the front of the room where they lit a purple candle for their lost boy. Tonight two extra candles were set on a separate table. My parents lit one and Mrs. Frolander lit the other.

The forty-six candles provided ample light. Once all were seated, the program opened with *The Battle Hymn of the Republic,* Peggy accompanying on the organ.

I followed the motions, after years of commemorations they were automatic, but this one went by in a blur. Eddie wasn't dead, this was all wrong. I couldn't understand why everyone accepted the captain's news without question.

His words returned. "They died in the Battle of Heartbreak Ridge," the captain had said.

I searched the rest of the conversation for any truth or holes. Aside from general comments about heroic sacrifice and where they died, he didn't share many details. What if there weren't any to share, because it was all a mistake?

I grasped the sides of my chair with such force my nails dug into the wood. "No, it's not true," the words repeated in my mind. Everyone else would find out soon enough and the commemoration didn't hurt anything. Another story to tell the boys when they returned, and wouldn't they just laugh to hear it? Then they'd be mad because their families had cried for no reason. From the commemoration, the townspeople formed a procession to the Weeping Place. We covered the tombstones and memorial monument with fresh cut flowers and ribbons brought to honor the fallen of both wars.

I lifted Melvin's trumpet to my lips to play the poignant notes of *Taps*. Did anyone notice my faltering start? The last note hung on the air.

Anna's Journal

I'm not sure why my heart still continues to beat.

Two Wars, Three Brothers

Two Wars
Three Brothers
One Mother left to mourn
Distant Thunder
Bombs

Did you lay scared, trembling
Under night skies lit day bright
Waiting for a morn
Out of reach
Forever
Out of a mother's embrace.

Telegrams

Strips of paper
Letters, cold impersonal
Bear news of intimate
devastation
From officers who never knew
The subject, my sons
Not once, Not twice
But thrice
Heart crushed beyond repair
From the news contained
In a few lines of type

Chapter Twenty-One

Maxine

WE SHOULD HAVE BEEN prepared for The Leaving, but I didn't want to believe it could happen. Not that there weren't signs.

In late 1952, the men sat in a circle at the store, you know, in the area we kids used as a dance floor. They'd made a habit of gathering most Saturday afternoons. One particular Saturday afternoon their conversation shifted. They started speaking in lower voices. I didn't catch on at first, but the sudden quiet got my curiosity up so I snuck down the aisle closest to them to listen. What I heard just about broke my heart.

"My Mary was beside herself last night. Damn if there's not a night that goes by that she doesn't cry herself to sleep," Mr. Bauer said.

Mr. Ackerman from the bank spoke up then. "I don't know how you handle it. My wife says whenever the quilting bee gets together, they keep rehashing the events. Each mother, each sister, each girlfriend sit around the circle and repeat word for word the stories of either how the captain brought the news or the day they received the letters and telegrams in the mail. When she comes home from one of those she's a mess the rest of the evening. I'm lucky if I get supper on those nights. No matter what I say or do doesn't have one iota of an effect on her mood. Ruth refuses to go, says she doesn't want to dwell on the past. Hate to say it, but she's always had a good head on her shoulders and her outlook makes the most sense."

"The mine is having rumblings again about closing." The last came from Doc Brennen. "Leastways, that's what you told me, right, Soderlund?"

"Yep," Mr. Soderlund agreed in a typical clipped response.

"If that happens, I just don't know how the bank will survive. I've held on these many years, but without the mine money..." Mr. Ackerman's sigh punctuated the sentence.

"Times are tough around here, that's for sure," Mr. Bauer returned to the original subject. "But it sure enough doesn't make it any easier with our wives not being able to get past the loss of the boys."

"Not just the wives, daughters too." Mr. Bracht said. "Susie writes Eddie every day and it's been well over a year now. Every time I look at one of those letters I think this is the day I'm going to rip it up, confront her and have it out. I just don't have the heart to take her hope away, even if it's false."

"A year? Shoot, it's been more than seven since the war ended. I'd be so happy just to get through a day without Liv stomping around the house looking for someone to snap at." Mr. Soderlund's former reticence ended. "Between Liv and Eva I'm ready to go AWOL. Or at least back to California."

At that the men broke into half-hearted laughter. The chairs scraped the floor and I hurried back to the register.

"I've got a couple of cows to tend," Mr. Bauer said. "But if anyone comes up with any new thoughts on what we can do to help, let me know."

Maybe I should have talked to Liv or some of the other women, but looking back on it now, I'm not sure anything would have helped.

From then on I have to admit to eavesdropping on the men's conversations. They were all similar. A couple months later, I knew it was past time to warn the women. It was the last Saturday the men came to the store. I took up my customary position in the next aisle and the men's conversation started much as before.

"Mary's constantly in tears." Mr. Bauer said. "When will these women stop their mourning?" He sounded tired and more aggravated than ever before.

"I hate to say I told you so," John Waterhouse said, "but I did. When the Council chose to inaugurate the commemorations and the meditations, I opposed it. It's just not right to be stuck in the grief like they are. We're all unable to let the past go if we continue on as it is."

Mayor Chester spoke up. "I voted for the commemorations. A way to honor our boys and there's nothing wrong in that.

But the women have taken it too far. What can we do to help shake them out of this?"

A chair creaked, and Mr. Bauer spoke, "I don't know. They're pretty determined to keep on with the rituals."

"My idea's pretty harsh, but it could work." Mr. Waterhouse's normally robust voice was hushed.

Liv's uncle Jim asked for him to explain.

"If the men all threatened to leave, maybe they'd break out of it." Mr. Waterhouse snapped his fingers. "Probably just like that."

"Whoa," the mayor said. "That's harsh all right. If we threaten it, we'd have to do it. Idle threats never work. Not with my wife anyway."

"Don't you think there's any other way? I don't want to leave Mary." Mr. Bauer's voice broke.

A foot stomped on the floor, evidently Mr. Waterhouse. "If it works...if it shocks them out of this extended sorrow, we won't have to leave. Understand?"

The men muttered in agreement.

The bell rang at the front of the store and the men grew quiet. I tiptoed to another aisle just as Doc Brennen entered. "Hi, Maxine. What's happening?"

"Nothing much, the men are in the back." My cheeks heated, and I prayed he put the redness up to exertions in the store.

When Doc's footsteps receded toward the other men I waited before resuming my listening post.

After a round of greetings to Doc, the men continued their conversation in whispers. I had to strain my ears to hear.

Liv's uncle Jim spoke first. "We've been talking about the women. How they don't seem to be able to let the boys go and get on with life."

"So we've all noticed." Doc scooted another chair over. "It seems the women have been affected more by the loss of the boys than most of us men. The men are sad but they processed their grief. They've not sunk into the sorrow like the women. I've been wondering. It may have something to do with the Spring waters. But I have no proof."

Sebastian inclined his head. "Do you mean if we stop drinking the water, the problem would be solved?"

"We can't stop drinking the water," Doc said. "We'd have to move out of town. The water is part of our life here, not only out of the faucets, but it's what we irrigate the crops with, so it's in our food as well.

"Besides, when people leave after drinking the water, they want to come back. We heard that over and over again in the boys' letters. The longing never goes away. The wish for the well-being, peace and that zing of energy when you first drink the Spring water doesn't seem to fade. Even Michael in his last letter home, expressed a desire to have a drink. Sometimes I wonder..."

Sebastian asked, "What?"

"Nothing...I...nothing."

A long silence stretched out and I was about to return to the front when the whispers started again.

The mayor broke the quiet. "You think if we left, we'd always want to come back?"

"Quite possibly," Doc answered. "Because we've always kept the Spring secret, we've never had any studies done as to the properties of the water. I can only go by what I've heard and observed over the years. It's not scientific, but my notions take into consideration all of the residents I've known."

"Doc, I appreciate your thoughts. It's something I think we all know, but haven't taken time to analyze. It seems as though you've give this a lot of ponderin'."

"That, I have."

After another moment of silence, Mr. Waterhouse said, "Well, is it worth it? Telling the women we're leaving if they don't give up the mourning? If they made the effort, I think we'd all be happier in the long run. Personally, if I have to listen to more crying and sobbing, I'm liable to wish I was six feet under at daggummed cemetery." I noted he didn't call it the Weeping Place.

Doc said. "Don't even joke about something like that."

"I've been thinking," Mr. Bauer spoke. "Would Mary give up the mourning in order to keep me here? She might. We've weathered a lot over the years. Certainly she'd not want me to leave if she understood the only thing she needed to do to keep me. Even if I left, I'd bet within the week she'd ask me to come home. It might work. It's worth it to give it a go. If it works, great, if not well I guess we can find work in Albuquerque. From what the papers say they're looking for hard workers. Who else is with me?"

I couldn't believe my ears. Sebastian Bauer leave Mary? They were the happiest couple I knew. Truly a couple where you could see the love they shared even after all their years together.

The others grunted.

Mr. Soderlund said, "Yes. I think it's our only choice now. If not Albuquerque I'll head back to California. Things are booming out there. The mine is closing for sure at the end of the year. Suppose Ackerman will need to close the bank anyway."

A shuffling of feet and chairs had me scurrying to the front.

At the door the men stopped to shake hands.

Mr. Waterhouse, back to his regular volume said, "Let's meet here at dusk if they don't agree to stop."

Dusk? That left only a few hours.

"Good luck, men." Doc said. "I won't be joining you. Of course, my wife died, so I'm not seeing things on a daily basis like you are. My main reason is the town needs a doctor. I have a duty to stay. But I wish you all the best."

When the last of the men left, I put my 'back in ten minutes' sign on the door and hurried over to Liv's, thinking to catch her before her father broke the news to her and her mother. Since Mr. Soderlund entered not long before I knocked, I anticipated he might answer the door, but thankfully, I saw Liv's face instead.

"Can you come over to the store for a while?" I asked.

"I guess so. Do you need me to watch it?"

"No, we need to talk, now." I gave her the urgent signal, widened my eyes and jerked my head toward the store and mouthed, *now*.

Once back at the store I locked the door. It would do no good to be interrupted during our conversation. "Do you know what the men are planning?"

"Plan? I haven't heard."

I pulled her over to the soda fountain. "They're talking about leaving town."

She shook her head. "Leaving going where?"

"Liv, do you understand what I'm saying?"

"They headed to town?"

"No, try to follow. I mean leaving, as for good." I went around to draw us each a Coke.

"No." She squeezed her eyes shut. "Father would have said something. Why would he leave again? It doesn't make sense."

"You haven't heard them talking. The men—"

"What do you mean?" It was like she hadn't heard me before.

"For weeks now, it's been the same thing every Saturday, they're complaining to one another about their wives, daughters."

"My dad?"

"Yes, but he's not the only one. All of them. Mr. Bracht, Mr. Ackerman, your uncle and Mr. Waterhouse, everyone. You know, they always come to the store and hang around Saturday afternoons. They're tired of the grieving. So they plan to give the women a final opportunity to choose to move on or they will leave town."

"We have to tell the women." Her eyes opened wide. "I have to tell my mother." She didn't stay another minute; she raced out of the store.

Chapter Twenty-Two

Ruth

WHEN PAPA CAME HOME and reported the bank was closing, one part of me regretted it. Much as I disliked being cooped up in Weeping Women Springs, it was home. What would we do now? In the next breath, he talked about heading up to Albuquerque.

"You mean we're moving?" I asked. "Does Mama know?" Not knowing why, I spoke in a whisper, aware my mother was busy in the kitchen.

"I'm moving, but I'm not sure your mother is coming with me or not. We haven't discussed it yet. Regardless of what your mother decides, it's your choice, Ruthie. You're a grown woman so you can make your own decision. You can stay in Weeping Women Springs, or you can come with me and hopefully your mother, whatever you choose to do. I'll make sure you're both taken care of whatever you decide."

Mother set the meal on the table. "Supper's ready."

During the quiet of our meal I waited for Papa to break the news, but he didn't speak until he had swallowed his last bite of apple cobbler. He leaned back in his chair and crossed his arms over his stomach. "I'm closing the bank at the end of the month. With the mine closing and most of the men likely leaving town, it's not going to make it. The men are just plain tired of their wives' tears. I can relate. Whenever you come home from the quilting bee, you're miserable. We need to get out of town."

"No, the women have suffered enough." Mama put her napkin down. "Their husbands can't leave too. That will devastate them."

"The men will give them a chance to decide," he said, "but they're hoping they will have a change of heart. I have to ask, because I know how close you've become to the women, and how you have been so supportive of your sister over the loss of Adam. Will you leave with me?"

"I don't know." Mama paled a little.

"Surely you don't mean that, Mama." I knelt beside her. "You have to go with Papa. It's time you got out of Weeping Women Springs anyway. I can understand where the men are coming from. If I learned anything in California it's the fact that men don't bluff, except for poker, but if they've made the decision, they aren't likely to back down." The image of Mr. Beirman setting down the law for me at the studio flashed in my mind. Even after more than eight years the ache and seeing the end of my dreams still hurt.

Papa nodded. His face appeared older as he waited for Mama to say something. In the end, he left the table.

Knowing I couldn't stand by and watch the two people I loved most in the world break one another's hearts, I headed outside.

I walked aimlessly before my path took me to the Bauers. Aside from running into Mary in town now and then, I had avoided them, and especially going to their place. It was too hard seeing Mary and Sebastian without Joe there, even almost a decade later.

Sebastian bounced on his tractor seat, maneuvering it alongside the barn. When it stopped, he slid more than climbed off the tractor. He wiped sweat from his brow. Before he caught sight of me, I glimpsed the exhaustion, which settled around him.

Guilt almost made me head back home. I should have visited them regularly. "Hi, Sebastian."

He rolled his shoulders and stood straighter. "Well, I'll be. What brings you here, Ruthie?"

"Don't know. I was out walking and thought I'd stop by."

"I'm sure Mary has some supper ready." He motioned for me to follow him to the house.

"I've already eaten, so I shouldn't intrude on your supper."

"Nonsense, you're family." The words brought a haunted pang, a wish for how things should have been. Family, yes we would have been related. Most probably I would have had a couple of children by now, Mary and Sebastian their grandparents.

We entered the house and nothing had changed.

"Mary, look who's dropped by."

She came in from the kitchen. The lines on her face spoke of the passage of time, but more than that, the never-ending sadness. Her eyes red and swollen indicated the depth of her grief.

The scene I witnessed next, I never truly understood. It reminded me of the day we found out about Joe. A moment of privacy played out before me. Perhaps they did think of me as their daughter. After having seen my parents' discussion, I suppose it shouldn't have surprised me that the Bauers would have a similar talk. Almost as if he forgot I was there, he approached Mary and drew her to the couch where he sat beside her.

Sebastian took her hand and stared at it, fiddling with her wedding band. "I can't do this anymore. I can't watch you cry and mourn any longer. It tears me apart."

She pulled her hand away. "Don't ask me to stop mourning my son. I don't think I can, or even should. He'll always be a part of us. If I don't remember him, if we don't remember, who will?"

"We won't ever forget Joe. He was my son too. We just don't have to live steeped in sorrow."

"But it hurts too much to forget it. I don't think it's the same for you. You didn't give birth to him, nurse him. He won't ever get married. We won't ever have grandbabies. You understand, don't you?"

"Yes. I've understood for almost a decade now. I can't take it anymore. It's your choice, but if you continue, I'll leave."

Mary's gaze darted to him. "You're leaving?" she whispered.

Sebastian stood, shoved both hands in his pockets. "I don't want to, but I will. I can't live like this anymore."

"But why?" The disbelief I heard in her tone echoed Mama's.

He knelt in front of her. Placing a hand on her knee, he met her eyes. "I love you. It's tearing me apart to see you like this. Joe wouldn't have wanted our lives to end with his death. You know that."

"I can't help my feelings. I don't think any of us can. I can't just turn off the tears."

With stiff movements, he hefted himself to his feet. "I know. That's why I have to go. It's time."

"Where will you go?" Was it a note of panic that crept into her voice? Maybe she would gain the strength to go with him, let go of the sorrow. I prayed that might be the case. Mary and Sebastian were close to my heart.

"Albuquerque. It sounds like it's growing there and I can find work."

The silence stretched out. "Will you come back?"

"I don't think so. Not while this town is still called Weeping Women Springs." He took her in his arms. "I'll send you my address when I get settled. You'll know where to find me if you want to." He kissed her deeply, turned, picked up a suitcase by the door—evidently he planned ahead of time—and walked through the hall and out the front door. Did he wipe tears from his eyes? I couldn't tell for sure, but knowing how he felt for her, it wouldn't surprise me.

I followed Mary onto the porch. With nothing else to do, I put my arm around her shoulders, wishing with all my heart she would call him back, tell him she would stop the tears, stop the meditations, and put away the remembrances. But she didn't speak.

"This can't be happening. Not after thirty years together," she whispered, more to herself than me. I'm not even sure she knew I was there. "How can he abandon me? Why couldn't he understand and accept how the women chose to remember our boys? He loved Joe too. Why doesn't he understand? What will I do now?" Without acknowledging my presence, she went to the house, grabbed a jacket and hurried to follow Sebastian. I could barely keep up.

When we arrived in town, the men were gathered in front of the store. Each had a suitcase, and in groups of threes and fours they loaded into cars, ready to head to Albuquerque. The women came out of their homes, us in the street.

Mary asked them, "They can't be serious, can they? Are they bluffing?"

"Jim told me that he couldn't take my crying anymore," said Wanda.

"Sebastian told me the same thing," Mary said. "They won't really go, will they? Can we stop them?"

"No," Anna Frolander spoke, her voice rising above the women's cries of disbelief. "You don't want to stop them. They'd resent you for it. They have to leave and we have to mourn our children. That's the way it is." She turned and left for home.

The poor woman. I think she was a little crazy with grief then, if you ask me. Sure, she lost her husband years ago after the first war, then all three of her sons. I visited her with my mother, and I always left her home sadder than I arrived. It wasn't a good feeling.

Mary spoke to me. "How does she even wake up in the mornings? Lord knows, I struggle day after day, and I've had Sebastian to lean on all this time."

Well, I thought, she wouldn't have Sebastian to lean on any longer, not if she wasn't going to go with him and she didn't. Neither did the other women.

They stared after the men as one by one the men's cars pulled away and headed out toward the highway. When they could be seen no longer, Mary said, "I think it's time for my evening meditation. I'll include Sebastian and all the other men this evening." Without another word all the women drifted back to their homes.

I caught up with my mother just outside our house. "You're not leaving? We're not going with Papa?"

"I can't leave Anna." She bent her head and I wondered how long her hair had been so gray. "My sister's lost everything, I can't desert her now. If you want to join your father, I understand, but right now Anna needs me more."

I considered leaving too. Being stuck in Weeping Women Springs held no promise of a future, but I couldn't bring myself to leave my mother. Yes, she decided to stay for her sister, and I would miss Papa. Eventually I could talk Mama into leaving. I was sure of it.

Certainly it turned out to be a good decision, but at the time I thought my heart would shrivel up being stuck in a town of mourning women. Sure, I often wondered what our lives would have been like if Joe came back, but I didn't dwell, not like the others. Until after The Leaving, I hadn't even attended the quilting bee, but the next meeting of the bee, I made sure to go, if only to figure out what the women were thinking to just let their men leave.

Mary greeted us at Liv's door. "I'm so glad you could make it too, Ruth. It's good to have you here."

"Where's Anna?" Eva asked as we sat around the parlor.

"It's a bad day for her," Mama said. "She'll be here next time."

"Is she all right?" Liv made the rounds with tea.

"I won't say I'm not worried about her, but nothing is physically wrong, leastways, that's what Doc said." Mama took a teacup from the tray.

The women settled in to chatting about everything except The Leaving, which struck me as odd. Not one woman mentioned the men. It almost gave me the shivers, I'll tell you. They spoke about the lost boys as if any moment they would drive up Main Street, but not one word about their husbands and fathers.

"I know this is a quilting bee, but I wondered if we might like to do some embroidery?" Eva exhibited an embroidered cushion cover in front of the gathering. It read:

> *As I sit here I contemplate*
> *My loved one's sad heartbreaking fate*
> *Although he is gone from us in this life*
> *I pledge to honor him through joy and strife*

Maybe that's what they considered the men's leaving, a time of strife? It was a little morbid if you ask me.

"That's perfect," Wanda said. "It works for whoever we honor, sons and nephews alike."

"I thought about putting Dewitt's name on it, but couldn't bring myself to spend the time required to stitch it." Eva frowned at the cushion cover.

"I'd like to design a symbol to go along with it," Wanda offered. "Would you mind?"

"What kind of symbol?" Liv asked.

"I'll come up with something, but it needs to represent their sacrifice."

Eva smoothed a finger over her handiwork. "What about a flag?"

"I don't think so." Liv tapped her front tooth with a fingernail, that annoying habit she had when she was coming up with some silly idea. She'd done it as long as I could remember even as a child and we played house. We'd be playing and she stopped and tapped her front tooth and I was always sure things weren't going to go well after that, but Liv would have her way. "A flag is too celebratory. It was what took them from us." Her voice grated harsh. "The patriotism."

"But it symbolizes their heroic sacrifice," I said. "They put flags on the cemetery at Armistice Day and Decoration Day. Seems natural if you ask me."

"Well, no one did," Liv snapped.

Mary held up a hand. "Now, ladies, I'm sure whatever Wanda comes up with will be appropriate. Since there are so many of us, I think it might be better to meet at the high school."

"I can ask Mrs. Godair if we can use her classroom," Susie said.

"In the meantime, I'll order the thread and materials for us to get started," Maxine offered. "Just let me know what colors and how much you need."

I shook my head. Sewing silly cushion covers wasn't my idea of a good time, or something that would help anyone feel better about anything, but I kept my mouth shut.

Anna's Journal

November 22, 1952

I could not cry for Elizabeth's loss, and though I'm grateful for her staying, it makes little difference in the end. All my days are miserable. No light reaches the darkness in my mind.

Leaving

Let them leave
They cannot understand
The depth of distress
The women face daily
No respite
No comfort
Only unyielding torture
Of memories
Which will never come again

Chapter Twenty-Three

Susie

THE FOLLOWING WEEK AFTER the Leaving, I accompanied my mother to the quilting bee or what the women were now calling it, The Gathering. I sat in the back of Mrs. Godair's classroom, threaded my needle and stitched the letter outlines. I worked slowly; the words weren't true. My loved ones, Mel and Eddie, weren't gone. The war wasn't over yet. The news reported those missing in action were numbered in the thousands. They'd return. Missing in Action didn't mean dead.

"We need to have a Council election," Wanda said, interrupting the simple discussion revolving around what vegetables they planned to plant in the spring. When she had everyone's attention, she continued, "With the men gone it leaves just me and Grace. We need an election."

"Do we even need a Council any longer?" Ruth asked.

"Of course." Grace answered. "The Council handles a lot of things, the most important being the Spring."

"I can put up a notice at the post office," Peggy offered.

"Who can vote?" I asked. I wouldn't be eighteen, but I wanted to be a part of things.

"Everyone should be able to vote." Grace said. "Why don't we include anyone fifteen and over. They should all be included, don't you think, Wanda? Since we're the only members left we could decide right now. The Council can convene and decide the particulars of elections later."

Wanda nodded. "Reasonable. Why don't we set the election for two weeks from now, that gives everyone a chance to be notified?"

With the topic of the election decided, the women fell into their more mundane conversations again.

At the end of The Gathering, I hung back to talk with my friends.

Sandi asked, "Do you ever get tired of the constant memorials?" She tossed her dark hair.

"I don't think The Gathering can be called a memorial, since we don't say prayers or sing or anything. It's not like a service."

"Oh, really? And you think embroidering these verses isn't a memorial?" Sandi pushed her black rimmed glasses up on her nose. "Between this and the commemorations, it's just too much."

"But we're remembering our loved ones. The commemoration keeps Melvin and Eddie here for me." I'd learned early on not to mention the fact I didn't believe they were really gone. People would shake their heads and pat me on the shoulder as if I were a child. "Isn't it the same for you and your family remembering your uncle?"

"I understand the need to honor them, but what about us? Our lives are passing us by." She scanned the street before leaning in close to me. "I'd like to find a boy, get married and have a family. Wouldn't you?"

I stared at her. "There aren't any boys left to marry. Who would you marry? Old Doc Brennen? He's the only man left."

Sandi wrinkled her nose. "No, of course not." She put her arm in mine and pulled me along the street. "We could leave town like the men did and find someone to marry on the Outside."

I froze. "Leave Weeping Women Springs? I don't think I could do that. My mother needs me, and I like it here. It's my home."

Throwing her arm around my shoulders, Sandi raised her voice. "We're only eighteen. We deserve more than to be living with a bunch of sad women." She swept her arm indicating the town.

Panic coursed through me. "They need us. We have a purpose here."

"Kate, Helen, Joan, Betty and Lola wouldn't agree. We're leaving next week for Albuquerque." She smiled wide. "I figure I'll look up my father and he'll help me find a job. We girls are going to share a place. It'll be fun. I might even go to college." She stopped and faced me. "You could join us. You can get out."

"No, I'm fine here." I avoided her gaze. "I don't think I'd like the big city."

Sweeping me into a hug, Sandi said, "Okay, but if you change your mind, we're leaving on Tuesday."

Later that evening I put down my latest read, *A Man Called Peter*. Catherine Marshall's love story with her husband, Peter Marshall, sent an aching echo through me. I stared at the bedroom ceiling. Perhaps I should go with Sandi and the girls. What if Eddie never did return? I pushed the thought away for the millionth time, but the next thought chilled me. What if he returned and I'd gone? He'd think she didn't love him, that I'd deserted our love. No. If there was the slightest possibility he'd think that, I'd wait forever.

Melvin's last words whispered in my mind, "They'll need someone to play at the commemorations." No one else could do it if I left.

On Tuesday, my friends drove away in Sandi's mother's car. I waved and then joined The Gathering in progress at school.

"I don't blame them for going," Liv said.

"Me either," I replied. "But I can't leave. My purpose is here in Weeping Women Springs. I want to honor our fallen soldiers." And pray for Eddie and Melvin's safe return.

Two weeks later we elected the new Council. The new members were Mary Bauer, Eva Soderlund and Anna Frolander. Wanda remained as did Grace.

The Council drafted a resolution which was posted in the post office where I first read it:

Resolution 1952-1
Whereas the town of Hope Springs is now to be known as Weeping Women Springs;

Whereas the town has experienced the Loss of their Boys in the conflicts known as World War II and Korea;

Whereas the Spring has ceased to be a medium of Hope as evidenced by our continuing sorrow;

Whereas the men of Weeping Women Springs chose to Leave (The Leaving)

Whereas the young women of Weeping Women Springs chose to Leave (The Second Leaving);

Whereas the women of Weeping Women Springs choose to remain;

We, the Council of Weeping Women Springs hereby resolve that the remaining Women are to maintain the memory of and commemorate the Loss as a lasting tribute to those Lost and forever gone to us.

The following amendments were added:

No one will be allowed to drink from the Spring without prior permission from the Council.

All visitors shall be routed through Liv Soderlund, hereafter known as The Guardian.

All residents of Weeping Women Springs are restricted to the township limits for their own security.

Any contact with the Outside will be regulated by The Guardian.

Part IV

The Echoes of Boots

Chapter Twenty-Four

Maxine

AFTER THE LEAVINGS, things got real quiet, not that Weeping Women Springs was ever a bustling place, but without the men around with their comings and goings, it became, well I guess the best word for it is ghost town. I hate the implications of that word, but it fits.

Then one day in early 1953 the store bell jingled. I couldn't have been more surprised a strange young man entered, bedraggled jeans and shirt and unshaven.

He took his sunglasses off and blinked.

"May I help you?" I asked from the counter.

"Hi. I was just wonderin' if you had something to eat, maybe a sandwich or somethin' quick." The poor man wore worn boots and dust streaked his face. He couldn't have been much older than a senior in high school. Under my inspection, he scuffed his boots.

"I can pay," he said. "I must look a sight. My mom would go bananas if she saw me like this."

"Oh..." I covered my mouth, unable to stop the trembling.

He stretched out a hand. "I won't hurt you."

"Well. Uh." I could not make another mistake regarding a stranger. I didn't know what the Council might do. I avoided his gaze as I struggled to think. He didn't look threatening, more likely he'd faint before harming anyone. It wouldn't hurt to feed the child. "I have a few eggs and some bacon if you'd like me to fry some up for you."

"That'd be cool," he said, and that confused me.

"What? It seems warmer today."

"I mean it would be nice, some bacon and eggs."

"You can follow me back to the kitchen if you like." I pointed to a door. "You can wash up in the bathroom upstairs."

A few minutes later, he came into the kitchen a few layers of grime lighter.

"That smells like the bomb!"

"The bomb? Is that good?" I flipped the bacon.

"Righto"

"You talk a little funny. Where do you come from, young man?"

"I'm from California originally, but I've been hitchin' and making my way east."

"I see. I'm Maxine Fiekens. I've never been to California or east."

"Wow, man. I mean, wow. You just stayed here in this hole in the wall joint?" His strange talk made me feel old at thirty. It had been a long time since we attended a movie or anything else Outside.

"It's not a hole in the wall. I choose to stay here in Weeping Women Springs."

"I dig you," he said.

"What? I don't need anything dug."

"I meant I understand you."

I shook my head. The boy confused me, but his energy brightened the room and my spirits lifted. "Well, I'm sorry I can't say the same."

"Name's Grant."

"Nice to meet you, Grant." I wiped my hand on my apron and shook his hand. "No one saw you come into town, right?"

"I don't think so. I wanna be under the radar anyway. I don't need no cops."

"We don't have any police here."

"Authority types?"

"We have the Council. That's the only authority that matters here." Mentioning it brought to mind that I needed to be careful. I should report him, but it could wait until after he ate.

"I don't mean no trouble, just trying to stay undetected. I have my reasons."

"As do we, Grant, as do we."

"What do you mean?"

I bit the inside of my lip. "Nothing. I'm just thinking that we may have similar goals if what you're saying is true. We've been staying 'under the radar' as you said for about a dozen years now."

"Why?"

"I can't say anymore at the moment." I set a plate at the table and told Grant to sit. "Here's your bacon and eggs."

He tasted the first bite. "Mmm. It's good." He mumbled around a mouthful of fluffy scrambled eggs.

"I'm glad you like it. While you're eating, could I get you some clean clothes? I'm sure I can find something in my late husband's closet."

"That's cool. Don't really need anything, but thanks."

"Young man, you certainly can use some clean clothes." I must have sounded like my mother. While Grant was older than any child I might have had with Billy, my mind couldn't help but wander to the 'what if.' "There's nothing to be ashamed of in taking what is offered."

"Okay, but I can't stay long. I need to be splittin'."

"Split what?"

"Leaving."

"Not before you get some clean clothes on." I shook a finger at him.

"If you say so."

I left to go upstairs. After pulling some jeans and shirt out of the closet I returned to the kitchen, but it was empty. Panic engulfed me. Where had he gone? On automatic I went to the back door.

There he was, across the little bridge crouched by the Spring.

My mouth dropped open. "You haven't taken any of the water have you?

"No. It sure looks good though."

I hurried over and took his hand to draw him back toward the house. "You can't have any, not without permission."

Grant stopped and shook off my hand. He grinned. "Okay. May I have some water? It'd wash down the meal I just ate."

I stood speechless until I could think of something to say. "No. You'd better not. At least not yet. The Council would have to approve."

He squinted at me through narrow eyes. "The Council would have to approve of me taking a drink of water? Why? I've never heard of anything so uptight."

"There are just certain protocols we have. I told you we're under that radar thing. That means we don't have many visitors here. You have your reasons for being under the radar, and so do we."

"My reason's simple," Grant said. "I don't want to die."

I stepped back. "Someone wants to kill you?"

"The government."

I gripped the clothes tighter. "Why? What did you do?"

"Nothing yet. That's their problem. They want me to go kill or be killed."

"Who do they want you to kill?"

He let out a bark of laughter. "Whoa lady, you really are under the radar aren't you? Don't you get television out here?" When I shook my head, he continued. "The Koreans or Chinese."

"Oh, the war?" I whispered. How was it possible that war came to Weeping Women Springs again? I wondered, then I studied him for his reaction. "You don't want to go to war?"

"No." He paced in front of her. "But the government wants me to. If they find me, they'll put me in prison."

I looked at him as if seeing him for the first time. Werner's words about men loving to fight came to mind. Could I believe Grant? "I've never met a man who didn't want to go to war before."

Grant turned, hooking his thumbs in his rear pockets. "I'm not the only one." He couldn't keep the defensive tone out of his voice.

I put a hand on his shoulder. "I didn't say you were. I just find it interesting. We've spent so much time...I can't say more. I need to talk to the Council."

Spinning around, he grabbed my hand. "Oh, please don't tell them I'm here. I'll leave peacefully."

"No, that's not the point. I want to know if I can tell you more about us. Maybe you could stay here. I'm not promising anything right now of course. It's up to the Council."

"Really?" he said.

"No promises, but there's a possibility that they'll allow you to stay. Now tell me, why do you not want to go to war?"

"Y'know it just isn't me, man. I don't think bad of others that go. It's just not for me. I don't want to kill anyone, and I don't think it's the way to solve problems."

"You make a good point. Is there any other reason you need to stay under the radar thing as you said? Any other reason someone might be looking for you besides the government for your war duty?"

"No. Nothing. I've been in college until recently."

"What did you study?"

"Veterinary medicine."

"You're a veterinarian?"

"I worked for a couple of years at veterinary clinic. I've studied enough to be a veterinary technician, that's the step below a full veterinarian."

"All right. Let's get you a Coke for your thirst." I led him back to the store and settled him at the soda fountain and gave him a glass. "I'll be back as soon as I can."

"I'm cool. I'll be here." He lifted the Coke toward me in a salute.

I smiled again at the young man's strange language as I made my way over to Liv's.

As soon as she answered the door, I launched into my story. "I'm telling you, this young man needs Weeping Women Springs and we need him. He doesn't want to go to war and he's avoiding the draft. Since we're off the radar as he puts it, it'd be perfect for him here. Plus, he's a veterinarian and I think the Council will see that as a way he could contribute to the community, don't you?"

"Let me talk to them." Liv said. "But I don't know. We'll see if they agree with you. Does he have family that would want to know where he is or try to find him here?"

"I'm not sure. Since he's been hitchhiking, I sort of doubt it, but I'll check while you talk to the Council."

"All right. I'll report back to you at the store."

"Thanks. I don't think you'll regret it. This young man's a hoot." I stopped. "I keep thinking too, if Billy and I'd ever had children, they would be a few years younger than Grant, you know? If we had kids someday they might be in the same position of not wishing to fight in a war."

"I understand. Don't get your hopes up too high, but I'll see what they say."

Liv left and I headed back to the store.

Soon as I opened the door, Grant jumped up from the counter stool. He shifted from foot to foot with his hands in his pockets looking like an eager child. "Well? Can I stay? What'd they say?"

"We won't know for a little while. We have to be patient."

Grant stared at me long enough that I almost started shifting on my feet. "Could I ask you something?"

"Sure. I may not have the answer though."

"Why're you helping me?" he asked.

"You remind me of someone. Or could have been someone."

"Could you explain?"

I considered whether it could hurt to tell my little story. "When I was younger, I was married to a wonderful boy named Billy. We had such plans for our future, including having children, running this store and spending our lives together." I cupped a yellow rose bud in the vase on the counter, leaning in to sniff its perfume. "He went off to the war in 1942 and didn't come back. I've always dreamt of what our life would have been like if he'd survived. Our son, if we'd had one, could be in your same position someday. I hope someone would help him."

"Thank you." His eyes watered and he blinked. "World War Two was a different kind of war. That war I'd say was necessary, but even a just war causes death and destruction."

I nodded, and wiped away a tear.

"You never remarried?"

That question brought Werner to mind, and I wondered where that thought came from. Sure Werner crossed my mind now and again, but my focus was always Billy. "No. There wasn't anyone left to marry. No real need or want after the war."

"I see. It's sorta sad."

"Life has a way of being sad sometimes, you know." If that wasn't an understatement I never heard one.

"I suppose so," he said, nodding. "I've been so busy trying to avoid letting the sadness catch me."

The need to share the pain warred with the need to protect this young man, but connecting with him won out. Perhaps he'd understand. "There's a difference between avoiding sadness to avoid the pain, and reveling in sadness to avoid the joy, but the two become the same somewhere in midstream of consciousness."

"Have you reveled in the sadness? Does that mean you accept it?"

"Yes," I spoke slowly. "Acceptance is part of it, but reveling in the sadness tends to invade all aspects and hangs large over a life. There becomes no room for hope or joy to enter. It saps life out of you: this sadness called grieving." At that point I'd spent many years meditating on this point, but for the first time I put it into words for another to understand.

Several minutes passed before he responded. "You must've loved him a lot."

"Yes. And the memory and the hope of him." It was the first time I'd admitted that to anyone, even myself. The mourning was as much for the hope lost as it was for Billy.

"You keep his memory alive within you," he said. "No one could ask for more than that after they die."

I pressed my lips together. "It's an honor. I can do nothing more or nothing less."

Silence except for the clock's ticking, always the clock ticking, but nothing filled the time. I wondered if perhaps it might be better to not keep track of time at all.

The jingle of the bell interrupted my thoughts.

"Hello." Liv held out her hand to Grant.

"Liv," I said. "You have news?"

"Yes. The Council had a quick meeting. Based on what you've told me, they agree. Grant can stay, but it won't just be for the duration of the war. He'll need to stay always. Is that acceptable Grant? If not, you should go now."

"You mean I hafta stay in this town forever? Why?" The thought seemed to startle him. "I just need a place to chill out for a while. Not forever. What do I have to do?"

"Everyone contributes here," said Liv. "You'll be expected to contribute as well. Maxine told me you're a veterinary student. With all the farm animals we have around, you could be helpful in that area. We also have certain protocols that you'd need to understand and agree to abide by. They aren't difficult, just things you need to know and also some things you'd be expected to participate in if you're a member of the community."

"I see. What kinds of things?"

"For one, we have meditation every afternoon for an hour to remember the fallen." Liv said. "Next, we have a weekly commemoration ceremony to memorialize our loss. We take time every week to tend the cemetery. These are all community activities each citizen takes part in. Another rule is no contact with the outside unless approved by the Council. That means no contact with family or friends living outside of Weeping Women Springs. Would that be a problem?"

He closed his eyes for a few moments then reopened them. "No. My family doesn't approve of my actions anyway. They've disowned me for my stance on the war. My old man is a World War One vet and thinks country comes above everything, even if the war isn't a good one. My older brothers did their bit in dubya dubya two. They don't much understand either."

"What about other relatives or friends?" Liv asked.

"No," he said. "I can't think of anyone that will try to come looking for me. I can't think of anyone who thinks I matter enough to search for."

"One last thing." Liv put her hands on her hips. "There aren't any young women here. Everyone in town is dedicated to maintaining the memory of their loved one. They've made a decision not to have families. Are you okay with that?"

"Whoa, no girls?" Grant didn't say anything for a space. Then in measured words said, "I think I could live with that." In the short time I'd known him, I could tell he wasn't being completely honest, but I let it slide. He'd figure it out soon enough.

"Maxine, it appears he's made his decision. Right, Grant?"

"Yeah, I guess I have. I want to stay here."

"You may give him a drink." Liv nodded at me.

With that we took him back to the Spring. I dipped the bucket into the pond and brought up a dipper of Spring water for Grant. I offered it to him solemnly.

He received it and drank deep of the sweet Spring water. "I think I do belong here." A deep sigh followed.

In July we received word the Korean War, excuse me, Korean Conflict, was over, they signed a peace treaty. Grant kept his word and stayed, content to live our quiet life and treat our animals. Something about having him here seemed it might be a sign for our future.

With an overhanging threat of the bombs they'd exploded not far from here the world was at a place of strange peace. Cold War is what they called it in the news. How any war could be cold always puzzled me.

Anna's Journal

February 1, 1953

After the Council meeting Susie came over for a visit. She was beside herself when she found out about Grant, a conscientious objector, being allowed to stay in town.

"It's disrespectful to all our Lost Boys to let him stay. How could you allow it?" She squinted at me. "You're on the council, but you've lost all your sons to war. They were brave enough to fight, and yet this coward doesn't have the guts to do his duty when asked directly by his country? It's repulsive."

I tried to explain. "It's the least we can do for the man. He feels the same way about war we all do. Giving him a place to call home, well it seems fitting to me. The Council deliberated on this point and the vote was unanimous. I think the Councilwomen felt moved by his plight and some of us wish—"

"What?"

I shook my head and told her never mind. But the poem below expresses the thought that went through my mind.

A Conscience

Man possess a mind
which guides his choices
right or wrong.
Some say those
who refuse to fight
are betrayers, deserters of duty.
Yet how much courage
might it take for a man to go against the norm
to stand up and say no regardless
of consequence
Should they be commended
for abiding by their conscience
or shunned?
In some little way I wish
my sons
might have had such a conscience.
If so, I'd be able to hold them close

Chapter Twenty-Five

Susie

THE FIRST TIME I MET Grant was after church. That's not to say that he attended church. It was a little odd. He never attended services, though he took part in the commemorations from the first. I was walking home after church and he was outside the store, standing with his hands in his jeans pockets. His jeans were rolled up at the cuff and he wore a simple white t-shirt, nothing over it. His hair was longer than any other boy I'd seen, and slicked back into a ducktail with one unruly curl hanging over his forehead. To put it bluntly, he looked like a hoodlum casing a potential burglary or some other nefarious deed. I'll admit my imagination was colored by many mystery novels.

I knew who he was. The news was all over town and the Council even put up a notice in the post office so everyone would see. I suppose they figured to be ahead of the curve and stop any potential panic of a stranger in our midst.

With as much nonchalance as I could muster, I walked passed him. Not for one minute would I acknowledge him with a glance. Oh, I'd spoken with Maxine, who went on about how nice he was even though he talked a little oddly.

She'd said, "He's different. A boy who doesn't want to go to war. He's avoiding the draft."

That told me as much as I needed to know about the stranger. He avoided his duty, letting others do their part for the Korean Conflict and letting others die for him. Eddie and Melvin volunteered, but this man—I hate to even give him the satisfaction of being called a man—fled his duty when his country required it.

"Hey." His low voice reached me before I'd taken one step away from him.

I suppose I could have rushed on toward my house, but good manners wouldn't allow me to ignore a direct greeting. "Afternoon."

"What happens here on a Sunday afternoon?"

"Much the same as any other day." I barely lifted my head toward him.

"No picnics or basketball games? Nothing?" he asked.

"Some go out to the Weeping Place."

"Where?" he asked.

"I guess you are a newcomer. The cemetery." My tone was sarcastic, I won't deny it, but I finally met his gaze.

"Then why do they call it the Weeping Place?"

My first thought was that the man must be dense, slow even. "You know our town. What else should we call the place which is the center of our purpose?"

"Oh." He pulled a comb from his back pocket and ran it through his hair. "What are you doing?"

"Me? I'm headed home to Sunday dinner with my parents and then we'll have our meditation hour. It's the same thing I do every Sunday. Now if you'll excuse me—"

"Hey, not so fast. Aren't you going to," he sauntered over to me, "I don't know, invite a newcomer to dinner? Seems the polite thing to do."

"No. The idea never crossed my mind. To my way of thinking it seems the rude thing to do to force an invitation." Once more I took a step away from him.

Just then Maxine came out of the store. "Grant, great. I was headed over to invite you to dinner, unless you have somewhere else you've been invited. I see you've met Susie." She took her time looking from me to Grant and back to me.

He smirked and joined Maxine in staring at me.

I refused to be tricked into inviting him to dinner. "Don't let me keep you from your dinner." I headed down the street.

"Nice meeting you, Susie."

"Susan," I flung over my shoulder. It was never like me to be rude, but then I'd never met anyone like Grant before. The image of our boys dying haunted me. The whole idea galled me—that someone like him sauntered his way through life unharmed, ducking the draft and hiding, taking it easy at home. He acted like he was on a holiday somewhere. I fumed all the way home.

From now on, I promised myself to have little or nothing to do with him. The Council might have approved his petition to stay in town, but that didn't mean we had to like it.

Chapter Twenty-Six

Maxine

IN MARCH, I WAS SWEEPING the store when Liv burst inside, the bell jangling overhead.

"Maxine, come quick. There's someone here you must meet. He's come looking just for you." She whisked the broom out of my hand and grabbed my wrist.

"What's going on? Is something wrong?" Her urgent manner rather startled me, and you know, made me wonder if someone was hurt. I didn't know what to think.

"No, I don't think so. His name is Earl Wilson—did Billy ever mention a man by that name?"

"I'm not sure, maybe," I pulled my hand back, "let me think. Yes, he wrote about a Wilson being a buddy of his."

"That's what he said. Evidently Billy told him about us, Hope Springs. He said he's been searching for us for eight years. I guess I really did hide the road." Liv grinned. "Come on. I left him alone in the parlor. Mother went to round up the Council, but she said it would be okay for you to talk to him."

My mind reeled as thoughts chased one another. Wilson knew Billy. When had he seen him last? Was he with him at the end? "I should clean up." I took the scarf off and fluffed my hair a little.

"Silly goose. There's no need to impress."

She was right. "Well, at least let me make sure I don't have dust on my nose." I made a quick trip to the bathroom, put some lipstick on and hurried back.

Liv led me inside her house. In the parlor a young man in dusty clothes waited, his rucksack on the floor.

He stood and offered his hand. "You must be Maxine Fiekens. You are just as pretty as Billy said."

Unsure, I glanced over at Liv, then held out my trembling hand.

Liv introduced us.

"I'm so glad to finally meet you." His wide smile echoed his words. "Billy spoke of you often. He always said, 'Maxine's the prettiest girl in Hope Springs.' When he showed me your picture, I had to agree. Of course, Miss Soderlund is pretty too." Wilson dipped his head in a nod to Liv.

At the compliment, heat flooded my face.

"I'll be right back with some refreshments," Liv said.

Sitting next to him on the davenport, I asked, "So you were with Billy in the war?"

"Yes. We met before the battle of Kasserine Pass when I was assigned to the 2nd Battalion. We were buddies from the start. Billy was a real standup guy. He always compared the climate of Africa to the desert of New Mexico. Some of us were really uncomfortable in the intense heat. Billy'd just laugh and say, 'Yeah boys, but it's a dry heat.'"

I couldn't help asking, "And...were you with him...?"

Wilson became more solemn. "We'd been marching along a road. All of us were pretty exhausted, hot and ready to take a rest when a unit of German tanks came around the bend. The firing started before we had a chance to dive into the ditch."

The poor man's fist balled up and I covered it in a small comfort.

"I dragged Billy down with me, but it was too late, he'd already been hit bad in the stomach." Wilson closed his eyes, and gnawed his lip.

It was a moment before he continued. "Billy knew he wasn't going to make it, and made me promise to come see his best girl. He'd told me all about you, Mrs. Fiekens. I promised if I made it to the end of the war, I'd come see you and tell you that his last thoughts were of you."

I nodded, and the tears escaped.

He lifted a hand to my wet cheek, and brushed them away. "I'm sorry I've upset you. It wasn't my intention. Thought you needed to know what happened."

I sniffed, gaining control. "Thank you, Mr. Wilson. It means so much that you made the effort to come here and tell me, especially after all this time." My hand tightened over his. "Thank you. I'm glad he had as fine a man as you with him at the end. I'm sure that gave him great comfort."

Wilson wiped his eyes. "He was such a good guy, and he couldn't wait to get back to you. He was funny too. Always making fun of me and my goofy clumsiness. I didn't know quite what to do with my two left feet." He chuckled, shaking his head.

I smiled. "Yes, he could move with such grace, and danced with the best of them, you know. We were always the talk of the school dances."

He shook his head. "Billy tried teaching me some dance steps, but I just couldn't get the hang of it."

Liv returned with a tray of three Coca-Cola bottles. "That sounds like Billy." After offering us each a bottle, she sat in the opposite chair. "I thought this deserved something special, for one of the boys." She leaned forward and clinked her bottle against mine and Wilson's. "To Billy."

We sat in silence for a moment. He drained his bottle. "Well, Mrs. Fiekens, I probably should be going. I just came to deliver Billy's message."

Was this going to be it? Something was wrong. Billy left and never came back, now this man would leave just like that? It didn't seem right. I gritted my teeth and gave Liv a nod.

After a pause, Liv asked, "How did you find us?"

"Been looking for a while now. Ever since the war ended, every vacation I had I came out here. I knew I had to be missing something. The people in the towns around told me what direction to head, but they also said they hadn't been there for a long while. In fact, whenever I asked, they'd never seen anyone from Hope Springs. Course, that might be because you changed the name."

I caught Liv's eye again, our plan worked to hide our town.

"Today I decided to go on foot," he said. "I'm not sure why, but it seemed like the thing to do. So I started out from Las Cruces," in his accent it came out lass, "heading east. It was supposed to be thirty miles. I knew it had to be pretty green since Billy had told me about a natural spring that irrigated the land."

"He told you about the Spring too?" Unable to remain sitting at such news, Liv paced in front of the mantel which served as the altar to Dewitt.

"Yes, ma'am. We did a lot of that in the service. Talking about home passed the time."

"Go on. You were telling us about your trip here." I brushed his knuckles. Touching a man's hand felt so odd, any touch, we weren't much for physical contact.

"I searched and watched the landscape. Sure enough, it became greener. I still couldn't see the town though. Then I saw the cemetery filled with flags and fresh flowers. Someone had to be nearby."

He sat up straight and his voice rose. "I came to a fork in the road. It wasn't apparent at first that it was even a road. The main road went straight and off to the right was a path, if you could call it that. It reminded me of that Frost poem. You know the one about the two roads? I memorized it in English class. I still remember it, 'The Road Not Taken' I think it said something at the end about feeling good about making a difference. The poem seemed to tell me where to go.

"The one road was hardly even a road, obviously not traveled in some time. I thought, well, it was worth a chance this untraveled road might lead to the place I was looking for. I had to scramble over some brush and continued down the road and it led me directly here. That's when I saw you on the street." He finished and looked at Liv.

I squeezed his hand. "I'm so glad you didn't give up."

Liv paused in front of Dewitt's picture. "Where are you from?"

"Back east. Brooklyn."

"Do you have a wife and family?"

"No, ma'am. No family. I never married, and my folks, well they're gone now."

"Where will you go, soldier?" Liv perched on the edge of her seat. "It's getting late."

He ran a hand through his hair. "Hell if I know, ma'am." His lip pushed out. "Sorry. I guess I'll head back to Las Cruces and then home."

I raised my eyebrows toward Liv in a silent question. Liv nodded. In unison, we said, "I'm sure the Council would approve."

Then Liv hesitated. "Let me ask them just to make sure. They're over at Aunt Wanda's. Stay here for a moment, Wilson. I don't want to delay your journey, but we have an idea." She didn't wait for a reply.

I sat with Wilson in silence.

"Nice little shrine they set up here for her young man." He indicated the flag draped mantel piece with the picture of Dewitt at the center with an unlit purple candle.

We all had variations of the same in our homes along with the little stool with our verse embroidered on it.

"So, Miss Soderlund lost someone too, I guess?" he asked.

"Yes. Most everyone in town lost someone or knows someone who lost someone."

"I'm sorry to hear that." After that he asked a little about the town, how many people lived here and, you know, little details, before he asked what was really on his mind. "Is the water as special as Billy told me?"

"Seems to be, for most folks, I guess." I wished for the days where the water brought me hope for the future, but that time had long passed.

Liv arrived out of breath from rushing. She stood just inside the room and searched his eyes. "Would you like to stay here?"

Wilson opened his mouth but didn't speak, closed it again and then said, "Does Weeping Women Springs need a clumsy man like me? I'm a mechanic by trade."

"A mechanic?" Liv almost screeched. "We need someone to keep our old machinery running. Especially since...Maybe I'd better not say anymore until you talk directly to the Council."

"I'm in between jobs at the moment. Suppose I could stay." A relieved expression crossed his face as he wiped his brow. "I never expected when I finally found Hope Springs, I would find a new home. The search has taken years, but maybe it was worth it."

"In the meantime, Maxine, why don't you get him a glass of our famous Spring water? I'm sure you could use a cool drink."

Wilson jumped up. "Now that's almost the best idea I've heard yet."

At Liv's nod, I led him across the street to the store.

Chapter Twenty-Seven

Ruth

FIRST GRANT AND THEN WILSON came to town. I began to think we might actually be moving on. Sure, several of the women like my Aunt Anna for example would never get to that place, where she could let go of the past pain, but life started taking root again. Not anything major, nothing like the construction going on in California or even Albuquerque, but still, for Weeping Women Springs it was positive thing.

I suppose Al's story is mine to tell. He wandered into Weeping Women Springs almost by accident, at least that's what he always said. On April 21, 1953, he made it, about a month after Wilson. For a town that had hidden for over a decade, our little road became rather well traveled that year. There Liv goes again trying to hush me. I'm not saying anything out of turn. I always thought it romantic how the people who found us were the same kind of people who never came back. Sort of made me wonder if our lost boys were watching overhead. I'll get to that in a moment.

Al said Joe told him about our town during their training. He repeated it on a freezing night on Attu. Let me read you something from his journal.

> I know Joe talked about a real place.
> Impossible as the story sounded in my
> memory, I remembered Joe's expression
> and voice telling of his home town and
> the Spring. No one acted that good, so
> there had to be a real Hope Springs. This
> is the last trip I'll make searching for it. If
> it exists I will find it, and if not perhaps it
> was like Shangri-La, a fantasy of
> someone's imagination.

I wish Al was here to tell his own story, but he told it to me so many times I can practically recite it too.

On the evening of May 11, 1943, the southern force had made little advance in the fog.

Al shivered, teeth chattering and then no movement whatsoever. He'd never been so cold. Mired with his buddies in the Alaskan mud, no one spoke. The gunfire had stopped for the moment, but if they moved the Japanese would fire again. He ached with cold during the frozen offensive against the enemy, longing to feel a thaw of temperature.

This was hell, not fire, but ice. He couldn't feel his fingers or his toes. He pulled his uniform closer, but the lightweight jacket did little to ward off the icy chill. The fog blanketed the terrain, but brought more cold, no heat.

Daylight faded into darkness though it was after ten at night. He searched the night. The waves crashed on the distant shore. Perhaps some wood for a fire could be found? But in the fog and mist he couldn't see much of anything more than five feet away.

His rifle lay beside him. The stock was wood.

"Can't burn your gun," Joe said as soon as Al lifted it up and took his utility knife out of his pocket.

"If we don't survive the cold, it won't matter if we have a gun or not."

Nearby, a couple of the other guys mumbled agreement. His clumsy, numb fingers unscrewed the stock and trigger, while his buddies did the same. He flicked a match, then another holding it to the wood. Nothing doing. "Come on, catch."

"Need some kindling." Joe said. He removed a knife, scraped it against his own rifle stock and the shavings curled into a small pile. "Try it again."

Al struck another match and the flame licked at the curls flaring them into a miniature fire.

They let out a soft cheer when the wood ignited. Al fed the flame with the stocks of their rifles. Other guys crawled over and contributed their own stocks. Still, the fire supplied little comfort against the frigid temperature. He lit a cigarette, but the smoke only teased him with heat without providing any warmth. After the last puff, drowsiness enveloped him.

A couple more hours till daylight--if they could hold on they'd survive, but to do what? Fight another day? It was never truer.

His mind wandered. What wouldn't he give to be back training in the Mojave Desert? He'd never complain again about the heat. He struggled to remember what heat felt like, maybe he could trick his body into feeling warm.

His eyes drifted closed.

"Don't fall asleep," Joe said.

Al jerked awake at the nudge on his shoulder. "Hey, why don't you tell me about Hope Springs, Seems like we could use some hope here."

"Again, Al?"

He never tired of the story and Joe had teased him endlessly about being like a kid with a fairytale.

"Please?

Joe grinned. "Hope Springs is just about the greatest place on God's earth. When I get home I'm gonna ranch on my folk's land. It'll be mine someday. I'm gonna marry the beautiful Ruth Ackerman and we'll have at least a half a dozen good looking kids. They'll help work the ranch. We'll raise a herd of cattle and probably some chickens..."

Al leaned in closer. "Tell me about the Spring."

"Right in the middle of town is our store. At the back of the store is a pond from a natural Spring. Out of this Spring comes the sweetest water you'll ever taste.

"You forgot the roses."

Joe laughed. "Yeah, it's surrounded by yellow roses. The water cures just about anything that ails a body. The first settlers arrived about eighty years ago worn out and exhausted." Joe pulled his thin jacket closer. "Their wagon master had been killed in an Indian attack and they were lost, almost ready to drop since they'd been crossing the desert for at least a week without fresh water. They'd lost any hope at all. The story goes that most were nearly dead from thirst. They happened upon this Spring not marked on any map."

Al finished the story for him. "They saw the Spring bubbling from the cliff into a small pond and were saved. It revived the whole wagon party. They were filled with hope so they called it Hope Springs and decided to end their journey west right there."

Joe chuckled, low. "That's right, buddy. Everyone who drinks the water is filled with hope. Plus, I think the water makes people want to stay."

"If it's as good as the story goes--it probably does."

"It's healed people too... I can't wait to get back." He turned his face away. "I sure miss the Spring water."

Reaching in his pocket, Al took out his Indian Head nickel, flipped it in the air and twirled it between his fingers. "Could I visit when the war's over?"

"Sure."

"Your town sounds so perfect. Like the home I never had." After returning the nickel to his pocket, he laid back, arms behind his head and stared at the fog. "The ranch sounds good too. What're your folks like?"

"Hard working and generous." Joe's teeth chattered. "Nobody ever goes away hungry from Ma's table. She cans all of our vegetables, so in the winter when they we can't get fresh, we have plenty."

"Mmmm. My ma died when I was seven. Papa, didn't pay much attention, busy working all the time and I grew up on the streets. Gangs everywhere and everyone wanted a piece of me. I had to fight or run just to stay one step ahead. Your home and ranch, they sound like a dream." He reached his hands closer to the fire. "Uh, hey d'you think after we get out of here that I could work for you on the ranch?"

Joe shrugged, and rubbed his arms. "Maybe. We can always use another pair of hands."

Al dozed, imagining a desert oasis and a home. Something awakened him.

Joe hadn't spoken again. He glanced over to see his buddy unmoving.

Al rasped, "Joe, hey, Joe, wake up."

But Joe did-didn't open his eyes. He wouldn't open them again. I'm so sorry, this part of the story always chokes me up, no matter how many times Al tells me.

Dawn came, but the short freezing night had ended, taking several of his buddies into an icy sleep. Al remembered little of what happened afterward. Several days later he awoke in a hospital recovering from his frostbitten toes sustained in the Battle of Attu and a bullet wound that had grazed his forehead.

Al spent two months in recovery. By the time his head wound was healed, he had learned how to walk, minus two toes, with the help of a cane. His war days were over.

He walked with a slight limp, but whenever he's on his feet for long periods of time the limp grows worse. That's how it was when he finally came to the road. His limp worsened, forcing him to slow his pace. He stopped, wiped his brow and leaned heavily on his walking stick. A break in the trees ahead led off to a path. He took his lucky Indian Head nickel out of his pocket. Heads, he would take the forgotten pathway; tails he would head straight down the road. Heads it was, so he headed into the path under the trees.

Like a mirage or an oasis, the town materialized in the distance. Greenery inundated the otherwise barren desert landscape. The brush took on new life. The trees offered shade and respite from the late afternoon sun. A cemetery filled with fresh flowers with a sign: Weeping Women Springs was off to the right. Had Joe been mistaken about the Spring? Or maybe a spring other than Hope Springs existed.

A couple of miles later his weary feet raised dust on an empty street. He whistled a cheerful song.

Liv was the first to spot him. She approached him with long purposeful strides, and stopped. "Hello. What brings you here?"

Her question struck him as odd. Well, of course, it would now, wouldn't it? "Uh, well, I'm looking for a place called Hope Springs. Do you know where I might find it?"

"Why?"

"I'm sorry? Why, what?"

Her direct stare didn't flinch. Liv's nothing if not direct as I'm sure you've noticed. "Why are you looking for Hope Springs?"

Attempting a smile, he said, "I had a buddy during the war who always spoke of his hometown. He spoke of it as if it was a mystical place. He planned to come back, ranch, get married and have at least a half dozen kids he always told me. I told him I always wanted a hometown like he talked about. I grew up on the streets of Chicago. He promised to take me to his hometown and find me a girl to marry and land to buy." Al scuffed his cane in the dust. "But he died during the war."

She clicked the tip of a long fingernail on her front tooth, her old habit. An uncomfortable few seconds stretched out. Poor Al, it's a wonder he stayed what with Liv and her inquisition. I know it was necessary back then, or they thought it was, but it never made a lot of sense for the boys who searched so long and hard for the Spring. "Who might your buddy be, soldier?"

"Joe, Joseph Bauer."

Another long moment passed before she answered, "You've found Hope Springs."

Al inclined his head squinting at her. "Really? But from your reaction, I thought perhaps this was another place." He pointed behind him. "And the cemetery sign said, Weeping Women Springs."

"Yes, that's right. That's our new name as of a couple of years ago."

"Oh. Then this is really Hope Springs?" He circled round taking everything in. Had he found the desert oasis he'd dreamed of for a decade? he wondered.

"Yes. It is. Though there is little hope in our town anymore."

He swung back to her. "The Spring--it's still here, isn't it?"

Her eyes narrowed. "Joe told you about the Spring?" A small grimace crossed her features. He thought she was mad at him. I must say, I feel that way a lot when talking to Liv.

Al nodded. "What's wrong?"

"Nothing."

Guessing she denied something, Al repeated, "But is the Spring still here?"

Again she stared at some point beyond him. "Oh yes, the Spring is still here and it still has water bubbling from it. It's the town that doesn't have any hope."

"I don't understand."

"It's not important right now."

"Do you think I could have a drink of the Spring water?" he asked.

"If Joe told you about the Spring, you know once you drink you may lose the desire to leave."

"I don't intend to leave, so it doesn't make any difference." Always the charmer, he grinned. "For eight years I've only had the desire to get here. This was going to be my last shot at finding it. I'd almost given up hope."

She led him to her house. "My name's Liv Soderlund. I have someone I want you to meet. Joe would've wanted you to meet her."

"I'm Al Caldarelli."

"Sit here and rest for a moment while I get her."

Of course, she was talking about me. She came and told me she had someone to meet me. We returned to her house.

Standing, he held out a hand toward me. "You have to be Ruth. You look just like the picture Joe showed me."

I started to speak but then remembered I needed official permission, well I already had it I guess. Liv came to me. However, I wanted to make sure. She nodded, and I took Al's hand and gave him a trembling smile.

For some reason I've never understood, I was speechless.

Liv gestured for us to sit in the parlor. "Al, that's right. This is Ruth Ackerman. I've told her about your friendship with Joe. I'll get some refreshments."

I sat on the edge of the davenport clasping my hands together. "You knew Joe?"

"Yes. We were both in the same unit. A great guy, so full of life and hope. Always happy. He amazed me."

"Did he talk about me?"

"Just before—" He cleared his throat. "Just before he died, he was telling me he was going to marry the beautiful Ruth Ackerman."

"Really?" I couldn't keep my joy out of my voice.

"I know now he wasn't exaggerating," he said.

"You're so kind. I must look a sight." I covered my face.

Al touched my forearm, gently moving my hands away. His eyes met mine.

"And, Maxine just never gets in my brand of cosmetics anymore." I was babbling I supposed. "Well, a girl has to make do, doesn't she?" Then I gave him a little batting of my eyelids. I have to stay I hadn't lost my touch.

"It makes sense Joe never stopped talking about you, Ruth, and Hope Springs. He knew that if he got back here, everything would be swell."

"A long time has passed." That's when it dawned on me. "And he brought you here."

"I suppose you could say that."

I grasped his hand and squeezed. "Yes. It seems as though I've been right in feeling Joe has always been watching out for me, though he took his sweet time about it."

Reentering the room, balancing a tea tray, Liv broke in, "Who took his sweet time about what?"

"Joe took his sweet time about getting Al here." I clapped my hands. "But you're here now."

"You had a hard time finding us because we've made sure to keep hidden, since the wars," Liv said.

"I wanted to come." Al didn't take his eyes off me. "I need a home like this town."

Liv searched his face before placing the tray on the table. "We're not what we once were. We've lost the hopeful spirit we had since the founding of our town. Whenever we think of our town we become sad, rather than hopeful. Do you think you would still want to stay here, since we call it Weeping Women Springs instead of Hope Springs?"

"Of course, he does, Liv. What a question." I laughed at the ridiculous thought Al would leave after meeting me.

"Do you need a hard worker who wants a town to call home?" he asked.

"See? I told you he'd want to stay."

"We can always use a hard worker." Liv said. "In fact some of the older women need help with their ranches. Can you round up cattle?"

Al pulled his gaze from me to look at Liv. "I grew up in the city, so I've never done it, but I could learn."

"Joe's mother needs some help," Liv said. "Ruthie's been helping Mary since Sebastian left, but she needs assistance with the plowing and planting. You could be a big help there, right Ruth?"

"That's a great idea. We could certainly use the help. Lately, I don't think she's wanted me around much. I suppose I remind her of Joe."

"Swell." Al said. "Just point me in the right direction and I'll get started right away,"

"First, why don't you relax? I'll take you across the street and you can have a long cool drink from the Spring," Liv offered.

"Could I? Gee, that would be such a gas! I've dreamed of being able to drink from *the* Spring."

"Come along then. We'll get you that drink," Liv said.

Al limped across the street, leaning a little on his walking stick. He told me later that he was thrilled because he'd found a home and, if he read me right, perhaps a new girl. He cast me a sideways glance.

When we entered the store, Maxine voice called, "May I help you?"

"Maxine, we have a young gentleman who needs a long cool drink of Spring water," Liv answered.

She came darting out from behind a shelf unit. "Did you say a young gentleman?" That's how starved we were to see men.

While Liv introduced them, I watched him carefully, but other than being polite, shaking her hand, no spark flared, not like it had with me.

"Welcome to Weeping Women Springs. It's nice to meet you. Did I hear correctly? You want a drink of the Spring water?"

"Yes ma'am. I've searched a good long while for the town, and now that I've found it, I'd like to stay. Liv said it would be okay, and I might be able to help some folks with their ranches."

"In that case, I've got a big tall glass of Spring water for you. I'll be right back."

"Ma'am?" He ducked his head in that adorable way he has. "I mean if it'd be okay could I... I mean would you let me see it? The Spring? You see, Joe told me about it, and it just seemed so--I don't know, almost magical when he described it." He spread his hands palms up. "And I guess I'd just like to see the actual pond. Would you let me?"

Maxine looked at Liv who gave her a slight nod. Al wondered why everyone turned to Liv for guidance.

"Sure, you may see the Spring. It's right back here." Maxine led the way followed by the other three. We wound our way through the store, through the back office and storage area out the back door to emerge on a covered patio.

He always says he will never forget the first sight of the little pond, how the vegetation, contrasted with the rocky cliff. Rose perfume wafted over him. It reminded him of the picture gardens in Grant Park where greenery and cement pathways blended together into a feast for the eyes. The Spring bubbled up through red rock cliff and ran over some black lava rock into a small pond. Maxine took the ladle and dipped it into the water and offered it to him.

Liv said, "Are you sure? There won't be any turning back after you drink."

"Yes. I've never been surer of anything in all my life."

"Then go ahead," she said. "Go to Maxine and taste the water of our Spring."

Al took the dipper with reverence and drank. The last part, he always looks rather stunned when he tells it. I find it compelling because I'd grown up with the water and don't remember my first drink. He said he felt the sacredness of the act deep in his soul. The water tasted sweet and pure and quenched thirsts both physical and spiritual.

After that his little limp virtually disappeared. He swears it was the water.

We watched his reaction. A peaceful expression crossed over his features. The Spring worked. We had wondered about the Spring even after Grant and Wilson arrived. We had our doubts whether the water retained the power.

Liv turned to me. "It works. I hoped it would, but I had my doubts since it hasn't helped us in the last few years. Perhaps it doesn't work on us anymore because we don't believe in its healing force."

"I think it's something more than that," I said. "The Loss had a great impact on us. It damaged something deep within each of us, you know. The water still works, but it just doesn't work on us. We lost all hope."

"You may be right." That had to be a first, Liv telling me I was right about something. "I'll tell the Council about this. I'm sure they'll want to hear it's not just Wilson and Grant affected by the water."

I agreed. "He's quite handsome isn't he?"

Shooting a glance at me, Liv nodded slowly. "But of course, well you know...there can't be anything..."

"Oh, of course not, the memory of Joe is safe." Well, I wasn't lying. Joe's memory would be safe forever, but that didn't mean I couldn't embrace love if it happened.

Across the pond, Al finished the dipperful of water. "Wow, this is the best water I've ever tasted. There is something special about it, just like Joe told me."

"We've always thought it pretty special too. Welcome to your new home," Liv said. Turning back to me, she said, "Why don't you take him up to meet Mary? I'm sure she can find a bed for him."

I nodded. "She'll be happy to have the help again."

"Not happy, but she will be helped. That's the main thing now."

It pained me to say it, but she was right. "Happiness is too strong a word."

Maxine led Al back across the pond and he almost skipped with new vibrancy.

"You'll like staying at Mary's," I said. "She's a good cook. I'll take you there now and make the introductions."

Filled with exuberance, Al's eyebrows rose. "Why don't you drink from the Spring?"

We all shook our heads. "No. To us it's just like drinking any water. Nothing special," Liv said.

"You're kidding! I can't believe that."

"We couldn't at first either, but it has remained true ever since the end of the war," Liv said. "Go on over to Mary's."

We went to leave, but behind us I caught Maxine and Liv's conversation.

Maxine said, "It's good to know it still works on some. My job won't be worthless now."

"Never worthless. Water does sustain us, even if it isn't Hope Springs anymore."

"It just isn't the same."

Liv heaved a sigh. "I know, believe me I know."

Chapter Twenty-Eight

Maxine

A CAR MOTOR CAUGHT my attention in September of 1954. I ran to the door and as soon as I saw the source, I went into the street. Everyone else had the same idea. The car with the star was back. It made no sense. No one from town was at war. What could it want? It drove slowly up Main Street. I searched the dismayed faces around me. Everyone was visibly upset, but none more than our guardian, Liv.

She approached the vehicle as a man in a sergeant's uniform stepped out.

"Wait a minute." She shook a finger in his face. "We don't have any young boys and there aren't any young boys at war either. I can't imagine what business you might have."

He stepped back, bumping into the car. "But—"

"You can turn this monstrous car around and head back where you came from!" she snapped. "Who are you to think you can just drive in here?"

He held up his hand in a gesture of defense. "Whoa. I'm not here on any official business, if that's what you're thinking. My name is Vern Cooper. I'm only here because I've missed Hope Springs the last several years. During the war I drove this very car here several times when Captain Richards needed a driver. Ever since then I've thought of this place, dreamed of it. It's been a while, but when I finally mustered out of the army, it was the only place I wanted to go.

"After my last visit, I was transferred to the Pacific Theater of the war and spent time in several places before being shipped over to Korea." He searched the crowd and I offered him a smile, the pathetic man, all he wanted was to come back here.

Wilson stepped up to him and I leaned in close so I wouldn't miss anything.

In a low voice Wilson said, "It was called Hope Springs until just before the big war ended. The Council changed the name when the young men didn't come home."

"But you're here. What do you mean they didn't come home?" Sgt. Cooper asked.

"This town didn't see a single one of the boys that went off to war return." Wilson gestured for Al Caldarelli to join him. "Me and Al, we arrived after the war, but we aren't from around here. We both ended up here for different reasons," he added.

"Oh," The sergeant cast another glance over the crowd. "Why are they so upset with me? I didn't do anything. They can't think I came because of the war."

"Well, they're upset at the arrival of the army car. The women associate it with the arrival of the news reporting the loss of their boys," Al explained.

"I guess I can't blame them. Stupid of me to have used the car, but I sort of missed it too. Do they hate me too?"

Al shook his head. "I don't think so. It doesn't serve them any purpose to hate people. What I've learned since I've been here is that the women don't want the loss that war brings. They dedicated themselves to remembering their Lost Boys and making sure no one else from here ends up in war."

"My name's Wilson. They haven't had any boys here for a little while. Until Grant arrived, during the Korean war, then last year me and Al came, not too different from you except we hadn't been here before."

Vern took that in. "Is there a way I could stay here, like you boys have?" he asked. "How did you get to stay?"

"I came to see the widow of one of my buddies from the war. I'd made a promise to him. When I arrived, it just seemed right to stay. It was like I'd finally found my home," Wilson said.

"After the war I just had to find my way here." Al said. "Both me and Wilson help out the women here. I'll tell you, both of us had a hard time finding it. The people of this town don't want to have anything to do with the Outside."

"We had a time finding it during the War. The last trip I thought my Captain was like to kill me for the delays. I'd like to stay and help, too, if that would be okay. I've dreamed of this place for so long. It's more home than my home is."

"You should meet with Liv and ask her." Al swept a hand to the store. "By the way, Vern, did you happen to ever drink from the Spring while you were here?"

"Yeah, funny you should mention it. One time the car overheated and I went to find some water. I found the Spring and drank some of that cool sweet water. I've dreamed of it ever since."

"Yeah," Wilson said. "That's the way it works. Hey, Liv, what do you think?"

She stepped forward. "I remember that. The car was parked outside Doc Brennen's and you were checking the engine. I didn't realize you went to the Spring."

"Needed water for the radiator. Took a drink too." He shrugged and gave a sheepish grin.

"The Council would have to approve it. And it would mean you couldn't be a soldier anymore. We couldn't have you going off to war again and something happening to you."

"Okay with me. I was going to try to make my twenty, but I've had it. I'm out, as civvy as you boys are."

"Let me check with the Council," Liv said.

She walked to the Council who were gathered off to the side whispering. After a short consultation, Liv returned to Vern. "You may stay, but you must take this car away. We need to see your discharge papers with you when you return to Weeping Women Springs."

Vern swept a hand across his face, obviously relieved. "Thank you, ma'am." He pumped everyone's hands. "I will make myself as useful as I possibly can. Oh, and, Ma'am? Would it be possible for me to get a drink of that fresh Spring water you have here?"

She smiled. "Of course, Vern. You know that's most likely the reason you couldn't get our town out of your dreams. Once someone drinks from the Spring, they want to stay here. It quenches a person's thirst for water and for a home."

"Not sure I understand that, but it sort of makes sense."

In a rush I ran back to the store and filled a glass of water and returned. "Here, Vern."

"Thank you so much, ma'am."

"You're welcome. This will ensure you will hurry back," I said, offering a smile.

"That I will. I'm going now and I will be back as soon as I can."

After Vern's return to Weeping Women Springs, he joined in our routine. Though he didn't know the boys we honored, he took time to remember his fallen comrades on the battlefields of two wars. He was a general handyman to the town.

A couple of weeks later, he approached Liv when we were at the soda fountain. "I think there was a way the ancient Romans made ice. Could you find a book at the library for me?" He handed her a slip of paper. "When you go to town next week, ask the librarian if they have anything on ancient Rome inventions.

When Liv brought him the book, he spent a few hours poring over the book at the soda counter. "It helps me think."

I'm not sure what he meant, but I was happy to have the company.

After a several attempts, he discovered a way to make ice even in the summer. He dug a pit close to the rocks in the back, lined it with straw, put water in it and then covered it with a metal polished shield, which reflected the heat of the sun. When the ice formed he cut the blocks out and stored it in the ice house he built for the store. Filled with sawdust, which he collected wherever he could, it kept ice cold for quite some time.

One day, he hauled in a block of ice to the soda counter. I finished packaging a sale for Mary. When she left, Vern picked up a candy bar at the counter. "Put this one on my tab."

"Never mind." I waved away his offer and poured him a glass of water. It never grew old, the expression on their faces when they drank. "Thank you for the help."

"You know, Al, Wilson and I've been talking. We really appreciate being a part of this community. Is there something more we can do? We'd like to be able to offer some comfort to the women."

"That's kind of you. But—"

"Y'know, we just feel somehow you don't share everything with us." He took a drink. "Maybe there's something we can do besides chores. We feel out of the loop sometimes."

I sat at the counter. "I'll ask, but I can't think of anything." I covered his hand with mine. "We care about all of you, but you can't replace our husbands, brothers and sons."

Already we referred to the four of them as distinct from the Lost Boys. Grant, Al, Wilson and Vern were always the "new boys."

"I don't believe any of us want to do that. We just want to help ease your sorrow. I know we love this town. It's soothed my soul." The way he said it made me wonder what horrors he saw during the wars.

"We're adamant you four remain safe, out of harm's way. You know that's why we don't lump the Lost Boys with you." I puzzled it out in my mind. "Maybe, we're afraid if we become close to you boys, we might lose you, too."

Vern took my hand. We sat in the quiet for a while.

"You know what I miss most?" I asked. "The sounds of the children playing. It's so quiet, as if all we have are the echoing sounds of memories."

With no further words, he squeezed my hand. Sometimes that's enough, to know someone is listening even in the silence.

Chapter Twenty-Nine

Ruth

"MAXINE, COULD YOU PLEASE remember to ask Liv to get some 'Cherries in the Snow' lipstick from Revlon?" I sipped a Coca-Cola at the fountain counter. "It's very important."

"Why?" Maxine popped up from behind the counter where she was putting away clean glasses.

"Well, I shouldn't say anything." I spun the stool then leaned back against the counter. "But I'm sure, absolutely positive, Al is going to pop the question."

"What? But—"

"No buts, we've been keeping company for a few months now."

"I assumed you'd been talking about Joe."

"It started out that way, but we've moved past that. He loves me. He said so last week, and I don't think we'll want to wait."

"What about Joe?"

"He's gone, isn't he? Of course, I was devastated when it happened, but it doesn't mean I have to stop living does it? I'm ready to move on. Honestly, Maxi, we're thirty years old" I refused to add the one. It hurt enough not to say twenty anymore. I went to the cosmetics aisle mirror.

"Have you talked with the Council? Or Liv?"

"No, but why should they mind?" I ran a fresh coat of Max Factor "red, red" over my lips.

Maxine clanged some glasses together. "No reason, I guess, but it might upset some people."

"Well, some people, as you say, get upset over just about anything. I'm sure I don't know why it should be any of their business if Al and I marry."

The doorbell jingled announcing another patron.

"Don't tell anyone yet." I whispered. "I'll do it in my own way."

"Max?" Liv called out.

"I'm at the soda fountain. Come on back."

"I'm just here to get your order for my trip into Cruces. I'm headed over tomorrow. I have eggs and a few chickens from Mary." Liv laid a notepad on the counter. "Wilson said he'd have a trailer of corn harvested by then too."

"Sounds like there's enough to buy a few items we'll need." Maxine said.

I spoke up then. "Don't forget my special order, Maxine."

Liv barely acknowledged my presence before continuing, "The Martinez' have some tomatoes and other vegetables to sell at the market."

"With my pension check, there might be enough to do a real stock up," Maxine said.

"I figure I'll take Wilson and we'll do a stint at the farmer's market."

The two women continued making their lists. I fidgeted with the cosmetics. "Al and I are planning to marry." I'm not sure what made me blurt it out.

Liv stopped mid-motion. The pencil clattered to the floor. "What did you say?"

"You heard me. We're getting married. I don't want a drawn out engagement so it will most likely be before Thanksgiving."

Liv paled. "No. They won't allow it."

I barely restrained rolling my eyes at her dramatics. After all, I was the actress. "Who do you mean? The Council?"

"You ninny, of course, I mean the Council. It goes against everything they've set up here."

"How?" I strode to the counter. "There's no rule against it."

Liv's voice grew louder. "The resolution after the Leaving specifically states, we *'are to maintain the memory of and commemorate the Loss as a lasting tribute to those Lost and forever gone to us.'*"

It didn't surprise me she had the resolutions memorized because she was odd that way. "So? Just because I get married doesn't mean I can't do that." I slurped the Coke and slammed it down on the counter.

"Please, girls, don't shout. Can't she just ask the Council for permission?" Maxine asked.

"Permission?" I asked. "Since when has anyone had to ask someone's approval to get married?"

Liv picked up the pencil from the floor and tapped it on the pad in a drumbeat reminiscent of the Commemoration processions to the Weeping Place.

Maxine's hand covered Liv's, stopping the beats.

"They'll have to know. I'm not sure what they'll do. You know as well as I do, things have never been normal in this town, more so since The Loss and The Leaving."

"What could they do?" I asked.

"Maybe nothing. Maybe ask you to leave Weeping Women Springs or anything in between."

"You mean like exile me? That's barbaric." I put the empty glass down.

Maxine took it up and washed it under the faucet.

Not since such vessels had been called chalices did a town exile someone for breaking a rule, I thought. In Romeo and Juliet, hadn't the Prince exiled Romeo? The banishment didn't result from Romeo and Juliet's marriage, or had it? I couldn't remember. Then there was the story of a man without a country we read in eighth grade. It haunted me with the greatest sense of isolation and sadness after reading it. What had the man's crime been? It hadn't seemed to fit the punishment. I shook my head. Nonsense.

"Think what it would mean for the rest," Maxine's soft tone pleaded. "We all spend our days honoring the Lost Boys."

"That's their choice. But I want to move on."

"What about children?" Liv asked. "Wouldn't it be cruel to raise a child in this kind of environment?" It sounded just as strange then as it does to repeat it. Why were we living like this?

"Wait a minute. I didn't say anything about having children," I said.

"Why else would you get married?" Maxine smiled. "It'd be nice to have children here again."

"Then have your own," I snarled at her. "I'm not sure I want to have any. Al hasn't mentioned them either."

"No. I can't. My husband is dead." Maxine grasped the feather duster and wandered the aisles slapping at cans with the duster. Tin clattered, threatening to tumble from the shelves.

Liv leaned in to me with eyebrows raised. "Now look what you've done. You've upset Maxi. Ruth, have you no compassion?"

"I'm up to here with compassion." I raised my hand above my head. "When I could have stayed in California, I stayed, and when I could have gone with father I stayed just to comfort Mama and Aunt Anna. Compassion? I've had my fill."

"Has he asked you to marry him?" Liv asked.

"No, but it's only a matter of time." I touched my hair, running a hand over the set curls. Maybe I should order a Toni permanent refill kit too, I thought.

"Not counting your chickens, are you?"

"No. Al loves me. Maybe you're just jealous of what I've found."

Liv jumped from her stool. "Jealous? Of course not. I'm determined to protect our town from further heartache.

"Further heartache? How can my marriage cause pain?"

"You're being selfish. You have no idea what effect your plans will have on Mary or your aunt."

"They'll probably be happy for me. Why wouldn't they be?" I was fed up with their attitude most of the time anyway, though I hadn't spoken to my mother about the plans.

"You really have no idea." Liv hit the counter. "They've lost their sons. Joe was supposed to marry you. Don't you think his mother will be sad at the reminder? Especially marrying his war buddy?"

"There's no need to be sad. A wedding might be just what this dreary town needs."

Liv tossed her curls. "Leave it to you to think you're what this town needs." She left the store flinging her parting words over her shoulder. "I'll report to the Council. Let them decide."

I waited until Liv was well gone before I left. On my way out the door, I called to Maxine, "Would you put a hair permanent refill on the list? Toni is my brand." No matter the date, I planned to be ready.

The following week, I received the summons to meet with the Council. I jerked my shoulders back, took Al's clammy hand and marched up the street. Darned if I was going to let these spinsters ruin my life too.

"Ruthie, I don't want to upset anybody. They've been real nice to me since I arrived." He pulled his hand out of my grip.

"Nonsense, sweetheart, if they're upset, it's not our fault." I followed a trickle of perspiration drop from his side-burn to run down his jawline. "My goodness, you weren't this nervous when you popped the question."

Liv had delivered the summons. *Please meet with The Council at our next meeting on October 15th at 3:00 p.m. at Wanda's to discuss your marriage plans.*

After my talk with Liv I expected it, but it still irked me and now Al's behavior added to my exasperation.

Ever since I'd told him, he had been jittery.

"I'm afraid, Ruthie."

"What of?"

"This is the only home I've had. I don't want to lose it."

"They can't make us leave." I gripped his hand again. "We live in a free country."

I stopped at Wanda's door, brushed down my skirt, patted my hair then inspected Al's appearance. He'd shaved and wore a fresh-laundered white shirt with a tie. Presentable. I grinned. "Don't worry, sweetheart." Ready to get this over with, I knocked.

Wanda invited us into the front room where the Council members sat staring at us. I returned the appraisals, and jutted out my chin before sitting in one of two kitchen chairs placed in front of the members. Inquisition chairs I thought, then smiled at the fantastic notion.

Grace, the mayor, spoke, "Thank you for meeting with us. Liv reported your news to us. Is it correct you are planning to marry?"

Al cleared his throat. "Yes, Ma'am. Ruthie agreed to be my wife. We'd be happy to have your blessing."

I clutched his hand, pulling it into my lap. "But it's not required."

The Council members' eyes locked onto me as one. Grace spoke. "It may not be required, but you know how things stand here. Our duty, by resolution, is to honor the memories of our Lost Boys. It is the Council's responsibility to make sure the citizens of Weeping Women Springs carry out this responsibility.

"It seems contrary to our duty," Eva Soderlund crossed her arms, "that you would wish to marry."

"Some have indicated that it represents a certain forgetfulness of your obligation to honor Joe's memory." This came from Wanda who gave Mary a sidelong look.

Mary wiped her nose, as if ready to burst into tears. I bit the inside of my lip to keep from offering my sympathies. For more than a dozen years I'd tried to comfort her, but it was never enough.

Al stood. "Mary, it's not my intention to dishonor Joe's memory, or to bring any distress to you. Joe was my buddy. If you think my marrying Ruth would go against your wishes or what he would have wanted, well—"

"Just a minute, Al." My chest tightened. It wasn't supposed to happen like this. These women wouldn't stop me from attaining my goal. I *would* marry Al. "We're not doing anything wrong. We love one another, and wish to marry. End of story."

He sat again and took my hand. "Honey, if it would bother people too much, we can wait."

"Wait for what? Nothing will change. It hasn't changed since the war." Something inside me slipped. I lifted my chin, certain what they wanted to hear. "Joe will always have a place in my heart. I will never forget him, or neglect his memory. I'll hold meditation for him each day, honor him at the Commemorations, and tend his grave. Al will do this also. Our marriage will not be a time of forgetting Joe, but a way for us to honor him. I believe in my heart that Joe would be happy for us. In some way, he brought us together." Refusing to flinch, I met each woman's gaze.

"It will be up to the Council to make the final decision," Grace said.

"What's to decide?" I asked.

"Whether it's appropriate to allow you and Al to remain in Weeping Women Springs."

"Remain? I've told you, it will not change anything to have us marry."

Grace pressed her lips together.

My aunt, Anna Frolander gasped. Her grief was carved into the lines on her face, layered in her all white hair. "If Liv was engaged to Donnie and now wanted to marry Wilson, I'd have to object. This doesn't keep their memory sacred. You are being completely selfish. There is no room in someone's heart as you say to hold two men in the same regard. Either you hold the memory of Joe sacred, or you marry. One or the other. We grieve for our sons, brothers, nephews and friends. There is no place for a new beginning."

The Council members rumbled in agreement.

I searched their faces for compassion—the same thing Liv accused me of lacking.

Liv's fists crumpled her skirt. All around the room the women displayed various expressions of hurt, anger and sorrow. Never since I left my Hollywood dreams on the backlot in Hollywood had I faced the utter desolation and hopelessness that filled the room.

No one moved.

"Let's go." I jerked on Al's hand and started toward the door. "They aren't willing to listen."

Al remained in his seat, removing his hand. "Ladies, this is my home. Since you allowed me to stay, I've felt a peace and belonging I'd never thought I'd find. I'd be grateful if you allowed me to stay."

I opened my mouth and closed it again. Desperate, I returned to my chair and cupped his cheek. "Al, stop. Think about what you're saying. The Council is refusing to allow us to stay if we marry."

"I know, Ruthie. If it means I have to leave town, well. . . I love you, but this is my home."

"No." My voice cracked. It was like I didn't know him after all these months we'd shared. I fled the room.

Anna's Journal

July 15, 1955

Putting one foot in front of the other has become a difficult task most days, but to keep up appearances for the others, I never neglect my mail collection chore every Monday. We each take our turn, be sure the mail gets to those who need it and check to make sure the road is still covered. Today was my day, my final day for the mail collection I think. They never guess that some days I never rise from bed. Those days my sister or niece don't check in I rarely get up or eat. Soon I may choose to stay there forever. Maybe tomorrow. No one will miss me. My sister would be free to go to her husband at last, and Ruth would leave to marry her young man, no longer held back by me or the Council. My death will be best for all.

In the late afternoon I pushed a wheelbarrow over the rough track. The hour's round trip to the road lengthens with each trip. Every one of my sixty two years pressed down on my shoulders, and I stopped often to stretch creaking joints and take a sip of water from the thermos. I didn't rush. No sense in it these days—not much mail arrives except for Susie's news magazines and occasional catalog mail orders for other residents.

Intent on maneuvering the wheelbarrow, I almost bumped into the stranger seated against the lock box. "Who are you?"

The man roused, shaded his eyes and tilted his head toward me. His voice rasped, with a German accent. "Weeping Women Springs?"

"Who are you? How do you know Weeping Women Springs?" My mind couldn't grasp anything except the German accent.

He ran a tongue his lips. "Please, water."

"Not until you tell me who you are and what you're doing here." I gripped the handles of the wheelbarrow so hard my nails dug into the wood.

"Werner." His chin sank to his chest then.

"My God, you're one of them. A Nazi. Aren't you?"

"War ist over. Long ago." The horrible man had the nerve to claim

"Not for me. It's never over. You people killed my sons."

"Please, water."

I spat on the ground. "No. Never will I help a German. A Nazi." I rounded the wheelbarrow and headed back. No mail today. I wouldn't spend another moment with that Nazi.

"Wait," his voice called.

Bile clogged my throat. To think that man lived and my sons died fighting the Nazis. Then because of his brothers, my poor Eddie enlisted in the Korean War. No. The man could wither away in the sun far from water or hope. This small act I could do for my sons.

Anger gave me energy, the walk back to the village went quickly.

Maxine swept a small billow of dust out the front door of the store. She waved at me. "No mail today?"

"I wouldn't give the time of day to a Nazi, much less a drop of water. So no mail today." The fiery words sprang out of my mouth.

"Are you all right, Anna?"

"No I'm not fine, nothing is fine. He got what he deserved."

"Who?"

"Who?" My mind went blank then. Nothing made sense. Why was I here in the road? "Um, I need to get home. Yes, home."

Maxine asked if she could help, but I told her, no just take the wheelbarrow back to Peggy.

I continued on to my house. Once in the front yard, my hands shook so violently I could hardly open the door. On warm days like this the child ghosts screeched as they sprayed one another with the hose. Eddie and Melvin, inseparable friends, chortled. I called to them, but they didn't come to dinner. When I entered the house the altar with the three purple candles called to me. Then I remembered. Eddie wouldn't be home for dinner. Melvin either. They weren't playing in the yard. They died far away just like Sam and Donnie. All dead. Soon I would join them. I lit the candles. The flames wavered, flickering over the photographs of my boys. Confusion melted away, and now I know what I must do.

Chapter Thirty

Liv

IT'S SOMETHING I'LL never forget, coming home from my trip to Cruces and finding the stranger. The '48 Packard station wagon rumbled, bouncing us along the road. I nudged the accelerator another increment wanting to make it back to the village before nightfall. The mountains were dark shadows in the moonlight when we arrived at the turn off. I almost missed the dark shadowed form slouched against the mailbox.

I stopped the car. "Who's that?"

"I hope it's not whoever collects the mail today." Wilson got out.

I swung my door open. "It's Monday, so that would be Anna Frolander."

"It's a man," he said.

"Who? Doc?" I worried about Doc Brennen since he was getting older, but he refused to cut back on seeing patients or his daily walks, or his daily whiskey.

Wilson knelt beside the man. "I don't recognize him."

"Is he okay?"

"He's out cold." Wilson placed fingers at the man's neck. "His pulse is pretty weak. He's burning up."

"Let me help you get him in the car. We'll have to put him in the front seat between us."

We hefted the man and half carried, half dragged him to the car.

I started the engine. "You think he's a hitchhiker, like Grant?"

"Doesn't seem so. He doesn't have a backpack. Looks like he just has the clothes on his back."

The man didn't look well. No sign of a canteen or water container. He must not be from around here. Desert dwellers know better than to take off without water.

The man mumbled, seeming to rouse himself. "Water." It came out sounding more like *wasser.* He had a German accent.

Wilson reached in the back for our emergency canteen. He tipped it against the man's lips, but more dribbled down his shirt.

The man spoke again. "Weeping Women Springs?"

Wilson met my eyes over the stranger's head. "How do you suppose he knows about Weeping Women Springs?"

"I have no idea. I've never seen him before." I drove up Main Street. "Should we take him to Doc's?"

"Yeah. I think so. He's in bad shape from what I can see."

"Maxine," the man croaked.

I wasn't sure if he had regained consciousness or spoke in delirium. "Did he just say Maxine?" I braked the car to a stop.

His eyes sprang open. "Maxine."

"You know Maxine Fiekens?"

The man's face registered recognition. "Please, I may see Maxine?"

Wilson curled his lips. "Guess that's our answer as to where to take him."

"But doesn't he need medical attention?"

"Please," the man's voice scratched.

"Okay." I parked at the store. We draped the man's arms over our shoulders and hitched him into the store.

Chapter Thirty-One

Maxine

"MAXINE," LIV CALLED from outside. "Come quick."

"Just a second, let me finish wiping up in here," I shouted from the storeroom. "I'll help you unload the car."

"Now!"

I wondered what the hurry was, but tossed the rag onto the shelf. "All right. What's the urgency?"

Inside the door they supported a man between them. They leaned him against the stool, and Liv ducked out from under his arm. "He asked to see you. He needs Doc, so I'm going to get him. Wilson and I will be right back." She hurried back out the door.

The man slumped on the counter.

"Who is he?" I asked, but Liv and Wilson were already gone.

I approached the man. He looked up at me, his face sunburned and wrinkled but filthy, just like the first time I saw him at the Spring over a decade ago. His white teeth flashed inside a smile. "Mein Angel of the Spring."

I reached out a tentative hand to his unshaven cheek. "No, it can't be. Werner?"

He nodded, but the effort seemed to require more energy than he possessed. Keeping himself upright proved too much of a struggle, and he slid to the floor. I tried to support him, but failed.

I crouched beside him. "Are you okay?"

"Water, please?"

I rushed to the faucet and returned with a glass of water. In the moment I was away, he'd slipped further. He lay prone on the linoleum. "Werner?" I held the glass to his lips, but he didn't open them.

"Oh, my Lord. Werner?" I lifted his head to my lap. "Please, talk to me. Wake up."

I shook him gently and then a little harder, but received no response. After all this time why did he come here? I searched his pocket and found a wallet. Was he breathing? I couldn't tell. I leaned my ear to his chest. When I heard a soft breath, I closed my eyes. "Please, Liv, hurry."

A little while later Liv rushed in ahead of Doc and Wilson.

"Doc, he's passed out." I slipped the wallet into my apron.

Doc moved slower, he was about sixty-five by then, but he bent over the patient, grasped his wrist and held a stethoscope to his chest. "We may be too late. I'm not hearing a pulse."

"No!" The word screeched out of me.

"Lay him flat. I'll try something I've just read about. It's something pretty new, mentioned in a journal I read, but—"

I scooted out from under his head and laid it gently on the floor.

Doc knelt at his side, pinched his nose and blew a breath into him. He thumped the man's chest and continued pressing, lifting, pressing in a rhythm.

"What's wrong with him, Doc?" Liv asked.

"From what you said, and looking at his face, I'd say he's dehydrated. Doesn't take long in our desert sun, especially if he had any kind of medical trouble." He pinched the nose again and blew.

I rose. No one spoke for the next few minutes. Only the sound of Doc taking breaths and blowing into Werner's chest broke the silence. I backed away, hugging my arms tight around my stomach, but my gaze never left Werner.

After a few more breaths, Doc checked his pulse again. "Nothing. I'm afraid it's no use. He's gone."

The silence jangled my nerves, gave me time to think. "Mrs. Frolander. She did this, but I didn't understand. If I'd only known what she was talking about."

Liv put an arm around me. "Max, what are you talking about?"

Holding back sobs, I said, "Several hours ago Mrs. Frolander came by talking about Nazis. I didn't pay her much mind. You know how confused she is sometimes, but she said something about not giving a drop of water. She must have seen him when she went for the mail."

"I'm not understanding." Liv drew me to the end of the counter.

"I don't either. Why would she do such a thing? Is this what it's come to, attacking strangers?" Impossible, and yet, Werner lay dead on my floor.

Wilson hovered next to us. "I'm not sure I'd call it an attack. We don't know what happened for sure."

Doc asked for a blanket. "Just something to cover him with."

I left to retrieve it and remembered the afghan I laid over him on his visit. When I returned, Liv and Wilson sat at the counter and talked, trying to sort out the events.

Doc joined their speculations. When they didn't seem any closer to answers, he said, "I searched for a wallet, but I didn't find one. No identification at all that I could see. I'll have to notify the county sheriff we have a John Doe."

Liv clicked her fingernail on her front tooth, thinking. "Do we really need to do that right away? I think we should talk to Mrs. Frolander. We need to investigate further. We don't want to get anyone in trouble, do we?"

"No," Doc answered, "but it's my job to make sure the proper procedures are followed."

"And it's my job to make sure Weeping Women Springs is protected." Liv swiveled her stool. "Max, how did this man know you?"

I shook my head, but couldn't speak. Werner had been my secret for so long. I fingered the wallet in her apron pocket. Now wasn't the time to share that encounter as it would cause more questions than it would answer. I held the memory to me. Why had he come back? Perhaps he had returned my feelings even after all this time. The thought brought a flash of heat to my cheeks.

"Talk to Mrs. Frolander." I waved them off, everything was too much. I needed to think. "She might know something."

"I guess we'll have to," Liv agreed. "Wilson, will you come with me?"

He shook a thumb toward the door. "Should we unload the car first?"

Doc picked up his medical bag. "I guess we should get help to move the body. Get him into the car and take it over to my office."

"You're right, Wilson. Let's unload the car, take this man to Doc's, and then we can check on Mrs. Frolander. Max, would you go tell Grant and Al to come over? I guess you'd better not tell them what for—they'll see soon enough."

I couldn't take my eyes off Werner and I knelt beside him. From far away I heard Liv's voice, but it didn't register until Liv touched my arm.

"Max, did you hear me?"

I jerked. "Yes, I'll get Grant and Al." With a last glance at Werner's covered body, I headed outside. The hot breeze swept the lingering fog from my mind. I hurried to both Al and Grant, explaining they were needed at the store.

"What's going on?" Grant stepped out of his office and closed the door.

"I need some help."

"I suppose they need some help unloading," he said, and I didn't correct him.

Back at the store the three of us met Wilson unpacking the car. The men each took an armful of goods and trudged to the storeroom. Al stopped and stared at the body on the floor.

Liv came in from the back hall. "Oh good, you're both here. We need help getting him over to Doc's."

"Who is he?" asked Grant.

"We don't know," Liv said. "He was out by the mailbox. Wilson, is the car empty now?"

"Yes. This is the last of it." He set a box on the counter.

The air around me shimmered in a long tunnel. I opened my eyes, confused as my cheek was resting on the floor. "What happened?"

Doc knelt beside me. "Looks like you've fainted, young lady."

"I'm sorry. I don't know—"

"You've had a shock. Grant, will you help me get her somewhere to lie down?"

"There's a sofa in my office. But I can walk." I rose up on my elbows and braced myself on Grant's arm. When I stood, my legs felt weak.

"Hey, Maxine, you don't seem too steady. Let me carry you."

"I hate to be such a bother."

"It's no problem. Let me help." He lifted me, strode into the office and laid me on the couch.

Doc hovered over me, took my pulse and such. "Doesn't seem to be anything serious, but you need to take it easy. You stay here. Rest. Sleep if you can."

"But—"

"No buts, Max." Liv handed me a glass of water. "We'll take care of things, and I'll see you in a little while. Try to rest."

I closed my eyes. I should tell them something. What was it? Oh, Werner. I should tell Liv, but as soon as the thought occurred, it disappeared once more. I drifted to sleep, dreaming of blue eyes sparkling in the sunlight.

Anna's Journal

Undated Entry

Dickinson said death kindly stopped
I hoped he'd stop for me
He stays so far from me
when I, with open arms spread wide,
invite him to my breast
begging him to embrace me
with his cold heat.
So exhausted from
the battle of my soul
am I.

Chapter Thirty-Two

Liv

BY THE TIME WE RETURNED with Doc, the poor man was gone. After Maxine fainted, I grew more curious about her relationship with him, but went with the men to Doc's.

Once they moved the body, I drew Wilson aside. "We need to go talk to Anna."

We walked up the street to her house. "This shouldn't take too long. I appreciate you coming with me." I knocked.

When Anna opened the door, she was tying the belt of her robe. "What in the world?"

"I'm sorry to disturb you so late, but something's happened, and we think you may know something about it."

"What? I was just lying down to sleep." Her tone scolded as if I should know better.

"A man was out at the mailbox this evening. Did you see him earlier?"

She looked confused. "Man? Who?"

I widened my eyes at Wilson, wondering if he had an idea of how to get through to her. "We don't know his name. He's a stranger."

"I'm sure I wouldn't know him. No men, none in town, none here, no men." Her ramblings were worse than ever.

"No. You probably wouldn't, but you went to collect the mail didn't you?"

"Is it Monday?" Her brow furrowed.

Wilson touched her arm. "It's Monday. Did you see anyone when you collected the mail?"

"Mail, no mail. Someone needs to get the mail. Dirty Nazi." Anna's mumblings grew almost incoherent.

"Yes, he was German, that's him." I nodded. "Did he say anything?"

"Just asked for water," she said.

"And?" I prodded.

In a firm clear voice, Anna said, "Didn't give it to him." Her lips twisted. "Wouldn't cross the street to spit on a Nazi. Why would I give him water?"

"He died." Wilson said, his tone somber.

Anna recoiled, and then shrugged. "It's not my fault. He should have had water with him."

"Your actions could bring the authorities here," I warned. "The Council will have to be notified. I'll let you know if they require your presence. I'm not sure, since you're a member of the Council."

Anna shook her head. "I have nothing to apologize for. Let the Council do what they will." She slammed the door.

"I know she's been hurt." I couldn't fathom what I'd just heard. "But I never would have guessed she'd do something so sinister."

"Maybe she didn't realize how bad a state he was in."

The warm night air didn't stop the coldness that ran through me. "That's just it. I think she knew and did this deliberately. To me, that amounts to murder. Let's see what the Council has to say about it. I'll notify them in the morning."

The following morning heat singed the earth early, promising record temperatures. I was up early and notified the Council members that a situation needed their attention, and they gathered at Aunt Wanda's house at ten o'clock.

The fluttering of hand fans rippled a gentle movement of air around the Council table.

Grace called the meeting to order, then asked, "Where's Anna?"

"Since this is about her, perhaps she wanted to sit this one out," I said.

"We would ask her to abstain from voting of course," Grace said. "But it's highly irregular not to have all members present. We should send for her."

"Why don't we conduct a hearing of the situation first?" Mary suggested. "If we need to, we'll call her in later."

The members' eyes landed on me. "A man, we still don't know his name, was found at the road into town yesterday." I explained what happened. "Anna says she didn't give him water, and Doc says he died as a result of dehydration."

A collective gasp chased by disbelieving murmurs followed my statement.

"You're kidding." Grace said. "Anna didn't give a thirsty man water? That doesn't sound like her. I don't believe she'd do such a thing."

"I'm afraid that's exactly what she told me last evening when I asked what happened."

"But why?" Wanda asked.

"She says it's because he was a Nazi," I said.

The clock's ticking drew attention to the quiet.

"Will the war never leave us alone?" Mary said. "It's been over ten years and it still haunts us. Not only our grief, but now this a new horror. One of our own commits this heinous act."

"It's unspeakable." Wanda rubbed her forehead. "What, if anything, should the Council do?"

"Doc says he needs to contact the sheriff," I said. "I'm concerned for Anna's welfare and the town's. What if reporters come? Anna doesn't deserve to go through that, not after losing three sons. I'm sure she wasn't in her right mind."

"I still can't believe she did it on purpose," Grace said.

"I told her to be available to speak to the Council," I said. "Do you want me to get her?"

"We'll have to talk with her—hear her side of the story," Wanda said.

"She's also a member of this Council, so she should be present," Grace repeated her earlier concern.

"That's something else." Mary raised a point. "Perhaps we should remove her from the Council—if she admits she did it."

Wanda met the eyes of each woman. "Should we consider turning her over to the authorities?"

"I'd hate to see that happen." I drummed her fingers on the table, thinking. "We've made Weeping Women Springs a sanctuary. If we bring in the authorities, others could be at risk. Think about Grant, we don't know if they'd prosecute him after all this time."

Wanda gave me a tight smile. "That's why we've appointed you Guardian. You think of things like that, by looking at the whole picture and the whole town's situation, rather than the individual pieces."

"That said, I don't think we can just let this go and sweep it under the rug," I said.

"Go, fetch Anna." Wanda pointed to the door. "We need to speak with her before going any further."

I followed my aunt's instructions. Everything could change so quickly. My job: protecting the townspeople, dealing with the Outside, all weighted my steps. Anger rose up in my tight chest against the stranger for daring to disturb our peaceful village. No one asked him to come. His whispered, 'Maxine' echoed in my ears. How could he know Maxine? She never left town and we had no visitors. It must be a coincidence, but Maxine's actions of the previous evening weren't those of a distant stranger. She'd been visibly upset. A flutter of a crow's wings drew me back to the present.

At Anna's door, I received no answer to my knock so I opened it. "Anna?"

No response. "Hello?" The house remained silent. I checked the kitchen and then the bedroom.

What met me there, a pale face lying against the pillow made me gasp. Blood soaked the bedding and a razor lay on the floor. I rushed to Anna's bed. "Are you all right?"

Anna rolled her head. "I'm feeling a might peaked. Just don't have the energy to get up." Her breath came in a rattled whistle.

"I need to get Doc."

"Hate to bother him." She let her head flop to the other side. "I'll just sleep a while."

Anna's chest rose and fell slower and slower. Then stopped. I shook her gently. "Anna?"

A crow landed at the sill of the window and pecked at the glass. *Caw.*

I STARED, DISBELIEVING. Not sure how much time passed before I went to Doc's. "It's Anna. I'm afraid she just died," I reported what had happened.

Doc's bushy eyebrows drew together. "Can't say I'm surprised. I've been worried for years this might happen. I've tried talking to her, suggested she go to Cruces get some help, but she refused. The psychologists would say it was depression. Poor woman, she suffered every day."

"I knew she was sad like the rest of us, but I never guessed she might do this. I'll inform the Council. We'll probably never know the answer of what happened with the stranger yesterday."

I returned to Aunt Wanda's dining room where hand fans still fluttered. "Doc's going to verify it," I said after explaining how I'd found Anna.

The women expelled a collective moan.

With a voice on the edge of breaking, Wanda said, "We'll adjourn for now."

"Don't we need to decide to do something about the stranger? At least tell Doc what to do?" I asked.

Grace stood. "In my opinion, the stranger should be buried and forgotten. We don't know who he is, why he was here, or where he was going. Nothing will be gained by bringing in the outside authorities. Besides, Anna's memory deserves to be treated with respect. She sacrificed everything for this country. If she wasn't in her right mind at the end, well, I'd sure not like to have her memory sullied for an act done while in that state." She reached for her purse.

"But what about Doc's coroner report?" Wanda asked.

"Why not just say it was natural causes?" I said. "That's not being untruthful. Doc said that she was depressed. As for the stranger, the same would apply, he was dehydrated."

"We'll hold separate services for Anna and the stranger," said Wanda.

TWO DAYS LATER AL and Grant dug the graves at The Weeping Place. I stood with Maxine alongside the men at the stranger's graveside.

"How should we mark the grave?" I asked.

Maxine bit her thumb.

"Maybe just a simple cross," Al said.

Maxine stumbled away, and fell to her knees.

I stroked her back. "What's wrong? You've been acting strange ever since this happened. Are you okay?"

Maxine dragged a hand over her mouth. "Ever since what happened?"

"The stranger, well..." I assisted her to stand. "Since the stranger died at the store."

"I—I don't remember any stranger." Maxine spoke slow and steady.

I gritted my teeth until my jaw ached. Not Maxine too? She sounded a little like Anna. Maxine didn't lie. She had swept the event from her mind. Somehow the stranger's death stole something from her that not even Billy's death took all those years ago could take.

I patted her arm. "Let's get you home."

"I need to get some roses for Billy." Maxine approached his grave and ran her hand across the marble etched with his name. "How could I have forgotten?"

"It's getting warm. Why don't I take you home and we can do this later, when it cools off a little?"

"I miss my Billy."

"I know, hon. Let's go." Gently, I drew her away.

Chapter Thirty-Three

Ruth

TRAGEDY, EVERYTHING IN THIS TOWN was tragic. Aunt Anna's death almost destroyed my mother, but never one to give up, I took the opportunity to remind her of things that were possible.

"Mama, you can go be with Papa. His letter last week said he got the manager's position at the Bank of New Mexico. I know he won't ask, but he would be happy to have you finally join him. There's really nothing to keep you here."

I didn't add only one thing prevented me from leaving. Al Caldarelli. The man wormed his way into my heart deeper than any other, and I refused to give up on us.

After our meeting with the Council the year before when they objected to our marrying, I must say I doubted his true feelings, but not two days went by before he knocked on my door.

Dark circles under his reddened eyes confirmed I wasn't the only one not sleeping.

"Ruthie, we need to talk. He reached for my hand.

I avoided his grasp, not wanting the distraction of his touch. "I don't know why you think you need to talk to me now. You seemed more concerned with what everyone else thought than me. That hurt." I blinked away the moisture in my eyes.

"Please? I've missed you. Can we talk?"

Reluctantly, I let him lead me to the field outside of town, the site of the last night before Joe left. Does it ever feel like important events in your life have a thread? Well, mine did. Anyway, we were careful since it wouldn't do to have anyone see us since who knew what the Council might do. "Al Caldarelli, why are you—"

"Sh." He put a finger on my lips. "Let me just look at you." His dark gaze traveled over me, and my skin tingled in awareness. He squeezed my shoulder, then lifted my chin.

"You're the best girl a man could have. I'm sorry for what I said at the meeting. For the last two nights I haven't slept."

"Me either."

His mouth drew closer and he moved his lips over mine. Butterflies skittered through my stomach. I hugged him tight. Finally, he understood we were meant to be together.

For several minutes we stood kissing, embracing. Then he backed away.

"What's wrong?"

"Nothing, not now. It's only that I need you, honey."

I threaded my fingers through his and sat in the grass, pulling him down with me.

"I'm yours," I said, and put my arms around his shoulders.

A long while later I left him in the field, his arms cradling his head and grinning.

By the time I got back to the house, the sun had slipped over the mountains. I had no doubts about his feelings any longer and I knew before long we would have our wedding.

Months passed. We sneaked out to the field every chance we got, but he never mentioned a wedding. Whenever I brought it up, he put me off. It's not a good time at the ranch. Let's wait until the weather cools, or warms. He always had a reason. Lost in our stolen moments, I didn't catch on at first.

The heat of July came and still Al made no move to set a date. I made excuses for him, saying it had only been a short time, but finally I couldn't ignore the obvious.

A week before Anna died I met him up on the cliff above the Spring.

I fingered the buttons of his shirt, teasing the little hairs on his chest. "Al, I've always wanted a fall wedding. Do you think it's time to get our invitations ordered?"

He captured my wrist. "You've never said anything about this before. I thought you understood. With things the way they are with the Council, we can't flaunt our relationship. I want to marry you, but I don't want to leave town."

"Even after what we mean to each other? You can't expect me to live like this, not at my age. I'm ready to leave Weeping Women Springs. I have a life to live and so do you. We're stuck in this place and it's doing neither of us any good."

"You want to leave town?" He squinted, as if that might make things clearer for him. "I never really thought you were serious about leaving. Your mother's here and your aunt, and me. I thought we were doing just fine."

"Fine?" I kept my voice level, but I wanted to screech at him. "This is not fine, we aren't fine. We have to sneak off to be together. It's not okay. Not by anybody's standard. I love you, Al. I thought you loved me too. Maybe what they say about not buying the cow when you can get the milk free is true. I shouldn't have given you any milk." I jumped up and hurried down the path.

I waited for the sound of his footsteps racing to catch me. They didn't come. That evening I wrote a letter to my father, asking if I could stay with him.

Before I received a reply, Anna died and not two days after that Al came to see me again.

I almost slammed the door in his face, but he stuck his foot in to block it.

"Ruthie, I know you're mad. Forgive me? Please? I just can't stand not seeing you, not having you."

I went outside, not wanting my mother to overhear us. "It's over. I'm going to Albuquerque."

With a sigh, he lowered his head, only to lift it again. "All right. I understand. Everything that happened over the last couple days, well it's changed my thinking. Maybe it takes a tragedy to bring us together, or tear us apart. I'm sure sorry about Anna, Ruthie."

"Yeah, me too. I don't want to become like her."

He half laughed at that. "Never, Ruthie. You're too strong. Stubborn true, but strong. You just might be the bravest person in this whole place. I'm not sure I'm that brave."

This sweet man who had faced an enemy, and endured the bitterest cold, how could he doubt his bravery? It didn't make sense.

The proverbial lightbulb went on in my mind. "Is that why you don't want to leave town?"

He didn't answer.

People around here have called me selfish, and maybe I was, but if I knew one thing, it was that you made your own way. Sometimes people needed help, but you had to make the choice, you had to choose to move. It was that time for me. After Joe died, I chose to go to California. It didn't help Joe, and it didn't work out, but I moved. When I came home from Hollywood, I took comfort in having a place to lick my wounds, but it was time to move again with or without Al, it was time.

I touched his arm. "I can't make a choice for you. I love you, but you have to choose whether you want to stay in Weeping Women Springs, or go forward and make a life somewhere else with me by your side. We can go to Albuquerque or anywhere, it doesn't matter to me, but I choose life, not to be surrounded by death. Not anymore."

"Could we go to the Spring? I need a drink and the water helps me think."

"Sure, just so you know, I'm not changing my mind."

"Ruthie, I know you." He put his arm around my shoulders. "Once you get your mind set on something it's going to happen."

We went to the Spring and Al took a long drink. When he offered me the ladle, I sipped. The cool water tasted fresh, unlike the saltiness I'd tasted since the war. For the first time in so long, the heaviness lifted off my chest. My choice was right. Somehow being able to let something, well someone go, opened up more possibilities. Yes, Al might choose to stay here, but my choice was right for me.

While I waited for Al to speak, I absorbed the peacefulness. Several quail scurried among the rose bushes. A little bunny hopped out from behind a rock. All this life existed in a place that dwelled on death. I'd never taken notice before. I reclined on the grass and closed my eyes.

Al put his arm under my head and held me, but didn't say anything for a long time. He sometimes has a tendency to chatter, but not that day. When he finally spoke, I twisted to look at his face and saw a tranquility there that I hadn't seen since he took his first drink of the Spring.

"Ruthie, in your arms I feel warm. I want you to know that. I'd be all kinds of stupid if I didn't snuggle up to that heat and take all you have to give. I need you more than this town, that's the truth of it."

"Does that mean?"

"Yes, if you'll still have me for your husband, we'll go wherever you like."

I smothered his face with kisses. "Oh my, of course, I'll have you."

When I returned home, I told Mama the good news. "You'll come with us of course. We're going to Albuquerque."

"I'm not sure I can leave. I've lived in this house for thirty-five years. We can't just leave it all."

Taking her hand, I led her to the sofa. "What's more important, your things, or being with Papa?"

Her gaze scanned the room, the furniture, paintings, crystal, all the things that made our house a home.

"Mama, we don't have to take much. I'm sure Papa will take care of it. Why don't we just pack the very best things? The art, china, silver and some clothes we must take, but the furniture can be left."

She studied me. "My Ruthie, you've grown up into a lovely woman. You're right. What's important is not in this house, it's in our hearts."

"We've needed this for a while. I'll go get some boxes."

Her hand kept me from leaving. "Who will tend the graves for Anna, Sam, Donnie, and Eddie? Who will light the candles?"

"Mama, they're gone. The Commemorations, the Weeping Place, all of that is for the living, not the dead. We're alive. Can't we say prayers for them from wherever we are?"

The melancholy I'd seen on her that we'd lived with for so long lifted with her smile. A sad smile, but it was a start, a new beginning.

The car, loaded down with boxes and crates, left barely enough room for Mama in the backseat, but we managed. We drove out of town, around the barrier and out onto the main road. I didn't even look in the mirror to watch Weeping Women Springs fade into the distance. Instead I looked down the open road, toward our future.

Chapter Thirty-Four

Susie

ALMOST A DECADE HAD PASSED with no definitive word on Eddie. People thought I was crazy to keep up the vigil, but when you don't know for sure, hope reigns, at least mine did. Most women my age were either married or had finished college and then married.

I made do with the library books Liv brought from town, and I spent most of my time reading news magazines. More news came about the Cold War. The Russians and Cuba all scared me. They tested the first nuclear bomb not far from here. Just because Weeping Women Springs was out in the middle of Nowhere, New Mexico didn't mean we were safer.

I visited Mary, she was the only one still left to talk to about Eddie and Melvin besides my mother. When Ruth left I made a point to go more often. After Anna died, we all took a special interest in making sure no one else suffered the same fate.

Poor Anna, I still blame myself for not seeing the signs. The night before she died, she knocked on our door and asked my mother to see me.

I came downstairs. It was late and I'd been about ready to head to bed. Anna obviously planned to do the same as she wore her robe. Her disheveled hair should have been a clue to her state of mind.

She thrust something at me, a thick little book, and then another. "These are for you. You're the only one who could possibly understand." She touched my cheek with an icy hand. "You've loved the written word as much as I ever did. I'd have been completely lost long before now if I hadn't had my writing and my books. It's time someone besides me read them. Because you live and fly through words, accept this without judgement."

"What is it?" In the dim candlelight I couldn't make anything out, but inside I saw the pen marks of handwriting. "Is this what I think it is?"

"My journals a few of my scribblings. The remnant thread of my life and someone who cares should have such a thing."

She gave me a hug, unusual in itself and left. That was the last I saw of her, her bathrobe flaring behind her trailing in the dusty street,

The glimpses into her mind and life, the town and its decisions were just a few of the words on those pages. The words she left behind, though I didn't know it at the time, became a profound insight into her world and ours both Weeping Women Springs and beyond. I want to share the journals with you, because you may find them useful in your project. I think Anna would like that. It's all part of our story, which is what we wanted you to tell.

Anyway, as I was saying, after Anna's death our lives returned to normal, I suppose. I spent my time visiting Mary Bauer or going to the Gatherings working on one project or another.

One day, while out at the Bauer Ranch, I ran into Grant. I avoided him whenever possible, even at the Commemorations. I'm not proud of my feelings, but I couldn't get past the fact he deserted. When other boys did their duty, died for their country, Grant ran. It wasn't fair that someone like him lived while Eddie and Melvin didn't. Then I immediately backtracked the thought, telling myself Eddie still lived. Couldn't he be a POW and out there somewhere dreaming of home?

Outside the barn, Grant was stroking a recently born foal in the corral. The animal, so adorable, played by bounding toward Grant and then to his mother, then back again. I leaned on the fence to watch his antics.

Grant came over. I'd still describe his movement as sauntering, yet I sensed energy just below the surface. "Hey, he's a cutie isn't he?"

"When was he born? I knew she was due."

"Yesterday, about sunset. I came by to check on him and his mom." He didn't look at me, just the animals, which gave me the chance to observe him.

He pushed back his hat and the light fell on his face, tanned and even to an uninterested party such as me, he could be called handsome with his blond hair and brown eyes.

Maybe he felt me staring because he turned quickly and smiled. "Do you ride?"

"No. Well not in a long while."

"Would you like to? The horses could use a little gallop." Far from being cocky and offensive as he was the first time I met him, the friendly invitation tempted me.

"Not these horses I assume." I laughed, wondering where my good humor came from and reminded myself to take care.

"No, there's a couple in the other corral. Come on."

"I really shouldn't. Mary—"

"Is just fine, she's fixing supper. I told her I'd stay to eat. Why don't you go say hi and I'll get the horses saddled. Meet me here in fifteen."

He left without waiting for my response. I watched him saunter away. No matter how friendly and good looking he was, I determined to remain distant. Riding reminded me of Eddie, I hadn't been on a horse since before he left for Korea.

At the house, I gave Mary a hug and apologized that I wouldn't be staying to visit.

"That's great. You should go. You're way too young to be cooped up with your books all the time or with an old lady like me. I'm fixing plenty of food so you go on your ride and you and Grant can eat when you get back. We'll have time for a nice visit then."

"You sure? I can stay and help you around the house if you need it." I half hoped I could get out of going with him. Being alone with a man, especially Grant, made me nervous. "I don't think he likes me much anyway, but I don't blame him."

"Nonsense, child. I think he might have a little spark for you. He's a respectful young man, and has a good head on his shoulders."

"I don't need a spark, you should know that." I frowned before agreeing. "I guess it won't do any harm."

"Go on, have fun. It's been a long while since you've ridden the horses."

Back outside I paced. What would we talk about? I doubted he knew much about world happenings. He just didn't seem that interested in anything outside of the animals from what little I gathered about him. Our previous interaction left me thinking he was out for a good time. Maybe the animals would be a safe topic.

Grant approached the barn, the horses following behind, one the white stallion, Spirit, and the second the brown gelding I'd named years ago, Santiago. Though dusty from his work, Grant's face was strong, his body lean and muscular, a likely result from lifting hay bales and exercising the animals. All things told, a nice looking fellow, much as I hated to admit it. I gave myself a mental scolding and tried to hold Eddie's memory close in my mind. It was something I did frequently, always imagining him as a hero in my books. Many of the women in town said their memories of their loved ones had faded over time, but I never had that problem.

"Why the scowl?" Grant asked.

"I haven't ridden in years." The falsehood came easily. I'd never acknowledge he was the subject of my discomfort, not the horses.

"It's like riding a bike and you'll feel fine once you're back in the saddle."

The refrain of the old song playing on the radio hit me. I was just a kid back then, and my father played the Grand Ole Opry every Saturday. The memory took me back before the pain, before I knew what war was, what longing was, back when the only trouble we knew was the Council's disapproval of that same radio. Rather than dwell on nostalgic times which would never happen again, I pushed the song out of my thoughts.

I patted the nose of my old friend. "Hey, Santiago. You ready to ride? I bet it's quite some time for both of us." Lifting my leg as far as I could, I still didn't reach the stirrup. Before I could ask, Grant linked his fingers together and offered me a boost. Then I was up and in the saddle which creaked as I settled in. I grasped the reins and waited while Grant mounted the stallion, a bigger and more powerful animal that chomped at his bit, raring to go.

We walked the horses around the corral and into the fields. Without warning, Grant nudged Spirit into a canter. Santiago pulled against the reins signaling his desire to join the romp. I let him have his way and caught up with Spirit and Grant. After a few minutes, Grant encouraged his mount to greater speeds. Buoyancy surged through me. I gave a nudge to Santiago to follow their lead.

With the wind blowing against my face, clarity overtook my mind. For the first time in years I allowed my heart to lighten, to let myself feel joy in the moment without holding back waiting for Eddie. My fears about Eddie, about the Cold War, about nuclear devastation fled on the breeze.

I whooped, urging Santiago faster and faster. Spirit had power, but Santiago had heart and being sleeker, he possessed speed too. We passed Grant and I laughed and wheeled my horse around a tree. "Last one back to the house washes dishes," I called over my shoulder.

"Oh, the race is on," Grant shouted.

I leaned down over Santiago's neck and we flew through the fields. He huffed and reached for greater speeds. Out of the corner of my eye, I glimpsed Spirit's great head gaining on us.

"Come on, boy, you can do it!" As if he sensed my urgency, my need for victory over this small aspect of life, Santiago shot forward with another burst of speed just as the barn came into sight. He never lagged, only pressed forward until we got to the corral. Only then did I pull back on his reins. "We did it! We won!"

While I couldn't forget the last time I'd raced with Eddie, the abandon I felt riding and winning the impromptu race with Grant rivaled that earlier time. Exultation and confusion tangled with my emotions. Ignoring Grant, I walked Santiago down the drive toward the road to cool Santiago down. When his breathing returned to normal, I returned to the corral, but I needed time to process my strange feelings so I dismounted and led Santiago into the barn. The monotony of horse brushing and grooming had always given me the necessary minutes to collect myself after my long conversations with Eddie. Perhaps it would do the same after my ride.

I already gathered the brushes and combs to groom Santiago, when Grant entered with Spirit.

We worked without talking, the only sound the brushes against the horses' hides and an occasional whinny from one of the animals. By the time I finished brushing down Santiago, my feelings were no more sorted than they were when I began. In some ways they were more confused. Eddie was further away than ever. No longer could I pretend he was still in Korea. Sure, rumors circulated of prisoners of war that were still held captive in some back country of North Korea, but the thought brought no hope, no comfort. It was worse, thinking of him in the hands of the enemy who would hurt him. The certainty slammed into me. Eddie wasn't coming home, ever.

Shuddering, I accepted that fact with an agonized heart. "Santiago, he's not coming back to us." My muscles ached, and it was more than my exertions with the ride. This tenderness encompassed my entire body. I stilled my actions, assessing the hurt. My eyes were dry, although I burned to let out my grief in tears, they didn't come. Even in this I was denied being a true participating citizen of Weeping Women Springs. The cruelty overwhelmed me and I stood frozen beside Santiago. He nickered and prodded my shoulder in a show of concern.

Engrossed in my misery I completely forgot I wasn't alone with the horse. Only the footsteps coming up behind me brought me back. I shook my head, not wanting to look at him.

"Um, could you put him in the stall and I'll go get cleaned up and—"

Grant placed his hand on my back and stroked, the exact same motion I'd seen him use with the horses, a gentling touch. No wonder he was good at his job.

Maybe it was the unexpected tenderness, but within seconds whatever dam had held back the tears ruptured and overthrew any composure I thought I possessed.

Using the same calming touch, he turned me toward him and embraced me, simply held me.

The emotional flood soaked his shirt, and it didn't stop, not for a long while, but he held me close, making soothing sounds in my ear and rubbing my back in a peaceful rhythm.

I'm not sure how long we stood like that, me in his arms weeping, but eventually I stepped away from him, careful to keep my head down. Looking him in the eye was beyond me. I was too embarrassed after my breakdown. Instead, I ran out of the barn and up to the house.

The screen door slammed behind me.

"Is that you, Susie?"

"Yes. Let me wash up and I'll help you in the kitchen." I couldn't let her see the evidence of my tears. It would only upset her and I didn't have the words to explain.

In the bathroom, I washed my face and tried to repair the damage my outburst had caused. No amount of washing helped hide my red and puffy eyes. Finally, I gave up and went into the kitchen.

"The table's all set," Mary said. "I just need you to get the corn out of the pot and we'll be ready as soon as Grant gets here." Fortunately, she didn't turn around.

I put the corn on the platter and carried it to the table, careful to avoid her line of sight.

When Grant came in we heard the door again. "I hope you don't mind me making a pig of myself, Mary. I'm so hungry I could eat a herd of cattle."

She laughed, but still didn't look up from tossing the salad greens. "Just bring your appetite. I'm sure we can fill it."

"I'll be in there in a second."

Not two minutes later, Grant arrived, his hair wet and his face cleaned of all the grime from his workday. At the doorway he waited. Though I hated to, I met his searching gaze. I hoped a slight shake of my head served as a warning to not discuss what happened in the barn. I poured the iced tea and sat, determined not to engage him further.

Before Mary came to the table, Grant took the chair beside me and leaned over to my ear. "You okay?"

I gave him a jerky nod, and distracted him and myself by offering corn and mashed potatoes.

The room was quiet until Mary reached her chair. She took a good look at both of us. "What in the world is going on? My word, Susie, you've been crying."

"Yes, ma'am." There was no point in denying the obvious.

"Grant Donaldson, what did you do to her?" Her tone took on a chill. "I have to say I'm shocked."

It was a second before it dawned on me what was going through her mind. "No. Mary, it's not what you're thinking."

The tears I thought were finished filled my eyes again, making everything shimmer. I blinked them back. "I realized today that no matter what I've hoped not to be true, Eddie won't be returning."

Mary didn't say anything for a long time, while Grant stopped eating. He put a comforting hand on my arm resuming the same soothing motions he'd made in the barn.

Her sharp gaze didn't miss the gesture. I wanted to snatch my arm away lest she get the wrong impression, but the reassurance of his touch provided me strength I never remembered having.

"I see." The way she said the words told me she guessed much more than what I intended.

"I'm not sure you do, but for now it's enough." I slid my arm away from Grant. "He's been nothing but kind."

My defense of this man came as a surprise. From the time he arrived in town I resented him for being alive after shirking his duty. Did a few moments of consolation erase all of his previous actions? I rebelled at the thought, yet the anger I'd fostered had disappeared, or at least diminished significantly.

The rest of the meal passed with Grant giving updates on the animals, the new foal and the dam.

When we finished, I cleared the table. "You just relax, Mary. I'll wash the dishes."

In the kitchen I filled the sink and scrubbed the dishes with unusual vigor.

Behind me, Grant said, "If you scour those plates any more, they'll be dust. Let me do it. Why don't you dry?"

I grit my teeth, the familiar anger flowing through me, before I stepped aside and grabbed a towel.

My shoulders ached with the tension, but I couldn't let go. "This doesn't change anything."

"Never thought it would," he said. "The ride was fun. Thanks for going along. I haven't raced like that in a long time, and so's you know, I've never lost. Spirit was sulking. I don't think he's ever lost either. Probably irked him a bit to be bested by his son."

"I'm not sure what got into me, it was almost like when I was a kid, racing with my brother or Eddie. I'd forgotten what it was like, the power of the horse and being free as the wind." I rolled my shoulders, the stiffness vanished.

"So you'll ride again? I could use the help."

"Yes." The word escaped before I could draw it back, and I thought of changing my mind, but didn't. "I'm looking forward to it."

He grinned. "See? We can have a civil chat."

"Yeah, well don't get too used to it." The old antagonism took over.

The smile didn't leave his face. He probably sensed the heat was no longer there.

"Um, thanks for the," I jerked my head the direction of the barn, "what you did out there." Flustered I didn't know what else to say. "Thanks."

"It's nothing. You'd do the same. Don't be afraid to ease up on yourself, go with the flow. Not everything needs to be studied in a book. Sometimes you need to go with your gut."

My shoulders tensed against his words. It sounded like Mary had been talking about me. "Books help. What have you got against education?"

"Not a damn thing." Evidently I provoked his reaction. "Sometimes you have to put the books down and see what's around you, live life."

"I see plenty. I see this conversation is over." I wiped the final dish and placed it in the cabinet. Back in the living room, I shoved my hands in my pockets. "Mary, I've got to go. Thanks for everything." I kissed her cheek and left.

"Isn't Grant going to walk you home?"

"No. He needs to check the animals." I didn't know if it was true, but even if it wasn't, it didn't matter.

"It's pretty dark already." Her concern was evident.

I needed to get out. "I've walked this road in darkness many times. I'll see you in a couple days."

Outside, the balmy air cooled my skin. My heated anger faded. Why had his words about books irritated me? The old emotions rushed back—being left out and not being able to pursue my studies—all the resentment I'd tried to let go over the years returned. What did Grant know about any of it? He had lived out in the world. All I had were my books to take me away from Weeping Women Springs, away from the pain of missing Eddie. The books were my life. Without them I'd shrivel and I might as well be dead. "Live life." His last words haunted me. Wasn't that what I was doing as best I could? Then I remembered the rush of passion that engulfed me when we were racing. That was life. Perhaps the answers weren't always in books. By the time I arrived home I was more confused than ever.

Part V

The Whir of the Helicopter

Chapter Thirty-Five

Susie

I TOOK UP GRANT'S CHALLENGE, so that's how I ended up running into the army in the fall of 1958. Since the spring with that first ride, I had made a concerted effort to get out of the house, out of my books. Besides the rides with Grant, I also took long walks. In early October I went out along the main road. I took time to observe a lizard perched on a rock at the side of the road, how he darted his tongue out to sniff or taste the air. A coyote ran into the road, stopped when he saw me and stared. His yellow eyes blinked, then he cocked his head. I didn't move. Soon he resumed his trek across the road and he disappeared into the underbrush. Seeing the coyote was unusual because they normally only came out at after dark. A tingle of awareness ran along my skin.

Not long after, an army jeep roared down the road. As soon as they saw me they screeched to a halt and both soldiers got out and confronted me.

The taller one, a sergeant, spoke first. "What are you doing out here?" His gruff voice and hard expression made me take a step back.

"Just walking."

"Why would you be walking out here in the middle of nowhere?" said the shorter, younger one. While he too was stern, his youth gave off an aura of openness.

"Because I like walking?" I couldn't keep my voice completely steady, but I was not going to let them bully me either.

"This is army land. Let's see your identification," the sergeant said.

"What? I don't have any."

"Driver's license, anything?" he asked.

"I don't drive."

"Come on, sister. You expect us to believe you got all the way out here without a vehicle of some kind?" The sergeant spit onto the road, barely missing my shoe.

"Listen, you could be in real trouble if you don't tell us the truth." The younger soldier narrowed his eyes.

"It is the truth. I don't have a driver's license and I'm out for a walk, enjoying the fresh air. I haven't ever seen any army cars on this road, at least not for a long time. What are you doing here?"

"We'll ask the questions," the sergeant said. "Where do you live?"

"Am I doing anything wrong?"

"You're on government property," he said. "No one is allowed here without government permission."

"Since when? I have walked here all my life and it's never been government property before."

"I'm not authorized to give you any further information."

"Well, I'm afraid I'm not either, not unless your superior officers explain themselves." I felt quite proud of myself for thinking of that one. It occurred to me that a sergeant probably couldn't make decisions.

The sergeant stepped back to the jeep, motioning the private to follow. They put their heads together and whispered.

"We'll be back." They got into the jeep and drove away toward the highway. The only sign they'd been there was their footprints in the dusty pavement and the cloud that drifted in their wake.

When they were out of sight, I hurried back to town. I first thought of going to Liv, but I needed to talk to someone else, to get some feedback before informing the Council. I knocked on Grant's door.

It wasn't the first time I'd visited, so aside from his eyes crinkling at the corners when he smiled, he registered no surprise until I rushed past him. "I just met some soldiers on the main road."

"Soldiers? What were they doing there?" Grant indicated I should sit, but I shook my head.

"They wouldn't tell me, but they said it was government property. I need to tell the Council, but I wanted to, I don't know, talk to someone. I found myself here."

He came toward me and held out his arms. Except for that first day in the barn, we had been careful not to touch. With my emotions roiling and fear of what I'd seen shuddered through me, I sprinted into his embrace.

"What are we going to do?" My words came out muffled against his shirt. Then I backed away. "You need to leave as soon as possible. They said they'd be back."

"I'm not going anywhere. This is my home."

"But what if they want to prosecute you for dodging the draft?"

"Then they prosecute me. I'm not running. I promised myself when I agreed to stay in Weeping Women Springs that I wouldn't ever run again." His demeanor was so calm, but I was nervous enough for the both of us.

"What do you think they mean that it's government property?" I asked. "They can't just do that can they, just decide they want some land?"

"Yeah they can. Remember during the war the government took lots of land for air bases and naval stations and whatnot. If the army wants something, it usually gets it. National defense and all that."

"I suppose that's true. But what would they need our land for?"

"Same things. They've taken all of White Sands as a testing ground. Probably something to do with that." His forehead crinkled. "Damnation."

It hit me then, the implications. The army wanted our land to test bombs, maybe even atomic bombs. "We can't ever escape them."

"Escape who?" Grant gave me a puzzled look, but from his curse I could tell he was worried.

"The wars, the hurt and devastation they cause. Now they're going to take our homes too."

He took me back in his arms. "We don't know that's what is happening."

"It is. I'm sure of it." From the reading I'd been doing about the Cold War and the threat of nuclear attacks, and the rocket programs, it all became clear. "We need to tell Liv and the Council."

"All right. Let's go. He took my hand and instead of pulling back, I let him hold it. These last few months I'd fought the attraction, telling myself it was only a friendship and that's all it could ever be. I was careful to not let it go too far, but on that day it didn't matter what anyone else thought. I needed his steady strength. I needed him.

In the light of what I guessed might happen next, perhaps it wouldn't matter anyway.

Chapter Thirty-Six

Liv

ALTHOUGH IT HAD BEEN OVER FIFTEEN years since I saw you, I recognized you immediately when you got out of your car. Then I saw your eyes. Who could forget those? I sound rather like a silly goose, don't I?

I'm glad it was you who came to us. You'll be able to tell our side of the story, explain to people what happened and why. I trust you to tell it right, and it's what I told the Council, "Bob Perry wrote a good article about our boys. He'll write an accurate accounting of Weeping Women Springs."

Susie and Grant arrived to tell me the news about the jeep a week ago, Thursday, right after she saw it. I called for a meeting of the Council immediately over at Wanda's. We sat around her dining room table as we'd done so often.

"What exactly did the sergeant say?" Grace asked Susie.

While she repeated the story for the Council, I studied the women around the table, remembering when I'd first come to the Council all those years ago. The men were all gone and these were the ladies who had taken up the reins of leadership for the last six years or more. Aunt Wanda's eyelids drooped lower than they ever had. She had little lines around her eyes that I hadn't noticed increasing over the years. Grace's hair was almost all dark gunmetal gray. My mother, still elegant, but her blue eyes had faded. Peggy, who had been elected after Anna died, had all white hair. All of the women were in their sixties now and should be cuddling grandchildren, but their grandchildren had never been born.

"Our guess is they want to incorporate our land into the White Sands Missile Range, what they're calling it these days," Susie said.

I'm sure I wasn't the only one who caught the looks passing from her to Grant, but that was far from our minds during that meeting.

Once Susie finished her report, Aunt Wanda asked, "What should we do?"

"Maybe they won't find us," I said. "After all the jeep Susie saw didn't come up the road, didn't cross the barrier we have. Perhaps we have no need to worry. Weeping Women Springs has remained hidden for more than fifteen years already. There's no reason they should find us now."

"The army knows where we are," my mother said. The pain I saw in her eyes when Captain Richard called on us to report Dewitt's death had never really left. "Remember they always seemed to find us from Ft. Bliss."

"True," Grace said. "We can't be certain they won't find us again, but our barrier has worked. I agree with Liv. We're panicking when we have no confirmation yet."

"I'll keep a particular eye out for the time being," I told them.

"Good. Keep us posted if you see anything out of the ordinary." Grace banged the gavel. "I adjourn this meeting."

The next morning a sound we'd never heard came from the sky. A terrible whopping whir as the helicopter landed at the end of Main Street. I had already been out to the road into town, but saw no sign of anyone.

I hurried down the street, but for the first time everyone else remained in their homes. No one had made any such orders, but everyone stayed behind their doors. I'm not sure why except they were afraid.

By the time I neared the helicopter, a major and a sergeant got out and ducking their heads, ran from the helicopter. I approached them. Every other time I confronted the captain or even when Vern came to town, I never hesitated to speak my mind, but something about the manner of these men made me hold my tongue. Blustering wouldn't work as a strategy, not that it ever had.

The major yelled over the noise. "Is this Hope Springs? We found it marked on an old map."

It served no purpose to correct him. "It is."

"You have one week to pack whatever belongings you wish to take with you and all residents are to relocate out of the area. This is now government property and you are considered trespassers."

"No." I wanted to shout the word but it came out an inaudible whisper. Stiffening my shoulders I knew I had to say something. "These are our homes. You can't expect--"

"Not only expect but require your cooperation, Miss?" He waited, his mustache wriggled as he grimaced. No doubt I was just a bothersome gnat in his day.

"Soderlund."

"Your country requires your sacrifice, Ms. Soderlund. I will post the notice on the post office door. My men will be back in one week's time to verify your compliance."

With no further words, he and the sergeant hurried to the post office, where they stuck the notice up and rushed back to board the helicopter which rose into the air. I stared at it, long after the whine of its rotor could be heard.

Numbness entered my limbs. I'm not sure how I remained standing. I went into the store. "Maxi?" I called.

"I'm out back with the roses."

Yellow roses and the Spring—everything normal, and yet it wasn't.

I ran out to her. As soon as she saw my face, she knew.

"It's time isn't it?"

It was reminiscent of the conversations we had during the war, every time we received a letter. For the last years since the issue with the stranger, Maxi's mind sometimes was befuddled, but that day she was clearheaded.

I nodded. "They said we have one week. I have to tell the Council. I'm sure they'll let everyone know, but--" I stopped when she shook her head.

"That's it? I can't leave," she said.

"Maxi, it's over. Weeping Women Springs is over. We can't fight them. They'll be back to make sure we leave. To be honest, I'm not sure I even want to anymore. Nothing's changed. Sure we've honored our boys, but at what cost?"

Maxine stared at the Spring. "Do you ever think it could have been different?"

"What do you mean?"

"I'm the Guardian of the Spring and even I'm not sure we always did the right thing. Maybe the founders were wrong all those years ago. I can't say it hasn't come to my mind before. Possibly we had it wrong all the time."

"I don't understand. What do you mean?"

She dipped the bucket into the pond and handed me a ladleful of water. "This water. We hoarded it. Maybe it wasn't meant to be a secret. Isn't it possible that by hoarding the water we've deprived others and maybe that's the reason the boys never came back?"

"No." I sipped the water. "You don't think? No, that's impossible."

"I'm not so sure. We've always hidden it because that's what the founders set up, but nothing bad ever really came whenever someone else drank from it, did it?"

The faces of all the new boys came to mind, watching them drink the water for the first time. "No, in fact I guess we could say the opposite. Since Vern, Grant, and Wilson's arrival even Al, they've been good for us, for the town." A shadow lifted off of my mind and in its place sunlight streamed in, illuminating everything. "Oh my word, Maxi, what have we done?"

"Nothing. It's all right." She patted my shoulder. "We did only what we had to. My job was to guard the Spring, yours was to guard the town. We've tried to do our duty, just like the boys did theirs."

My sweet gentle friend put my mind to rest. My limbs tingled with feeling again, but they weren't tense, the constant aches in my shoulders lessened. Yes, I could be angry at the army again, but where would that get me? Weeping Women Springs was asked again to make a sacrifice. The cost of this surrender was much less than the original. We would do it with our heads up.

Bob, you arrived just before the Council meeting that afternoon. I couldn't believe it when you said you'd heard rumors about the town from the air force base, but then you always got the scoop on the local happenings didn't you? For the first time ever, the Council agreed to let you, an Outsider, sit in on their meeting. Once more we sat around my aunt's dining table, and I reported the army orders.

"What if we stayed, refused to leave?" Mary asked. The dark circles under her eyes were mirrored on all the other Council members' faces.

"This may be something bigger than anything we've encountered before," Grace said.

"They say it's our duty to leave, that the army needs the land," I said. My urge to fight had left and I wondered if this is what the boys felt at the end. Maybe it was just that they didn't have the will to fight any longer.

Grace put her hand to her head. "I doubt it would matter if we said we were going to stay."

"Liv is the Guardian of our town. We've appointed her because she sees the whole picture. What is your true inclination?" My mother's gaze pierced me. She wasn't asking as the person who raised me, or as the woman who tried to fix me up with any eligible young man. Instead, she was asking as a Councilmember and resident of Weeping Women Springs.

"While we could put up a fight," I said, "in the end it is, as the government said, our duty. If we think about leaving as some small thing we can do for our country, it doesn't make it better, but it does give a good reason to leave. No matter what I've done, no matter what we've tried, the world intrudes on us. We have to face facts." The words came out of my mouth effortlessly. Me, who had struggled against everything since the beginning, I didn't struggle then. It was perhaps the easiest thing I'd ever done.

"True," Peggy said. "We'll all be cast out of the town into the world. Maybe we will never see one another again."

"What should we do about the mail?" I asked her. Talking about the mundane helped me face the fact of the end.

"You can leave forwarding addresses and I'll put in a special request to forward any mail addressed to Weeping Women Springs to be sent to the postmaster over at Doña Ana."

"I have an idea, if the Council agrees." I said. "We could each sit down with Bob Perry to tell our story. If he shares the story of Weeping Women Springs, maybe our efforts here will mean something. I hope I'm not being too presumptuous in assuming that's what you wanted to do, Bob, get the viewpoint from our residents."

"Yes, that's precisely why I came. It's an interesting story for our readers."

"I suppose nothing is secret any longer, not even our Spring," Grace said.

"After the army takes possession, I doubt the Spring will make any difference to anyone," Aunt Wanda said.

"I think we could take a remnant of our lives here," I suggested. "Maybe everyone can take a jug of Spring water with them when they leave."

"That's it then." My mother made a motion to allow residents to tell the story, all of it.

"I adjourn the final meeting of the Weeping Women Springs Council." Grace rapped the gavel. "I hope you will keep in touch, when we all have to depart."

From your first article in the paper last Sunday, Ruth learned about our situation. It's another thing I never expected, that she would show up at the end, but maybe it shouldn't be so surprising. She was always one for the attention. I'm glad she was able to tell her story too.

We'll be leaving in the morning. You can record that too. Let people know of our sacrifice, make it not be in vain, our boys, and us. Maybe our story can help someone. Maybe someday the world can see that war only causes pain, even to those who win.

For the first time in so many years, I'm looking forward to the future with an eye toward preserving our memories.

Final Reporter's Note: Liv's interview is the last tape of the women of Hope Springs AKA Weeping Women Springs. On November 11, 1958, the women packed their mementos, the flags, medals, pictures and their little cushions each had embroidered into their cars.

The women made a pilgrimage to the Spring for one last view. One by one they filled jugs to take with them. Many tears, but a few smiles too as they shared this final moment. This reporter wished they might find hope again in the future with a sip of their precious water.

After Grant and Susie led the animals out onto the range, they mounted two horses and prepared to follow the small, slow caravan.

In the first car, Ruth waved at me, holding Al's hand. Her husband drove in from Albuquerque. In the next car, Maxine bowed her head, her tears hidden from prying eyes. Mary patted her shoulder. Then came Grant and Susie on horseback.

Another car held Eva Soderlund and Wanda. They held their heads high, proud. In this way the people of Weeping Women Springs left their homes. Many of the women looked back until the town disappeared behind them. This reporter put his arm around Liv's shoulders and guided her to my car. We followed the rest and the army jeep took up the rear.

After a short stop at The Weeping Place, where prayers were said and Susie played "Taps" a final time, the women drove away from their village.

I touched Liv's cheek. It was conceivable she might leave the memories in the past and move into the future. I planned to be there when she did.

There are those that will say Weeping Women Springs is not real because it has never been marked on a map. I bear witness to this place which I visited on two occasions, both during the war and when I heard at the base they planned to evacuate the village of Hope Springs. The women's stories speak for themselves. Anyone who has faced such indescribable heartbreak such as these women, deserve to find their joy once more.

–Robert William Perry

A Note from the Author

Historical events often prove captivating to the fiction writer because they can provide an amazing backdrop to a novel. I delight in discovering the lesser known elements of the past and incorporating them into my stories.

While writing *Weeping Women Springs*, I let the developing story lead me to several obscure corners of history which begged to become a part of the tale.

From the original news broadcasts of the Pearl Harbor attack, I learned that most Americans didn't even know where Pearl Harbor was, nor that a part United States was invaded by Japanese Forces. If you followed Al Caldarelli's ordeals in the Battle of Attu, the descriptions of the adverse weather and poorly equipped soldiers are based on little known but well established fact. Unbelievably, soldiers did burn their rifle stocks just to keep warm while their summer uniforms were of little protection from frostbite.

The "bat bombs" reported on by Bob Perry in the book were an actual military weapons experiment and did result in inadvertently turning portions of remote New Mexico military installations into blazing infernos. The uncontrollable success of the program resulted in it being halted and the bat weapons never did roost in the wood and paper houses of Japan.

The escaped Prisoner of War, Werner Koch's story developed from the many escapes from POW Camps scattered all over the west and southwestern US, including New Mexico, Arizona and Colorado. I have enjoyed exploring many of these now abandoned camps, and getting just an inkling of what it might have been like.

The military taking over the village of Weeping Women Springs in this book emanates from actual events. The military thirst for remote sites to develop secret weapons during WWII gobbled up western ranch lands with little compensation. The patriotic landowners were told it was for national defense, and were promised their land would someday be returned, though much of it never was. Even in 2015 we hear the echoes of history, where a Nevada family is currently being threatened off their land by the Air Force.

All the historical references have a basis in actual fact, while some modification of the story elements helps them fit within the framework of my novel.

Dearest reader, I hope you enjoyed this glimpse into the little magical place of Weeping Women Springs. Thank you for reading. I would appreciate you taking the time to review the book on Amazon.

Tamara Eaton
South Dakota, 2015

About the Author

Tamara Eaton is a "western woman." She divides her time between Nevada, New Mexico and South Dakota where she and her love spend their summers renovating an old school. Wide open spaces of the desert and prairie are often portrayed in her work.

A former secondary English teacher, she grabbed the opportunity to create her stories after she left the classroom. When not writing, she works with other writers editing and polishing their stories and poems.

Find out more at http://tamaraeatonnovels.weebly.com/ and be sure to sign up for her Reading Group to keep posted on other projects as well as share your thoughts on current reads. You'll receive a short story direct to your inbox.

Find out more about her editing services at http://tamaraeatoneditingservices.weebly.com/

Made in the USA
San Bernardino, CA
16 October 2015